Gideon's jaw dropped in stunned disbelief.

No boy on God's green earth had a chest like that. Not swelling out like small twin melons, their stem ends standing out like pink coral beads. The conniving little heathen was a— He wasn't even a—

Disbelief was slowly replaced by a deep-seated rage as Gideon stared at the long, rounded thighs. Fists curled impotently at his side, he breathed in a rasping lungful of air and expelled it in a soft burst of profanity.

God, what a fool he'd been! How could he not have *known?*

What other lies had she told him, he wondered as he watched her bend forward to wring out her hair.

Anger burned deep inside him. While he stood hidden in the shadow of a giant cedar tree, Haskell—or whatever her name was—waded up out of the water, revealing a body that was so flawlessly made, he felt himself hardening in spite of his bitterness.

Furious at this further betrayal, Gideon eased deeper into the shadows. Forcing himself to ignore the desire that raged through his blood like a fever, he deliberately stoked his anger.

Before he was done with the little witch, she would rue the day she'd ever set out to make a fool of Gideon McNair!

Dear Reader,

Once again, as we will every month from now on, Harlequin Historicals brings you four new historical romances for your reading pleasure.

Bronwyn Williams is back with a delightful love story that captures the joy and pain of a young girl growing to womanhood under the uneasy tutelage of a handsome whaling captain. Set in the outer banks of North Carolina, *Gideon's Fall* is a book you will want to read again and again.

And we are very pleased this month to be publishing *Stardust and Whirlwinds,* a Western by first-time author Pamela Litton. With astonishing skill, Pamela has written a heartrending tale of a refined Eastern lady and the gun-slinging drifter who becomes her protector.

With Jan McKee's *Sweet Justice* and Caryn Cameron's *Wild Lily,* this month is packed with romance and adventure. We hope you will enjoy all four titles, and we look forward to bringing you more of the same in the months to come.

Yours,
Tracy Farrell
Senior Editor

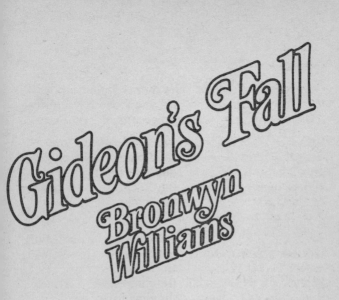

Gideon's Fall

Bronwyn Williams

Harlequin Books

TORONTO • NEW YORK • LONDON
AMSTERDAM • PARIS • SYDNEY • HAMBURG
STOCKHOLM • ATHENS • TOKYO • MILAN

Harlequin Historical first edition March 1991

ISBN 0-373-28667-8

GIDEON'S FALL

Books by Bronwyn Williams

Harlequin Historicals

White Witch #3
Dandelion #23
Stormwalker #47
Gideon's Fall #67

BRONWYN WILLIAMS

is the pen name used by two sisters, Dixie Browning
and Mary Williams. Dixie Browning had written over
forty contemporary romances for Silhouette Books
before joining her sister to write their first historical.
A former painter and art teacher, currently co-owner
of a craft shop in Frisco Village on Hatteras Island,
Dixie divides her time between her home in Winston-
Salem and North Carolina's Outer Banks.

Mary Williams is married to an officer in the Coast
Guard and has lived in such diverse places as Hawaii,
Oklahoma, Connecticut, Virginia and New Jersey.
The mother of three grown children, she now lives on
Hatteras Island, where both sisters grew up.

Their second historical, *Dandelion*, won the presti-
gious Maggie Award for best historical romance of the
year from the Georgia Romance Writers and was a fi-
nalist for the Romance Writers of America's RITA
Award for best series historical.

Prologue

June, 1725

Urias was dying. Even as his life's blood seeped into the sanded decks of the French brigantine, *Saint Germaine,* he could see the flames climbing higher in the rigging of his own proud new ship. The foremast had been shot away in the first barrage, and now the mainmast was canted at an angle that told its own tale. Within sight of Jamaica, she was sinking fast.

A grimace of pain twisted his face, but the pain soon ebbed away, leaving behind only a growing coldness and a deep sense of loss. He would not live to see his son grow to manhood, nor his daughter into a taller, bolder image of her mother, his own beloved wife.

Blanche. The name formed soundlessly on his pale lips as his mind reached out to the wife who had died so long ago. Urias was not a praying man, yet he found nothing out of the ordinary in speaking silently to his dead wife.

The damned bastard finally caught up with me, love. For nigh on twenty years I've looked over my shoulder, expecting that sniveling Frenchman to come after me. He was a sly devil, cheating from the very first, but I beat him at his own game. It's not my nature to cheat, as you well know, but the man would have stripped me of all I owned had I not turned the tables on him. I took my winnings and made a bloody

fortune for you and the babes, and I would have soon dou-
bled that. But old Delarouche has reached out from the
grave to win the last toss.

The man who stood over Urias, his handsome young face
twisted by bitterness, had taken great pleasure in introduc-
ing himself as Delarouche's son the moment Urias had been
dragged aboard his ship. The weasel-faced captain was evidently a cousin of sorts, for he, too, bore the name. The
barkentine had come gliding out of a fog bank just after
dawn, firing what had probably been meant as a warning
shot across the bow of the *Pride of Portsmouth.*

Either the gunner had been remarkably unskilled or the
twenty-pounder had misfired. The shot intended to bring
Urias's fine new schooner about had gone wildly amiss,
holing her at the waterline. Taken unaware, Urias's crew had
been unarmed and unable to defend themselves when Delarouche's men grappled her and swarmed aboard. Urias
had managed to bring down two men before he was taken
prisoner, but most of his crew had been killed in the first five
minutes. The few survivors were taken aboard the Frenchman's ship; Delarouche's men had made a frantic search of
the crippled schooner.

Unfortunately, in their zeal, the French privateers had set
her afire, and she had gone up like a torch. If he hadn't been
mortally wounded, Urias could have laughed at Delarouche's impotent fury as he danced about, trying to force
his men down into the schooner's blazing hold.

"Speak, you devil's spawn!" he shouted now. But Urias
was too far gone to feel the pain as the flat of a broadsword
caught him on the side of the head. "Tell me where you have
hid my father's gold!"

Spitting a mouthful of blood at the dandy's well-shod
feet, Urias managed a weak grin of defiance. God, didn't
the young fool realize what he had just done? Urias had sold
everything he owned back on Portsmouth and put it all into
the fine ship and a cargo that would have brought him another fortune had it reached the market for which it was

bound. And now the witless young jackanapes had sent it all to the bottom!

Urias thought again of his gentle and lovely wife, who had given him a fine set of twins. When she died of a sudden fever, he had installed her widowed mother in his home to look after his children.

Pride and Prudence. They were all any man could wish for in his heirs, although he admitted to having wished more than once that his daughter had less pride and more prudence, and his son the other way around.

He had taken pleasure in teaching them both how to get on in the world while keeping their skins whole. Though Pride was as fine a son as any man could want, Prudie was his secret delight—although mayhap he should have heeded their grandmother's advice to let her try and make a lady of the girl before it was too late....

Too late...

They would be destitute now, thanks to Delarouche, may his nuts roast in the fires of hell!

Urias groaned as another blow was directed at his head. He closed his eyes. Above the whisper of the seas against the hull and the wind in the rigging came the distant sound of crashing wood, crackling flames and screaming, cursing men. His own crew, or what was left of them, God rest their souls.

"Where is my father's gold, son of a Yankee dog?"

Urias managed to gasp out a profane response and shut his eyes again.

Spittle flew from the French dandy's mouth as he shouted out his frustration. The cousin looked on silently, stroking his pockmarked chin and nodding occasionally in response to a word from his quartermaster.

"Where, damn you, *where?*" the dandy snarled. "My father told me many times before he died of the great fortune you stole from him—more than enough to buy a hundred verminous islands like your own!"

Urias suffered another vicious kick as he lay bleeding at his captor's feet. Something fell from his pocket and clattered across the deck. The cousin stooped to pick it up, and Urias felt a stab of sadness at seeing his favorite pipe of briar root inlaid with ebony and ivory held in those bloodstained hands.

With a shrug, the French captain slipped the pipe into his own pocket and sent a well-aimed boot to Urias's groin. *"Toute sa fortune a été réduite à zéro."*

"Non! It cannot be gone—it cannot be! The son of a dog, he has hid it somewhere!"

Too weak now even to shiver with the fearful chill that had crept into every part of his body, Urias managed to find the strength for one last act of defiance. "'Tis hidden well," he whispered, "and buried deep...held...forever in my...mistress's keep...."

Moments later, his body was thrown to the sharks.

Chapter One

November, 1728

Prudence eyed the rose-colored silk with its ruffled stomacher and circular skirts with distaste. It had belonged to her mother. Her grandmother had insisted she wear it, and so wear it she must. Which meant corset, hose, slippers and the entire foofaraw that went with playing lady.

"Pru-dence! Aren't you dressed yet?"

"Almost, Granna. I'm doing my hair." Hastily she twisted the thick brown braid into a coronet.

"Shall I send Lillah up to help you?"

"No, thank you, Granna—I'm nearly done!" A note of panic crept into Pru's voice with that last, for if Lillah caught her looking the way she did now, she would tell Hosannah, and then, not content to restrict her to her room for a day, that grand lady would see that she didn't set foot outdoors until the spring of '29!

Prudence stripped off her boots—Pride's boots, actually, outgrown three years before—and snatched up her chemise and petticoat. She began scrambling into her clothes before her grandmother's freedwoman, Black Lillah, could come tromping up the stairs to see what was keeping her.

She would have to suffer Albert Thurston again, no doubt. She'd seen the extra place at the table when she crept past the window on her way up the oak tree that served as inlet and outlet for her daytime hunting and fishing excursions as well as her nocturnal activities—or rather, those of Haskell and Nye.

Haskell and Nye. Had they been real men, or just two imaginary adventurers in all those wonderful tales her father used to tell? She could see him now, nursing his favorite pipe and spinning outrageous yarns about the two fearless young seamen....

Well, make-believe or not, they were real enough now. For the past three years—since their father had been murdered by pirates, who had sunk his spanking new schooner with her entire cargo of rare pelts, mountain tobacco, indigo and fine lumber—Pru and her brother, Pride, disguised as two young ruffians named Haskell and Nye, had taken their revenge on every freebooter who swaggered ashore to drink, whore and game away his ill-gotten gains.

But what had started as revenge had soon become necessity, for their grandmother, Hosannah, had refused to allow Pride to go to sea, and there were few other means of earning a livelihood on the tiny island.

With a snort of disgust, Pru yanked the white silk hose up her long legs and anchored them carelessly below her knees with strips of cloth, her garters having long since been lost. Now for that damned corset! If men had to go through such a mommicking before presenting themselves to society, she thought, the world would quickly come to a screeching halt!

Picking up one of her boots, she slammed it against the wall that separated her bedroom from that of her twin brother, Pride. "Sssst!" she called softly to him through the thin partition. "Are you near ready to go downstairs? Granna's serving up Albert for dinner again. If you don't draw him off as soon as we finish eating, I'll likely say something awful and then Granna'll send me to my room for a week, and Lillah will feed me on stale biscuit and water!"

"You'll be glad enough for stale biscuit and water if our luck don't soon change. That one-eyed devil near about caught us last night. Blast it all, Pru, did you have to go af-

ter his pistol? He was too drunk to prime, much less fire,''
Pride said.

"I'd have got it, too, if I hadn't tripped over that damned
root!''

Her hair was sliding from its coronet already, its chestnut color glistening with golden highlights as she prodded
and poked at the tumbling hairpins. What a bother! Who
but Granna would insist on going to the trouble of dressing
for dinner each evening, when it was all they could do to put
food on the table?

At least when her father was alive, the dinners had been
worth dressing for. Now they were lucky to have more than
pokeweed salat and cornmeal pone along with whatever they
could shoot or catch in their net. And to think even that was
to be wasted on a lump like Albert, who ate like a pig, only
with worse manners.

Granna was determined Pru must marry before she withered on the vine. But who on this benighted island was there
to marry? Her friend Annie Duvaal could smirk and sigh all
she wanted to over the likes of Albert Thurston and that
redheaded Oleck boy, but not Pru. Her father had always
claimed there wasn't a man on the island good enough for
her, and he'd been dead right. She would sooner live alone,
like Lillah, turning up her nose at anything in pants, than
suffer the indelicate indignities of marriage to Albert.

Only it was not Albert Thurston who rose from the best
chair when Pru entered the front parlor, but a dark and
dapper young gentleman, sporting a flared pink knee coat,
a blue silk waistcoat and altogether more frills and ruffles
than Pru and Hosannah could manage between them.

"Sir, I present my grandson, Pride Andros, and my
granddaughter, Prudence,'' Hosannah said proudly.
"Children, this is Mr. Claude Delarouche, the man who
now owns your father's business.''

"I thought it belonged to Mr. Simpson,'' blurted Pride,
while Prudence stared at the dandified specimen before her.
He barely topped her own five foot four, and fairly reeked
of cologne.

"M. Simpson wished to retire." The Frenchman's accent was thick, his manners oily. Long before Lillah called them in to dinner, Prudence decided she would have preferred the slovenly Albert to this slippery French eel.

"Gad, we'll starve for a month to make up for this," Pride whispered as he held his sister's chair for her. "Gammon, roast mullet and stewed goose, foolberry jam, plum dumplings... What got into Granna to turn out the larder for a slick-un like this?"

Pru knew very well what had got into her grandmother. It had taken no more than the Frenchman's speculative looks and her grandmother's pointed references to her own privileged girlhood at Hunt House on the Albemarle and Urias Andros's golden touch, which had turned a barren sand spit into a thriving port, to know that she was being placed on the market.

All of which touched a streak of perversity in Prudence that never lay far beneath the surface. "Is this the goose I shot yesterday, Granna?" she asked, knowing full well it was, and that Hosannah had meant to lard it down, in order to serve it up, one measly joint at a time. "I only stunned him at first, and he nearly took my ear off when I waded out after him."

Ignoring Prudence, Hosannah smiled and passed to her guest a plate of plum dumplings, made from the last of the wild plums Pride and Pru had gathered in the summer. "The dear girl does like to tease," she explained to her guest. "Takes after my own dear husband in that respect, for Mr. Gilbert had a delightful sense of humor for a man of the cloth."

The Frenchman scarcely took his eyes off Prudence all evening, making her distinctly uncomfortable. Her eyes, large, and of a nondescript gray-green color, seemed to tilt even more than usual when she was angry, and after the first five minutes with Claude Delarouche, she was furious, for no real reason at all but that the man made her flesh crawl.

"Oh? I find stormy weather quite pleasant, Mr. Delaroach," she replied to a complaint of his about the persistent cold wet wind.

"Dela*rouche, s'il vous plaît*," he murmured, a pained expression on his narrow face. He was not unhandsome, yet there was something about his expression that made her uneasy.

Somehow, the evening passed. Pru was yawning well before Hosannah called for the port and apologized for its quality. "When my dear son-in-law, Urias, was alive, he would never have tolerated such a poor wine in the house," she said, and then grew flustered as she realized she was spoiling the very image of wealth she had hoped to create.

The Frenchman was slick, Pru decided she would have to give him credit for that. He managed to excuse the wine, to compliment their home—ignoring the darker places on the rugs where the finer pieces of furniture they had been forced to sell off had stood—to remark on her grandmother's obvious breeding, Pride's courage and Prudence's beauty in one long, flowery sentence, and all without batting an eye.

Pru thought she might lose her dinner, but held on because it would be a terrible waste. Tonight's dinner might also be tomorrow's breakfast and nooning.

"Granna," said Pru as soon as the door closed behind their guest, "he's awful! How could you invite him here?"

"He was a business associate of your father's. Naturally he called to pay his respects, and I invited him to dine."

"Huh! Well, I don't like him and I don't trust him, not one little bit. If Mr. Simpson had never talked Papa into selling—"

"Hush, child. No one could talk your father into anything, and well you know it. Urias was bound and determined to go to sea again. I told him no good would come of it, and I was right."

No good, thought Pru, amazed as always that her grandmother could swallow a horse and balk at a housefly. "Well...just so you don't expect me to make up to some toad in fancy silks and silver buckles," she said grudgingly.

"He's a handsome man, Prudence, and quite well off, I should think."

"I'd sooner stay an old maid."

"Nonsense, child. Your father's gone now, and I won't be here to look after you forever, you know. It's time you were settling down."

It had never occurred to her grandmother, Pru thought with a rush of affection, that it was Pru who had been looking after the old woman for a good many years.

In one way or another, life had left its mark on the six men gathered on the deck of the sloop *Polly.* There was Ned, the young striker, who had been beaten and left to die when Gideon McNair found him. Now a sturdy seventeen, the lad would have willingly died for his captain.

The heaviest and most fearsome of the lot was Gouge, who had lost an eye in a fight. His mates swore that he could see more with an empty socket than most men could with two good eyes and a looking glass. Back at their whaling camp, Gouge shared his pallet with a pet pig, which he guarded fiercely whenever rations were running low.

Crow was a lean and handsome half-breed, whose dry sense of humor came as a surprise to those used to his more stoic side. Gideon had pulled him more dead than alive from a bear trap some years before and nursed him back to health.

Tobias Burrus was the eldest at sixty-nine. He had come to the banks penniless from Barbados, claiming his great-grandfather, Will Burrus, had been deported there from landed gentry in Jamestown. Pretensions to gentility notwithstanding, Gideon had recruited the old man for his whaling crew, and they had been together ever since.

Lear had been sword-whipped, his face healing in an unfortunate manner, the left eye drooping to meet the left side of his mouth, which was drawn up in a perpetual grin. Less brawny than his mates, he had been drawn to Gideon perhaps for the reason that Gideon, too, was blemished.

These men, as well as the others left back at the whaling camp, owed allegiance to one man—Gideon McNair. All had been castaways rescued by the young man who was determined to make a new life for himself as a whaler.

Hardened now by bitter experience, Gideon had fled a cruel stepfather as a boy, only to find himself trapped into serving aboard the infamous pirate ship, *Morning Star.* He had learned many bitter lessons, one being that some men were born without souls. But he had also learned that no matter how low a man fell, most still had at least one redeemable quality that, given the opportunity, could turn their lives around.

To a man, his crew would have laid down their lives for him, yet none had been allowed to broach the wall of aloofness that seemed to surround the tall young captain.

"Two days and a night," Gideon cautioned his men. "That should give you time enough to trade your shares and spend a bit on rum and a bit at Quick Mary's. The rest you can send to your families or put away for your old age."

The words were greeted with the usual groaning protest, but none dared to debate the issue. Gideon was a good man to work for. He knew whaling, he paid well, and he looked after his crew, but he was *not* a man to cross, under any circumstance.

"Watch your backs," he warned as they lowered the launch.

"Aye, Cap'n, them cutpurses'll not take one o' us," Ned replied, patting the knife at his side.

Gideon nodded grimly, his pale hair whipping in the northeast wind as he watched his men pull away toward shore. Anyone seeing him in his linen shirt and leather vest, his oiled jackboots pulled well up on his powerful thighs, might be struck by the flawless cut of his features, the unusual depth of his blue eyes.

But lest strangers be gulled into thinking him handsome, he would deliberately turn his face, presenting them with the large blemish that marred his right cheek. If there was one thing Gideon had been taught to despise, it was falseness, in word, deed or image.

Satisfied that his crew would stick together for their own protection, Gideon crossed to his cabin, where the manifests waited to be completed before he could go ashore. It had been a good season so far, starting earlier than usual. They had already tried out near two hundred barrels of whale oil, with every hope of tripling that number.

Two hours later, his oiled packet of papers secure under his vest, Gideon took the small launch and headed for shore, leaving old Tobias on watch, with Crow scheduled to relieve him at eight bells. Crow usually went ashore only long enough to trade his shares and make a few purchases, for he was not overly comfortable drinking with white strangers, being of mixed blood, half Negro and half Indian. Powerful enough to break an oar barehanded, he was also smart enough to avoid trouble whenever possible.

After attending to his business with the clerk at the countinghouse, Gideon headed for the largest of the island's two pubs, the Leaky Cask. A dram would not come amiss on a night like this, though he was not a hard-drinking man. Responsibility weighed heavily on him, for all he was not yet thirty years old.

The pub was hot, smoke-filled and noisy, altogether a cheerful place for a man bent on having a good time. At a table near the door, several of his men were gambling, and he'd a mind to caution them not to walk out alone with their winnings. More than likely, cutpurses weren't all they would have to fear, for he'd heard tell that since Andros had sold out a few years back, cheating was not only tolerated, it was expected.

Quietly he placed his order with the buxom barmaid and glanced around the crowded room. There were a few familiar faces other than his own crew. In fact, he could have sworn he remembered some from his days with Will Lewis on Ocracoke, when the whole island had swarmed with freebooters.

Most likely they were only inlet pilots and fishermen he'd seen in various ports around and about. During the off season, Gideon often hauled freight on the inland sounds, and one saw a lot of familiar faces in one port or another. For some reason, he was unduly edgy tonight.

"The damned bastard held a gun on me!" The indignant voice rose above the noise, and Gid looked around, but could see nothing amiss. Someone laughed. Someone else called for another round of drinks.

This was Portsmouth, he reminded himself—not New Providence, which had harbored the worst scum of the seas a few years back, and for all he knew, still did. How in God's name had he managed to live through those years aboard the *Morning Star?* An innocent lad of fifteen, he'd gone to sea with his uncle and come back at twenty-two a pirate in name, if not in deed, with his skull laid open and his arm nearly severed from his body, left for dead on the wharf at Ocracoke.

There was more than one man alive who could testify that Gideon McNair had once sailed on one of the most notorious ships to ply the freebooter's trade, but few would know that it had been only out of respect for the uncle who had taken him in as a lad. Nor had Will Lewis become a pirate by choice.

But Will had been a weak and sickly man—no match for his wily quartermaster. Turk had led the men in a slow, but effective mutiny that had cost the captain and crew their lives. Had it not been for an Ocracoke widow named Barbara, who had nursed him well and patiently, Gideon would have joined them in hell.

Absently, he stroked the strawberry mark on his right cheek. The mark of the devil, some had called it. It had earned him a certain awed respect from the more superstitious among men, and for that he'd been thankful. He had needed all the help he could get at the time—a green kid, trying to make his way among the roughest men on land or sea, when half the time he'd been so damned seasick he couldn't look at a dry biscuit without his gut turning inside out.

Nursing his ale, Gideon was oblivious to the covetous stares of the few women present. For reasons that escaped him, women had always seemed to be drawn to him—those who weren't repulsed by his blemished face—and there had been a time when he took full advantage of the fact.

But not lately. Turning away an offer from one of Quick Mary's girls, who plied their trade at the tavern during the early hours of the evening, he said gently, "No thank ye darlin', I fear I'd be no good company at all tonight."

The girl was comely enough, and in truth, he didn't know why he wasn't tempted. A man had certain needs and would likely sicken if those needs weren't met, but tonight, for reasons he couldn't fathom, he was in a strange mood.

Barbara. They'd have been married eight years had she lived, but she had died of the yellow fever that awful winter of '23, along with their infant son, Adam.

Gideon lifted his hand to call for another ale, and asked for a rum instead. The wind was from the northeast tonight, wet and cold. His shoulder ached, but his soul ached even more. It was at times like this that he asked himself why he continued to work so hard, with no one of his own to care. He had a sister, Maggie Rawson, living up the banks on Hatteras Island—that was all. Maggie's children would likely be his heirs, for he couldn't see himself marrying again. He had learned to his sorrow that anything a man could possess, he stood the chance of losing. First his father, then his mother, then his uncle, his wife and his son. A man could bear only so much sorrow in one lifetime.

A surge of restlessness overtook him and he paid his tab and left. There were times when the walls seemed to close in on him for no reason at all. He was too edgy to sleep and in no mood to drink himself into a stupor or lose himself at gaming or a tumble at Quick Mary's.

Portsmouth Island was less than two miles wide at its northern end, narrowing as it strung out toward the southwest. There was no town to speak of—little of interest other than the row of warehouses, taverns and bawdy houses that lined the waterfront just inside the main channel.

Narrow paths meandered across vast stretches of creek-riddled marshland, leading past houses sheltered in groves of scrub pine and cedar against the fierce storms that raked the island. Gideon stared at a small weathered cabin, a bleak expression darkening his eyes.

Once, he had lived in such a house. Barbara's house, left to her by her first husband. After she and the boy died he had boarded up the house and left. Later he had heard that the storm of '25 brought a giant cedar down on the roof, smashing it to bits.

Some men were meant to abide ashore—some weren't. And a man like Gideon, it seemed, could find contentment neither on land nor sea.

Pru waited until she was certain Lillah had left to go to her own house to the south'ard before she eased out of bed. The floor always creaked, and the young Haitian woman had ears that could hear night fall. Even worse, she was of an unreasonably suspicious turn of mind. At times Pru was almost certain the freedwoman knew where the coppers that paid her wages had come from. Copper was all Pru and Pride dared spend. Silver was scarce enough, gold rarer than possum eggs. The gold guineas and Spanish silver they took from their drunken prey continued to pile up in the bottom of the sewing basket, a hedge against a time of even greater need.

But Lillah said nothing, and Pru and Pride continued their masquerade whenever a suspicious ship was sighted lying at anchor. The brigantine *Good Friend* had dropped anchor just after midday. By now the crew should be more than ripe for plucking. All knew that the *Good Friend* was likely to hoist the skull and crossbones as soon as she cleared the inlet, though none dared point an accusing finger. Pride had been waiting at the Leaky Cask since dusk in order to pick out the most likely target for tonight's activity. Any moment now the crewmen should begin stumbling, a few at a time, along the Haul Over Road on their way to further entertainment at Quick Mary's.

Pru had already decided how some of tonight's take would be spent. To begin with, she would barter for a decent case of port wine, so that Granna would never again have to apologize to the likes of Claude Delarouche. And perhaps a new rug to keep the draft down. In rainy weather or whenever the tides were unduly high, water stood under the house and the damp crept up through the floor planks, stiffening poor Granna's joints until she could scarcely move.

By the light of the moon, she darkened her face with soot from the inside of her lamp chimney. Quickly she twisted her braid around her head, wishing for the hundredth time that her hair was not quite so long, or so thick and unmanageable.

"Pru! Open up."

Startled, Pru tiptoed to her window and threw it open to see Pride, sooty-faced, sprawled along the nearest branch. "What are you doing back here?" she demanded in a fierce whisper.

"What's keeping you? If we aren't in position in five minutes, we'll likely come up empty-handed. Half the *Friend*'s crew are dead drunk, and the other half're arguing over whether to go on to the Bait and Bottle or head straight for Quick Mary's while they're still able."

Pru jammed the stocking cap down over her head and snatched up the heavy flintlock pistol that had belonged to her father. "I had to wait for Lillah to leave, and she took forever tonight."

The pair quickly descended the oak tree and dropped silently to the ground. Keeping to the shadows, they hurried along the path that led to the Haul Over Road. There was a certain grove of palmetto, yaupon and scrub cedar at a bend halfway between the taverns and Quick Mary's that served them well as a hiding place.

They hadn't long to wait. The four men were still arguing, albeit so drunkenly as to be almost unintelligible, when they approached the bend.

Two youths, known only to themselves as Haskell and Nye, waited until the men were well into the grove before slipping silently from their cover.

"Stand and deliver," cried the first lad, while the other slipped deftly around and aimed an unwavering barrel at the level of the crewmen's chests.

Some twenty minutes later, the one who called himself Nye slipped through the second-story window with a whispered word of caution. "Mind you don't trip over the window seat this time."

"Just see that you don't drop your damned boots," Haskell called up quietly from the shadows under the giant live oak. "Last week I had the devil's own time convincing Granna the noise was nothing but a branch rubbing the side of the house."

Prudence waited a good five minutes before following her brother up the tree. Silently the shadowy figure opened the window and slid one long leg over the sill. Shivering in the damp cold air, she quickly lowered the window and then lit a single candle.

Off came the stocking cap, to be tucked under her mattress along with the linen binder that served to flatten her bosom. Down came the long thick braid. Prudence dug her fingers into her scalp and scratched freely, glad to be rid of her confining disguise. Recently she had enjoyed these late-night excursions less and less, yet how else were they to earn a living? Granna would never hear of her going to work in one of the taverns, and in truth, Pru didn't think she could stand it. Pride had tried to find work at the wharves, but paying work was scarce, and those who held such jobs guarded them jealously.

For themselves it wouldn't have mattered so much, but Hosannah had never known need. She had grown up in a house of wealth, and since Urias died, her mind had begun to slip its mooring, causing her to grow more and more demanding as she forgot the family's changed circumstances.

Pru dearly loved the woman who had raised them both from babes. She would have worked day and night to provide for her, but there was simply no work to be had for a decent woman. Unless she married—and then, of course, her work would never cease.

Not even for Hosannah could Pru bring herself to settle for either of the island's two eligible bachelors. They were both toads, Albert being the bigger toad, and Jeremy Oleck being merely a fool who, like most other islanders, seemed to think the Andros family was still made of gold.

If it weren't so aggravating, it would be funny. She had told them over and over that she was lucky to have a sixpence, but they only grinned, unconvinced. Not even the fact that she could afford only the meanest of goods seemed to make a difference, for rumor had it that Urias had hidden a fortune on the island. No matter how many times she told Albert and Annie that he had poured every shilling he owned into that damned schooner and her prime cargo, only to lose it all, no one believed her.

For the most part, Pru ignored the occasional remarks. As long as she could take her revenge on her father's murderers, and at the same time keep food on the table and pay Lillah's wages, then people could think what they wished, and the devil take them. Pru had all her mother's old things—Blanche Gilbert Andros must have had a gown for every day of the week and two for the Sabbath—but they were all nearly twenty years out of date. It was a good thing Lillah was skilled with a needle!

Not for the first time, Pru wondered what they would do without the freedwoman. What if she should up and leave as suddenly as she'd come? She had made them no guarantees.

Pru had been eleven years old when the tall, haughty black woman stepped off a schooner one hot May morning and asked to see the master. Someone had directed her to Urias's house, and she had shown up on their doorstep wearing a high-necked black gown and a starched white headdress and apron, a blazing sun scattering blue highlights on the inky skin of her high brow and proud cheekbones.

"You be needin' me?" she asked as coolly as you please.

It was Urias who answered. He had been home later than usual, as Hosannah had fallen the night before and had to be helped in and out of bed. "Damn right I be needing you. Where you from, woman?"

"You make me a place to live, pay me good, I work for you."

"Anything," the harried man declared. "Get them young'uns down from that attic before they fall through the ceiling! I'm coming, Hosie, just keep your drawers on," he had muttered to the sounds of distress from the room beyond.

Lillah had been with them ever since. She was a fearsome creature, tall as a man and proud as a peacock, a Haitian by way of South Carolina. To this day they didn't know why she had chosen to come to Portsmouth Island or how she could have known that Urias Andros was in desperate need of someone to take over the care of his two wild twins and his ailing mother-in-law. Over the years, they had simply come to accept the fact that Lillah "knew things."

Prudence was too keyed up to sleep. She had tiptoed to the front hall and slipped the coins they had collected tonight—more copper than gold this time, thank Providence—into the basket, taking care not to clink them against the other coins there. Lillah would be paid for another few weeks, and Granna would have a new wool shawl and enough port wine and laudanum to keep her in possets for the rest of the winter.

But how long could they go on? What would happen to Granna if they were caught? The disgrace alone would kill her, for she had somehow managed to convince herself that Pru, who along with her twin brother had been taught the arts of fighting, riding, gaming and shooting by a doting father, had outgrown her wicked ways and was now ready to settle with the first likely young gentleman who asked her.

It was partly Pru's fault, for she had worked hard to please her grandmother as the old woman grew more helpless with age. She would do anything in this world for her except marry Albert Thurston or Jeremy Oleck. Or that snail turd, Claude Delarouche.

Pru shuddered. Clad in her night rail, which was too thin for warmth and too small for comfort now that her bosom had sprouted out in such an ungainly fashion, she perched on the window seat in her room and stared out into the night, idly combing her fingers through her long hair as she watched a skein of clouds drift across the face of the moon.

Not too far away, in the well-appointed captain's quarters of the French brigantine, *Saint Germaine,* two men sat talking over cognac.

"Why do you not get rid of that fool, Simpson? He cannot find his own ugly nose," growled the taller of the two men.

"Ah, Jacques, have patience. It is there—did not Andros himself tell us where it was to be found? In my mistress's keep, he said. Do you suppose he could have meant one of the women from the bordello?"

"There is no talk of such a thing. If the man kept a mistress, he was discreet."

Claude's narrow face darkened with anger. "He was a filthy, cheating cur. But for him, I would have been a wealthy man—I will *still* be a wealthy man!" He stood and turned to pour another drink, not bothering to offer the bottle to his cousin, who was, after all, but a by-blow of his father's weak-minded brother. Jacques had proved useful, but once that usefulness was over...

"We have searched the warehouses and the ordinaries. Will you now turn the old woman out of her home and search there? I could be persuaded to go through the bordello once more, for I confess I might have been distracted the first time." The French captain's grin revealed a row of rotting teeth.

"*Non, mon ami.* I have a much simpler plan," Claude mused, crossing his legs so as to admire the length of white silk stocking above his spool-heeled slippers. "The gold is within that house. I can smell it! It belongs to the boy, but if he should happen to have an accident . . ."

"There is still the girl."

"Marriage is a simple matter. What a woman brings to a marriage becomes the property of her husband. And wives, unfortunately, do not seem to live long in this unhealthy climate."

Jacques turned in his chair and poured himself a drink, lifting his glass to his younger kinsman. "Felicitation, cousin."

Chapter Two

After a long spell of warm, dry weather, late December turned cold, windy and wet. Hosannah, bedridden most of the time with swollen and aching joints, eased her misery with frequent possets and drifted more and more often into the past. Pru read aloud to her for hours on end from a tattered novel, one of the few on the island, which were lent freely among the people who could read.

With seas running high and seagoing traffic at a seasonal low, Haskell and Nye had little to do, for they would never knowingly strike an honest target.

But on December 31, a notorious freebooter dropped anchor for provisioning. That night they relieved two members of her crew of a purse containing two gold sovereigns, three guineas, a jeweled ring, a handful of coppers and a curious stump that turned out to be a shriveled human thumb. Pru retched herself inside out at the sight. She'd had just about all the revenge she could stomach.

Lillah muttered constantly about "doings" and "goings-on" that should shame a decent body. Still, she managed to see that Pride had his favorite sweet at least once a week, and took the time to insist that Pru plaster her face with a sticky concoction guaranteed to render her pale and lady-like with faithful use.

Claude Delarouche remained a constant source of irritation, for Hosannah had taken a liking to the young swell, and nothing would change her mind. He was a frequent guest in the household, full of questions and curious about the least little thing. One evening, Prudence had seen him fingering the cypress paneling near the mantelpiece, as if fascinated by the perfectly ordinary texture of the wood. When he noticed Pride watching him, he'd made some remark about the fine handmade wall coverings that were available in his own country.

"If he likes his own country so well, why don't he go back home?" Pride grumbled, having finally shown their guest the door.

Pru tossed a knot of driftwood on the fire and dropped into the high-backed settle to stare fixedly at the leaping blue flames. "I don't trust the man. He's got eyes as cold as a dead mackerel, and besides, he wears too many ruffles."

Hosannah, dozing in her chair, roused in time to hear that last remark. "A gentleman considers it his duty to dress well, my dear. Claude's father was related to one of the oldest houses in Europe."

"Just the same, I hate the way he looks at me."

"Any man worth his salt will notice a pretty girl, and you've your mother's looks, more's the blessing. I dislike to think what I would have done with you if you'd taken after your father."

With a grimace, Pru leaned forward to straighten her grandmother's woolen shawl. "Yes, Granna. Are you getting sleepy yet?" Hosannah would doze half a dozen times each evening before finally giving in and allowing Pru to help her to her bed.

And so the evenings went, with the wind howling to get in and the tide creeping up from the nearby marsh to stand under the house, giving rise to a damp chill that only a roaring fire, a hot brick and a warm blanket could chase away.

To please her grandmother, Prudence continued to comb her long, chestnut hair with a bone comb and polish it with a scrap of old wool until it gleamed like bronze silk. Each evening she would dress in one of her mother's fragile old gowns, and wear Pride's hand-me-down boots and woolen stockings underneath for warmth.

And each evening, for Hosannah's benefit, she pretended that she had lolled away the day in a series of ladylike pursuits instead of fishing for winter trout, hunting the bays for wildfowl or gathering the last of the acorns to parch on the hearth.

To Pru's great disgust, Claude came at least twice a week, always making a fuss over Hosannah and beguiling her into telling him about the grand days when Urias was alive, and theirs was the most prosperous household on the island—indeed, on the entire banks, some said.

Along with her anger and frustration, Pru was beginning to feel increasingly restless. Annie Duvaal blathered constantly these days of marriage and babies, hinting broadly that she found Pride more than pleasing to the eye. Not quite eighteen, however, Pride was wary of entrapment. He made himself scarce whenever he saw the pretty young blonde flouncing up the path.

Being twenty minutes older than her brother, Pru had always lorded it over him, especially as she'd been born with a competitive spirit that made her strive to excel in everything she attempted. Not only was she the faster runner and the better rider, she was a finer marksman and even a better gamester, thanks to her delighted father's tutelage.

All of which exasperated Pride and provoked Hosannah no end. "Prudence Andros, you'll be the death of me yet!" her grandmother would say. "The next time I catch you skylarking about in those wretched trousers like a fallen woman..."

Actually, the only fallen women Prudence had ever seen were those who worked at her father's bordello—not that Urias had ever admitted to owning it, but it was general knowledge that he'd owned all the businesses on the waterfront before he sold them to Mr. Simpson, who turned around and sold them to Claude Delarouche.

"Yes, Granna." She didn't bother to point out that, on the whole, the fallen women at Quick Mary's dressed considerably better than the unfallen ones, thanks to the generosity of the sailors who frequented the establishment.

If January had proved stormy, the first week of February was no better. Shipping was still down, and most of the pirates who regularly preyed on the merchantmen had left for warmer, more productive waters. The whales, however, had shown up earlier than usual this year, which meant that business at the taverns was nearly as brisk as ever.

The *Polly,* with her rounded hull of cypress logs, rolled relentlessly as she made her way into the harbor, and Gideon's normally bronzed features took on a faintly greenish cast. As steady a ship as any man could wish on a stormy sea, she was devilish dancey on a light chop.

"Ready, Cap'n?" shouted his grizzled mate.

"Aye, lower away," Gid muttered, and turned away from the rail. On the day he actually lost his dinner in front of his crew, he would hand over ownership of his sloop to Tobias and wade across the shallow sound until he reached the mainland. He'd been chopping corn and cotton when he was scarcely big enough to lift a hoe—he could always go back to such work if he had to.

"Where ye going to find crew at this time of year, Cap'n?" the old man asked as they set out toward the wharves of Portsmouth.

Gideon seriously doubted that he would find the men needed to fill out his stricken crew. Experienced whalers were in demand, and the season was well under way. "We'll leave one boat ashore and switch around so that every able man has a turn in the other two if we have to."

"Damned shame, so many of 'em coming down with the heavin' trots jest when the season gets hetted up," Toby muttered as he bent to the task of rowing them ashore.

Gid stood in the stern, wind whipping his hair forward as he stared out across the water. He mumbled something in response, his mind on a dozen more pressing matters—among them the price he could command for his oil, the ability of the men he'd left behind to manage without him and whether those blasted cutpurses were still operating in the area.

"It was the pork," Toby grunted as he bent his back to the job. "Damned pig weren't salted down near good enough to keep. I told Ben to throw it out."

"Hmm? Likely you're right," Gid allowed. He spared a look of concern for the wiry figure huddled in the heavy canvas coat. For all his years, Toby could still outrow most men half his age.

Gid had grown fond of the old steersman, but he was careful not to allow it to show in his manner. It would do neither of them any good, and would be deucedly bad for discipline.

"I notice you didn't eat it," he said blandly as he made ready to cast a line around one of the wooden bollards that marched along the docks.

The old man grinned, revealing a gaping lack of teeth. "Weren't stewed down enough, that was all that kept me from it."

"Take my advice—keep away from bad meat, bad rum and bad women and you might manage to live to a ripe old age," Gid retorted, permitting himself a quick grin.

By dusk that evening, Gideon had more than the falling price of oil and the lack of crew to worry over. Word had spread rapidly in the Leaky Cask of the recent activities of the pair of thieves who lay in wait for unwary seamen on their way between taverns and bordello to relieve them of their earnings. Or winnings, if by chance they had been lucky at gaming.

"Three men off'n the *Good Friend* was waylaid not a week ago. I heard they didn't even have a chance to lift a gun, the pair was so bloody fast."

Young Ben downed his rum and tried not to grimace. "I wouldn't fret none over the likes of them," he said. "Way I heard it, the *Good Friend* finds most of her cargoes out to sea, and ain't real particular about keeping up with bills of lading or witnesses, either."

"That's as may be," another crewman put in, "but I vow I near 'bout met my maker once at the hands of them devils. Two of 'em, and young, from the looks of 'em, but mean as forked lightning. If Gouge and Lear hadn't come onto us while they was a turning out my pockets, likely they'd have left me with my skull stove in."

Gideon listened as the tales, fueled by rum and freedom, grew more and more outrageous. Evidently, this had been going on for some time now. The devils were smart, he'd grant them that. Waiting until some poor fool was three sheets to the wind, they would jump him between tavern and bawdy house and take from him whatever coin he still possessed, disappearing into the night.

Dammit, it was bad enough that nearly all of his second crew was laid up from eating bad meat, but when the few healthy men left to him were threatened by a pair of thieving scoundrels, then something had to be done!

Gideon stood, scraping his chair on the gritty floor, and threw down a handful of coppers, letting them ring out clearly. He held up one gold sovereign so that it flashed in the lamplight. It was a lucky piece he had carried for years, the only gold piece he was ever likely to own in this lifetime.

Tonight it would serve as bait.

Glancing about the smoke-filled room for anyone appearing overly curious, he deliberately swayed a bit. Then, tossing the gold piece onto the table where several of his men were rolling dice, he said loudly, "Play this out for me, Gouge, for I fear I've had too much to drink. A bit of air will likely clear my head."

Ignoring the startled looks from his men—for Gideon neither gambled nor drank excessively—he lurched out. Goggle-eyed, they stared after him. "Reckon what got into the cap'n?"

"Hell, he's a man, ain't he? He ain't no saint."

"Saint or not, I never knowed him to act like that."

"Reckon we ought to go after him?"

"What, and see him puking his guts out in the bushes? Ain't bloody likely he'd thank ye for it come morning."

A few of them laughed. A few more looked thoughtful. Someone said, "Ain't bloody likely he'll be thanking the sun for rising come morning. I don't doubt me he'll be sore as a skint bear."

Laughing, the men returned to their gaming, but Gouge slipped the captain's sovereign into his pocket for safekeeping. He'd lost an eye, not his brains. Come morning, Captain McNair would be regretting the loss of his lucky piece.

No one noticed the slender youth in ragged britches and a dark coat who slipped out soon after Gideon.

Avoiding the road, Pride took to the bushes, splashing through marsh as he hurried toward the grove of cedar, yaupon and palmetto. He hadn't truly expected luck to ride with him tonight, for most of the commerce in wintertime was whalers.

It had been the flash of gold that alerted him. Whalers weren't paid off in gold. Both his father and old Simpson had paid more often than not in letters of credit, with a bit of currency to recirculate through the taverns and Quick Mary's.

Then he had seen the man's face, with that blazing red mark as clear as day. God, there couldn't be two such men! He had heard that face described more than once when talk turned to the pirates who frequented the area. Young, yellow-haired, with the devil's brand on his right cheek. Some said he'd been the only one to escape when Will Lewis's *Morning Star* went down.

Pride could hardly credit his good fortune.

"Sweet Jesus, Pru!" he cried breathlessly a few moments later. "Either I've just seen a ghost, or one of old Will Lewis's men is headed this way!"

"Will Lewis! The pirate? Are you certain?"

"Tall as a mast, broad as an ox—leastwise through the shoulders. Hair near as pale as a baby's arse, just like Pa used to say."

"Huh! Since when have you ever seen a baby's—"

"Just hear me out, will ya? The man was throwing gold about as if it was cockleshells, and he had the devil's mark on his right cheek. I saw it, Pru—I mean Haskell—plain as day. There was this dark red thing the size of a gull's egg right where Pa said it was."

Even in the dark, Pru could see the excited sparkle in her brother's eyes. She sometimes thought their activities were more of a lark to him than a matter of revenge and necessity. "Is he drunk?"

"Drunk as a coot! He just went out to clear his head, but he's coming this way. Now ain't you glad I talked you into trying tonight?"

"Talked me into nothing," Pru retorted. With no more coppers for cornmeal and oil, what else could they do? "But I won't rob an honest seaman, Pride, not even for Granna."

"He's a bloody pirate, I tell you—I saw him with my own eyes!"

"Is he alone?"

"Near's I could tell."

"Then we can take him," Pru declared without a moment's hesitation. She tugged the heavy flintlock out of her belt and hitched up her trousers. "Get over there." She pointed to a dense thicket on the other side of the narrow path. "Wait'll I step out, then slip in behind him and poke your stick in his back."

"Ah, dammit, Pru, it's my turn to carry the gun!"

"Just do it! I hear him coming now!"

They had only the one pistol, for they had long since traded its mate for the milk goat and a barrel of pickled beef. And although she wasn't one to brag, they both knew that Pru was a far better marksman than Pride would ever be.

Besides, in a moment of panic on a moonless night, what drunken pirate would know the difference between a stick nudging his backbone and the cold barrel of a second gun?

Gideon forced himself to walk slowly, remembering to stagger a bit. If the cutpurses were about their nefarious business tonight, he might as well let them think he'd be easy pluckings.

The white sand gleamed palely under a sliver of moon as he neared a thicket directly ahead. It was the most likely place for an ambush, and Gid slowed his steps. He pretended to fumble at his trousers, as if to relieve himself in the nearby marsh, all his instincts quivering and alert.

"Stand and deliver!"

No sooner did the boy leap out before him than Gideon whipped out with his belt, striking the pistol that was pointed at his chest and sending it skittering along the ground. He sensed more than heard the second one behind him, and with one hand clamped around a skinny wrist, he spun about and sent the second thief sailing tip over tail.

"Dammit, you said—" the first one cried out, his voice shrill with fear. Or anger, Gid didn't know which.

"Pr—"

"Shut up! Blast you, Nye, can't you do anything right?" *Great God, they were only children!*

"The both of you pipe down," Gideon roared. Whipping the lad's arms behind him, he secured them with his belt. The other one was still flat on the ground, and Gid yanked him to his knees. He hadn't wanted to kill the young scoundrel, but he didn't mind one bit roughing him up. It was time someone taught them a lesson. "All right now, I'm taking you home, and you'll not try anything along the way if you know what's good for you."

The one on his feet was quaking like a halyard in a full gale. Gid felt himself begin to soften and steeled himself against it. Dammit, if they were old enough to go about waving guns under a man's nose and robbing him of his hard-earned wages, then they were old enough to take their punishment. And since there was no law closer than Queen Anne's Towne, he would see to it that they got a good taste of homegrown discipline!

"Lead on!" he barked. "If your own father don't peel your britches down and blister your backsides, then I'll damned well do it for him! You're lucky I don't haul you across the sound!''

"You lay one finger on me and I'll carve out your liver and stuff it up your—'' the skinny one cried, and Gid yanked hard on the belt that bound his wrists, jerking it upward. He heard the sharp gasp of pain, and wished he hadn't yanked quite so hard, but dammit, the mouthy little bastard had stuck a gun in his face, and that riled him considerably.

"Tell me where you live!"

"Nowhere!'' cried the mouthy one, while the other one mumbled what sounded almost like an apology.

"Want to try that again?'' Bending over, he shoved his face into that of the lad he had bound up with his belt; runt or not, Gid was fairly certain he was the ringleader, for the other poor wretch, even though he was some taller and considerably broader in the shoulders, was nearly in tears.

"Nowhere,'' the runt growled at him. "I told you, we don't have a home—we—we're orphans!''

"Now, why the hell don't I believe you?'' Gid mused. The little devil was shivering so hard his bones were fairly knocking together. Gid turned to the other one, unconsciously moving to stand between the runt and the sharp, cold wind that blew in off the sound. "All right now, lad, let's have the truth of it.'' He was almost sure they were lying. Still, he couldn't very well turn them loose to continue this nasty business.

"Sh—my brother's right, sir. Our mother died when we were babes, and our pa was killed by pirates.''

"Humph! More likely he was strung up for thieving,'' Gideon muttered.

"That's not so! He was took by pirates. One of the crew made it to shore by hanging on to a pickle barrel, and he described the whole thing before he died. Honest, if it ain't the truth, may I turn blue and drop dead. We thought you were—''

"Someone else," the runt finished for him. "We would never have dared stop you if we'd known you were—ah, I mean you weren't—"

Gideon found he was quite enjoying their discomfort. The young heathens deserved to be roasted over a hot fire, and even at that, it was probably too late to save them.

"We promise not to bother you—or anyone else—ever again," vowed the trembling one. But Gid wasn't about to be taken in by the young whelp. Not after the tales he'd been hearing.

But what the devil was he going to do if they were telling the truth and there was no one about to straighten them out? Momentarily distracted, Gideon allowed his grasp on the end of the belt to loosen and his attention to stray from the scrawny scrap of devilment moping along before him.

It was all the chance they needed, for even as the one jerked himself free, the other took flight.

"Oh, no, you don't, you young bastards!" With the swiftness learned in his earlier years as striker for a northern whaling crew, Gideon reached out and caught one by the shoulder, the other by the shirttail, and brought them together as hard as he could.

Heads cracked. Curses heated the air. Gideon wondered belatedly if he had broken their brain boxes.

"Blast it, if you won't give me a straight answer, I'll damned well deal with you as I see fit!"

"You'll let us go?" whispered the runt, who was clutching his noggin and swaying from side to side. Gid wanted to examine the boy to see if he'd done any permanent damage, but he didn't dare. The little blighter would likely knee him where it would do the most damage and take off again.

"I'll do better than that," he vowed darkly. Swinging the pair around before him, he began marching them toward the docks.

Prudence was thinking furiously, a process hampered by the pain in her head and the fear in her heart. They could admit to having a home and a grandmother to mete out punishment, but would he believe them? And if he did, and dragged them home looking like this, what would Granna do?

He would tell her what they'd been doing, and she would look them in the eyes, and they would all die of shame! Dear Lord, how had they come to this? It had seemed so logical at the time—taking care of Granna, and at the same time taking their revenge against the kind of men that had murdered their father.

Never mind the few mistakes they had made—what else could she have done? Gone to work for Quick Mary?

"Move, or I'll heave you into the swamp and leave the snakes to chew away at your filthy hides!"

Pru was more than willing to risk it, but she was given no chance. The great hulking brute dragged her along by her bound wrists as if she were a half-wild animal.

"You don't have to break my arm," she grumbled, hurrying so as to ease the strain.

"I'll break more than that if you give me cause."

She had to believe him. The man had probably murdered more men than she would know in a lifetime. "Umm...you could leave us here at the foot of the path," she said, her husky voice quivering with cold and fright. "We promise never to do it again."

"Do what?"

She thought fast. If she admitted they'd been relieving men of their purses on a more or less regular basis for nearly three years, he might not be so willing to let them off with a dressing-down. "P-play at being robbers?" she ventured.

"Play? Ha! It don't strike me as play when a pair of stinking little cur pups tickles a man's nose with a blasted flintlock like it was no more'n a goose feather!"

"It wasn't loaded." Papa's pistol! Where the devil was it? "That is, I wouldn't even know how to fire it. You see, we found it, and—that is, we—I—"

"Stole it, more'n likely."

As the row of warehouses that lined the wharves came in sight, Pru and Pride bumped along together, their wrists caught up behind them by the great ox, who took one stride to their three. Pru could feel his breath on the back of her neck where her stocking cap had slipped awry in the tussle. If the thing came off and her hair came tumbling down she would be discovered and poor Granna would likely disown them, and at her age, and in her condition, she needed them. Lillah would stay only as long as her wages were paid. She reminded them of that fact with depressing regularity.

"Where are you taking us?" she questioned.

No answer. Her lips tightened mutinously, and she looked at Pride. *Do something,* she willed silently. *You're the man—can't you think of some way to make him turn us loose?*

They were forced to scamper up onto the wharf—it was either that or have their arms jerked out of their sockets. Then, before they could even get their bearings, they were both flung facedown into an open boat. "You stinking blackguard!" Pru shouted, spitting grit and bilge water.

A large booted foot came gently down on her neck. "Unless you want me to drown you right now, guttersnipe, you'll pipe down."

The words were less than reassuring. As was the fact that before she could wriggle out from under the boot, she felt the boat lurch away from the wharf and head out into the open channel.

Beside her, Pride lay unmoving. Was he dead? Had he broken his neck when that devil-marked bastard had flung him into the boat?

She would kill him with her own bare hands. She would make him pay, if it was the last thing she ever did!

Pride, damn you, don't go off and leave me alone, for I can't bear it! You're a part of me—I need you! Dammit, don't you dare leave me alone this way!

Could she take him by herself? Could she leap up and surprise him enough to throw him overboard?

He was too big. Too powerful. Entirely too vicious. The next time, he would kill her without a second thought.

Sitting up, she watched the man closely, for her eyes were well adjusted to the darkness. The boat was meant for at least six men, but he rowed it easily, digging deep and handling his sweeps with ease.

Voice quivering, she asked, "What are you planning to do with us? I fear my brother is hurt bad."

"Not bloody likely. He's too wicked to die young."

They were drawing away from the shore, the sounds of revelry fading fast. Pru snaked out a hand and touched Pride's arm. He was still warm, at least. "Are you going to make pirates of us?" she ventured.

"Ah, so you want to know your fate, do you?"

Her mouth snapped shut at the sound of his laughter. It was not a pleasant sound, nor did it interfere in the least with his stroke.

"First off, I'm going to teach you some manners, you devil's spawn."

Manners? She would believe that when bluefish rode horseback. "You plan to drown us, don't you?"

"Oh, no. I've something entirely different in mind for the pair of you."

"We didn't harm you! We were only taking back a bit of our own!"

"A bit of your own! Before I'm done with the pair of you, you arrogant young pup, you'll know what it's like to do an honest day's work for an honest day's pay. Then you might be in a better position to judge what's yours and what's not!"

That did it! The bloody bleeding cutthroat had finally got her riled! "Honest day's work! Why, you blasted murdering heathen, you wouldn't know honest, if it slammed you in your devil-marked face!"

"Heathen, huh? I been called worse. Now batten your trap before I give you something to bellyache about. I've never been known for my patience."

Pru stared sadly back toward the shore, now barely visible in the distance. In a few more weeks they would have turned eighteen. Granna had promised her a party, which she'd hardly wanted at all, there being no one interesting to invite.

Now, perversely, she found herself longing for a gathering of good friends, for cake and mulled cider, for singing and dancing . . . even with that pig, Albert Thurston.

Chapter Three

"**N**eed a hand, Cap'n?"

"Aye, Crow, I'll need a line. These lads are a mite stove in."

A line snaked down the side of the hull, and Gideon reached for the toughest of the pair he had captured, the runt. "Any of the men back yet?" he called up softly in the darkness.

"Be the taverns shut down yet?"

Prudence could scarcely make out the shadow of a head and shoulders leaning over the rail above them. This was to be their fate, then—they were to become pirates themselves?

"Give me a hand with this pile of dung, will you?" the big man commanded, and then, to Pru's horror, he whipped the line about her chest and knotted it to one side, checking to make sure it would not slip.

Furious, she shoved his hands away and tried to step out of range, only to stumble over her brother. "Hold there, damn you, or I'll feed the pair of you to the sharks! If I weren't so blasted shorthanded—"

She was still protesting when she found herself being hauled painfully up the side of the tall sloop, her knees and elbows bumping every inch of the way. Before the line had quite succeeded in cutting her in two, she was dumped unceremoniously onto the deck, where for a moment she simply lay staring up into the darkness, struggling to catch her breath.

Unseen hands removed the line, and a flash of white that could have been a smile shone above her. "Found your men, eh, Cap'n?"

"I'd not call them men, but they'll serve well enough in camp to free up Lear and Ben. Leastwise we'll be doing Portsmouth a favor by ridding them of this pair of lice."

Before Pru could arm herself with a blistering rebuttal, Pride was dumped out beside her. He groaned, and she nearly drowned in relief. He was alive! Alone, she didn't know what would have become of her, but together, they could surely manage to outsmart this stinking boatload of cutthroats.

Reaching out, she touched his reassuringly warm body.

"Oh, Pru, what are we—"

"Dammit all, *Nye,* stop your blubbering!" she whispered fiercely. For all she loved him dearly, her brother had never been one to keep a cool head when things began to go awry. They were of an age, yet he seemed years younger, leaving her all too often torn between mothering him and clinging to him for protection.

There'd be no clinging now, not until they were free of these devils. "We'll get out of this somehow," she reassured him without the least notion of how they would manage it. They simply must, that was all.

"But how?"

"Never mind how. I'll think of something. Just keep your wits about you and wait for my signal."

"Pru, what's Granna going to think when we don't come downstairs in the morning?"

"Hush! Lillah'll make up some story. Didn't she cover for me when that damned stallion threw me down to the south'ard and I had to walk all the way home?"

"Yes, but that was a single night. This is likely to be forever!"

"We'll just have to find some way to escape before she misses us. Now, cry off," she whispered fiercely. "They'll hear us!"

The two men were talking quietly between themselves as they secured the launch, and Pru tried in vain to make out what they were saying. Did their captor suspect? Dear Lord, if that blemished devil should ever learn about Granna and go telling tales, she would never forgive him!

"Ssst! Pru, you mustn'—"

"My name is *Haskell*, you noddy, and don't you forget it!"

"Yes, but you mustn't ever allow them to learn that you're naught but a girl," Pride warned, and she nodded, grabbing her aching head at the resulting pain. They were huddled together where they had landed, Pru rubbing her sore head and Pride his bruised backside.

But he was right, of course. If they ever found out she was a woman nearing her eighteenth year, it would likely be the worst for her. She'd heard horrible tales of how such men treated their female captives.

Not that she'd fully understood them. But by the time she'd grown curious enough to ask questions about the things a man did to a woman, there'd been no one to ask except her friend Annie Duvaal, and she wasn't fool enough to believe half of what Annie had told her.

Oh, her father had taught her well enough how to use a sword and pistol, how to spot a card cheat, how to use a knife for everything from skinning out a muskrat to chinking up a leaky seam. He had taught her how to swear in four different languages, and even taught her how to lure a wild boar into a pitfall without getting herself gored in the process. But when it came to those mysterious things that happened to a woman when she turned a certain age, she'd had to look to Lillah, who had stressed that she must never *ever* allow a man take "liberties" with her person.

But when Pru had tried to find out precisely what a "liberty" was, Lillah had shut up tighter than a clam at low tide. And Granna was worse than useless.

She'd known for years about kissing and hugging. Albert Thurston had caught her mending net out behind the shed when she was fourteen and bussed her flat on the mouth. Naturally, she'd shoved his face in the mud and held it there until Pride made her let him up.

But all that silly nonsense she'd heard from Annie, who could believe that? Any man fool enough to shed all his clothes in this weather would freeze stiffer'n a dead mackerel. And even if he didn't, and he found a woman witless enough to climb jaybird naked into bed with him, all that poking and prodding sounded silly, and damned uncomfortable, besides!

She had begun to hope she and Pride had been forgotten when she saw one of the two men coming back. It was the big one, his boots surprisingly quiet on the hollow deck.

"You two limbs of Satan found anything to say for yourselves?" he demanded. "No? Then we'll see how long it takes you to come around. Crow, come and tie 'em up."

"Aye, sir." Like a shadow, the other form crossed silently and knelt beside them. Pru flinched, but his touch, though firm, was gentle enough.

"Watch yourself, they're a wicked pair. The runt would as leave blow your head off as bid you the day." The captain stood back and watched while his mate bound them both, hands and feet. Not until they stood before him, tightly secured fore and aft, did he address them directly. "We'll see if we can't work some of the rocks out of your gizzards, lads. A few weeks of hard labor should do it."

"You bloody bast—"

"Toss 'em in the hold, Crow. They'll keep until we get back to camp."

"There be coffee boiling on the stove and a pan of bread. Do you think—" the dark one began, when his captain cut him off.

"I do not. Don't let their tender years fool you. They're the devil's spawn right enough. I'd have been lying in a marsh somewhere with my gut blown open and my pockets turned out if I hadn't been ready for them."

"That's not true," Pru squeaked. And then, remembering to lower her voice, she cried, "We never in all our years harmed a soul, and that's the honest truth. Did we, Nye? Never, I swear it!" And though it fair killed her to do it, she added a grudging, "Sir."

The tall devil with the marked cheek grinned, his teeth gleaming in the light of a half moon. For the first time, Pru felt herself go limp as anger fled, to be replaced by fear.

Everyone knew a pirate would torture for profit, but to torment for the sheer pleasure of inflicting pain on another human being—and to *smile?* Why, that wasn't even human!

A low moan escaped her, and Pride hobbled closer, supporting her with his wiry strength. Was he, too, remembering Lillah's tales of those dreadful creatures who came back from the dead, who walked right up out of the ocean with their teeth gleaming in their evil skulls and their eyes all empty and staring?

"Are you a—a *jumbee?*" she queried before she could bite her tongue.

"Am I a *what?* Why, you little heathen, who's been filling your noggin full of such tomfoolery? Dammit, get a move on there, Crow, before I forget myself and take a strap to the pair of them!"

Prudence had no way of knowing how much time had passed when she awakened to near darkness. In attempting to lift her hands to press them to her throbbing temples, she was reminded painfully of how she and her brother had been bound up and lowered into this freezing hellhole.

Groaning, she struggled to sit up, tugging impotently against the salt-hardened ropes. Tears came to her eyes, and she stared malevolently at the slit of gray light visible overhead.

The thieving, murdering, seagoing heathens! At least they were human, she decided, for no rotting hunk of waterlogged Haitian ghost could have tied them this securely!

"Pride!" she croaked, twisting about to peer into the thick darkness. As her eyes gradually adjusted, she could make out what appeared to be stacks of wooden barrels arranged neatly on their sides all around them.

"Pru? You all right?"

"My headbone's splitting open, and I'm all trussed up like a blasted boar hog, but other than that, I'm just lovely!"

"Leastwise, you had a stocking cap and all that hair to pad the blow. If the pain in my noggin is anything to go by, I'm alive, at least. What went wrong?"

"That miserable scar-faced bastard wasn't drunk, he was just gulling us. It was all a wicked trap!"

Pride scuttled closer, and Pru was glad of his warmth, for it was fearsome cold in the bowels of the ship. Overhead, she could hear the wind howling in the rigging, and she shuddered. As nearly as she could make out, it was just about daybreak. If the wind blew this hard with the sun on the horizon, it would soon be spitting a full gale.

"If we tell them who we truly are and that we never meant them any harm, do you think they'll let us go?" Pride ventured.

"Don't even think about it! Can you imagine what would happen to Granna if that ugly devil were to show up on our doorstep and tell her he'd caught us trying to rob him with Papa's pistol? Her poor heart would likely give out on her, and even if it didn't, we wouldn't see the light of day for the next ten years. He'd have her believing we were nothing but a pair of thieves!"

"I reckon we are, at that." Pride's voice broke. He sounded cold and miserable and hungry—more little boy than man. Pru suspected she would have her work cut out for her keeping him from surrendering them both.

"We were never thieves! Not in the ordinary way, at least—we were only taking back what was rightly our own," she said.

"Yes, but Granna—"

"Lillah will take care of Granna. She knows what's in the sewing basket, I'm convinced of it. More'n likely, knows how it came to be there, too. And if we don't come back, she'll look after Granna and find some story to set her poor old mind at rest. Lillah won't see her hurt, Pride—er, Nye, that is."

They both fell silent for a time, and then Pride said, his voice more unsure than ever, "What happens when the coins are all used up? There's still a good bit of gold, but you know as well as I do that a black woman, even a freed one, can't go sporting gold 'thout stirring up trouble for herself."

Prudence fought against the tears that were a sign of weakness—a weakness she could ill afford. "Pity sake, we'll be back home before you know it! There's bound to be a way—all we have to do is wait our chance. Just keep your mouth shut and your eyes open."

"And my nose pinched."

"That most of all! She's truly foul, isn't she? A whaler, from the smell of her. I wonder what they did with the rightful owners?"

"Don't think on it, Pru. We'll get away, never doubt it."

By the time the hold was thrown open and the twins were led up to meet their captors, a bright coppery light had spread across the sky, touching everything with its warmth. Prudence, her circulation sorely impaired from having been trussed up for so long, swayed on her feet as she tried to sum up their circumstances in a single glance.

It was the man called Crow who came for them. Pru wondered at the name. She couldn't make out if he was Negro, like Lillah, or Indian, like the men who came to fish the lower end of the island.

Could he possibly be a slave? Even the Indians had slaves, she had learned—members of other tribes, bartered for or taken by force.

This man was no slave, not if his bearing was anything to judge by. By the time he had helped them climb out of the hold, Pru had lost much of her fear of him. For all his massive strength, there was no cruelty in his hands. He could easily have broken them into fishbait.

"Aren't you going to untie us?" she asked, remembering to keep her voice pitched to Haskell's husky tones.

Ignoring her question, Crow led them across the deck, allowing them a moment to stare over the railing. It was the first they realized that they were riding at anchor. "There be food soon," the dark-skinned seaman told them, but neither Pru nor Pride could have forced down a bite.

Where the devil were they? There was a narrow, unfamiliar inlet off to the northeast, but little else of note. No warehouses, no houses of any sort. Yet there were three sharp-ended launches of a considerable size, all filled with deck cargo and making for the low and barren shore.

Hearing a sound, Pru turned warily. Behind Crow, who stood as tall and silent as a burnt pine, three common seamen stared, their faces without expression. She waited for her fate. When nothing happened, she shifted her gaze back to the man called Crow, lifting her throbbing head proudly. Both her hands and her feet were aching fit to fall off, but she'd be damned if she would let on by word or deed.

A footfall sounded behind her, and she spun around. The devil-marked bastard had snuck up behind them! Unfortunately, fear had always made her more reckless than reasonable. "Dammit," she exclaimed, remembering just in time to lower her voice, "why don't you just chop off our heads and nail them onto the bowsprit and be done with it? Fair lot of good we'll be when our hands and feet rot and drop off!"

In the darkness the night before, she'd barely been able to make out his features. Here under a blazing sun, she had no trouble at all in recognizing him. Few men stood so tall or so broad across the shoulders. Yet for all his breadth, he was surprisingly lean in the flank. Sun had bleached his thick blond hair until it gleamed more like silver than gold, and his eyes were surely bluer than mortal man should possess.

She'd always imagined angels would possess such coloring, but if this man were an angel, he was an angel of Satan, come to spread his wickedness among decent, God-fearing folk. There was nothing faintly heavenly in his salt-stained chamois vest, his snug canvas breeches or his well-worn, buckleless boots that had been oiled until they looked soft as silk.

Abruptly, the pirate captain turned away to dismiss his crew, leaving Pru with an image of a high-bridged nose, a stern, yet curving mouth and a formidable jaw. For a man who made his livelihood preying on others, the bloody bastard was remarkably handsome, Pru admitted grudgingly, hating the way her eyes clung to him in spite of her disgust.

Abruptly, he turned back to face her. Pru shivered, her gaze torn between the devil's mark on his right cheek and the cold blue fire of his eyes. Pride, who had seen him more clearly in the tavern, had told her about the mark on his face, but he'd failed to mention the stunning intensity of those eyes.

For what seemed a lifetime, no one moved. Wind keened through the rigging. Wooden rings clacked against the mast, and overhead a fish gull squawked loudly. The spell was suddenly broken by an old man who cackled and said, "Caught 'em red-handed, did ye, Cap'n?"

"Aye, but they'll soon learn an honest trade. We'll see how they like stripping, chopping and tending kettle."

Stripping, chopping and tendenkettle? Stripping who? Chopping what? And what the devil was a tendenkettle?

"An honest trade!" she scoffed. Pride clutched at her coattail with the fingers of his bound hands and tugged, but she was beyond caution. "And what would the lot of you know about honesty? At least not a one of you ever came to harm at our hands, which is a bloody lot more than you can say for your own victims!"

"Prudence!" Pride hissed.

"Th' lad's bleating nonsense," muttered a galleon-sized seaman with an empty eye socket and a hideous smirk.

"He's plumb daft." The growl of agreement sounded more puzzled than angry, but Pru was too het up to take note. She glared at the lot of them, gallows bait all. She'd seen pirates aplenty in her day, but a more scurrilous crew than this she had never seen!

"You'd rather spare the whales and burn mossbunkers in your lamps?"

She blinked, momentarily thrown off course. Mossbunkers? They were the fattest, rankest of all the fish, so why would she want to burn one in her lamps? And *whales?*

Before Prudence could make sense of any of the comments, the ringleader moved to stand before her. "What name do you go by, lad?"

"Uh—uh—"

"Haskell and Nye," Pride put in quickly. "He's Haskell, I'm Nye." He glanced nervously at Pru and was relieved to see her nod in agreement.

"Last name?" barked Gideon.

"We ain't got any other names," replied Prudence, getting into the role she had so often assumed before.

"Family? Surely there's someone."

"Got no family at all. I told you, our ma died and our pa was kilt by them thieving, murdering bast—"

"He means—uh, freebooters, sir," Pride put in diplomatically.

"But there's a woman what feeds us now'n again, name of Black Lillah. She'll likely wonder what become of us." She glanced at Crow, who stood still as a statue, never letting on by so much as the flicker of an eyelash that he cared the least bit what became of them. "If some'un could get word to Lillah, sir, I'd be obliged."

"Not family, you say?"

"She's a Negro, sir, but she belongs to herself. She's got paper that says it."

"All right, lads, I'll consider it. I don't have to explain why you're here, for you well know that what you were doing was wrong. You'd have been caught sooner or later, and you can thank Providence I was the one to do it."

Pru's green eyes blazed again. "Thank—" she began, when Pride elbowed her sharply.

"My brother means, thank you kindly, sir."

Gideon looked suspiciously from one to the other. Finally, he nodded once and began speaking. "Happens I need men. I'm shorthanded for a spell, and the roads of Portsmouth Island will be well rid of the likes of you two. Just so you know what's in store for you, hear me out now, for I'm not given to repeating my words."

Pru's mouth had opened automatically to register a protest, but this time she subsided without a murmur. The deck was teeming with silent, battle-scarred men, a rough sort who could make things infinitely worse if they were of a mind to.

Gideon seemed to tower over them. There was only one man who came near his height, and that was Crow. Thoroughly intimidated for once in her life, Prudence clamped her mouth shut while Gideon said, "You're to settle down and cause me no more trouble, else I'll haul you up to Queen Anne's Towne myself and see you in irons. *Now,*" he continued, glaring right into Pru's rebellious eyes, "God knows how long you young hellions have been running wild, but when you made the mistake of holding up the first one of my men, you cut your own throat. It's long past time you learned some manners, and as neither of you seems to be acquainted with the notion of a day's work for a day's pay, I've taken it upon myself to broaden your education. How long have you been without a father?"

"Three—" began Pride.

"Ten years." Prudence wanted all the sympathy she could garner, and the man seemed to have some feeling for their being orphans.

"Liars, too, I see. Ah, well, we'll soon change all that." His derisive glance raked over Pru's costume, from the shapeless knit cap that covered her hair and half her grimy face, to the threadbare coat and breeches Pride had worn out years before, and the boots that were several sizes too large, the soles tied on with netting twine. "You'll be issued a coat, a blanket, a set of 'skins, a pair of boots, two shirts and two pairs of breeches a year. You'll be—''

"A year!" Pru yelped.

Ignoring her, he went on. "You'll be fed two meals a day and given a blanket and a place to sleep. For that, you'll carry out your assigned tasks to the best of your ability for a period of time that I deem suitable."

"And then you'll let us go?" asked Prudence.

"Stow it! I'm not done talking yet!"

"Well, what about this pay you keep blathering on about?" she demanded.

With an icy glare, Gideon said, "Each member of my crew gets a share of the proceeds. The pair of you will pay your shares over to the men you've robbed until each man has been paid in full."

"But that's not fa—"

"Make no mistake—any man here will gladly dispatch you to the hereafter if you so much as shirk a single task. Do I make myself clear? There's whales out there waiting to be taken. And once they're taken, you'll haul arse until the carcasses are beached. And once they're beached, you'll chop, strip and haul blubber, and then try out oil until you're sick of the sight and the smell of it, and then you'll damned well do it some more!"

Whalers. *Whalers!* Not pirates, but honest, law-abiding whalers!

"Do I make myself clear?" Gideon roared again, to the amazement of his crew, for their captain was not a man to show emotion of any sort.

Both twins nodded hastily in agreement. It was hardly the first time they had made a mistake and robbed honest men instead of pirates, though they had tried their best to be sure. This time, however, their mistake was to cost them dearly.

The camp was huddled down between two ridges, nearer the ocean than the sound. All supplies, therefore, including nearly a hundred barrels, had to be hand-carted across the low shore, past the woods, through what seemed miles of deep, soft sand.

"It appears to me a man with half a brain would get an ox to haul his carts," she grunted to no one in particular. There were six men pulling and three more pushing.

"Aye, it 'pears that way, don't it?" replied the man called Thomas. "Onliest thing is, he'd have to haul hay to feed the beast, and it don't seem reasonable."

"There's grass on the dunes." She turned and planted her bottom against the back of the cart as the wooden wheels dug in deeper.

"Last about a day, it would. Without the grass, the sand'd soon come a-blowing down onto the camp, and then the sea'd come a-washing over us. Don't hardly seem worth it when the critters can't do nothing but walk."

By the time they finished hauling provisions across the narrow island, Pru would have traded any one of them, including her own brother, for a single ox. Her hands were bleeding and raw. Her feet, in the wet and worn boots, were little better. Each time she felt the captain's gaze light on her, she doubled her efforts, until Crow appeared beside her and led her off to one side, where he smeared some foul-smelling substance on her hands.

She was too spent to resist, too spent even to thank him, although she knew he meant it kindly. Unless he was in league with the captain and was trying to poison her. At this point, she hardly cared.

It was nearly dark by the time she was allowed a moment to size up her new home. It stank. That was her first impression. As if the smell of whale offal weren't bad enough, there was a pigpen and a net enclosure housing a dozen or so scrawny chickens to add to the stench and the noise.

She would never endure it. Not for a single day, much less a week. Much less a year!

During the endless trips across the island, she had noticed a dense grove of trees some half a mile distant from the camp. Thick enough to hide in, it seemed to stretch nearly down to the sound shore. An idea began to take shape. Ships were bound to pass close by. Fishermen were bound to work these waters....

She would wait for a chance to slip away, but first she had to recover from this dreadful, endless day.

"You mean this is where I'm expected to *sleep?*" she squawked a short while later. The shack that the man called Gouge had pointed out to her was small and dismal, little more than a hut made of brush and rough plank. "I wouldn't ask a pig to sleep in that filthy hovel!"

"He don't. He sleeps with me."

Pru could only stare, wondering if she'd fallen asleep and was caught up in some endless, hideous nightmare. "I'd like to see the other accommodations, if you please."

The mutilated face twisted into what could only be a smile, and Pru cringed, wondering where Pride had got to. "This here'n is the onliest one left. Them what slept here with Crow 'n Ben was took real bad off. They're over to Ocracoke, so you 'n yer brother kin have their places. Bugs ain't too bad this time o' year."

Bugs! Crow and Ben—And she was expected to *sleep with them?* "You can take your stinking hovel and burn it to the ground before I'll set one foot in it!" She was bent over, one hand on the small of her back, with strips torn off her shirttail wrapped around her bleeding palms.

Pride, coming up behind the pair of them, felt an upsurge of sympathy. If only he'd had the courage to speak up in the beginning and take his punishment from Granna. If only he'd had the gumption long ago to put an end to this business of revenge and reprisal, and getting back their own from their father's murderers.

Pru had always been too bold for her own good, and Papa had encouraged her, laughing when she outdid them both. Now Papa was gone, and it was up to Pride to protect his twin sister from her own recklessness.

The trouble was, he hadn't the least notion how to go about it.

"I think he means we're both to share it, Haskell," he said, his voice gentle even though he was in nearly as bad shape as she was. "The both of us'll sleep there—we'll do well enough."

She turned on him, her gray-green eyes tilted dangerously. "Do you know we're expected to share this—this pigpen with two of these stinking . . . *sailors?*"

"We be whalers, lad, and don't ye forget it," growled the hulk towering over them.

"Oh, yes," she said sweetly, "and this one claims to sleep with a pig!"

"Now, now, Haskell," Pride said, his voice heavy with silent warning. "We're well and truly caught, so you may as well stew down."

Pru got the message. She was acting missish, and he was right to scold her. Pirates or no, they were still men of the roughest sort. If word should get back to Portsmouth that she'd been picked up by a crew of whalers and brought to their camp, she'd be ruined. No decent man would ever look at her, not even Albert, which suited her well enough. But the shock would kill poor Granna.

She blustered a bit more from sheer habit, but when Gouge went about his own business, her face fell. "I'm not fighting, Pri—Nye, I'm just so tired, and so scared, and so hungry. Don't they *ever* plan to *feed us?*"

"Forget your belly. Just stop calling attention to yourself. You want 'em to take off your shirt to flog you?"

Pru's eyes widened, and she cut a nervous glance at the group of men gathered around the farthest hut. A canvas awning extended out to form a shelter of sorts, under which several crude tables and benches had been placed. She would probably be expected to eat there, along with all the others, which was bad enough, but what was even worse, it had just occurred to her that she would have to wear the miserable chest binder for days on end—perhaps even for weeks—until they could find some way to escape.

"Pru?"

"Yes—that is, all right, I'll behave," she said dispiritedly.

And then deep down inside her, a small spark began to flicker and glow—the flame of competitiveness that had been bred into her by her father and fostered until the day he left home to triple his fortune. If what the blemished devil wanted was a worker, why then, she'd be the best darned stripper and chopper and kettle tender he'd ever seen. If it killed her, as well it might, he would have no cause to complain that Prudence Andros was a shirker.

The tent with the awning was indeed the cook tent. That night, Pru waited until the others had eaten and gone to their huts to sleep, all save the single lookout left posted in a crow's nest built in the highest dune. Waiting to be sure his attention was focused on the moonlit water beyond the surf, she hurried on back to the crude necessary, which was little more than a brush wall around a trench in the sand.

After that, she slipped across to the trying area, where a row of fifty-gallon iron pots waited to be filled with blubber, which would be melted down and strained through the series of rush-filtered wooden troughs and eventually into the barrels.

Glancing about to be sure she was unobserved, Pru collected enough soot from the try kettles to keep her in "beard" for a week or more. It would hardly stand close scrutiny, but it did serve to disguise her downy, too soft cheeks. If they thought her too slovenly to bathe, all the better—at least she wouldn't stand out in this motley company.

Pride greeted her in a whisper when she ducked into the dark hut. "You all right, Pr—Haskell?"

She murmured a response, and heard him begin to snore within moments. She must remember never to slip and call him Pride—or to answer to anything except Haskell.

Fortunately, like all the others, she was expected to sleep in her clothes. Despite the draft that filtered through the walls, the air was fetid. The one called Ben—a boy, really, despite his swagger—was snuffling in his sleep like a hound dog after a hunt, but at least Crow remained silent, sleeping on his back with one hand on the hilt of his knife and the other clutching the sandy floor. It took only a bit of imagination to picture him coming suddenly awake, hurling a handful of sand in a body's eyes before plunging with his knife.

Moving silently, she sought a place on the far side of the hut, and then nearly cried out in relief when she lowered herself onto her own thin pallet. Her blanket was thick enough, though it smelled of whale, as did everything else that didn't smell of pig or chicken. She rolled up in it, pulled her cap down over her face and fell into a deep, dreamless sleep.

Morning came too soon. It was pitch-dark when the men around her began stirring, grunting and swearing under their breath. Before the uneven line leading to the necessary thinned out sufficiently for her to even think of making the trip herself, she found herself eyeing the distant woods longingly.

Perhaps today they would find a chance to slip away....

There was a lot to be learned. Rather than risk a flogging, Pru made herself heed every word. Whether by design or otherwise, she and Pride were set to different tasks so that they scarcely had time even to speak. The captain, whose name she had learned was Gideon McNair, had assigned Crow the task of educating her.

Fortunately for her, the man had a wealth of patience. No matter how many times he had to explain a task, he never lost his temper. Had it been the captain himself instructing her, Pru suspected the two of them would have been at each other's throats before the first hour had passed.

"The dead ones, they be called drifters. Sometime they come to us, sometime we go to them." Crow wore no coat, despite the raw damp nor'easter that kept most of the other men returning often to the cook shack for a mug of the rum-laced coffee that was always on the hob.

"What about the live ones?" she asked. Surely she wasn't expected to go to sea in an open boat and conquer a giant whale on its own territory.

In his oddly accented tones, Crow explained how the three crews of six men each would launch the boats and row out to where the whales had been sighted, taking care not to alert the sensitive beasts before they closed in to make the kill. "With holes no bigger than a stem of sea grass, they can hear the smallest noise. They hear, they be frightened. They be frightened, they sound—go down deep, deep," he said, his voice rumbling quietly.

In spite of herself, Pru was fascinated. "And you lose them?"

"No," he told her with the merest hint of a smile in his amber-colored eyes. "The oarsmen, they change to thin paddles that do not cut deeply the water. It be the work of the steersman to guide the oarsmen. It be the work of the striker to sink the iron. It be a great honor to sink first iron, but more be needed."

There was too much to take in all at once. Steersmen and oarsmen, strikers and irons and ears as small as a stem of grass in a creature big as a warehouse.

"Is that all?" she asked, shoulders drooping tiredly, although it was scarce midday.

This time he smiled, his broad face creasing unexpectedly. "There be your job," he said with a hint of laughter in his voice.

And so she learned about cutting and toting wood to keep the fires burning, carving strips of fat off the beached hulks with a razor-sharp shovel, cutting that into lengths, holing it, poling it, hauling it up to the kettles, then boiling—or trying—it, until the fat became oil and straining it until the oil became clear.

"But how will I know when it's done?" she asked, more intimidated than she had ever been in her life.

Before she had her answer, Pride joined them, looking none the worse for his first morning's instructions. "Are you all done here, Haskell? After we eat, you're to chop rushes and I'm to cut firewood. That don't seem so bad, does it?''

"Rushes?'' she asked faintly.

"To strain the oil,'' Crow reminded her, and she nodded absently, her mind too full of five dozen facts to absorb one more.

Before the day was done, she had visited the woods, with no chance at all to escape, for Ben was with her. It was he who showed her the water hole where they refilled the butts, a job she would be expected to take on in turn.

"We all serve turnabout when there's no whales sighted. Ye'll take a hand at cooking, like the rest of us, and tending the hogs and fowl, too.''

"Cooking! But I can't—''

"Hell, neither can the rest of us, but it don't make no difference. Cap'n say it's your turn to cook, you cook or lose a half a share o' pay.''

Gouge's pet pig ambled by, lean and mean as any wild hog Pru had ever laid eyes on. She stepped back, eyeing the beast warily, and young Ben cackled aloud. "Ha! Don't lay a hand on Lucinda, or ye'll never hear the end of it!''

"Lucinda?'' As ignorant as she was in some respects, Pru knew a boar when she saw one.

"Lear took to calling him Lucifer, but Gouge got his dander up, so we changed it to Lucinda. Mostly, we just call him Lucy.''

Pru shook her head, wondering, not for the first time, if this crazy nightmare would ever end.

As day followed day, each bringing its own special agony, Prudence worked harder than she would have thought possible at the most boring, disgusting, miserable tasks imaginable. Crow had neglected to tell her what an impossible task it was to drag a ton or more of dead meat up the beach away from the tide.

It had been a young sperm whale—a calf, according to her mentor, who had worked alongside her, doing more than his share to make up for her lack of strength. Of a mouse color, it had been shiny and shapeless—rather flat, altogether, with an enormous mouth and shoe-button eyes.

They had all pitched in, working furiously with the high tide to beach the creature, and then hacking with sharpened shovels to strip away the blubber while the tide was out. By the time the day was ended, Pru was sick to death of the sight and smell of fat and blood.

"Dear God, if I ever get away from this awful place, I'll never fill another lamp with whale oil as long as I live! Tallow candles are good enough for anybody!"

During the next week, two more drifters were brought in, one some distance from the camp, which made their work doubly hard. After each carcass was stripped, including the bone from the right whale, all three crews joined in a noisy celebration.

But not Pru. For all she might have won a bit of respect had she joined them in gaming—something she had not yet managed to do otherwise—the thought of carousing about a bonfire and joshing with such a smelly, unmannerly lot made her flesh crawl.

Of the entire crew, only two men stood aloof. Crow was not one for carousing, nor was Gideon McNair, who stood apart from his men, even though he was not above bearing a hand at the most onerous task should it be needed.

Besides, once the rum began flowing at night, the talk invariably turned to whoring. Pru always managed to find some excuse to retire early, which suited her well enough, for dawn came all too soon, and the whole routine commenced again. Whether or not a whale was taken, there was work enough to break the back of a team of oxen, with each lot of blubber taking days to render.

Pru had all but forgotten her earlier intent to slip away to the woods and hide until she could escape, for the opportunity never seemed to present itself. Even when she was sent to refill the water butts or chop firewood, she was invariably accompanied by one of the others—usually Crow, who seemed to have adopted the pair of them.

By the end of the second week, her hands were hardened, her muscles had all but ceased protesting, and she sometimes managed to get through an entire day without burning herself on the scalding oil as they rendered, strained, restrained and barreled the wretched stuff.

By the end of the third week, she could hold her own with the best of them at most tasks, and was determined to be given something more exciting than the lackey work. She could certainly row a boat. She'd been boating all her life.

Come to that, she could probably do better at hurling the iron than the strikers, if they'd only give her a chance.

February 3, 1729. Generally fair weather all day, with N.W. wind for the first part of the day, switching to N.E. during latter part. Three drifters taken since last sell. One right, two sperm, one a calf. Gouge reports schooner ashore north of inlet, no lives lost. She struck just after sunup, loaded with lumber and pitch from Bath Towne, some 180 tons burthen.
By my hand, Gideon McNair, the south banks.

Having sent Crow off to Portsmouth in the small shallop to inform the woman, Lillah, that her charges were alive and well, Gideon lingered over his last pipe, sniffing the wind for that peculiar scent that meant whales. Perhaps he only fancied he could smell it, but his fancies had proved correct more than once.

The weather had held well for February. The take had been fair enough, considering how many northern whalers were working the Hatteras grounds this season. His crew was close to full strength now, with the two new lads turning out to be far handier than he'd expected.

The runt, Haskell, remained a puzzle. More than once he'd found himself watching the boy, half expecting him to cut and run. There was no real reason for the strange awareness. They'd settled down quickly enough once they saw he meant business. For a pair of rapscallion cutpurses, they commanded far more of his thoughts than was necessary.

Gideon grunted and drew on his pipe, discovering it had gone out in the meantime. Knocking it out on the heel of his boot, he stood and wandered to the door of his quarters, staring out over his camp. There was Haskell now, sitting apart, as usual. Could it be that the lad was still pining for his father? It had been—how long? One had said three years, the other ten. Liars, the pair of them, and not to be trusted out of his sight, yet there was something engaging about the little runt, galled though he was to admit it.

Nye was training for an oar in Toby's crew, since Bully's game shoulder was bothering him lately. Next thing they knew, Haskell would be wanting a seat, as well. Spunky little bastard. If a man weren't careful, he could find himself getting attached to the little blighter.

Come the end of the season, he'd send them away. Like as not, they'd soon go back to their old ways, but at least he'd tried.

Of course, if they wanted to stay on, that was a different matter. It was a hard life and a dangerous one—many a good man had been killed when a whale had sounded at the wrong time, or brought a fluke crashing down on a hapless boat and crew.

No, he'd best send them on their way come the end of the season. He'd soon forget he ever laid eyes on the young bucks. Just because he'd lost his own son...just because the little runt had stood up to him like a man twice his size...

Gideon sighed as the haunting loneliness that had ridden his back for so long began to close in on him again.

Chapter Four

March 5, 1729. Rising pressure, high N.E. winds. Some fog, cleared by midmorn. Cloudy. No whales sighted. Bully's arm swole up some, but not paining him much. By the hand of Gideon McNair, the south banks.

Under any other circumstances, Prudence might have found life at a whaling camp a glorious adventure. She'd been standing watches alone for almost a week now, taking her turn along with the others, having finally been able to convince Gideon that she could be trusted. She had mistaken a small waterspout for a pod of whales the very first day and been jousted unmercifully by the rest of the crew, but in good nature.

That was not to say that she no longer took her turn at other tasks. Scouring down the troughs with sand was not so bad, but she'd hated having to salt down meat and pack it in a barrel when Lear butchered one of the few remaining pigs.

"Dammit, Nye, it's not fair," she complained one evening shortly after her brother came in from his first stint as oarsman. While he was out on a practice run, she'd been salting away joints of greasy pork and was filthy from head to toe. "I've handled boats since I was big enough to lift an oar!"

"Fair! You sound like a whining girl, Haskell," Pride was quick to retort, reminding her that there were others about. "You ain't got the strength to match Toby's oarsmen, and you know it."

It was true. Yet anything was better than staying in this stinking camp week after week, getting bitten by the ever-lasting flies, and bound up tighter than a tick to keep her bosom from showing. At least out at sea, she wouldn't have to breathe this awful stench!

It couldn't be all that difficult. After all, there were three and sometimes four oarsmen to a boat.

Of course, it was not without danger, she supposed. She'd heard enough tales of how this whale or that would look a man in the eye and then do his bloody best to kill him. Yet they continued to go out, and bring in their prey. And dammit, she would rather do anything than be stuck in this wretched camp another day!

"Ho there, Haskell, come join in!" called Ben two nights later. "We need you to make up the numbers."

"A card game?" Mutinously she upended the huge scouring pot on a post and rolled down her sleeves, having scrubbed the last trencher and fork. While she was cleaning up after the evening meal, the crew had been celebrating the monthly toting up of shares, and more than a few, her own brother included, were already three sheets to the wind.

It would serve them right if she won their entire shares and more before they sobered up enough to know what she was about. And she could do it, too. Urias had taught her to read in the set of a player's shoulders what he kept carefully hidden behind his eyes. He'd claimed a man didn't need to cheat if he kept his wits honed.

He'd admitted, though, to cheating when he won his first fortune. Some poor drunken dandy had tried to snooker him, and rather than call him out, Urias had simply cheated more skillfully than the other man and won.

"I ain't swingin' Gouge no more, and that's the plain, pickled truth! Come along, lad—me feet's itchin' to dance!" someone called out, while someone else struck up a tune on

an out-of-tune fiddle. It was soon joined by the eerie pip-
ing of Crow's wooden flute.

Dancing? Mouth agape, Pru watched as a pair of grizzled whalers began to lurch and prance about. Good Lord,
even old Tobias! Who would have believed it?

"The lad can't dance, mates. Why his feet's too big fer his
scrawny carcass," cried one of the men.

That was all the challenge she needed. Hands still stinging from the harsh lye soap, Pru churned across the sand
and pushed her way through the ring of men who were
sloshing their drinks as they clapped in time to the music.

Ben handed her a tankard of rum. She snatched it up, for
once not bothering to water it down from the canvas-
covered butt, as she usually did.

Off to one side, a few of the men were wagering their
shares with a toss of the colored bones. The instant Bully
tossed them into the air, all began shouting at once.

The white bone fell into the hole, all the rest had tum-
bled onto the sand. No winners.

Distracted, Pru wandered over to watch. "Make way. Let
Haskell toss the bones," Lear muttered. After working with
him for hours on end without so much as a word from him,
never mind a smile, she had dubbed him the Dour Corsair.
"The lad's still got enough salt on his tail to bring ye luck,
I vow."

Pru glared at him, and to her amazement, his weathered
face cracked into a grotesque grin. "Aye, let the lad toss
'em!" he cried.

As the fiddle sawed and Crow's flute competed with the
wail of the wind, Pru joined in the revelry, for once feeling
a true part of the crew. She dropped to her knees beside one
of the steersmen. "I'm not sure I know what to do." She
had never played at this game. Besides, since that fateful
night in early February when she'd made the mistake of
challenging the wrong man, luck seemed to have been running against her.

There was a ragged, cheerful chorus of instructions. "Kiss 'em and rattle 'em, toss 'em and bury 'em, sparin' the white to bleach in the light!"

Ignoring Gideon, who had come up silently to watch the goings-on, Pru gathered the handful of dyed bones and blew her breath across them as she shook them gently in her palms. Fastening her gaze on the small holes that had been dug in the sand, she threw them into the air.

There was a gasp and a reverent oath. All but the white had disappeared, and the men cheered noisily.

"Hey, Ned, better watch your arse, or Haskell'll learn to strike. With a dead eye like that, he don't need heft to 'im."

"You play cards, boy?" someone asked.

Feeling enormously puffed up, Pru grinned cockily. "Happens I'm a dab hand at any game you can name."

"Knew the runt had to be good fer something," someone said.

"Cor, that bloody settles it," another man swore reverently. "Next time we heads into port, Haskell goes with us. Mates, we'll be rich before the first night's done!"

Even Prudence was surprised at her continuing run of luck, for the colored bones invariably fell into the holes. Willing hands kept her supplied with rum, for gambling, she discovered, was a mighty thirsty sport.

Pru's head was fairly reeling by the time she heard Crow's quiet voice saying, "The lad will soon own your souls. Leave him be now."

There was a chorus of agreement, and without bothering to tote up her winnings, which Lear had marked down on a clear patch of sand under one of the tables, Pru sat back on her heels, swaying gently as the music commenced once more.

It was Lear who tugged her to her feet, saying gruffly, "Best go empty yer belly, lad. There's lard to render come morning, and ye'll likely have a head on ye big as a pun'kin."

Pru swallowed hard at the thought of the day ahead, but her belly remained quiet. It was her head that was trailing off into the clouds. As she leaned against one of the peeled poles that supported the cook shed awning, listening to the thin screech of a single fiddle and the wail of Crow's flute, she was transported to her childhood when she and Pride had visited Great-uncle John Hunt at Granna's girlhood home on the Albemarle.

Hearing music in the night, they had crept out of bed and down the hall to peer through the balusters at the colorful silks, the great white wigs and the flash of silver buckles on dainty heeled slippers. For a long time afterward Pru had relived that evening, picturing herself wearing such a gown, dancing on the arm of some kind and handsome young man....

Her sigh lost in the sharp wind, she stood, staggered and began to move her booted feet in the sand. *One and two and dip and turn, one and two...* She would be wearing a lovely silk gown and bowing over her hand would be a tall, blond stranger, more handsome than any man in the entire ballroom, and he would whirl her away....

"Well, look at you, brother Nye, swaying like a willow in a hard blow." Pride, looking fuzzy about the edges, appeared before her, and she beamed at him, hiccuped and held out her hand, wrist bent gracefully under the filthy cuff of her canvas coat. "Dance with me?"

"It ain't me that's swaying, you noddy. How many of those have you had?" Pride reached for her tankard and she stumbled against him with a giggle that was suspiciously feminine. Someone began a bawdy song, and soon others joined in, some dancing, some merely reeling in place with a vacant grin on their faces. Suddenly, it all seemed the greatest adventure in the world, and Pru was determined to waste not a moment of it.

Lear and Ben Tolson were performing a creditable jig, considering the depth of the sand and their lamentable lack of sobriety. Not to be outdone, Pru lifted her coattails and set out to show off what little she knew of dancing.

Several of the men began clapping and cheering her on, and suddenly it was all so dreadfully funny. She laughed and laughed as she whirled about, spilling the last of her rum and finally tossing away her tankard. When she veered too near the circle of men who were watching, chanting and swaying to the wild music, one of them would push her back into the center, where she would dance some more.

The sand was growing deeper and deeper, until she could hardly drag her feet through the stuff. Faces blurred, the sound of Crow's flute grew faint, and suddenly, her stomach began to turn on her.

That was the last thing she remembered.

It was Gideon, his face as hard as hickory, who caught her before she reached the ground. Glaring at the others, who were mostly too drunk to notice, he stalked away, his features as rigid as if they'd been carved out of granite.

Not until he was well away from the firelight did his guard drop. Gazing down at the unconscious form in his arms, he sighed, a bleak look replacing the stoniness. "You're a mighty swiller, my lad. No doubt you'll pay for it on the morrow."

Behind him the revelry continued unabated. Gideon did his best to ignore the slight figure draped over his arms, the head jostling against his chest at every step. For a lad who was naught but skin and bones, he was surprisingly soft, he thought, and then he stopped dead in his tracks, shocked at the direction his thoughts had taken.

He snorted in disgust, and was assailed by an even wilder notion. Swearing fervently, he ducked through the low doorway and dumped the boy onto the nearest pallet, brushed off his hands as if he'd touched a live coal and backed out again. Sweet Jesus, he needed a stiff drink and a short visit to Quick Mary's!

Make that a bottle and a long visit!

For hours, Gideon lay awake, staring up at the sky. After Barbara died, he'd spent months without the least urge to bed a woman. Then had come a spell when he'd spent every spare moment fornicating, doing his damnedest to erase all memory of the past.

Two years had passed before he'd settled onto an even keel, and now this! Was it but another phase he was entering? In his arms, it had suddenly seemed to him that young Haskell was not only feminine, he was downright dainty! Under all the sweat, the smoke and the whale stink, he'd even *smelled* like a woman!

And that giggle of his. Of course, it could have come from a boy, but it had sounded remarkably girlish from where he'd been standing, some distance away from the celebration.

But the worst of it—and he'd kill the first man who said as much to his face—was that the scrawny young pup was beginning to get under his skin. He had made himself a promise nearly six years ago that he would never again allow himself to care for anyone, man, woman or child. He'd kept that promise.

Gideon's home was his sloop. Besides that, he had the small shallop, his fleet of whaleboats, a lease on some thousand-odd acres of prime whaling land and a loyal crew. A man could count himself lucky to have far less than that.

He still missed Barbara and the boy. After six years, the pain had dulled so that he could go for days without remembering, but something about the runt . . . holding the cocky young devil in his arms must have put him in mind of the way he used to carry his new son about when the babe refused to settle of a night.

Dammit, it was time that young pup grew up! And Gid was just the man to see to it! The lad wanted to tackle something more challenging than scrubbing, salting and cooking? That could be arranged, he thought with a bitter curl of his lips. He would set him to rowing, and if that didn't build him up, he'd think of something else. The first time they made a haul, he would take the lad across to the mainland and fix him up with a fresh young whore! That should set his juices to flowing!

Prudence had never felt quite so miserable as she did the following morning. Pride was in no better shape, but when he began to regale her with tales of her own misdeeds, she buried her face in her arms and prayed to die.

But the morning watch was hers, and some remnant of sanity made her drag herself out of the hut before Gideon could send someone to fetch her. She could do without any more reminders of her misbehavior.

Crow was sharpening an iron just outside the door. He looked up when she emerged, but Pru was in no condition to read the concern in his eyes.

She grunted a greeting of sorts, and then remembered something she'd heard the night before. "Didn't you—uh, go to Portsmouth recently?"

"Aye," he said quietly.

"You didn't—that is, I don't suppose you happened to see anyone?"

"Aye." Crow hid his smile as he surveyed her greenish pallor. She was paying the piper. And while he had no sympathy for whites, be they English, French or Spanish, he had harbored a small weakness for this one ever since he had realized that she was female. Having had to fight for his life more times than he cared to remember, he could admire bravery in anyone, and especially one so small.

"There is a woman who calls herself Lillah," he told the trembling figure before him, who had bundled herself in layer upon layer of clothing against the raw wind. "I say to her that my captain has took to his crew two young whelps, to teach them a trade."

"Lillah," Pru breathed, feeling the starch go right out of her bones. "Did she say—that is, did she ask—"

"That woman, she give me the sharp side of her tongue."

"Oh, that's just her way. She didn't mean anything by it."

Crow had cause to doubt that. That woman would have taken a knife to him from the look in her eyes. She was a proud one, that Lillah. But then, he was a patient man. Nothing worthwhile came easy.

"Did you tell her—uh, how long we might be here?"

"I say to her the season will soon be ended. I say to her the captain did take two lads. I say he will return two men."

For reasons that quite escaped Prudence, the half-breed seemed to find this whole exchange enormously entertaining. After trying once more to get a bit of information from him, she gave up and headed for the necessary, turning her head away from the odors that emanated from the cook shed.

"Salt mullet and fried mush," called Ben as she hurried past the tables. "It ain't good, but it don't outright kill you."

With a groan, she turned away and emptied her belly onto the sand. A spate of rain blew against her back, and she turned her face to it. After a moment, she kicked sand over the evidence of her indiscretions and went on her way.

By the time she had done her business and was headed down the beach toward the crow's nest, she was feeling some better, except for her pounding head and the awful weakness that made her want to curl up and sleep for the next three weeks. Perhaps she would catch a chill and die. It would be a fitting end to what was rapidly becoming an unbearable situation.

Toby had kept the night watch, which was maintained if there was the least chance of seeing out over the water. The clouds had not moved in until morning. He called down from the crude lookout tower as she approached. "How ye farin', son?"

Pru lifted baleful eyes and encountered, not Toby's gray-bearded countenance, but Gideon. He stood midway of the ladder, looking far too big, far too stern and so beautiful she felt like crying.

"You're relieved of watch, Haskell. Go back to bed."

"But, sir, I—"

"Go!" he barked, and go she did, tears streaming down her face as she stumbled toward the shelter of her hut.

Gideon stared out after the retreating figure, willing himself to an objectiveness he was far from feeling. They were good lads, both of them, considering the life they'd been leading when he caught up with them.

Of course, Haskell would always be a runt, and likely the butt of many a joke because of it. There were times when Nye was a bit too protective of the boy, but sooner or later, Haskell was going to have to fight his own battles. The poor little blighter couldn't count on his big brother to haul his ashes out of the fire for the rest of his life.

Certainly Gideon knew a thing or two about brotherly responsiblity. Hadn't he lived with it every day of his life since he'd run off and left his mother and sister with that pious bastard his mother married after his father died?

And if Johnson weren't bad enough, his son, Nimrod, had been a monster. Never a day went by that Gideon didn't think of what could have happened had his sister Maggie not managed to escape the farm and find her way to safe harbor.

Maggie had long since forgiven him. Even more, she claimed she'd never blamed him for running off, for their mother had died happy, knowing at least one of them had escaped the hell she had made of their lives when she married Zion Johnson.

Gideon found it much harder to forgive himself, even knowing that if he'd stayed on at the farm, he would have murdered the bastard, and that wretched son of his, too, only to hang for his troubles.

As it was, he had taken refuge on his uncle Will Lewis's ship, fully intending to earn enough to make a home for his mother and sister and go back for them. Instead, he'd found himself caught up in a web of piracy and intrigue, unable to save his uncle and barely able to save himself.

He had failed them all. For his sins, he had lost first his parents and his uncle, then his wife and his son. If he spent the rest of his life trying to make amends, it would not be enough, but mayhap setting the feet of a pair of erring lads like Haskell and Nye on the right path would count for something against his massive debt.

There was a great deal of competition among Gideon's three crews. Pru had not been in camp a month before she was itching to join in.

Old Toby was the one who finally agreed to let her take one of his oars during a dry spell, when no whales had appeared offshore for more than a week. In order to stay primed, the crews often made practice runs, coming in drenched to the skin and chilled to the bone, to huddle around a blazing fire, drinking rum and telling outrageous lies.

The same quirk in Prudence's personality that had made her strive to outdo her brother from the moment she popped into the world twenty minutes before he did now compelled her to prove herself before the whole company.

And it happened to suit Gideon's plans very well. He was determined to push the boy, to broaden those narrow shoulders, strengthen those skinny arms, so that the lad could at least fend for himself in a fight. The next time he might not have a gun at his side to even the odds.

"Damn me if the lad ain't after me own seat," Tobias teased the first time Pru found herself calling out commands before the old steersman could voice them. "I'll give ye this much—ye're spunky as a fresh-shed crab, for all ye ain't no bigger'n a cricket." He grinned and spit safely against the wind, a rare skill of which he was inordinately proud. "By the time ye've lost as much hair as I have, son, ye just might have the makings of a passable steersman."

Pru had already lost more hair than old Toby would ever lose. Their second night in camp, she had snitched a knife from the cook shed and prevailed on Pride to saw off her braid until it was no longer than his own hair, figuring she would worry about what to tell Granna later.

"You've no worry on that score, old man," she shot right back, "for I've decided to have Ned's job, instead." Ned, Toby's striker, tossed her a side of salt mullet, and she caught it in midair and dropped it into the hot fat. It was her turn to cook, and they had all learned to help out if they wanted to be able to eat.

"Takes more'n a bit o' sass to make a striker," said Ned, who had a tongue as sharp as his eye.

"Try me," she challenged. "Draw your mark and I'll cover it five times out of five."

"Remember the bones, Ned. Ye'd best watch yer arse!" Lear warned.

"The day you can bury an iron in a blowhole off'n a rolling deck, then I might let you tend my gear for me," said Ned, filling the captain's plate with greasy fish, hard beans and scorched pan bread.

Sitting off to himself, Gideon listened to the byplay, pleased to see Haskell holding his own. The lad was coming along. Except in the matter of cooking, he thought with a grimace.

His meal half-finished, he abruptly shoved back his bench and stalked away, unaware of Pru's gaze following him as he crossed the compound.

While the last of the mullet in the enormous skillet curled up and turned from brown to black, Pru sighed. By all rights she should despise the arrogant devil. Yet he continued to fill her thoughts to the point where she no longer even considered escaping, not even when she slipped away to the freshwater pond for a hurried wash.

The routine continued, growing easier as time passed. Pru found herself standing in whenever there was a small injury, smearing lard and sugar on cuts, flour paste on burns, and dosing the occasional raw throat with treacle, black pepper and vinegar.

She was privy to all manner of small confidences, such as Ben's ambition to one day own a whaling camp of his own, and Gouge's secret longing for a woman who had died more than twenty years before. She even learned that Lear had once owned a dog, the closest thing to a family he would admit to having, which had been killed by an injured bear.

Gideon noted all this, and if he wondered at the lad's popularity with his men, he kept it to himself.

Between chores, the men often threw knives at a mark on a piece of driftwood. As with gaming, it soon became evident that Pru could more than hold her own against the best of them. If she sometimes glanced around to see if Gideon was admiring her marksmanship, it was only natural, she told herself. He was her captain, after all.

If he happened by and applauded her skill, she glowed like a firefly.

If he was nowhere to be seen, she felt unaccountably depressed.

Gideon had problems of his own. Ruthlessly honest in his dealings, with himself no less than with others, he confronted the fact that the two lads were beginning to get under his guard, young Haskell most of all. He'd always had a feeling for the underdog, he supposed, and the runt was all of that!

They'd both proved themselves to be good workers and reasonably honest, although Haskell's run of luck at both bones and cards was little less than remarkable. There was no way a man could cheat with the bones, but at cards?

No, the young pup was nimble-minded, that was all, Gid told himself. Quick of mind and sharp of eye, he was as fine a marksman as any among them. In truth, he'd have made a fine striker but for his slight build. It seemed that no matter how high the boy piled his plate, nor how many times he went back to the pot for more, he was doomed to remain as thin as a willow whip, his shoulders scarce broader than his hips.

But it took more than a sharp eye and a quick hand to be a good striker, as Gideon knew from experience, for he had worked every position in the trade when he'd first taken up whaling eight years ago with a crew on the northern banks. He'd been hard driven at the time to overcome the stench of piracy that hovered around him.

It occurred to him now that young Haskell exhibited much the same sort of drive. Like more than a few of the assembly of misfits and castoffs Gideon had gathered around him, not excluding himself, the runt had been a likely candidate for the hangman's noose.

"Needs a father," he muttered aloud, not even wondering why he felt none of the same paternal interest in Nye.

With a soft oath, he recalled the night a brash young outlaw had shoved a pistol under his nose and ordered him to stand and deliver. Bloody limb of Satan, he thought with a reluctant grin. It was a wonder the little bastard hadn't long since had his throat slit and been tossed in a ditch to rot by one of his own victims!

A totally unexpected pain sliced through him at the thought, and he reached for his pipe. It was none of his damned business! He'd taken the lad to fill out his crew—he hadn't taken him to raise! It was just that for all his brashness, the young pup was not all that—he was not particularly—

Again Gideon swore. Dammit, the plain truth was, the lad was not especially masculine. Nye had claimed they were twins, giving their age as a month shy of eighteen at the time, but in that case, why hadn't the boy's voice settled? He had screeched like a girl when he spilled hot oil on his hand that first week.

On the other hand, Gid reminded himself, he had quickly clamped his mouth shut—a mouth that was curiously vulnerable for a youth verging on manhood—and not once had he let out a yelp while Toby had dressed it, even though he'd been in mortal pain.

The sound of a quarrel broke into his meandering thoughts, and Gideon turned toward the trouble. It had happened more than once of late. He'd give ten barrels of spermaceti right now to hear the watch cry out, "Whale off!" The men were growing restless.

And damned if he wouldn't race them to the boats! He needed a challenge tonight. With the last drifter stripped, boned and tried, and not so much as a porpoise sighted for nearly a fortnight, they were all growing edgy.

As a cold wet March withheld even the promise of spring, bathing continued to be a major problem. Prudence was no stickler, yet she couldn't see going for weeks on end without a thorough stem-to-stern scrubbing. Save for the massive iron try kettles, there was not a tub on the island, but she could hardly climb into one of those before the whole camp.

Not that any of the others seemed overly fastidious. Thank goodness for the frequent dousings in saltwater, for without those, she would have long since suffocated. She managed to stay upwind of her mates whenever possible, and in particular of Gouge and Lucy. And by the time she fell onto her pallet each night, she was usually far too exhausted to worry over a small thing like the stench of a few unwashed bodies.

Who would have thought that rowing would be so difficult? She had been rowing, paddling and sailing all her life. Small boats, to be sure, but all the same, she hadn't expected her back to be broken nor her arms to threaten to fall off after merely helping to row a small whaleboat a mile or so beyond the breakers and back again. The craft was heavy. Still, she'd had three men to help her.

At least her hands had been no problem, for they'd long since grown hard as boot leather. Now all she had to do was harden the rest of her body.

The weather held fair, the days rapidly growing longer, and still not a single whale was sighted. There was talk of going to Portsmouth or Bath for supplies, but as everyone grumbled over who was to go and who was to stay, nothing was done about it. Even Gideon seemed distracted.

"Season's finished," vowed Gouge.

"Finished! Why, we took seven whales 'twixt May and June in the year of '26," argued Toby, to which young Ben Tolson promptly replied that if he'd not been so greedy three years before, there would have been more for them all this year.

"Never you believe it, lad. There'll be oil enough to light up half the world when my grandbaby's young'uns is a hundred and ten years old. It's them that come down from the northern banks in their big ships, is what it is. They'll take enough oil and bone to fill their holds and scare off the rest for pure cussed meanness."

"And run like hell for home afore the king's man can claim his tenth," added another old hand.

"Water's too warm," James said thoughtfully.

"Warm! It's too damn cold," rebutted Ned, and Prudence had to agree. While the freshwater pond grew passably warm by midday, the ocean was still cold enough to make her bones ache each time she got drenched—which was far too often for her liking.

They were seated around the fire, having finished the evening meal, which Pride had helped with that night. Surprisingly, he had turned out to be a more than passable cook. Bully was on watch in the crow's nest some hundred yards away, and Pru had drawn first daylight watch—which meant she would soon need to head for the hut and her pallet.

As weary as she was from having chopped and hauled firewood all day, she was not especially looking forward to the night. With the coming of warmer weather, many of the men had taken to going about in shirtsleeves. The air inside the hut was barely breathable of late. She was tempted to give up her weekly dips in the pond in self-defense!

"Crow, your turn at the cook shed tomorrow," said Gideon, and everyone groaned, for Crow was not among the camp's better cooks. "James, you take cleanup with Ben to help. The rest of you men can finish loading the sloop, for if this wind comes about by morning, I've a mind to head out across the sound two days hence."

"What about me, sir?" Pru asked, hoping to draw something more interesting than repairing barrels or scouring troughs.

He merely glared at her, and shrugging, Pru turned away. Her belly was sore, and her breasts ached from being bound up tightly. She had just finished her monthly flow, which always made them more sensitive.

"Haskell!" At the sound of that commanding voice, she stopped in her tracks. "You and Nye will be crossing with me. Make sure you eat before we set out, for you'll not get a hot meal until we make port."

"If ye're headed for Bath, better warn all the men at the One-Eyed Cat not to get into a game with young Haskell," said Ned with a sly chuckle. "I mind them on Portsmouth already knows to watch their cards."

"What, gaming?" someone else chimed in. "A hearty lad like our Haskell here? Why, he'll head straight for Miss Suky's Boardinghouse and not see the light of day until some'un hauls him back aboard ship, right, lad? Ask for Molly, she's as prime a piece as you'll find anywhere, eh, mates?"

There was a ragged chorus of agreement, and Prudence hurried off toward the necessary, glad of the darkness that hid her burning cheeks. She had heard more than enough of their bawdy tales to know that Miss Suky's Boardinghouse was on a par with Quick Mary's.

Two pairs of eyes followed her as she disappeared into the darkness. Crow wondered how long the lass could conceal her secret. And Gideon wondered why the thought of taking Haskell to Miss Suky's should suddenly seem so distasteful.

Chapter Five

March 29, 1729. Gale winds blew two days, moderated this morning. Heavy fog, but will likely clear off by midday. Schooner Hariette B. Carstairs *went aground six miles south of camp with cargo of sugar and molasses. All hands spared. Another vessel disabled but took under tow to Portsmouth. One drifter spotted this day, but she was too soft to get a line onto.*
By the hand of Gideon McNair, the south banks.

The fog had blanketed the entire camp with a damp chill when Pru stumbled out of her hut the following morning after a sleepless night. The others had already left, and Pru dragged on her coat as she headed for the feeble glow of the cook shed lanterns.

A dark form emerged from the fog, and Gideon said, "If the wind rises, we'll be setting out early on the morrow, lad. Best get your gear together today."

Pru huddled in her coat, staring up at him. It was as if a great yawning cavern had suddenly opened up under her bosom. She mumbled, "Aye, sir," and ducked her head. What on earth was happening to her? It wasn't fear, for he'd treated her fairly almost from the first.

Anger? Somewhere along the way, her anger had disappeared. And while she didn't exactly worship the ground he trod, as most of his men seemed to do—and with just cause, from the tales she'd heard—she had come to admire him, in spite of herself.

She waited for him to dismiss her, never more conscious of her windburned face, her callused hands and her hair shorn off in a ragged fringe. She needed to go to the necessary, and she was longing for a mug of steaming hot coffee, but she couldn't bring herself to walk away.

His voice broke the eerie fog-smothered silence. "You've not had much pleasure since taking up with us, lad."

Taking up with them? It was an interesting way to put it, at the very least. Pru mumbled some sort of response into the neck of her stiff coat, painfully aware of the ripe scent of her own body.

"Speak up, Haskell. If you're ever to get on in the world, you'll have to learn to speak out like a man." In the halflight, it seemed to her that his eyes were gleaming with laughter—but that couldn't be right. Gideon seldom smiled. No one, to her knowledge, had ever heard him laugh.

"Aye sir," she yelped. This time there was no mistaking it. He actually grinned at her, and her poor knees fairly buckled!

"We'll not call the season ended until June or thereabouts," he said abruptly, his smile fading so fast Pru decided that her eyes had deceived her. "Then, if you've a mind to, you and your brother can make a trip or two with me lightering freight across the sound—maybe up as far as Virginia. That is, if you've nothing better to do."

When she couldn't think of a thing to say, he grunted. "It's honest work. 'Twould serve well enough, unless you've a mind to go back to your old trade."

Gideon, you great golden-haired noddy, I'm no seaman, nor a thief, nor even a whaler! I'm a woman! Why can't you see that?

She was suddenly torn between wanting him to know and fearing that he would find out. She might long for his approval, but even if he could get beyond her lie, he could have only contempt for the rough-skinned, coarse-haired woman she had become. She would die before she let him see her like that.

"No? Well...never mind, 'twas just a notion. The whales will be back come November. There'll be a place for you here if you need it," he said gruffly.

Without another word, he stalked off, and Pru stared after him.

For the rest of the day, Prudence kept busy at any chore that would take her the farthest from her captain. There was always water to be hauled from the fresh pond. Anyone with time on his hands usually fetched a few buckets, using the shoulder pole that made carrying easier. Now that the weather was beginning to moderate, Pru tried to take a turn when no one else was about, stealing a few moments after filling her pails for a hasty wash.

As the morning fog burned away, the sun's heat bore down on the camp. Soon most of the men were bare chested—they'd been going without boots for weeks. Pru waited until two crews were out on a practice race, the others busy grinding spades, irons and lances. She had only to chop and tote wood, cut rushes and stand the evening watch—an easy day for a change. It would be a wonderful opportunity to bathe in the altogether, if she didn't freeze in the process.

As she had not seen Gideon for more than an hour, she reckoned him to be safely in his quarters bent over his books. There was always a might lot of reckoning to be done to keep up with totals and shares of bone, spermaceti and common oil.

The woods were quiet and peaceful, the pond as still as a teapot. Pru inhaled deeply of the resinous smell of sun-warmed pines and cedars as she knelt to fill her pails. She had never dared do more than a hasty wash, but now that all the men were busy, and the weather so fine, it was too good a chance to miss.

Looking carefully over her shoulder one last time, she quickly shed her boots, wriggling her toes in sand. Before she could lose her nerve, she shed her shirt and trousers and set to work unwinding her chest binder.

Blessed relief! Glorying in the moment, she stretched her arms over her head, inhaled deeply, then peeled off her drawers and waded out into the chilly water.

Gideon shoved aside his ledgers, restless for no reason at all. Toby and Gouge were still headed out, with the old man ahead by an oar's length.

Gideon grinned. Dammit, he thought, if he wouldn't like to be with them. He'd a good mind to take the other boat out alone and give them all a run for their money. He needed to sweat some of this confounded edginess out of his system; he'd slept no more than an hour during the entire night, and that sleep had been filled with dreams that had left him doubting his sanity, not to mention his masculinity.

As if that weren't bad enough, the first man he'd come upon when he'd set foot outside was Haskell. The young whelp had stared up at him with the sleep still fogging his sea-green eyes, his mouth all soft and trembling. Gideon had suddenly felt sickened by the unnatural way his mind had taken to working lately.

Christ, he had to do something! It was either take an icy header into the surf and have the men wondering if he'd lost his senses, or slip away to the pond and scour his hide with sand until he forgot those crazy dreams that had left him hard and needy and mad as hell!

He'd be first in line at Miss Suky's Boardinghouse, Gideon promised himself as he rapidly covered the ground between the quiet camp and the freshwater pond hidden in the nearby forest.

By the time he was halfway there, his shirt was unfastened, his trousers held on by a single button. He stopped just long enough to hook his boots under an exposed root and work them free, then left his clothes at the edge of the woods, hanging neatly on a dead cedar, boots aligned at its base. He was an orderly man by nature, having spent the most of his life at sea.

Oh, hell! Someone had got the jump on him!

Striding naked to the edge of the water, Gid called out a greeting, and then swore again when he saw that his companion was none other than the lad who had deviled his mind until he didn't dare even sleep at night.

"Isn't it about time you were getting back to work, boy?" he called out, not bothering to hide his displeasure. The slight figure on the other side of the pond sank even lower in the water, if that were possible. All he could see was a shock of hair standing on end, and those great gawking eyes that always seemed too big for the boy's thin face.

"I—I—I'm s-sorry, sir," the lad croaked. Then recovering a bit of the gumption that had made him such a favorite among the men, he blurted out, "Better me than Gouge or Lear—I'd sooner share a bath with Lucy than wallow in the same pond as those two."

The lad had a point there, Gid admitted silently, as he strode into the water.

The boy had turned away—too shy by half, Gideon thought, but he'd get over it. A shore leave or two with Ben and Nye, and he'd be rutting like any other young buck. He was old enough—just barely.

"I'd give a whole Spanish dollar for a chunk of soap, eh, Haskell? Nothing like the smell of sweet soap on a man's hide to soften up the ladies."

The little beggar was stubborn, he'd say that for him. Seemed he'd made up his mind not to talk—or even to face him, not after that first goggle-eyed look. It occurred to Gid that he might be jealous of his . . .

Come to think on it, the whole camp had teased the poor mite about not filling out his breeches properly. He had more in the crup than he did in the cod, and while Gideon had never had cause to feel deficient in either respect, he could sympathize with a boy who was late developing.

He reached for patience. "Listen, son, if you're nervous about meeting the girls at Suky's, you've nothing to be feared of. I vow they'll take to you like a duck to water. Women, they like to mother a man."

No response. Maybe that had been the wrong thing to say, with the boy being an orphan and all. Hell, he was probably a virgin, too. He hadn't even started sprouting a beard yet, while Nye strutted like a peacock over his straggly crop.

"It don't hurt none, you know," he called out encouragingly. He was beginning to feel a mite foolish talking to the back of the boy's head. "They'll be fighting over you before you even get shed of your coat, much less your breeches."

There was an anguished sound from across the pond, but be damned if Gideon could make it out. "D'you say something, boy?"

A groan was the only response. Shaking his head, Gid scooped up a handful of white sand from the bottom and plastered it onto his hair, squinting to keep it from dribbling into his eyes. He began to scrub ruthlessly, swearing under his breath. If the scrawny little whelp didn't want to talk to him, why then, that was just fine! It hadn't been Gid's choice to share his damned bath in the first place!

When there was no more sound for several minutes, Pru began to hope he had finally gone. Dare she turn around and see? What if she turned around and he was still there?

Before she could make up her mind one way or the other, Gideon spoke again, still from the other side of the pond, thank goodness.

"Y'see, it's kind of like whaling, lad. Has your brother told you anything about—uh, he-ing and she-ing?"

He waited. Finally, a small voice whispered, "Um, he-ing and she-ing, sir?"

"About bedding a woman?" Gid said impatiently. He reminded himself that under other circumstances, this might have been his own son in need of fatherly advice. "There's certain precautions a man should take, for his health as well as his pleasure. Don't ever lie with a sickly woman, boy. She might not be poxed, but if she is, you'll wish to hell you'd kept your pecker in your pocket."

"Oh, dear," Pru moaned, her face half-submerged under the water.

"The cure? Speak up, boy, I can't half hear you! The cure's no more or less than mercury, and you're as apt to die from that as the pox. Suky watches after her girls—likely you'll be all right there, but once you get back to Portsmouth, steer clear of all but the freshest of Quick Mary's girls. Since Andros sold up, things ain't run as careful as they should be."

Pru thought surely she would strangle—that is, if she didn't die of mortification first.

"But don't let me put you off, son. Bedding a woman is a man's duty as well as his pleasure. His duty to himself, you might say, for if he goes without too long, it can—ah, that is, he can—well, hell, I doubt me you'll be going without once you've dipped your wick a time or two."

Just as Pru gave an agonized cry and covered her ears with her hands, Gideon stretched back to rinse his head, submerging without a ripple and swimming underwater for several strokes. He came up with a great splash and tossed back his head, sending a spray of water fanning out across the quiet surface of the pond. "Damn me, but that feels good, don't it?" When there was no response, he said, "Haskell? Son, you all right? You ain't got a cramp or anything, have you?"

Pru shook her head vigorously, praying he would just leave her in peace. How could she ever face him after this?

"Ready to go back to camp?"

Again she shook her head. He stood staring at her averted face, wondering if he'd made a mistake in broaching the topic of mating with the boy who had more than once given rise to some damned unhealthy thoughts in his own mind. "Whaling, you understand?" he repeated, harking back to the beginning of their one-sided conversation.

She nodded her head jerkily.

"Don't be in any great rush, boy. A whaler learns to take his time, plan his moves and never lose sight of his target. Now, a woman, she's got more than one target. You'll need to go easy, search for the best way to get to her, and whatever you do, don't just sink your iron and run. There's certain things—that is, there's certain places—well, a woman's put together different from a man, boy. She's softer, for one thing, but there's parts of her that get—"

Ah, the devil! He was no good at telling a man how to pleasure a woman! No one had told him. Leastwise, no man had, though he'd had the benefit of a few good widows, including his Barbara.

"Just remember this boy. No girl sets out to be a whore, leastwise, not to my knowledge. And no man worth the name would ever hurt a woman. You'll do all right, son. Not a one of us but didn't start out a virgin."

A strangled gasp was the only sign his lecture had been heard, much less understood. Gid shook his head. It was like talking to a tree stump. But dammit, the boy didn't have a father, and if he was going on shore leave, someone had to set him on course.

Swearing softly at the back of the mule-stubborn head, Gideon thrashed up out of the water and strode across the clearing toward the dead tree where he'd left his clothing.

Hearing the commotion, Pru peered over her shoulder in time to see him wade ashore. Unable to help herself, she gawked. It had never occurred to her that a man's body—or indeed, any body—could be beautiful, but Gideon's was. Fascinated, she continued to watch the intricate play of light on the muscles of his back and his taut buttocks, wincing at the sight of several large scars. She'd thought there'd been one on the front of his shoulder, as well, but there'd been so much to look at when he first came down to the water that she couldn't be certain.

At the edge of the woods, he turned, catching her dead to rights, and her face burned hot enough to set fire to water. "Don't stay overboard too long, boy. A bath now and again don't harm a body, but staying in too long might cause your musket and balls to get rusty. A man can't be too careful about that kind of thing."

By the time they prepared to set sail the following morning, Prudence was able to hold up her head and even laugh

off most of the taunts that had come her way when the crew
realized that she had never before set foot inside a place like
Miss Suky's.

At least she'd not had to face Gideon again, for she'd
been too busy toting wood and filling the bungholes on the
troughs with fresh rushes, and then it was time to relieve the
watch.

It was late when she finally climbed stiffly down the ladder. She stopped by the cook shed for a bait of cold beans
and corn bread, washed down with the dregs of the coffee.
The last scrap of sugar in camp had long since hardened into
a brown, bug-speckled rock, but she could do without that.
It was milk she missed most. Even when Granna's goat ran
dry, there had usually been someone among the island's
seven families willing to trade for a bit of milk.

Pru slept poorly that night, tossing and turning until Ben
snatched up his blanket and stalked out to sleep under the
cook shed awning.

"Wha's the matter, Pr—Haskell?" Pride muttered
sleepily.

"Nothing!" she snapped. How could she tell him she was
worn ragged with wondering how to get out of visiting the
whorehouse? If he were any sort of a brother at all, he
would know!

"Go back t'sleep."

"Not bloody likely," she muttered under her breath,
jerking up her blanket to flop over onto her belly.

He had deserted her. Just because he'd taken to whaling
like a hog to a mudhole, he seemed to think she should be
every bit as happy here.

If only she'd been born a man, she thought as the first
light showed above the eastern horizon, none of this would
have happened. Or if it had, it wouldn't have mattered;
she'd not be lying here quaking in her boots, wondering how
on earth she was going to keep from disgracing herself. And
she certainly wouldn't have fallen tip over tail in love—there,
she'd said it!—in love with a stubborn man who was bent on
teaching her to make love to a—a woman!

By the time the camp had fallen behind that morning, both Pru and Pride were entranced with Gideon's sloop, the *Polly*. Their first trip hadn't counted, for they'd been too miserable and frightened to notice anything. But one had only to stand on her deck, to watch the clear, bottle-green water curve away from her bow, to appreciate her gracefulness.

Unlike the cumbersome merchantmen that plowed back and forth across the Atlantic under acres of canvas, the *Polly* was a single master, rigged fore and aft with two jibs, a mainsail, topsail, and staysail. She took wing like a gull lifting off the water, and Pru had to be called more than once to bear a hand.

"You know, I can almost understand why Papa wanted to go back to sea," she confided to her brother when they came together with time enough for a few words.

"Yes, well, don't get to liking it too much. Once the season's ended, I'm taking you home and there you'll stay, if you know what's good for you."

Pru's face fell. Of course she wanted to go home. Hadn't she thought of nothing but escape from the moment they were captured?

But that would mean leaving Gideon, and she didn't rightly see how she could do that. "Will you stay on?" she asked, knowing the answer in advance.

"If Cap'n Gid'll let me."

"He'll let you. He told me we could both sail with him if we wanted to, until time to—"

"Dammit, Pru, haven't you learned your lesson yet? You're naught but a female. You don't belong here!"

"I belong as much as you do," she shot back.

"Oh, indeed you do," Pride mocked. "Don't you even know how the whole crew laughs at you behind your back? They call you a sissy, a lamby-boy! For ha'pence I'd tell Cap'n Gid everything, and let him take you back home!"

Pru's mouth trembled. "They don't laugh at me, not really. They like me—I can tell."

"Sure they like you, you noddy," Pride said gruffly, for he'd never meant to hurt her feelings. "But that don't mean they want you for a mate. Cap'n Gid's always fetching some stray or other to camp. You heard what Ben said about stealing them cabbages and near getting his neck stretched for it. And Crow—did you know he near about died from getting caught in a bear trap? And you know how Gouge lost his eye, don't you? And how Lear got his scars?"

"I don't want to know about it! Besides, that's not why he took us in." She coughed and blotted her damp brow. It had turned unseasonably hot.

"Took us in! Have you forgot just *how* he took us in? And *why?* It weren't because of your manly muscles, I'll vow." He shook his head in disgust. "You and your tom-fool notions of taking revenge on the men who killed Pa—that's why he took us in!"

"You were in it just as deep as I was, Pride Andros! If you hadn't sworn he was a pirate—"

"Hey, Haskell," Ben Tolson called out from halfway up the shrouds where he'd gone to secure the running lantern. "Ye're goin' gamin' wi' me and the lads tonight, ain't ye? We're a-countin' on ye fer luck!"

Pru leaned close to Pride and whispered furiously, "There! You can see how much they despise me! I note they didn't invite *you* to go gaming with them!"

"Yes, well, if you've got half a brain in your bonnet, you'll break a leg before we reach port, or gaming ain't all you'll be sharing!"

As it came about, Pru did not have to break a limb. By the time the low smudge on the horizon grew into woods, plantations and towns with harbors and steeples and such, she was burning with fever, her face far more flushed than constant exposure to the elements could account for and her voice a chest-aching croak.

She might have managed to keep from being discovered had not a deep, rattling cough escaped her just as Gideon strode past. He wheeled about, searing her with those flame-blue eyes, and before she grasped his intent, he had pressed the back of his hand against her cheek.

She already felt as weak as water, and his touch just about did her in.

"How long have you been like this, lad?" he demanded as she tried not to sway on her feet.

"Like what, sir?" She lifted her chin with a careless air, but the effect was spoiled by a fit of coughing.

The stream of profanity that shattered the soothing sound of water rushing alongside the hull made her own talents fade in comparison. Nor did it do much to lift her spirits. "Dammit, you're ailing! I don't coddle my crew, but I damned well don't waste the bleeding bastards, either! Hit the fo'c'sle, son, and don't come up for air until I give you permission. Is that clear?"

"But Gideon—I mean, sir—I mean, dammit all, there's nothing wrong with me! You promised me I could—" Perversely, now that he had forbidden her to go ashore, she wanted to go.

"I know what I promised you. We'll still be here tomorrow, and if you're up to scratch, then you can go ashore with the others. But I'll not risk you dying in some whore's bed just because you've not got the sense of a boiled turnip! Now, *get!*"

Pru got. With the great hulking son of a sea serpent glaring at her, ready to pick her up by the scruff of her neck and heave her below deck, what choice did she have?

But he wouldn't have the last word. Sick or well, it wasn't in her to knuckle under to a bully. No matter how big a musket he carried!

Lying in her hammock, shivering under two coats and a scrap of blanket, Pru waited for Pride to come below. Surely he wouldn't go ashore without first coming to see if she were truly dying.

She was right. Shortly after the noise ceased on deck, she heard boots clattering down the ladder, and looked up to see Pride and Ben Tolson, both grinning broadly.

"You think you're both so blasted clever, don't you?" she rasped petulantly.

"Not half so clever as we're going to feel come morning," Ben returned, digging through his seabag for a fresh shirt. "Watch the shoulders, is that right, Haskell?"

"The shoulders?" With dull eyes, she watched the two boys get ready to go ashore.

"To see if a man's bluffing or not," Ben reminded her.

She nodded, trying hard not to be such a poor sport. It wasn't Ben's fault she was stuck here in this miserable floating prison. "He'll guard his eyes, but not many men can help bracing their shoulders if they're holding a risky hand. If they're plumb out of luck, they'll likely slump a bit, but when they lean back and sort of spread their shoulders like a puffing adder, they've got you where the hair's short, so you may as well throw in."

"Pru—dammit, I mean, Haskell! That ain't no way to talk!"

Suddenly, she turned to her brother. With his back to her, he'd been changing into his best breeches and shirt—which were, in truth, little better than his worst. "Well, that's what Papa always used to say," she muttered.

"You'd best save your voice." He glanced over to see if Ben had caught the slip, but the young oarsman was already on his way up the companionway.

"Come morning, you'll be feeling better," Pride assured her. Although he wished his sister only the best, privately he considered they'd both had a lucky escape: Pru because she would surely have been found out and disgraced before the evening was over; himself because he was looking forward to spending a night ashore with his mates without having a bossy sister looking over his shoulder. "I'll look in on you when I get back," he promised.

"Better say *if* you get back," Ben called down with a chortle.

Pru caught at her brother's sleeve, her feverishly bright eyes pleading. A mixture of sympathy and guilt made him draw up a stool beside her for a moment. She looked flushed and frightened and completely miserable. "Aye, little Haskell, there's no Lillah to bring you sugarcane to suck on this time, is there?"

"Little, the devil! You may have shot up like a weed and burst the shoulder seams on your coat, but we both know who's the oldest and the strongest, not to say the smartest!"

"Oh ho! Not quite at death's door yet, eh?"

"I caught a chill, that's all, likely when I washed in the pond, but—"

Pride scowled. "You mean you took a fool chance of being discovered, all for a bit of a splash?"

"Splash indeed! I itched, Pride. Not only that, my own stench was enough to turn away a boar hog."

"Devil take it, you ain't no worse than any of the rest of us. Leastwise, if you had to risk shucking your clothes, I hope you waited until after dark."

"What, and freeze? I'm not that great a noddy. I waited until everyone was busy at something and then took two buckets and went to fetch water." Should she tell him about Gideon? Never! She still burned with shame when she remembered the sight of him—not to mention his advice!

"Leastwise your bath served some purpose. If you hadn't caught a chill, you'd be getting ready for your first visit to Miss Suky's Boardinghouse," Pride taunted, even as his eyes warmed with sympathy. "Ahh, Prudie, what are we going to do? Shall we cut and run tonight, and make our way back home the best way we can?"

"Would you go with me if I said yes?"

He sighed, for he would truly hate to miss tonight's revelry. Pru was not the only one who had never before visited a whorehouse. "Aye—at least, I'd see you home safely and then return to camp. I've a mind to stay on with Cap'n Gideon. He's a fair man, no matter what his faults."

"Faults! Gideon has n—" Pru commenced coughing, and Pride backed away, more concerned than he cared to reveal. "Should I see if I can find a doctor, Pru?"

"And have him find me out? Not bloody likely. I'll be well enough come morning, you'll see. But, Pride, I've a favor to ask."

"Ask away, then. If it don't cost more than my share and yours, I'll do my best."

"I don't know what it costs, but somehow, I must have a bar of sweet soap."

"Soap! We got soap back at camp. Ain't that good enough for you?"

"I'm tired of making do with yellow lye soap. It burns my face and smells like hog fat, and—"

"Are you plumb daft? You go around smelling like a rose and see how long it takes for some'un to tumble to the fact that you ain't no man at all!"

"If you love me, you'll get me some soap." Pru's eyes, though overly bright, glinted with determination. Pride well recognized that particular look, for he'd suffered for it more than once.

"If you think I'm going to walk into any emporium and ask for a cake of sweet-smelling soap, you've gone soft in the brain!"

"And you're stubborn as a two-headed mule!"

Pride jumped up just as Ben called down to say that he was about to get left behind. "Dammit, Pru—"

"Don't do it then. Just because you're satisfied to go around smelling like a rutting goat, why should I care?"

Pride sighed, wondering if his life would have been any different if he had been the firstborn twin. He rather thought not. "I've got to go now, Prudie. But I'll look in on you soon's I get back."

"Don't bother," she said with a sniff, and flopped over onto her stomach, which gave Pride some notion of how far gone she was, for surely no sane person would lie in a hammock on his stomach.

"It ain't no bother, I'll just—"

"Nye! Have done and come along, or ye'll go it alone!"

"I'm coming!" And in a more gentle tone, "I'll see if maybe I can find you some soap, all right?" She was his sister, after all. And for all her wild, reckless ways, she was as dear to him as his own right arm. "Ah, the devil, darlin', I'll get you the sweetest cake of soap in all of Carolina. Now quit crying, or I'll send the captain down here to dose you."

"You'll do it? Oh, Pride, you're a wonderful brother!"

"Aye, and you're a royal pain in the butt—always were, leading me into more mischief than most men survive in a lifetime. All right, all right, come about now before you break your back."

Pru spread the hammock with her fists and managed to turn over without oversetting herself. With a great sigh, she gazed up at him and said, "I'll never ask you for another thing as long as I live, Pride, I vow it on my sacred honor."

"Sacred? You've not got the honor of a blue jay, but I reckon—"

"Nye! Are you coming?"

"Hold yer hawser, dammit, I'm on my way!"

Prudence stared after him, feeling desolate. She could well die right here in this miserable little hammock, in this miserable hole in the water, she thought, forgetting that only a few hours earlier, the *Polly* had seemed the finest ship that ever sailed.

Gideon stood in the shallow copper tub and poured a pot of cold water over his head, sucking in his gut at the shock. He was some disappointed, he couldn't deny it, for he'd been planning on leaving one of the others to stand watch while he went ashore and saw to his own business—both private and otherwise. But with the lad lying up there in the fo'c'sle, likely burning with fever, he didn't see how he could rightly put off his responsibilities on Gouge or Bully or one of the younger men. He'd see about going ashore tomorrow.

Swearing, he scrubbed his hard body with ruthless disregard for the sudsy spatters that flew about the tiny cabin. Two baths in one week was stretching it a mite, but he hated to go to a woman smelling of whale and worse. And Haskell had been so embarrassed at sharing the pond that Gid hadn't had the heart to stay and give himself a thorough scouring.

The little fool should have told him right out before they set sail that he was feeling poorly. Still, to be fair on the lad, he had pulled his weight on the way across the sound, scant though that weight was. He seemed flimsier than ever, even after a season of hard work. Gid had thought that rowing for Tobias would build up his shoulders so that the other men would leave off taunting him about being such a runt, but it hadn't worked.

Twins, they'd said. If those two were twins, then he was a buffalo's behind! Nye was growing up before his very eyes, but poor Haskell . . .

The truth was that some men were born scrawny and remained that way. That wasn't a mark against them, as long as they were decent and honest and pulled their load. Of course, Haskell didn't have the heft to make an oarsman—and so far, Gideon had not found the courage to tell him. Still and all, he was useful. And cheerful. A good sort to have around, never shirking, never grumbling, always jumping in to bear a hand, no matter what the task.

Gideon had worked long and hard to shape his whaling crews the way he wanted them. There was not one man among them who couldn't be trusted, and that was important when six men put out to sea in an open boat to pitch their skills against several tons of enraged whale. One mistake could cost an entire crew their lives—and had, on more than one occasion.

Gideon stood and toweled himself dry, dropping the damp square into the largest of the puddles surrounding the tub. It was unlikely there'd be any more whales sighted this late in the year, save the occasional drifter.

Of course, if he were a true seagoing man, he could take the lad on as his cabin boy. That way, he could teach him, guide him, see to his welfare and—

"Why don't you damned well adopt the poor bastard?" he muttered, glaring at himself in the small shaving mirror over the rimmed shelf.

Dressed in trousers and nothing more, he opened the hatch and lifted the tub, carrying it up and across to the rail to empty it over the side. His skin tingled from the scrubbing. Likely he'd end up catching a chill himself, from bathing too often. Still, it felt good to be clean again. Living rough for the greater part of each year, he had learned to do without bathing in self-defense, for none of his men seemed to miss baths at all.

The tub upended, he was preparing to go below again when he heard a thud, a cry and a string of curses coming from forward and below.

By the time he reached the lower rung of the fo'c'sle ladder, he was cursing himself for a selfish beast. While he had wasted time gussying up for all the whores who would have to do without his company tonight, that poor little bastard was lying down there all alone, probably heaving his guts out.

Though not actually heaving his guts, the lad was sitting on the deck, one hand on his head, the other on his stern, swearing up a storm in a voice that barely registered above a croak.

"Belly turned on you?" Gid inquired as he tried to sum up the situation.

"No, that blasted, bleeding, filthy damned hammock of yours turned on me!"

"Yeah, they'll do that, right enough," Gid muttered, looking for signs of a rash, a discoloration or anything that would indicate this was more serious than an ordinary chill. "Head hurt?"

"Like a busted pun'kin!"

Torn between sympathy and amusement at the boy's unfailing belligerence, Gid reached for his hand to help him up. Then, with an oath of his own, he knelt and scooped him up, depositing him in the nearest hammock. "Umm...ah, we'll see about laying you a pallet, so you won't roll out of it," he muttered, once more shocked at his own reaction to holding the slight bundle of skin and bones in his arms.

"How're you faring now, lad? Other than taking a tumble, I mean."

Pru had been trying to get up to fetch a dipperful of water from the barrel on deck when the hammock had spun over with her as neatly as if she'd been a button on a whirligig. "Thirsty," she whispered.

"I'll fetch you something to drink directly. How's your throat? Is it white?"

"How the devil would I know?"

Gideon looked at her thoughtfully, and Pru stared back resentfully. If she'd gone and caught the deadly disease that choked off a body's air, then she might as well go over the side and be done with it.

Tears of weakness, misery and self-pity threatened. She turned away from the captain's look of concern, lest he see and think her less than a man.

A man! She was sick and tired of being thought a man! All in the world she wanted to do was to throw herself into his great, hairy arms and have him take away the pain in her head, the ache in her bones and the burr that was lodged in her throat so that it hurt to swallow.

That and have him tell her he didn't mind one bit that she was homely and windburned and smelly and callused, because he'd always wanted a woman exactly like that.

Chapter Six

Pru focused her eyes on the heavy timbers overhead and forced her mind to ignore the man who was supporting her while she drank from the water gourd. To ignore the fact that he wore nothing save a pair of breeches that clung to his limbs tighter than pond scum in August. To ignore the great broad chest her head was pressed against, and the golden thicket of hair that was tickling her cheek.

Soap! All these months while she'd been ruining her skin with the harsh yellow lye soap, he had kept a hoard of French soap all to himself! Damn his hide, she could *smell* it on him, and he'd sworn just yesterday he'd trade a whole Spanish dollar for a bar of soap! And all the time, he'd probably had a barrel of the stuff stashed aboard his sloop!

She sniffed, feeling sorely done by.

It's the fever, you silly noddy! Fever always makes a body burn and ache and think all manner of daft thoughts.

But was it fever that made her stare so hungrily at the short curve of his upper lip, or the smooth thrust of his lower one? Was it fever that made her want to reach out and touch the single blemish that served to set off the rare perfection of his features?

"There, no more now, lad," Gideon said as he withdrew the gourd and eased her down on the pallet he had made for her against the forward bulkhead.

"Thank you . . . sir," she rasped, closing her eyes before he could read the confusion and longing she was too weak to hide.

"D'ye think you can keep down a bit of broth? There's the water the fish was boiled in still left—it's bound to be nourishing."

Sinking deeper into her lonely well of misery, Pru shook her head and then wished she hadn't. A low moan of pain escaped her, in spite of all she could do.

"Hurting, are you, son? I've laudanum in the medical stores, if you've a mind to take it."

Not bloody likely! She remembered how Hosannah's mind would weave in and out like a mosquito hawk when she took rum and laudanum toddies! "No, I . . . no," she mumbled.

He studied her for a moment through narrowed eyes. "Aye then. I'll just fetch a wet cloth and a bit of rum to help you sleep. Come morning, you'll be right as rain, or I miss my guess."

Come morning, I'll likely be dead, and you can sew me in a bit of rotten sail and slide me over the rail, and poor Granna will never even know . . .

A short while later, Gideon returned with a handful of dripping rags. Pru followed his progress down the companionway and across the cramped crew's quarters. Damn the man, why couldn't he put on a shirt? Did he have to flaunt himself this way, when she was too ill to resist?

With clumsy gentleness, he laid the sodden wad on her forehead, where it promptly filled both eye sockets and dribbled into the corner of her mouth. "This should ease the pain, son," he growled tenderly, and Pru felt his hand smooth the tangled hair away from her face.

"Good of you, sir," she said with ill grace. Lifting one chapped and calloused hand, she raked the water from her right eye and her tongue darted out to drink what had puddled at the corner of her lips.

She saw the captain staring down at her, a strange expression on his lean face.

"What are you..." she began, and then she gave it up and closed her eyes. Tomorrow she might try and riddle it out. Tonight, she was in no condition for any such challenge.

With hands that were far less steady than usual, Gideon poured himself a measure of his sister's fig brandy and downed it in one gulp. The fever had spread to him. It had to be that, for he could think of nothing else that would explain the way his gut had tightened on seeing that shiny pink tongue dart out and circle round before slipping back between the soft, full lips.

"The lad is *ill*, McNair! He's in your keeping, and you're a perverted bastard, for all you think you've turned into such a fine, upstanding citizen!" he whispered to the image in his shaving mirror....

The sound of a launch scraping against the side of the hull roused Gideon from his thoughts. He cleared his throat, wiped his watering eyes and reached for a shirt. The night was not ended yet; there was still time to go ashore.

The *Polly* weighed anchor on the turn of the tide the following morning. Gideon felt considerably more relaxed, having stolen a few hours after James and Gouge returned to pay a visit to a certain widow he knew. Immediately on returning to the ship, he had looked in on Haskell, to find the boy sleeping soundly. He had lingered just long enough to determine that his face was no longer quite so flushed, nor his breathing as troubled as it had been earlier.

Eighteen? he mused. He thought not, despite what the young imps had tried to make him believe. Sleeping, the lad looked younger than ever. Aye, he was wiry, and considerably stronger than he looked—but for all he could cast a hand line out beyond the breakers, and hit his mark with a throwing knife five times out of five, the lad was still a runt. Despite his windburned cheeks, his face remained as smooth as a woman's behind.

Dammit, that was no way for a man to look—not once he'd untied his mama's apron strings! Haskell's mouth was too soft, too full—even his blasted eyebrows were delicate! Half the camp was laughing at the slack in the poor lad's breeches, while the other half pretended not to notice.

Maybe he should have taught him to defend himself before he attempted to instruct him in the manly art of bedding a woman. Pity the young lad had missed going ashore with the others, though. A night of whoring was just what he needed.

God knows, it had saved Gideon's sanity!

With March behind them, the weather began to moderate. The air warmed up during the day, but the Atlantic was still cold and wild, causing fog to smother the banks more often than not. Pru was forced to remain on shore until all trace of her chill was gone. It was Toby who suggested she be put in charge of the drifters—the dead or dying whales they found and towed ashore. It was a great responsibility, he insisted, but Pru knew it was only an excuse to get her off his crew. She looked to Gideon, but Gid just looked away, muttering something about next season.

But come next season, Pru knew, she wouldn't be here. Somehow, without disgracing herself in either Gideon's or Hosannah's eyes, she was going to have to go home and start over.

Prudence had a goal. There had to be *some* way she could soften herself up, grow out her hair and learn to be the kind of lady a man like Gideon would want, so that when he went to Portsmouth again and saw her in the beautiful gown she would buy with her shares, he would lose his heart to her before he ever discovered who she was.

After a week of being dosed by Gideon and Toby with turpentine neck wraps and balsam sap on a lump of sugar, she'd finally stopped coughing. But she was sick and tired of smelling like a stick of pitch pine! The minute everyone set about their daily chores, she intended to slip away to the pond with the cake of lilac soap Pride had brought her, which she had yet to use. She could commence working on her skin this very day—and perhaps she would leave off the soot, for it invariably got washed off her face in the course of a day anyway. Let them think she was too young to grow a beard. If anyone asked outright, she would tell them she was fifteen. Ben had been fifteen when he signed on with Gideon. It was no mark against anyone to be young.

Sheltered in a grove of live oak, sweet bay, cedar and pine, the pond was wonderfully warm. Pru had brought along her clean shirt and breeches, both worn and stained from use, and her precious cake of soap, wrapped in a scrap of linen.

After a thorough wash, she floated on top of the water, watching the clouds move overhead from the southeast. She wondered if Gideon would smell the lilacs on her—and what he would think.

What a dreadful pickle she had landed herself in, living practically under the nose of the most wonderful man in the world and him thinking she was a boy! And a wicked, dirty boy, at that.

Scrubbed, tingling and thoroughly relaxed, she continued to dawdle in the sweet, dark water, dreaming of the day when Gideon would see her as a woman and fall in love with her. It never occurred to her that he would not love her. He had to. God simply wouldn't allow one person to love another so much unless that love could be returned—it would be too cruel.

Gideon had seen Haskell slip away to the woods almost an hour ago, carrying a bundle of clothes, and he hadn't yet returned. Whether the lad was set on bathing or laundry, it wasn't wise for him to go alone. The pond was a common resource, and most ships that regularly sailed these waters knew where all fresh water was to be found. If a man happened to be sailing shorthanded, he might not be overly fair in picking up another hand—Gideon had lost two men that way.

With Haskell, there was another problem, one that sickened him to think about. The lad was too pretty by half.

There were men who preyed on young boys, the more delicate ones being in the greatest demand.

And Gideon knew with cold certainty that he would kill the bastard who dared lay a hand on that boy.

Unreasoning fear sent him striding across the clearing. Not until he reached the edge of the water hole did he slow his step, and then he swore softly in relief. Pausing at the edge of the woods, he wiped the sweat from his eyes. And then he wiped them again and blinked.

Haskell, up to his neck near the middle of the pond, had suddenly stood up in the shallow water, lifting his arms to hold his hair off his neck.

Gideon's jaw dropped in stunned disbelief. No boy on God's green earth had a chest like that. Not swelling out like small twin melons, their stem ends standing out like pink coral beads. The conniving little heathen was a— He wasn't even a—

No damned wonder he couldn't fill out his codpiece!

Disbelief was slowly replaced by a deep-seated rage as Gideon glared at the long, rounded thighs and the sable triangle that sloped back between them. Fists curling impotently at his sides, he inhaled in a rasping breath of air and expelled it in a soft burst of profanity.

God, what a fool he'd been! How could he not have *known?* Day after day he had watched her. He'd even touched her—actually held her in his arms. Granted, he wasn't the most experienced of men, for he'd spent more time at sea than he ever had ashore—all the same, he should have known!

But hadn't he? In the deepest regions of his consciousness, hadn't he been drawn to the boy he'd thought her to be—drawn and disgusted with himself for his unnatural yearnings?

Tenderness, he'd called it. A father's affection for a lad who could have been his son!

But he'd known. His brain might not have been so quick, but his body had damned well been aware of her, causing him to suffer more doubts and more sleepless nights than any man should have had to bear.

And for what! For a common thief! For a snip of a girl with all the grace of a starving hound!

What other lies had she told him? he wondered, as he watched her bend forward to wring out her hair. It had grown longer since she'd been in camp, until now it reached past her shoulders.

Those pathetic shoulders that no amount of hard work would broaden, he thought, anger burning deeply inside him. While he stood hidden in the shadows of a giant cedar tree, Haskell—or whatever her name was, for she had probably lied about that, as well—waded up out of the water, revealing a body that was so flawlessly made he felt himself hardening in spite of his bitterness.

Furious at this further betrayal, Gideon eased back deeper into the shadows. Forcing himself to ignore the desire that raged through his blood like a fever, he deliberately stoked his anger.

As he watched her dance about on first one foot and then another, tugging a pair of threadbare muslin drawers over damp thighs and sleekly rounded hips, he came to a decision. He'd not charge her with her perfidy.

Perfidy, hell—with treachery!

But before he was done with the little bitch, she would rue the day she'd ever set out to make a fool of Gideon Mc-Nair!

Pru stayed on to chop the kindling she meant to use as an excuse for lingering. Then, with the canvas carrier slung over her shoulders, she headed back to camp, bent almost double to balance her load. Sharp edges pressed into her back, and she ignored them, breathing in her own sweet scent. Would Gideon notice?

Fool! She'd better pray he didn't! She should have rinsed herself more to rid her skin and hair of the scent of lilacs.

Pride met her just as she dumped the lot behind the cook shed. "Where the devil have you been so long? There's trouble!"

She straightened her back slowly, one hand rubbing the place where the load had poked into her tender flesh. "What's the matter, has Bully been threatening to make sausage of poor Lucy again?" she asked. Gouge's pet pig was the joke of the camp. Even Ben had pretended to chase the poor beast a few times with a cleaver, to the great amusement of all present.

"It ain't that, it's Ned." Ned was Toby's striker, and a favorite with the whole camp. "Bully had the watch—he sighted a drifter not more'n ten minutes after you left camp. We couldn't lay hands on the captain, so we set out to get a line onto her."

"We?" Pride now rowed for Toby, spelling the ailing Bully.

"Would you pipe down and let me tell it? Anyhow, Cap'n Gid showed up about then—I could see him on the beach, and they got another boat into the water and set out. But by that time, we were almost on top of her. Ned let go his iron—he had a perfect shot right down the pipe—only the damned thing weren't dead! She come alive and slung a loop around his feet, and over he went!"

Horrified, Pru could only stare. It was every whaler's nightmare—even the shore crew knew that much. "Did he—is he—"

"Dead? No—leastwise, he's stove up right bad, but he ain't dead. Toby went over the side after him. You never seen anything so fast in all your born days as that old man taking a header. The water was all bloody, and the cow had come down hard with her flukes when she sounded, just about upending us, and over he went, right into the middle of it!"

Pride's eyes glinted with excitement, but Pru felt a chill shudder through her body as she thought of what might have happened to her twin. It was time they both went home—past time! Whatever daring she had once possessed—and she'd had more than her share, she had to confess—it was all used up. She wanted nothing more than to return home and have Gideon come to her in a month's time—a week's time—however long it took her to turn into a lady.

"Poor Ned," she whispered. "Is Toby all right?"

Pride dropped onto a log, resting his face in his hands. "Yeah, they'll both make it, I reckon, but I don't mind telling you, I've never been so scared in all my born days."

Like Pride, Pru had come to think the world of the old man. That night after supper she made a point of stopping by his hut to offer her sympathy and whatever he needed in the way of nursing care.

Tobias was drawing on a black clay pipe, throwing out a cloud of stinking smoke. "Well, lad, ye come to pay yer last respects? Yer brother beat ye to it." He chuckled, and Pru, gagging on the foul smell of his pipe, mumbled something about being sorry for his discomfort.

"Save yer sorry fer Ned. The lad's not like to throw another iron fer many a day. Hit her square on, did he, and then, damn me if we didn't have to cut 'er loose an' come in light!" He swore with the same precision that enabled him to get away with spitting to the wind'ard.

Pru paused to stretch her protesting muscles. She'd been among those chosen to load the heavy barrels of oil onto the carts for hauling across the island. That done, she'd had the privilege of helping row them out to the *Polly* in readiness for the next trip into port.

She thought longingly of the days when all she'd had to do was chop and strip fat, tend the try kettles, cook and wash up after an army of gluttons. For some reason, it seemed that lately she had been landed with the hardest, most demanding tasks in camp. It couldn't be because of her debt, for they had long since repaid anything they had inadvertently stolen from Gideon's men.

It was almost as if Gideon were determined to make her cry mercy. Hadn't he said he would release them at the end of the season? Did he want her to go now?

She was willing. She was more than willing, for she had never been so weary. But she refused to beg. She had little enough in this world, but she had her pride. And love him or not, she would die before she would beg Gideon McNair for a single favor.

Gideon stood on the watchtower, his eyes shadowed from too many sleepless nights. He had shifted crews, taking on some of the duties himself, as they were once again short-handed. Toby would not be kept down much longer, for he was afraid of losing out to a younger man, and Gid would never rob him of his pride.

But Ned... aye, there was a problem. A good striker was hard to come by. Crow could have handled it. He could himself, but both were needed elsewhere.

A bleak smile shifted the planes of his face as he stared out across the moonlit water. There was one other who had bragged more than once about his—her—prowess as a marksman.

By damn, it would serve her right! As an oarsman she was of little use, for the others had to hold back or they ended up rowing in circles. But as a striker she would have to make the practice runs with the crews, which was no easy task in itself. She would do her part in maintaining the boat, and there was the gear to keep in shape—lines to check for fraying and irons to keep sharpened.

He'd been expecting the little beggar to cry mercy long before this. From his own hut, where he took most of his meals, he would watch her drag into camp after a day spent doing the work of three men.

But not a single complaint did she utter. More than one of his men had questioned his assigning the hardest tasks to the scrawniest member of the crew, but he'd cut them off short. As for that brother of hers, the poor lad had looked fit to scalp him on more than one occasion—nor could he blame him. But dammit, they were in it together, thick as thieves. All she had to do was confess and beg his forgiveness—she damned well owed him that much!

Gideon had already made up his mind that he would break her, or die trying. One way or another, she was going to pay for making a fool out of him—out of his entire crew! She would learn a lesson she'd not soon forget, and then he would wash his hands of the pair of them.

Chapter Seven

Lillah was on her way to the dock to buy fish when she saw him. With an innate pride that had brought her little but trouble in this life, she stiffened, lifting her head still higher.

It was the man who had brought her the message from the twins. Crow, he called himself. His hair might be crow-black, and straight as the feathers on a raven's wing, but he was like no crow she had ever seen. His skin was the tawny color of fine cane syrup—the color of swamp water when the sun shone straight down from overhead. Nor were his eyes the opaque black-brown eyes of her own people, but smaller, narrower—the color of ripening acorns.

"You bring more word of those children?" she demanded the moment he was within hearing. She hadn't intended to speak first. It was worry that made her rush into speech—worry for the mizzus. And perhaps just the smallest sliver of fear for those twin imps of Beelzebub.

He moved at his own pace—slow and deliberate, like an ox that would be neither prodded nor halted.

"Where be my mizzus's babies? You say they come home. You lie. Speak, mon!"

"Woman, I do not lie. My captain, he say tell the woman they do be fine. I tell you that."

"Time they come home now. The mizzus, she not fine no more." Lillah shifted her fish basket to the other hip, and Crow reached out and took it from her, gaining for his efforts a furious glare. "You want my basket, mon? Go weave you own basket. Have you woman make you a basket.'' She tilted her head higher, causing her long neck to rise like a night heron on the hunt out of the crisp white muslin fichu she wore tucked into the bodice of her faded indigo gown.

"If I had me a woman, she would have more to do than weave my baskets.''

Lillah drew back as far as the narrow path would allow. There was something wild and deep about this man, something she could not fathom, for all she could see behind the eyes of most men. Try as she would, she could have seen the dark side of the moon more clearly than she could see into the heart of this one.

"The children, tell them this for Lillah,'' she said. "Tell them Lillah say to get on home now, they Granna need them.'' The sewing basket need them, she added silently.

Lillah worked for no man who could not pay her wages. Her bargain had been struck by Mr. Urias, himself, long before he had sailed out through Ocracoke Inlet that fine March morning in the year of '25. She had stayed on for the sake of the mizzus and the children, but when they could no longer pay, she must go.

Lillah had learned long since that in this world, the white man valued two things above all—his money and his fish-belly skin. Lillah would not have traded her beautiful blue-black skin for all the gold at the bottom of the sea, but she had quickly learned that to live in a white man's world, one must have more than the white man's trade paper—one needed the white man's coin. A woman counted for little in any man's world—a black woman, still less.

But gold and silver, and even copper, were respected by all.

Lillah had once been the property of a sickly old man whose hateful son had treated her considerably better than he treated his wife, but not so well as he treated his dogs. Never again would she suffer herself to belong to any man. She would die first.

But so would the man who tried to claim her, for she had made herself that promise on the day her old master had called her to his room and given her a paper of manumission as he lay dying. His son had tried to stop him, but even near death, the old man had been the stronger of the two. Lillah had not even lingered to hear his death rattle, but had slipped out and made her way to the river before the son could send men to destroy her precious paper and bring her back in chains.

The man called Crow spoke again, his voice sending currents of uneasiness up her spine. "The girl, Haskell, she be—"

"Her name not be Haskell! She be called Pru-dence."

Something shifted in the depths of Crow's eyes, and though not so much as a twitch revealed itself on his face, Lillah had the strange feeling that he had known all this before.

She drew in a deep breath, and his gaze immediately dropped to the place where the fichu was knotted and tucked into her bodice. "Say what you come to say, mon, and be on you way. Company coming tonight. That old woman would have me make a feast from one small croaker and a handful of yaupon."

Actually, Hosannah had sent her to the docks for butterfish and China tea. That mincing fop Delarouche would turn up his nose at the fare of honest people. Fortunately, Lillah could work magic with anything that swam in the sea. Soaked in a bit of sour milk first, her fish would be fit for a king, and her good yaupon tea far finer than anything that came from any heathen country on the other side of the world. Far too good for that devil, Delarouche.

Head high, she turned and stalked away, telling herself that all too soon she would need all the spells old Mahadoo had ever taught her to keep them from starving. What she *didn't* need was this high-nosed stranger prying into her affairs, mocking her for staying on with a white woman who could no longer afford to keep her. That was her own concern, and none of his!

They had nearly reached the docks, where the island's few fishermen were unloading their catch. Lillah stared straight ahead, pretending the man called Crow was not sauntering along beside her, swinging her best limberjack basket on his arm. She walked stiffly, her arms, bereft of their burden, crossed over her bosom.

"That Pru-dence, she got the captain so twisted hindpart before, he don't know whether to fly or cut bait," Crow mused idly, as if speaking to himself. "He think she a man, with her coat all buttoned tight and her codpiece hangin' flat as a flounder. He think—"

"Hush, mon! Don' you say this wicked thing to me! Mizzus goin' whup her good with a willow switch if she come back wit' a baby in her belly!"

This time there was no mistaking the grin that split Crow's broad face. He uttered not a sound, but Lillah glared at him, telling herself he was *not* the most handsome fella she had ever seen, for his lips were too thin and his hair was too long, and he smelled of whale fat and wood smoke instead of clean, honest sweat.

"Ah, woman, you ain't fooling this man. You may be freedwoman, but these white folk got you bound up in the worst way they is."

"No white folk ever lay a hand on Lillah again. I be free to walk myself right off this island if I want to, and don' nobody forget that."

They were nearly at the docks, and several of the men working there turned to watch them, for other than Lillah, there were no Negroes on Portsmouth. She was known by all and gave equally short shrift to all. The villagers had come to harbor a grudging respect for the woman's independence, for it was a quality required of anyone who sought to survive on the bleak and storm-raked Outer Banks.

"Lookee yonder. First thing ye know, the whole blarsted island'll be overrun with blackbirds," one man said to his partner, who nodded, sized up the breadth of Crow's shoulders and turned back to planing the plank he'd been working on. Crow had been seen about the waterfront before. It was generally known that he was a member of one of the whaling crews working the lower banks. As a breed, he was a matter of some interest, but then, any outsider was held with suspicion by the handful of people who had chosen to make the island their home.

"I will have my basket now." Lillah focused her eyes on a point just above and beyond Crow's left shoulder. After a moment, she began to tap a small booted foot in the sand.

"Would you have it empty, or filled with fish?"

"Empty!"

"Then I believe I will make it full, just to see your eyes snap with devil fire again." So saying, Crow turned away and approached one of the fishermen who was emptying his nets onto the wharf.

After a few words, he stiffened and moved on to the next one. Lillah watched his progress as he moved from one man to the next, and to her dismay, found herself flinching inwardly each time he was turned away. She could have spared him that, for the fishermen all knew she worked for the mizzus. They would often throw in an extra fish, because despite the rumors of a hidden fortune, they felt sorry for any woman left alone with two young hellions to care for.

Finally, Crow went back to the beginning of the line. This time, he spoke longer, and dug deeply into his pocket. The fisherman held up two fish, and Crow shook his head and pointed to two others. There was a bit of laughter up and down the line, and then Crow walked away with his basket of—not croakers, but trout. Fine, fat trout, for which he had paid three times their worth.

Lillah accepted them with no thanks at all, for she had not asked the man to take her basket and do her business for her. She would have accepted croaker and made the mizzus think it was butterfish. As for what that Delarouche thought, she cared not one blade of grass, for that man was evil. She had looked directly into his eyes the first time he came to the house and a knowing had come upon her. She had seen great greed and wickedness, and something dark that burned like banked coals. Something that would one day bring danger and pain to those around her.

But not to herself. Lillah knew that she would not be personally involved. As for the mizzus, she could not say. She had not seen her there, in the knowing, but she had felt her pain. It was the children who were in the most danger from the Frenchman—this Lillah had sensed almost from the first.

Why? How?

But the knowing was done, and no amount of burning feathers and setting out cornmeal for the chickens to write in had produced an answer.

"I will be back to this place," Crow said as she walked away without looking back. "I will look for you, woman!" he called after her. His laughter followed her down the path, stiffening her back until her shoulders ached from the effort.

But despite her best intentions, Lillah thought of the brown man with the long black braids and the narrow laughing eyes more than once in the days that followed.

Pru was in love with Gideon. As much as she hated herself for her weakness, she loved him for his startling good looks, his unfailing fairness—at least with all but her—and even for the aura of loneliness she often sensed when he didn't know anyone was watching. It was sheer bad luck, for he'd done naught to encourage her. Not that he would, of course, thinking her a man.

All the same, she was getting tired of butting her head against that stony wall of aloofness that surrounded him. Lately it had been even worse. Lately, his harshness had bordered on cruelty. It was almost as if he delighted in seeing her humbled.

Scrawny, he called her. Weak as cambric tea. A sniveling little runt. Yet when it came time to hand out duties, he seemed to think she had the strength of three men, assigning her the most devilish tasks of all.

Not for all the gold in Spain would she have let a single word of complaint pass her lips, no matter that she nearly broke her back shifting troughs and chopping firewood, no

matter that she nearly severed three fingers trying to learn
how to set a barrel stave properly.

Did he appreciate it? He did not! More often than not, he
scowled at her as if she'd managed to bollix up the works.

"Ye're bein' a mite hard on the boy, ain't ye, Cap'n?"
asked Lear one morning when she'd been set to build a new
compound for the three remaining hogs, move them and
then shovel sand over the entire reeking fly-ridden site of the
old pen.

Gideon had fixed him with an icy stare. "Have you finished caulking number three yet?"

"Run plumb out of oakum."

"Then break out that barrel of pitch and start picking
hemp."

"Aye, sir, right away, sir," the disgruntled steersman had
muttered.

Pru had already gathered up her tools and was trudging
across to the hog pen. Of all the duties she could possibly
have drawn, this was the absolute foulest! Next, he'd have
her digging a new trench and moving the necessary.

"When you're done with that, Haskell, you can get
started on trenching over behind that line of dunes. May as
well set four corner posts and throw up a new brush wall
around it. The old one's too far gone to move."

Had she thought she loved him? She hated him! It was
nearly dark when she finally finished the first chore, having had to chase one of the blasted, squealing creatures all
over the beach before she finally thought to lure him into the
new pound with an ear of dried corn.

Come to think on it, she hated pig meat, too. It was tough
and stringy, and as often as not, tasted of fish from the
scraps they fed the wretched beasts! There wasn't enough
pickle or brine in the whole wide world to make it palata-
ble.

As dirty as she was, with the weather so warm Pru didn't
dare go near the pond to bathe. It would be dark by the time
she got there, and there were snakes as big about as her

thigh. Pride and Ben had bathed in the ocean just before supper, but she dared not.

Filthy, she fell into an exhausted sleep, never knowing that Gideon stood for a full quarter of an hour at the door of her hut, staring down at the small tanned feet that poked out from beneath the light blanket.

"We'll set a competition for striker," Gideon announced the next morning. He appeared gaunt-faced and dark-eyed just after dawn as the men were grumbling over their first mugs of Gouge's coffee, which was even worse, if possible, than Pru's. "All wantin' to try out, meet at the driftwood log in ten minutes."

Gideon avoided looking directly at Haskell, but he was deeply aware of everything about her appearance. She'd lost weight. Damn all, he'd intended to teach her a lesson, not kill her! If only she weren't so bloody stubborn! Why didn't she cry off? Why didn't she ask him to ease up on her?

He'd do it in a minute, but first, damn her, she was going to have to ask him! Pride in either a man or a woman was good, but there was such a thing as too much pride.

Yet it was that very pride he was counting on to save her. Or to save him—at this point, he wasn't sure which he was after. All he knew was that he couldn't go on driving her, for he was suffering for it more than she was. And the stubborn little donkey would break before she would bend.

Serving as striker when the season was done would be safe enough. She would have to keep her gear in order, but that was surely easier than sanding the massive fifty-gallon try kettles and greasing them against rust, setting posts, digging trenches and building brush fences, which had left her sleeves in shreds and both her face and her arms scratched and bleeding.

He'd damned near given in and begged her forgiveness when he saw her, she had him that addled.

Playing at being striker would keep her out of mischief for the last week or so of camp. It would keep her away from the woods, as well, for she'd nearly come to grief the last time she'd gone with Bully to chop firewood. If Bully hadn't seen that cottonmouth in time...

Gideon swore, something he'd been doing an inordinate amount of lately. He wiped his suddenly damp brow. Not for the first time, he cursed the day he'd ever brought her into his camp.

Thank God he'd soon be rid of her. They were merely marking time now, closing down the camp for the season, keeping an eye out for a late drifter. Another couple of weeks and he'd be rid of the little troublemaker.

When an inner voice mocked him, reminding him that he could have spared a man to sail her up to Portsmouth long before now, he refused to heed it. Just as he'd refused all along to heed the voice of reason, the voice of his own salvation.

"The pair of you, eh?" he asked a few minutes later when he joined Haskell and Nye near the great mahogany log that had drifted up onto the beach. The entire company had assembled there, too, ripe for a bit of entertainment to break the monotony of work.

"And me, sir," cried Ben, fastening his breeches as he hurried to join them. He'd been last in line for the new necessary.

"Three of you, then. Tobias, would you care to set out the rules?"

The old man, fully recovered from his ordeal, stepped forward and laid out the gear. An iron, with twenty fathom of line attached, to be coiled by the striker, was assigned to each contender, the mark drawn in the sand some fifty feet back from the log.

Gideon could see the excitement glistening in Haskell's eyes. He had counted on that wicked streak of competitiveness of hers to do his work for him, and it was turning out just as he had planned.

As long as she won, that was. Of the three, she had the least strength by far, but her eye was uncannily accurate. He'd seen her throw knives against half the crew, and there wasn't a man jack among them who could match her.

"Lay yer bets, mates," cried Ned, who had recovered enough to keep tabs on the wagers after being assured that his seat was not permanently at risk.

"If we've the crew for it, we'll mount four boats next season," he told them. *But Haskell won't be among them, you can be sure.*

Pru carefully coiled her line as she'd been taught, so that it would feed freely. Then she toed the mark, her ridiculously small foot wriggling in the sand for a purchase. She hefted the iron to get the feel of the weight of line that would be trailing it, lifted her face to sample the wind and then eased off.

The others were doing much the same, though they would throw in sequence, with Nye going first, Haskell second and Ben third.

"You ain't got near enough heft, Haskell," Ben muttered under his breath, but the wind carried his words to Gideon, who stood only a few feet behind the mark. "It ain't like tossing a handful of bones, you know."

"Just watch me," Haskell said calmly, and Gid felt his chest swell with pride. She was a cool one, all right. Outnumbered, outweighed and, God knows, a female striker was unheard of, but she was game. A man couldn't help but admire that unsinkable spirit of hers. If she'd truly been a boy, he would have been proud to claim her as his son.

Pride cut his eyes at his sister, his narrow face still taut with anger. He'd had only minutes to try to talk her out of this crazy notion after Gideon made his announcement.

He might as well have saved his breath. "Devil take it, Pru, just because you used to be a fair shot when we were younger—" he'd said.

"Younger! I can throw rings around you any day, and you know it!"

"Hush up! You won't win, anyhow, but even if you do, it won't do you no good. Season's over. There won't be any more whales coming up the coast now. All's gone north that's going. You'll be back home helping Lillah in the kitchen 'fore you know it, and I'll damned well shackle you to the doorpost if I have to, to keep you from getting into any more trouble.''

He might have known it would be the wrong thing to say. Pru's face had taken on that look she used to get whenever Papa had pitted them against each other, but she'd only smiled her sweetest.

This had given him no small amount of uneasiness.

"Get set, lads. Put 'er right down the pipe," Toby called out. There was a knothole turned three quarters to the top surface of the log, a perfect replica of a blowhole. That was to be their target.

They were all three poised and ready when the next call came. "Hup, Nye! Ready—set—*strike!*"

The iron skimmed over the top of the log and buried itself three feet in the sand. Nye groaned. A few of the men who had placed money on his throw cursed, and then it was Pru's turn.

This was not like squinting down to sight along the barrel of Albert Thurston's fowling piece, for she'd be shooting from above her right shoulder this time.

She drew in a deep breath and released a part of it, focusing her entire being on the tiny target. Her feet were spread, her whole body as tense as a bowstring when the cry came.

"Strike!"

Line sang past her ear, taking more than a few strands of her hair with it. Before she was even aware of the cold iron's having left her grasp, it was buried deep in the very center of the knothole, its shaft still vibrating as the line dropped harmlessly across the glistening sand.

A cheer went up, from both those who had bet on Haskell and those who had bet against her. For an instant, Pru felt only a deep sense of disbelief.

And then she was laughing and dancing about. Pride had run forward to yank her iron out of the log. He presented it to her, and she stopped just short of throwing her arms about his neck when Toby called out, "Ben, ye're up, lad. On yer mark—get set. *Strike!*"

He hit the lip of the knothole. Close, but there could be only one winner, and all knew who that was. With a long face, Ben came over to congratulate her, and Pru murmured something about luck and a bit of wind that had kicked up and thrown his iron off course.

If she'd thought to spend the day basking in her new-found glory, she was sadly mistaken.

"All right, Haskell!" Gideon said coolly, without so much as a single word of congratulation. "Your turn at cooking today, and you can start checking your gear in the meantime. Ned'll give you some pointers."

The devil take Gideon McNair! He was a closed-minded, woodenheaded noddy without a shred of common decency to his name!

"We'll just see who has the last laugh," she fumed, her mind working at a furious speed a few hours later as she chopped the tops off withered turnips and hurled them into the pot of muddly stew along with potatoes, carrots, onions, wild bay and salted pork.

Now that the days were longer, the crew sat about outside the cook shed long after they finished the evening meal—talking, gaming, drinking their last ration of rum for the day. And complaining about the stew.

Pru took it in good stead, for without enough to do, the men were growing increasingly restless. They complained about everything, but they meant no real harm, and she knew it.

"If ye're fixin' to make another pot of coffee, lad, I'd take it kindly if ye'd not put so much tar in it this time," said Bully. Pru caught the twinkle in his eye and jokingly reached for the box of salt. It came to her how much she was going to miss them all when she left this place.

There was no moon that night, which meant that there would be no night watch. Gideon was a stickler when it came to not wasting his men's energies.

Except where she was concerned, she reminded herself wearily. Seated on a chunk of firewood, she crossed her arms on her knees and rested her head for a moment, which brought her bare feet and the ragged ends of her trousers into her view. She needed new boots and new breeches, she thought with a sigh.

No, dammit all, she needed new gowns.

Oh, botheration! Sometimes she wished she had never laid eyes on Gideon McNair. He had her so confused, she didn't know what she was or wasn't—or even what she wanted anymore.

Oh, yes, she did. She sighed again, smelling the harsh lye soap on her hands. If she had learned one thing since her father was killed, it was to make do with what was instead of wasting time worrying over what could never be.

In the first place, she would never be a beauty. Her hair was plain brown instead of golden like Annie's, and her eyes were no particular color at all—neither blue nor green nor gray.

She'd been ordinary enough before, but now she had months of living under the most wretched conditions to overcome. It would take more than a few of Lillah's buttermilk facial soaks, and applications of sweet oil on her hair to restore their softness, and as for her hands and fingernails, she doubted they'd ever fully recover.

She'd just have to resort to wearing gloves. Not lace mitts, like those she'd found in her mother's trunk, but long silk gloves that would hide her raw knuckles and the calluses on her palms.

She would have to have new clothes, of course—even with her mother's old gowns, she had nothing at all suitable. Annie could help her choose, for Annie had always had an eye for that sort of thing.

Fingering her hair doubtfully, Pru wondered if it was totally beyond repair. It felt like a squirrel's nest, the ragged ends all stiff with salt, but at least it was growing again. All the men had grown shaggy over the winter months. Even Pride had sprouted a small beard, which looked rather nice on him. It occurred to her that her brother was turning into a rather handsome young man.

Not in Gideon's class, of course, but then, who was?

She sighed wistfully as a split callus on her palm caught in her hair. Once her hair had regained its luster—if it ever did—and her skin had softened and lost its ruddy tan, she would still be faced with the problem of finding Gideon again.

Would he even give her a second look? Would he recognize her? If he did, would he despise her for having gulled him all these months?

Pru stood abruptly and dusted the sand off the seat of her breeches. Instead of sitting around daydreaming over a man she might never see again, she'd best be thinking of how she was going to look after Granna. If Blackbeard himself had risen from the dead at that moment and offered her his purse, she'd have turned the other way. She'd had quite enough of playing highwayman, thank you very much!

She found Gideon alone in his hut, bent over a crude desk and marking wages and barrels processed in his daily ledger. Not waiting to be invited inside, she rapped on the door and flung it open, nearly tripping over his boots, which he had shed and left where they fell. "Captain McNair," she began in her deepest, most forceful tone, "Ned says he received another half share once he made striker."

Gideon's jaw hardened. He'd not shaved in three days, nor had he gone back to the pond since he found her there. "I'm aware of that. Now, if that's all you came to say, you may take your leave."

Or suffer the consequences of his damnably short temper, he added silently. He was tired. He'd not slept soundly since the day he'd seen her at the pond, flaunting her nakedness like some wicked wanton.

To make matters worse, he was five barrels off in his calculations. "Well?" he demanded. "Are you hard of hearing?"

"Then I may expect the same amount from now on?"

Making an effort to reel in his temper, he said with ominous quietness, "You may expect what you damned well wish to...Haskell."

Pru stood her ground, but she was not man enough—or woman enough—to prevent a small quiver of her lower lip. He had spoken her name as if it were a curse. "Have I done something to anger you, Gide—that is, sir?" As much as it galled her to ask, she couldn't bear for him to look at her as if she were no more than the dirt on the sole of his boot.

Gideon pushed back his lamp and stared down at his ledgers. She waited, wanting to run away, but wanting even more to smooth away the deep lines that creased his high forehead. A shock of sun-bleached hair fell over one eyebrow, gilded by the light from the oil lamp. If only he'd been put together differently, Pru told herself, she might have hated him. Truly, a man's looks were nothing—a matter of lineage, an accident of birth—that was all.

Yet no matter how she tried to harden her heart against him, she was drawn by something deeper than surface beauty, stronger than mere infatuation. She knew, without knowing how she knew, that she belonged to Gideon McNair, and he to her.

Only how the devil did she go about convincing him of that fact?

Gideon refused to look up, but he was acutely aware of her presence. Why didn't she go, damn her? Was she waiting to be thrown out? Was she about to offer herself to him and beg him to slack off with his demands and pay her two full shares?

Shares of what? There'd be no more whales this season. "Well? What are you waiting for?" he growled.

When she didn't speak right off, he made the mistake of looking directly at her, regretting it instantly. She was standing just inside his doorway, swallowed up by the coarse shirt she'd been issued and a pair of trousers that cradled her bottom and smoothed over her rounded hips, the codpiece draped mockingly over her flat crotch. It would serve her right if...

For a small eternity, Gid's deep blue eyes burned into her cooler sea-green ones, and he swore bitterly. If he didn't rid himself of her cursed presence this very instant, he would throw her onto the sandy floor and take her there, hard and fast and deep.

"Get out," he said quietly.

"But sir, you never said—"

"Get...*out!* You are about as noxious a bit of flotsam as ever I ran afoul of, and if you don't stay your flapping tongue and keep out of my sight, I'll have you flogged so that you'll truly have something to whine about! Is that quite clear?"

He turned away before he could reach for her, but not before he had seen her eyes flood with tears.

Damn her soul, what had she done to him? he thought. It was not in him to treat any human being, man or woman, the way he'd been driven to treat her.

Nor was Gideon the only one to notice that Haskell had been coming in for the rough side of Gideon's tongue more often than not—when he wasn't pretending the poor lad didn't exist.

"Cap'n didn't bet heavy on Ben to win the strike, did he?" asked one of the oarsmen, who'd been idly shaping another paddle to replace one that had split.

"Cap'n Gid don't gamble. Damn me if I know what's eating at him, but he's sure 'nuff got his tail caught in a crack over something."

Pride managed to stay close to Pru, standing between her and whatever trouble she'd managed to land herself in as best he could, but there was only so much he could do without giving the game away. And it was so near time to go home now, that it was hardly worth the danger.

Crow watched silently, a knowing look in his eyes. He would be taking the girl back to Lillah soon. Tomorrow would not be soon enough for him.

Chapter Eight

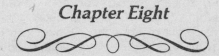

April 25, 1729. Wind beating out of N.E. for past week. Moderate temperatures, four inches of rain in the pan this morning. Sea tide running higher than normal. Huts leaking bad, men complaining of wet bedding. Will break camp by week's end if all goes well. No drifters, no porpoise.

By the hand of Gideon McNair, the south banks.

The entire crew, as sour as their own dispositions were, had taken to avoiding Gideon like the plague, for he was apt to bite off a man's head for the least offense.

Such as being late to relieve the watch.

Pru hadn't meant to dawdle at the pond, but she'd been increasingly out of sorts recently. The constant rain had been bad enough, but Gideon's snappishness made it worse.

She wanted to go home—and she wanted to stay on forever. She was worried about Granna, about how they were going to make ends meet. She was afraid of being found out now that it was no longer possible to disguise herself under layers of bulky clothing.

The truth was, she was beginning to despair of ever sorting out the mess she had made of her life.

Fully an hour late, she climbed the ladder to the crow's nest to relieve Pride, feet dragging and an apology on the tip of her tongue.

But it was not Pride she found there. "I will not tolerate slackers in my company, Haskell. You were to relieve the watch an hour ago."

Gideon. The words of apology flew from her mind—she'd been planning to plead the excuse of a miserable night that had left her practically afloat on a wet pallet.

Staring down at the toe of her boot, she was half tempted to blurt out the truth and take her punishment. She just wanted to go home! Now—this very minute. The season was ended, and all, including Gideon, knew it. Pru wasn't fool enough to believe he would ever have allowed "the runt," as he called her, to become a striker.

A drop of rain drizzled off her oilskin hat and guttered down her cheek as she stared up at him, willing herself to demand her freedom this very instant. The only thing that prevented her was the galling admission that she couldn't bear to leave him—not just yet.

What if he decided to go north and whale the Newfoundland grounds? What if Granna sent her to Hunt House to stay with Great-uncle John? Granna would probably tell him to marry Pru off to one of his stodgy neighbors, and that would be the end of her dreams.

And even if Granna and Uncle John were to hold off on finding her a husband, Pru knew for a fact that there were no whales up the Albemarle Sound. She would never see Gideon again.

"Well? Have you nothing to say for yourself?" Gideon demanded. He stood at the top of the ladder, rain dripping off his bare head, looking like heaven's messenger come down to earth. It occurred to her then that his blemish, if it could be called that, was so much a part of him that he would have looked naked without it.

"I have plenty to say for myself...sir." And she did, only some vestige of self-preservation prevented her from saying it.

"Well?" he barked after an eternity of silence had passed, filled only with the dripping of rain on the wooden deck, the seething of the surf, the keening of the wind and the demented laughter of the gulls—background sounds that were so constant she no longer even heard them.

Blinking, she caught herself up short. She'd been staring at his mouth. Hungrily, she feared. "Sir, I'm ready to relieve the watch."

Gideon's curses would have had more effect on her had she not been so accustomed to hearing them. To her knowledge, he hadn't smiled in weeks. And as for laughter, why, the very skies would come tumbling down before that happened.

Which they were doing this very moment, Pru thought with an irreverent urge to giggle. A trickle of rain had slid off her chin, spattered on her bosom—or what would have been her bosom had she not been bound up tight as a bung in a barrel of rum.

"Come along, Haskell, I don't have all day! If you've something to say, then speak up!"

"I'm sorry to be late, sir," she muttered into her collar. *And more sorry than you'll ever know that I once had the misfortune to hold a gun on you and try to relieve you of your purse.*

"What's that? Speak up, I can't hear you!"

Eyes stinging from the rain—surely not from tears again!—Pru threw back her had and glared at him. "I said, I'm sorry for not relieving watch sooner, sir! But he's not here, anyhow, so I don't see what—"

"He's not here because I had to spell him when he came down with the trots! You were nowhere to be found, and the others were all busy at their assigned tasks."

Pru looked up, her eyes wide with worry. Pride was ill? Why hadn't he told her? She'd spoken to him this morning, and he'd not said a word. "I'm sorry, sir." And she truly was.

Gideon continued to stare at her. "Never mind," he muttered. "Your brother'll likely recover. I've set three men to fishing. You'll be off watch by the time they bring in their catch. Scale 'em, gut 'em and salt 'em down. Use one of the new casks—I'll have Crow roll one out for you."

Pru's lips tightened. She hated gutting and scaling fish. The scales stuck to every exposed bit of her skin and stayed there until she picked them off with the tip of her knife. Her hands smelled like fish for days afterward, and she'd just got them to smelling sweet again after working the last drifter.

"Is that all, sir?"

"What? Oh. Yes." Gideon stood aside as she took the last rungs of the ladder. Then, without a word he moved past her and descended. Pru watched as he stalked across the sand toward camp, his back impossibly straight as his powerful limbs carried him easily across the deep sand.

He was bareheaded, barefooted and so damned beautiful she hated him. Hated him and loved him, and both were equally fruitless.

Back in his own quarters, Gideon wondered if he'd been too rough. He'd meant to ease up on her, after having pushed her so hard when he first discovered her deception.

The trouble was, just looking at her sent the blood coursing through his body until he was stiff as an oar, and each time it happened, he took out his anger on her poor defenseless head before he could stop himself.

"Poor defenseless head, my sweet arse," he muttered, ducking as a drop of rain spattered down on his nose. Damned rain! Damned leaky roof! Damned lying little heathen! If he worked her harder than he did the others, she had brought it on herself!

Besides, Crow would see that she didn't fare too badly. For reasons that defied logic, the half-breed had taken her under his wing, never saying much, never appearing to champion her cause, but never far away when she was struggling under what could have been a dangerous task.

Thank God for that, whatever the reason, Gideon thought. He might despise the little beggar, but that didn't mean he wanted her blood on his hands.

It was nearing midday when the entire camp heard Haskell scream out, "I *saw* one, I *saw* one! I mean, *wha-a-ale o-offff!*"

For an instant, no one moved. Several of the men had been mending a net, while others worked on sharpening the shovels. Crow was shaving down the blade of a paddle, sitting off to himself, as was usual.

Gid, who had been working on his books, was the first to the boats. He whipped off the rain cover and flung it aside, and before the others even reached the high-water mark, he was calling out orders. With Nye still suffering from dysentery, another man would be needed to round out the crews, he reasoned.

And he himself would be that man! He was in desperate need of the clean, sharp thrill of the chase and the kill to rid him of the miasma that had hung over him for so long. Ned would get his full share of the prize, whether or not he was in on the kill.

Toby's roar could be heard over the pounding of the surf as he cursed the tide for being too low. It had begun to flood only a quarter of an hour ago, which meant they'd have heavy seas and not enough water under them until they got past the first bar.

"Toby, you take Ben as striker and Thomas as first oarsman—I'll row for James—Crow can strike for Gouge!" Gideon ordered. It was hell having two men laid up at once and one a striker.

Gideon put his shoulder into one final shove and then swung himself into the boat just as the others came aboard. An instant later, all oars were in the rowlocks and pulling deeply as the crew raced to catch up with their quarry.

Not until they were safely past the outer bar did Gideon spare a glance for the other two boats. Gouge, the third steersman, was having troubles. He'd taken on water early on, and his striker was bailing hard as the oarsmen strained to get past the breakers.

Toby, his weather eye finding the smallest break in the choppy seas, had sent his boat darting ahead of James's by a length by the time Gideon turned around to catch a glimpse of a familiar figure hanging over the bow.

Haskell? Dammit, he'd told the old man to take Ben as a striker, not as oarsman! Only a fool would go after a live one with a green striker—and a woman, at that!

With no break in his rhythm, Gideon rowed and cursed. There was only one thing for it—Toby would have to lie behind until the kill had been safely made. If Haskell was determined to get involved, she could move in and sink her iron in time to help on the long shoreward haul. But only *after* the other two boats had worn the beast down.

Fueled by a dangerous blend of fear and anger, Gideon bent his powerful back to his work, forcing the others to dig deeper to keep up. Drawing abreast of the other boat, he shipped his blades and shouted, "Haskell, damn your hide, what the hell are you doing out here?"

"I'm striking for Toby! Sir!" she shouted back.

"Get the devil back where you belong! Ben can—"

"She blo-oows, she blo-oows!" Toby shouted, and to a man, the oarsmen twisted around to stare at the spume that was even now falling back onto the sea. "Come about three points to the east'ard, lads," he yelled, "and we'll be onto 'er!"

"My sainted soul, she's a monster," breathed the man seated in front of Gideon.

"We got us a prime sperm, or I'll eat my boots!" vowed the first oar, Lear.

But the gawking had cost them precious time. Toby's boat, already to the east of them, had now pulled ahead and was bearing down on the very place where the spume cloud had fallen back to the sea.

Gideon rowed as he had never rowed before, but the old man had the faster crew, and he'd been closer, to boot. Gideon found himself cursing under his breath with each stroke, covering fear with anger, and anger with fierce, backbreaking work.

But if Gideon was covering fear, Pru was covering something altogether different.

She'd been feeling sicker by the minute for the past hour. Rowing, no matter that it fair pulled her arms out of their sockets, always kept her mind off the motion of the water. But riding forward in the striker's seat was sheer hell, as the small craft rose crazily on the crest of one great sea, only to slam down into the trough of the next. She had pounded her behind to a pulp and now she sadly feared she was going to disgrace herself before the entire crew.

"Ease off a few fathom o' line and lay her ready, lad," Toby called over the heads of his oarsmen, and she swallowed and nodded.

"James is coming up abaft the port beam," Thomas called out.

Wonderful, Pru thought sourly. All she needed to make her misery complete was for Gideon to witness her disgrace.

Nevertheless, she turned about and began laying her line as best she could. Closing her fingers over the cold shaft of her iron, she prayed for a miracle.

Thus she suffered for more than an hour before Toby began to close in on his quarry. The three boats had bracketed the last sighting, with James and Toby taking the northeasterly station and Gouge the southwesterly. The whale could be expected to continue on a northeasterly heading at present.

"She's laying nearby," the old man said quietly, breaking the eerie silence. "I can smell the old bastard sure's I can smell me own sweat. Prepare to switch to paddles when I gives the signal, lads."

Tension grew until Pru wanted to scream just to relieve it. Or vomit.

"James is easing abreast," murmured Thomas, the oarsmen seated immediately behind Pru's precarious roost. She cast a baleful look over her right shoulder. The sight of James's small boat pitching about like a cork in a tempest did nothing at all for her belly.

"Breathe deep through yer mouth, lad," Thomas suggested, and she smiled halfheartedly and did as she was told.

Why now, God? I've been out nearly this far a dozen times without my belly turning on me. Why now?

Suddenly, something dark and enormous broke the surface not thirty yards away. The whale blew, showering them with spray even as the oars dug into the bottle-green water, but before they could get into position, the monster had settled back into the depths again.

Behind her, Toby was reading the surface of the water, his steering sweep still. The oarsmen sat frozen, arms extended for the next pull. Pru focused bleary eyes on the wooden loggerhead on the forepeak and willed herself not to retch over the side and scare the beast away.

"Bring her around gently to the port, lads—aye, easy does it. Get ready to change over." The old man continued to call out commands in a voice scarcely above a whisper. Reluctantly, Pru lifted her iron and freed the lock on the loggerhead. The first few fathoms of line would feed off the lay at her feet, the rest from the loggerhead. Silently, the oarsmen changed over to paddles, so as not to alert their prey.

"Think she's heard us yet?" whispered Thomas.

"She's sounding," Toby murmured. "Ease up, lads—I've a notion this lady is toying with us."

They waited. It was as if the world had suddenly ceased to turn. Pru clutched her belly with one hand, the heavy iron shaft with the other. More than once she had heard Toby brag that he could track a whale underwater as well as he could on the surface, but if there was a visible sign, she was blind to it.

Waiting.

If only they would give up and turn back, she thought longingly, she would gladly confess her sins and take her punishment. If only her stupid pride hadn't forced her into this impossible masquerade...

Waiting.

If only she had followed Granna's advice and learned to dress and behave in a womanly fashion, she might have met Gideon when he came to Portsmouth, and somehow made him notice her....

Pru was on her fourth "if only" when the beast broke the water practically under the boat.

"Christ, she's breaching!"

"Here comes James!"

"Work her in close, boys, she's ours!" Toby cried, not bothering to lower her voice, for the thing was practically upon them. He waved an arm at Pru. "Now, lad! Heave!"

It had an eye. Dear God, the creature was looking right at her—staring right at the harpoon in her hand. It even had hair!

"Haskell, blast it, strike!"

"Dammit, boy, do it!"

They were all screaming at her, and the whale was staring at her, and she froze. Before she could break herself out of the paralysis that had suddenly gripped her, Thomas dropped his oar with a clatter and snatched up the iron. Bracing himself against a cleat, he hurled the projectile directly over her head.

The iron embedded itself in the shiny black flesh all the way up to the hitches as Pru stared in disbelief.

And then the whole world exploded. The whale rose out of the water, and with a terrible crash of her flukes, sent a column of water some twenty feet into the sky.

They were nearly swamped. The sea around them was boiling as the animal disappeared, taking the line out so fast smoke rose from the loggerhead. Fifty fathoms—a hundred. She rose to the surface again and rolled, going down once more with a thrash of her flukes that sent spume flying over half an acre of ocean.

"Sweet Jesus, she's a big one!"

"She's a killer! I ain't ever seen anything like—"

"She'll stow down to a hundred barrel, easy!"

"Set to bailing before she breaches again!"

James's boat had come in close enough to get off one shot that had fallen short of the mark. With two boats acting as drag—better yet, three—they would have worn her out within an hour.

But there was only the one boat attached to the enraged sperm whale, and they could only grip the gunnels and pray as the ride commenced.

Pru had never thought past winning the coveted position as striker. Not in her wildest dreams had she imagined what it would be like to be in at the kill of something so massive and magnificent.

Oh, she'd heard tales aplenty, but nothing could equal the stark terror of knowing that they were anchored to a beast so big it could crush their boat as easily as she could step on an anthill—and they were being towed rapidly out to sea.

Dear God, what would happen if the whale should decide to sound again? Would they go down with her before they could cut the line?

James's boat had fallen far behind, and Pru stared back at Gideon's distinctive figure. Would she ever see him again? *Please, God, save us this time, and I'll not bother you again.*

After what seemed an eternity, the mad race began to slow. Not one of the men had spoken—praying, likely, as she was.

"James's boat's coming on fast," Toby said tersely. "If she don't sound before she breaches again, he'll likely be in position to get a line onto 'er."

Her. Pru wished they would refer to the thing as an "it." She didn't want to think of the whale as a female. She didn't want to think of it at all.

It had looked at her. Directly into her eyes, as if to say, why are you doing this? I've never harmed you or your kind.

"The oil," Pru whispered into the wind. "It's the oil, don't you understand? We need your oil, else how would we see? Tallow candles can't light a whole town." She was clutching the gunnel and staring ahead as Toby barked out commands and the oarsmen did their best to add drag with their oars.

And then the thing came up to blow, and James's boat moved in quickly. Pru saw Gideon stand and hurl an iron,

Gideon's Fall

and then there were two lines sprouting from the great beast's head.

Throughout the afternoon, the fight went on, the whale moving steadily seaward with both boats in tow. The shore had long since fallen away by the time she rose to the surface again, and even though it was obvious that the fight was near an end, there was no cheering from either of the two boats that rocked side by side near the stricken cow.

She had fought a valiant fight, but she had lost. Stained with the setting sun, the water looked like blood.

Suddenly, Pru felt deathly sick to her stomach again. With a soft moan, she leaned over the gunnel and emptied her belly in front of the astounded crews of all three boats, for Gouge had come up alongside. Kneeling on the slippery wet bow cap to one side of the loggerhead, she leaned over and dipped up a handful of water, splashing it on her face.

The silence around her was deafening. Pru felt she could have died with shame. A few of the men averted their faces out of sympathy, but the rest stared in disgust—all save two men—Crow and Gideon.

Perhaps that was why both crews were caught off guard when the whale gave one last thrust, her flukes striking Toby's boat a passing blow that splintered the starboard gunnel.

The old steersman was flung forward, striking the side of his head. Three oarsmen were thrown to their knees. Prudence pitched headfirst over the bow.

Down, down, down—there was no light, only the awful pressure on her chest. She struggled to right herself, kicking for the surface as hard as she could. Praying. Cursing.

Dammit, she wasn't ready to die yet!

By the time a pair of strong arms dragged her over the side of the boat, she was beyond struggling. Without a sound, she slithered to the bottom of the boat, limp as a wad of eelgrass.

It was the sound of voices that eventually aroused her. Her eyes still closed, Pru dimly remembered having been lifted back into the boat, pummeled on the back until she spewed up half the ocean and then held tightly against something warm, wet and hard. The homeward journey had been endless; she'd slipped in and out of consciousness, her throat raw and her chest aching.

"Damned fool. I should've known better," someone muttered aeons later. Despite the curses that accompanied the observation, the sound of that particular voice sent a warm current stirring through her chilled body.

"He's a right plucky little bastard, Cap'n. It ain't his fault his belly turned on him."

"I bring rum and more blankets." That was Crow, Pru recognized dimly, his voice sounding oddly strained.

"There's brandy in my chest," Gideon said tersely. "Fetch it."

"Is sh— Is he going to be all right?" Pride asked anxiously.

Pru tried to summon the strength to reassure him, but gave it up. She knew that he was concerned about more than her health, but she was beyond caring. It was enough that she was alive and no longer pitching about in an open whaleboat.

"Dammit, you didn't even have the guts to strike!" Gideon growled down at her as he carried her up from the boat. He sounded furious. His breath felt deliciously warm on her face, but his hands were biting into her flesh like grappling hooks as he strode along the shore holding her tightly in his arms.

"Now, Cap'n." That was Toby. Bless him, Pru thought, he must have been the one to pull her out of the water. "I seen it happen before when one of them big cows surfaces too close. Thing like that kin scare a man plumb out o' his wits. Fer all his spunk, Haskell's naught but a half-growed boy."

"You hold up there, Cap'n." Thomas, Pru thought drowsily. He'd been right behind her. Perhaps he'd been the one to drag her back into the boat. "It weren't the lad's fault he seized up. He ain't the first green striker to—"

"If all you men have to do is follow me up to camp and make excuses for—Haskell, then I'll oblige you to head back out and help tow the blasted cow in!"

"Aye, sir."

"We're onto it, sir."

"Will he be all right?" That was Pride again. He'd have to go out, Pru thought drowsily, for they'd be shorthanded without her and Gideon.

Gideon plodded on until he came to the cluster of huts. The boats had been beached some distance from the camp, as the tide had been running strong. At dusk it had been hard to read the shoreline. Gideon vowed he'd have someone's head for not lighting the signal fire, as he stalked past the place where it had been laid and covered with a tarpaulin, all ready to light whenever a boat had to be out after dark.

The voices fell behind as the men hurried off to the boats. Pru felt herself being jostled as Gideon ducked inside one of the huts, and she opened her eyes near pitch-darkness. He lowered her onto a pallet just as Crow blocked what little light fell through the doorway. "Brandy, Cap'n," he said in his strangely accented voice. "I will stay. This be my hut."

"You will go. I don't give a damn if it's Eden's palace."

Pru closed her eyes for a moment, and when she opened them again, there was a dim glow coming from the oil lantern just inside the door. Crow was gone. Gideon knelt over her.

Wanting nothing more than to close her eyes and sleep the summer through, she struggled to rise onto her elbows. Gideon slipped an arm under her shoulders and held a tankard to her lips.

"Easy now—it's all right. Sip this, and then we'll get you out of those wet clothes."

Summoning up the last shred of strength at her command, Pru pushed his hands away and sat up. Rather than drown in it, she took a large swallow of the drink and then gasped, pushing it away. "N-no thank you, I'll j-just stay as

I am." She had to get him out of there before he uncovered her secret. Quite literally.

"Don't be daft." He shoved the tankard at her again, and glanced about the room for the seabag with her name painted on it with tar.

Needing the courage it lent her as well as the warmth, Pru took another deep draught and felt it burn all the way to the pit of her stomach. "If you d-don't mind, I'll just c-c-cover up and sleep th-th-the way I am," she said when she could get her breath again.

"Dammit, you stubborn little fool, I'm just trying to help you!"

"Yessir, but I'm n-not really c-c-cold. Honest, sir, the b-brandy served quite well."

Rising from a kneeling position, Gideon towered over her. His fists curled at his sides. Pru waited for him to speak, to rail at her for endangering his crew and failing to carry out her duty. She had it coming; she would take it like a man, but she did wish he would wait until morning.

Or better yet, next July.

He crossed over to unsling her seabag from its hook, and the lamplight fell on his face, distorting his features so that he looked strange and threatening. Pru huddled under her blanket, wanting him to go so that she could change her clothes—wanting him to stay at the same time.

Wanting him to hold her, to accept her for what she was—to love her blindly, heedlessly, so that he no longer saw her rough skin, her ruined hair and her unladylike ways.

She swallowed another big gulp of brandy, liking the warmth it produced but not caring at all for the way it set her head to reeling. She might as well have been pitching about still in an open boat.

"Here's a dry shirt and a pair of breeches. Will you do the honors, or shall I play lady's maid?"

Pru felt her eyes cross with the effort of focusing. "Maidy's laid—tha's funny, Gideon." She beamed up at him, and then frowned. She must keep her wits about her, or else—or else... Something or other, at least. There was a very good reason, only she couldn't quite remember it.

"So sleepy, so-o-o slee-epy," she whispered with a sigh. Her throat no longer hurt—in fact, nothing hurt. She felt wonderful, as free as a bird.

"You're drunk."

Her eyes popped open, and she squinted up at him, noticing for the first time that he was as wet as she was. Still, wet was not so bad, not when a body felt all warm and drifty and balmy and sunny, and...

"Pooor Gideon," she murmured.

Gideon tossed her a towel, his face as dark as a thundercloud. "At least dry your hair before you pass out!"

"Passout? Passegarde, passementerie, passepied..." she chanted tunelessly.

His lips widened in a smile that held little humor. "That covers armor, dressmaking and dancing quite nicely. I must say, for a cheeky little cutpurse, your knowledge of things French is admirable. Thanks, no doubt, to my good French brandy."

Feet planted wide apart, he continued to tower over her, his wet shirt plastered to his body so tightly she could see the shadow of his chest hair, and his trousers clinging like a second skin to his knees, his thighs and his—his...

She swallowed hard, feeling the rawness in her throat again. "Th-thanks to Claude Dela-Dara-Deralouche," she said just as her eyes drifted closed once more.

"Another of your victims?"

But she was beyond response. Lashes fanned out across her unnaturally pale cheeks, she had slumped over the small heap of clothing he had tossed down to her and was snoring softly.

"God help me," Gideon whispered. Taking a deep, sustaining breath, he knelt beside her once more and lowered her head onto the pallet. Then he began to unbutton her wet, cold shirt.

Binding. He might have known she'd had to do something to hide those small, ripe breasts of hers. Hardening his resolve to remain unmoved, Gideon proceeded to unwind the length of linen, which meant lifting her and supporting her with one arm while he uncovered her with the other.

It was a tedious process. He was shaking and cursing by the time he had finished. The light from the lantern cast devilishly beguiling shadows, highlighting the hardened nubs of her nipples.

He managed to get her arms into the sleeves of her dry shirt, wincing as he smoothed the harsh, coarse fabric over her soft, satiny skin. No woman, not even one such as Haskell, should have to endure such a thing.

Unable to help himself, Gid allowed his gaze to linger on her rounded shoulders—a woman's shoulders. On her slender arms, which were surprisingly hard for one so small.

On her breasts. Small, but full and sweet, like ripe Spanish oranges, they invited his touch. He ached to cup them in his palms, to cradle their slight weight, to trace the faint blue shadows to their summit.

And her nipples...

Swallowing hard, he forced himself to look away as he hurriedly buttoned her shirt, but his mind could not be so easily distracted. He saw himself kneeling over her, lowering his head to take her into his mouth. She would taste of salt now....

So why did he keep thinking of lilacs?

The ill-fitting men's shirt buttoned up under her chin, Gideon steeled himself to finish the task he'd set out to do. Surely no more devilish chore had ever been devised than tugging wet trousers off a sleeping body.

He unbuttoned and peeled open the front, then, with a hand under her softly rounded behind, he lifted her and struggled to shove the stiff canvas garment down over her hips. His hand itself was in the way, which meant turning and shifting, leaning over her until his nostrils were filled with the heated scent of her womanhood, and he was hard as a throwing iron and cursing with every breath.

God knows, if she'd been wearing boots he would probably have ended up cutting them off with his knife. He was sweating by the time he got her nether regions bared, and he knelt over her, mopping his hair off his brow with one hand as he pondered the best way to set about getting her into her spare pair of breeches. For a man who'd been dressing himself for some twenty-nine years, he was proving remarkably ham-handed.

He dried her off, which he thought would help some, taking care not to stare as he worked. Yet it was impossible not to notice the slender perfection of her long limbs, the small dimple of her navel set in the subtle hammock of her belly. There was a speck over to one side that he mistook for a bit of gravel, for the stuff had a way of getting next to a man's hide and sticking tighter than a seed tick.

This was no speck of gravel, but a tiny mole. Had it been on her face, it would have been called a beauty spot, yet Gideon swore silently that no beauty spot he had ever seen on any woman of his acquaintance had ever affected him quite so much as the one on Haskell's belly.

He refused to look directly at the thatch of dark curls at the joining of her thighs, for to do so would have been the gravest discourtesy to an unconscious woman. Not to mention the fact that it would have undone him altogether. Not bothering with drawers, he hastily tugged the stiff dry trousers up one leg and then another, and then lifted her and pulled them up over her hips.

Swearing under his breath, he managed to button them, his knuckles brushing against her warm, soft flesh until he came close to losing control. Taking time only to pull a blanket up under her chin, he blew out the lamp and backed out the doorway, drenched in his own perspiration and shaking like a halyard in a high wind.

Two drams of brandy later, he stood in the door of his quarters and stared out across the water, searching for some sign of the returning boats. He had recovered enough to wonder why the hell he hadn't just taken her and been done with it. God knows, any woman who led a gang of cutpurses, who lived in a whaling camp, slept in an eight-by-eight-foot hut with three other men, was no saint.

She'd probably been laughing her head off at them the whole time, he told himself as he poured out another dose of brandy. For all they professed to be brothers, Nye could have been her lover all along.

Though they'd hid it well, if that was the case.

No. Gideon trusted his instincts about men, and his instincts told him that there was nothing like that between the pair of them. Brother and sister, more than likely. Which didn't mean that she was any virgin, for he'd lay odds against that.

The little bitch! If he'd even suspected she was a female, he would have paid her no more mind than he did any other passable-looking doxy. Flying her false colors, she'd managed to slip past his guard, and now he was going to have to break up camp with work still to be done just to get rid of her!

Gideon slammed down his tankard, scattering the papers awaiting his attention. He'd do no such thing! She'd made her bed—now she could damn well lie in it until he was good and ready to turn her out!

He just hoped to God she would never know what she had put him through in the moments after he'd seen her go over the side.

Crow had hit the water a split second behind him, but Gid, a powerful swimmer, had pulled ahead, reaching the site where she had gone under and diving while the other man was still some distance away. He'd stayed down until his lungs were fit to burst, and then he'd surfaced, filled his lungs with air and sounded again.

And he'd found her. She'd been floating shoulders high, and he thanked God at that moment for the slight buoyancy of her woman's breasts.

He'd brought her to the surface, with Crow supporting her until he could crawl over the side and take her from him. Nor had he let her go until he felt the boat drag against the shelving bottom of the beach, though it had brought him more than a few peculiar looks from the crew.

It occurred to his fuzzy-edged mind that Crow must have known it was no half-grown boy he'd handed up out of the water. But if he had wondered at the delicate frame, the revealing softness where there should have been only hardness, he had kept his own counsel.

And would continue to do so, Gideon had no doubt. Haskell's secret would be safe for the few days it would take to strip the whale, render her down and barrel her oil. A few more days, he promised himself, and he could send the crafty little baggage back where she came from. With his blessings!

Chapter Nine

May 3, 1729. Weather holds fair. Bully's arm much improved. Spermaceti cow taken yesterday looks to be biggest of season. With bone and oil, she'll likely make up near half a load. Men will draw bonus in addition to shares.
By the hand of Gideon McNair, the south banks.

The shouts of the men could be heard in the distance as they worked the carcass into the shallows and then awaited each wave to haul her in a few more feet. Abruptly pushing aside his journal, Gideon moved to stand in the door. He'd passed another sleepless night. This time, thank God, he had the excuse of tending the signal fires, awaiting the return of the boats that had gone to bring in the cow and thinking about that damnable girl, Haskell, and the sheer hell she'd put him through since he'd had the misfortune to come upon her. He had half a mind to march over to her hut this very minute and turn her over his knee!

One thing kept him from it—the knowledge that if he did, the tables would be neatly turned, leaving him to look the fool.

It was a distinct relief to see Crow cut away from the work crew and head in his direction. Gideon was not the only man who knew Haskell's secret; he was damned near certain that Crow knew, too. He was sorely tempted to charge him with it just to see what he had to say about the matter.

"There be trouble, Cap'n." Crow came to a halt some five feet away. Even with those he trusted, he never came closer than necessary, a holdover, Gideon suspected, from a past that he would neither discuss nor reveal. Nor would Gideon dream of prying.

"Trouble?"

"Some of the men say Thomas made the strike, Thomas take the striker's share." Like the other oarsmen, Thomas had signed on for the hundredth lay, which meant he would have earned a barrel for every hundred processed. A striker earned a bonus above that for each kill until his second or third season, when his lay would increase to one barrel of every eighty. Only the steersmen and the captain earned more.

"And you, Crow, how say you?"

"You be the captain, Gideon."

A humorless smile twisted Gideon's lips. "My neck's on the block, not yours, eh? Then I say Thomas takes the striker's share."

Crow nodded. Gideon knew the man well enough to know he would not have argued in any case, but the nod meant that Gideon's decision met with his approval.

"Haskell would likely not have accepted it in any case," he said, remembering the stiff-necked pride she'd revealed on too many occasions. It was that same damnable pride that had pushed her to work harder than any of the others, that had driven him to try and break her.

Something cold and miserable settled in his gut as he thought of the way her husky laughter would ring out over the camp, enticing the others to join in her merriment even when the lot of them were up to their ears in blubber and offal.

The wench was irrepressible, irresponsible—and to his sorrow, damned near irresistable.

"Is there something more, Crow?" he demanded as the other man continued to stand there.

"We sell to Portsmouth?"

"I thought we'd sell across the sound. Likely a better price."

"Inland ports pay in trade paper, not silver. At Portsmouth, there be more hard money. The men, they like hard money."

This time, Gideon's smile held more than a little amusement. He well knew his men preferred to be paid in silver. What whore wouldn't favor a seaman with pockets ajingle, no matter what his nationality, over a local whaler bearing a bundle of trade paper? "Portsmouth, eh? 'Pears to me you've grown right fond of Portsmouth lately, Crow."

The half-breed met his gaze boldly. "Aye, it be a good enough place."

"I reckon—leastwise, we've cleaned it up so a man can walk the roads without looking over his shoulder."

Crow said nothing. If there was a message to be read in his curiously light brown eyes, Gideon failed to read it.

"At any rate, I plan to sell this load across the sound, so Portsmouth will have to wait."

If Gideon had surprised the half-breed, he had surprised himself even more. He had fully meant to rid himself of his unwelcome guest at the first opportunity. But as his anger had grown, so had his need for revenge. This was a part of him that he neither recognized nor appreciated, yet he was determined to make her squirm like a worm on a hot griddle before he set her free.

The first confrontation between them was not long in coming. On her way from the necessary, Pru had overheard the men discussing the relative merits of selling up the banks in Portsmouth or crossing the sound to sell at Bath or Queen Anne's Towne.

She marched directly to where Gideon was working with several others in planning the repairs on Toby's boat. Seeing her approach, he met her halfway. "There's talk that you might be going to sell in Portsmouth this time," she said bluntly. With her head pounding like a flock of oyster catchers, it was all she could do to be civil, never mind the pleasantries.

Gideon appeared to study her for an inordinate length of time, making her painfully aware of the way she must look. Never noted for his tactfulness, Pride had told her when he woke her that morning that he'd seen better-looking things washed up after a storm.

"Well?" she demanded when she could bear his scrutiny no longer. "Will you be going to Portsmouth or not?"

"Can you think of a good reason to be going there?"

"Gouge says she'll try out at near seventy barrel, and you've half a hold filled from those last two drifters. What with the bone and spermaceti, you'll have a full load, and you're not likely to take another whale this season."

His eyes glinted dangerously. "You're the king's authority on whaling now, I take it?"

"You know what I mean," Pru muttered. "All the men said it's rare that one comes along this late in the season, and we're lucky she was so big, and a sperm, at that. I only thought—that is—"

"Hmm? Speak up, Haskell. I'd be mightily interested to know what you've been thinking all these weeks you've been sharing my bed and board."

Pru's head snapped up at that—snapped up and nearly flew off. Her eyes closed briefly, and then she recovered enough to say, "I'd hardly call myself a *guest* . . . sir! Since the first day you kidnapped me and dragged me off to this stinking, godforsaken sandbar, I've worked as hard as any two men for my keep, and well you know it!"

"What about yesterday? Did you pull your weight then? Five men to a boat, Haskell, and every man jack of 'em knowing his place. Five puny men against that great raging creature out there—" He stabbed a square-tipped forefinger in the direction of the massive carcass that even now was rapidly being peeled down in layers with the sharpened shovels. "Did you work as hard as any two men yesterday, Haskell?" He reached for one of her small hands and turned it palm up in his own. It looked lost there. "I see you're losing your oarsman's calluses. You didn't have to row all the way out to the grounds, now, did you? Nor did you have to read the waters and man a twenty-foot steering sweep. *Did you?*" His face lowered to hers, he raked her with the cold blue fire of his eyes. "No. All you had to do was make a single strike."

Against her will, Pru was mesmerized by the startling contrast of brilliant eyes against bronzed skin. By the strawberry-colored blossom on his right cheek. By the surprising darkness of his whiskers, which, normally shaved close, had been allowed to sprout these past few days.

At his last softly spoken charge, she stiffened like a bowstring. "Damn you, you know I didn't! You were there! You saw me freeze up, and you saw me lose my breakfast and go over the side—and you saw Thomas drag me back in again, so stop it! Just leave me alone!"

Spinning away, she churned furiously off through the soft sand, her eyes stinging with tears. The great bleeding bully! He knew damned well what had happened—knew better than she did, in fact. He'd seen it all, and she'd seen nothing after the water had closed over her head.

"Haskell."

She barely hesitated before continuing on her way, face contorted with anger.

"Haskell!"

This time she couldn't ignore it. Whirling about, she confronted him, drenched eyes shimmering under the morning sun, quivering chin thrust forward, small fists knotted at her sides. "What do you want? You want me to apologize? You want me to say I'm sorry I froze up and Thomas had to do my duty for me and then risk his life by going over after me? Then you have it, damn your filthy black heart!"

She spun away, and Gideon stared after her retreating back. He had wanted her apology, all right—but for something altogether different. Now that he'd wrung this much from her, he wasn't even sure *what* he wanted. All he knew was that he wasn't satisfied with what he'd got. Not by a long shot.

Pru avoided Gideon like the plague, and he seemed equally intent on avoiding her. She worked right alongside the others, taking on the worst tasks as if to make up for letting them down on the hunt. Under the heat of a blistering spring sun, the carcass ripened quickly, and they worked around the clock, shedding their filthy oilskins and falling onto their pallets for a few hours' sleep when they could no longer do without.

Sun baked down on them with late spring's fury, turning the protective oilskins to an oven. Most of the men gradually shed their shirts, some their trousers. All of them took to wading out into the surf every few hours to wet themselves down for comfort.

All save Pru. She worked on as the sun burned down from a cloudless sky, bleaching the top layer of her hair, deepening her golden tan and painting a becoming blush on her cheeks and the tip of her nose. She sweated profusely as her callused hands grew slick and softened from the rich blubber, causing her shovel to slip and nearly chop off her toes more than once.

"Ease up, lad, ye don't have it all to do yerself," one of the older men cautioned, but she continued to drive herself mercilessly, wanting only to be done so that she could leave this place and forget she'd ever known a man named Gideon McNair.

To think of all the foolish dreams she had harbored, even briefly. If she could only live through these next few days, it would be over. And then she could set about putting the entire experience out of her mind.

It was five days before the last barrel was loaded aboard the *Polly*. Pru, who had not spared herself, groaned and dropped down onto the shore beside one of the carts. Never again would she take for granted the oil lamps that made reading and sewing after dark possible. Never again would

FIND OUT <u>INSTANTLY</u> IF YOU GET
UP TO 6 FREE GIFTS IN THE
Lucky Carnival Wheel

▼ SCRATCH-OFF GAME! ▼

Scratch off ALL 4 gold areas

YES! I have scratched off the 4 Gold Areas above. Please send me all the gifts for which I qualify. I understand I am under no obligation to purchase any books, as explained on the opposite page.

247 CIH ACFV
(U-H-H-03/91)

NAME

ADDRESS   APT.

CITY   STATE   ZIP

◄ DETACH AND MAIL CARD TODAY! ▼

HARLEQUIN "NO RISK" GUARANTEE
- You're not required to buy a single book—ever!
- You must be completely satisfied or you may return a shipment of books at our expense or mark "cancel" on your statement and return it to us. Either way, you will receive no more books; you'll have no further obligation to buy anything.
- The free books and gifts you receive from this offer remain yours to keep no matter what you decide.

If offer card is missing, write to: Harlequin Reader Service, 3010 Walden Ave., P.O. Box 1867, Buffalo, NY 14269-1867

BUSINESS REPLY MAIL
FIRST CLASS MAIL   PERMIT NO. 717   BUFFALO, NY

POSTAGE WILL BE PAID BY ADDRESSEE

HARLEQUIN READER SERVICE
3010 WALDEN AVE
PO BOX 1867
BUFFALO NY 14240-9952

NO POSTAGE
NECESSARY
IF MAILED
IN THE
UNITED STATES

DETACH AND MAIL CARD TODAY!

she turn up her nose at one of the rank-smelling, rough-looking whalers who came ashore from time to time to spend their hard-earned shares.

"Weary, lad?"

She glanced up at Lear, seeing his grotesquely scarred face pulled into a semblance of a grin. "Bone tired is all. Nothing a week's sleep won't cure."

"Cap'n says ye'll be going out wi' the *Polly* come morning. Best have a wash and put on yer best bib'n tucker. There's a place called the One-Eyed Cat where ye can rest up in fine style."

"In Portsmouth?" Pru knew both ordinaries on her own island, and there wasn't a one-eyed cat among them.

"Cap'n be selling at Bath this time."

Pru muttered an obscenity that had not passed her lips in months, despite the provocations. He would take her to Portsmouth if she had to hold a knife on him! Enough was enough!

Lear was still roaring with laughter when Gideon spoke from behind them. "Glad to see you're still able to laugh," he said, sounding not at all glad to Pru's ears. A scowl on her face, she looked up at the man—and up, and up, and up.

He wasn't even looking at her.

"Haskell here sounds about ready to tackle shore leave, sir. Me, I'll be stowing my gear and heading north soon's you get back."

Gideon nodded absently, his mind on other things. "Fair enough, Lear. Reckon that lady friend of yours up Hatteras way will be about ready to make you welcome."

To Pru's astonishment, the scarred face flushed a deep shade of red. "Reckon she's done found some'un else by now, sir. How th' hell did you hear about Bess, if'n ye don't mind me askin'?"

Before Gideon could reply, Gouge charged down on the three of them. "Damn your wicked gizzard, you ugly bastard, you been feedin' Lucy hard crabs again, ain't ye? I told ye they gives 'im gas! Now he's a-bleatin-and a-carryin' on somethin' awful!"

Lear burst out laughing, Gideon was grinning from ear to ear, and even Pru couldn't hold back a smile. Poor Gouge doted on that scrawny pig of his to the point where he lost sight of all common sense.

"Gouge, I saw him just this morning when we carted out that first load. He was hock deep in the sound with his muzzle under," Pru said gently. "I think you're just going to have to fence off the whole sound if you want to keep him from stuffing himself with crabs. He fair dotes on them."

Gouge stalked off, with Lear three steps behind him, leaving Pru alone with Gideon. She was still sitting on the hard sand, her bare toes burrowing tunnels as she clasped her arms around her knees and stared out toward where she supposed Bath might lie.

Neither of them spoke for a while, and then Gideon said, "Lear told you we'd be leaving for Bath Towne come morning?"

"He did, sir."

"He tell you you'd be going along?"

"Yes...sir." She refused to look up at him. If he wanted her full attention, he would have to come down to her level, for she was not of a mind to look up to any man.

"Haskell! Are you being impertinent?"

Pru drew in a deep, shoulder-lifting breath and expelled it before she spoke. "Yes, sir. I reckon I am."

"Sweet Jesus," she thought she heard him mutter under his breath. And then, "What am I going to do with you?"

Unable to help herself, she looked up, hope filling her wide-set eyes. "Take me home, sir? You promised. The season's over, Lear's leaving. Portsmouth is practically on your way to Bath." Leastwise, she hoped it was.

"We'll see, Haskell. We'll see." She thought she heard him sigh, and then he was gone, leaving her to stare out across the sound to where she pictured her home might lie, and wonder why he'd been so moody of late.

So he refused to take her home, did he? On the deck of the *Polly,* bound across the sound, Pru seethed. She had tried appealing to Pride to make him see reason, but her brother had fallen under Gideon's spell. ''He'll see you safely home as soon as he can manage it, Prudie. He's a fair man. I'm going to see if he'll take me on permanent, for I'd a sight rather work for him than clerk in a warehouse or ship out with a man I don't know from Adam.''

Well, by damn, she wasn't licked yet! She would use his mule-headedness to her own ends. If Gideon was bound on hauling her off to Bath Towne against her will, she would use the opportunity to buy herself the finest gown her meager shares could pay for.

Something in lilac silk, perhaps, or if that was too dear, then at least a nice bright cotton with a fresh lawn fichu, and perhaps a pair of buckled shoes.

Her shoulders drooped. How could she? She'd need all she had for Granna. There would be no more Haskell and Nye to keep the sewing basket filled once she got home again.

On the other hand, if she were to double her money at the gaming tables, perhaps she could afford a single gown for herself and still have enough to take care of Granna until Pride could find a way to earn their living.

Gideon stood in the door of the smoke-filled ordinary, his expression one of distaste. It was noisier than he had remembered. How could a man, used to breathing clean salt air, endure this?

He would have a drink—two, perhaps—and stand his men to another before he took his leave. Then he would pay a visit to Letty, for he had to do something to rid himself of the perpetual randiness that had plagued him since the first time he saw Haskell bathing in the pond.

She'd gone ahead with the others, somewhat to Gideon's surprise. Truth to tell, he'd been expecting her to cry off. He'd been sure she'd find some excuse not to accompany her mates on an evening of gaming, drinking and wenching.

That deepened his conviction that she was no innocent, for all he'd not caught her in the act. If he'd been inclined to give her the benefit of doubt before, seeing her prance off toward town with Ben on one side and Thomas on the other was all he needed to convince him she'd been playing him for the fool all along.

Holding his anger just below the boiling point, Gideon had dressed hurriedly in his best pair of biscuit-colored breeches and a white linen shirt. He'd tied back his hair, still damp from his bath, with a narrow black ribbon. Disdaining a waistcoat, he'd shrugged into a dark buff kneecoat.

The clothes smelled faintly of camphor wood from having hung too long without an airing. He seldom bothered to get himself up in such finery, for he was a plain man with no pretensions of being anything more. Yet for some reason, tonight he wanted to look his best. For Letty, he told himself, knowing all the while that Letty would have taken him in if he'd come to her wearing canvas breeches and a tarred jersey shirt.

At the tavern it took Gideon but a moment to find Haskell. She was seated at a table with Ben and three strangers— a rough sort, Gideon summed up in a single glance, who would as soon slip a kris through a man's ribs as bid him the morning.

From the stack of paper before her, he deduced she was winning, which made it even more imperative that he ease her away before she brought the house down on her head. While the men claimed the little beggar never cheated— didn't have to, for her eye was uncanny sharp—Gideon wasn't so sure. She might have stayed her hand in camp, but that was no reason to believe she would spare the three gentlemen who were eyeing her narrowly across the scarred table.

He wished to hell he'd brought her brother along. Nye would have quickly put an end to this foolishness. Indeed, he'd never have allowed her to set foot in the place. But Nye was back in camp, learning the carpenter's trade by helping Tobias rebuild his splintered gunnel. And here in the tavern Ben was already three sheets to the wind, egging Haskell on while he stayed out of the game.

Gideon caught the eye of one of his men and nodded to the table where Haskell was coolly raking in another stack of silver and scrip. James stood and hitched up his breeches, then sauntered over to stand behind her. Bully and Thomas followed, and Gideon joined them there.

They fanned out behind the three strangers, arms crossed over their chests. Gideon watched Haskell closely, but for the life of him, he could detect nothing amiss. "If you gentlemen don't mind, I'd like to borrow your young friend here," he said politely.

"Bugger off, mate," snarled the one with the notched ear.

"I'm afraid I really must insist. However, as it might break up your game, I'm sure the lad will agree to dividing the take for the sake of fairness." Which should still leave Haskell considerably richer than she'd been before the evening began.

"Now hold on there, mister," cried the one with the beard. He was an ugly customer, one no seasoned man would have gambled with.

"No, you hold on." The three whalers began to close in while Gideon held the man's gaze. Clear blue eyes met glittering black ones, and the black ones fell.

"All right, divvy up then. The pukin' little bastard don't deserve nothin'. He was cheatin', and we was about to call 'im on it."

Gideon's voice was pure Arctic. "Haskell doesn't need to cheat. The lad works for the owners, uncovering weasels like you. If you value your skin, you'll be on the next ship out of here."

In the barrage of profanity that followed, Gideon grasped a handful of shirt at the back of Haskell's neck and guided her none too gently across the room to a table near the door. On the way, he signaled the barmaid to provide his friends with a round of drinks.

"All right, d'you want to tell me what you thought you were doing?" he demanded quietly after planting her firmly enough into a chair to jar her teeth.

"If you hadn't interfered, damn you, I was about to turn a few measly shillings into a small fortune! What right have you to—"

"I'll tell you what right, you little demon! You were about to get your throat slit, and I've no wish to be held accountable to your brother!"

The barmaid interrupted to place two tankards of rum on the table, and Pru, so furious she could have cheerfully crowned him with hers, downed it in one go, instead.

Gasping for breath, she leaned back and fanned her face.

"So now you're going to prove what a hearty tippler you are, eh? Go ahead. It should prove one hell of a lot easier to keep your scrawny little neck from being broke once you're snoring away under the table."

Pru was too busy trying to catch her breath to speak. Her father had taught her the proper way for a lady to drink, and but for a few notable exceptions, she had followed his simple rule—enough water to keep the spirits from numbing your brain, and enough spirits to keep the water from rotting your gut.

"The Cat don't water their drinks these days," Gideon said, as if he'd read her mind. "Rum's easier to come by than good water. Care for another?"

Her head came up proudly, and he summoned the barmaid with a knock on the table. One knock—not two. His own tankard was untouched.

"Well, 'ello, lovie," purred a buxom redhead in the yellowest satin gown Pru had ever seen. "You two gents look like you need comp'ny." Without waiting to be invited, she drew out a chair and sat down, so close to Gideon she was practically on his lap.

Pru snorted, furious with Gideon for pushing her into making a fool of herself. Like everyone else, Pru had been drinking watered spirits practically all her life. Only three times in her life had she imbibed enough to feel the effects.

And Gideon, damn his wicked soul, had been witness to all three of them!

Glaring at the friendly woman in yellow satin, Pru decided she didn't like her. For one thing, her hair was too red. For another, her gown was too tight. Not to mention the fact that it was cut so low that she looked like three gallons of cream in a two-gallon bowl.

The barmaid brought another rum, and Pru shoved it toward the redhead. Gideon promptly slid his own untouched drink across to her.

"I've had shufficient," she said coolly.

In the dim lighting, his eyes appeared to gleam like wet sapphires. Not that she'd ever seen real sapphires, wet or dry, but she'd envisioned all manner of gems when she and Pride first began relieving visiting pirates of their stolen goods.

"There be a lovely frolic over to Suky's place tonight, handsome," the overblown redhead crooned as she stroked Gideon's freshly shaven cheek. "How'd ye like to dance wi' Drucilla, hmm? I know steps that'll make a man lay right down and whimper like a pup."

Gideon snatched up the tankard and downed half the contents, and Drucilla slid off her chair and onto his lap, shoving her most prominent attributes up under his chin.

Pru snorted again. If only she could be certain her knees wouldn't buckle under her, she would get up and march right out the door and leave him to his fancy piece! Likely the painted sow would drug him, pick his pocket clean and then sell him to a crimp, and he'd end up being murdered in a brawl in some wicked heathen port!

Without thinking, she snatched up the remains of Gideon's drink and finished it off in one long swallow. It would serve them both right!

"I've never been much of a hand at dancing," Gideon mumbled. He was sweating. Pru, who had stared at him goggle-eyed when she saw him come in wearing his finery, was tempted to stand up and help him out of his coat.

With something of the kind in mind, she stood, and then sat down again when the room tilted and dipped about her head. "Whoosh!" she panted, trying to focus her eyes on something that wasn't inclined to move.

"You've had enough to drink," Gideon told her. His frown would have been far more effective had he not had to peer across the pale pink shelf of Drucilla's bosom.

Pru giggled, and the older woman looked at her closely for the first time. "Oooo-weee, ain't he a pretty lad! What's yer name, lovie?"

"His name is Haskell!" Gideon snapped, squirming under his considerable burden.

"You let Drucilla look after you, sweetings. I'll see ye has a ripe old time."

She wrapped a plump white arm around Gideon's neck and smiled at Pru. Pru willed her to come down with a sudden case of the cramping flux. "Is your hair really that red?"

Penciled eyebrows tented comically. "Don't it look red?" the woman asked, and Pru nodded half a dozen times. It most emphatically did. "Then it's red."

One couldn't argue with the truth. Pru had a vague sense of having somehow failed to make her point, but she couldn't think of anything more to say on the matter. Besides, it was becoming increasingly difficult to keep her tongue from tangling.

"If you'll excuse me, uh—Miss Drucilla," Gideon said firmly, "I'd best see my young friend here back aboard ship. 'Pears to me he's sinking fast."

Gideon stiffened. The doxy's hand had slithered down his chest to his lap, and was now squeezed between his belly and her own generous hips, setting a direct course for parts better left unexplored.

He eased the woman's hand aside and scowled at Haskell, who was beaming indiscriminately around the room. Things were definitely not going the way he had planned when he brought her across the sound with him. He'd looked forward to watching her try to wriggle out of going out with her mates, and he'd meant to push her just a bit.

Just a bit, the devil! He'd meant to drive her as far as he dared, just to watch her squirm! He'd fully intended to follow her right up to the door of Suky's place, if need be, and then rag her unmercifully when she made up some excuse not to go inside.

"Let's get out of here," he said gruffly, nearly dumping the doxy on her plump behind.

"Well, I never!" the outraged woman screeched.

Gideon tossed down a few shillings and grabbed Pru's arm at the elbow, levering her up off her chair. "Come along now. I'd hate to have to knock you out and carry you over my shoulder, but if that's the way you want it..."

Pushed as far as she cared to be pushed in one evening, Pru dug in her heels. "I b'lieve I'll have a round wi' Bossom and Tolly—umm, Thossom and Bolly..."

"You're sozzled!"

Swaying on her feet, Pru strained for a draft of the fresh air flowing through the doorway. "I am no' soz-sozzled."

Ben called across the noisy room, having seen them head for the door. "Ho, Haskell! Ain't leaving, are ye? We'd counted on taking ye to Suky's place with us!"

Pru's eyes flew directly to Gideon's and locked there. She blinked, willing him to stop bobbing around like a cork on a rough sea. Then she blinked again. "If you'll 'scuse me, Gileon, I'll shee you back on the ship, hmm?"

He bared his teeth in what was definitely not a smile. "Oh? Going whoring, are you? P'rhaps I'll just come along."

As groggy as she was, Pru knew that she had an errand to perform before she boarded the *Polly* again. Something she needed to buy—something special that would make Gideon's eyes light up when he saw it.

A gown. She brightened instantly. "D'you like lellow—yellow, Gileon? Lellow gowns?"

He scowled at her. They were still near the doorway, with people coming and going around them. "Yellow gowns? Aye—I reckon they're as good as any." He sent her a suspicious look, and Pru smirked. Yellow, then—and satin.

And cut low over the bosom, because Gideon had stared at Drucilla's bosom as if he couldn't believe his eyes.

"Then 'f you'll suscuse me..." she mumbled, intent on getting herself to the cloth merchant before he could talk her out of it. Surely the fresh air would unfuddle her brain before she got too far.

Gideon took her arm again and led her forcefully outside, and she breathed in deeply the mingled aromas of sewage, dead fish, stale spirits and warehouses filled with cured hides, tar, brined beef and pickled pork.

It was not a particularly welcome experience, coming as it did when her belly was inclined to reject that last draught of rum.

In the dim night light intended to discourage pilferage from the warehouses, Gideon studied her face. She looked unhappy, and faintly greenish. "I'd best get you back before you make a worse fool of yourself," he grumbled.

"You don't need t' concern yourself, shir—sir. I've shome shopping—some sopping—that is—"

Planting a large hand in the small of her back, he shoved. "Get moving! I've about had my fill of you!"

Pru stumbled ahead, and he caught her and clamped her arm under his. "Owww!" she burst out. "My gown!"

A cold smile crossed Gideon's stern features as he marched his young charge toward the place where the *Polly* was moored. He had her now. She was all but groveling, her masquerade ended. "And what might you be wanting a gown for—lad?"

Even in her condition, Pru could recognize a sneer when she heard one. Lad, he'd called her. And lad she must remain, at least until she could present herself in a far more favorable light. "It was a gift. For my—my lady frien'." At least the fresh air had served to untangle her tongue. Now if it could untangle her wits, as well...

"Oh? And this friend of yours—what might her name be, hmm?"

The reply came tripping off the tip of her tongue. "Her name? Pru. Tha's short for Prunence."

"Well now, it looks as if Miss Prune will have to wait a bit for her gown. And what were you going to use for money? Are you so flush you can afford to buy your lady friend an expensive gift and take care of your own needs at the same time?"

They came to the *Polly,* gleaming like silver in the moonlight, and Gideon grasped Pru's elbows and swung her over the low railing and onto the deck.

Fortunately, the deck was remarkably clear of hazards, unlike those of the bulky barks, brigs and brigantines she had explored as a child. Turning away, she headed for the fo'c'sle, already dreading the stifling heat held over from the day's sun.

Gideon caught her before she could take more than three steps. "Hold there, young lady."

At first she didn't catch it. Breathing in deeply, she willed her stomach not to rebel. "If it's all the same to you, sir—"

"And if it's all the same to you—Prudence Haskell, or whatever your name is—you'll join me in my quarters. We've a few matters to settle between us before I send you back where I found you."

Chapter Ten

The minute Gideon ushered the girl into his cabin, he knew he had made a mistake of major proportions. His quarters aboard the sloop were surprisingly commodious, but there was only so much space available aboard a seventy-five-foot, shallow-draft vessel designed primarily for cargo.

She hovered near the companionway for a moment, then moved across to one of the four open portholes, as if in desperate need of air.

Gideon's coat was suddenly too tight across his shoulders, and his modest neckcloth had gained a stranglehold on his throat. He wrenched it awry. "You may sit." It was more grudging command than gracious invitation.

She continued to stand at the porthole, seemingly fascinated by the few lights visible along Water Street. Despite the heat, she was wearing the short canvas coat she'd been issued, and he couldn't help but notice the way it billowed about her slender hips, making her legs look impossibly long, for all she came no higher than his shoulder. "Haskell—Prudence—what the devil is your true name?"

"Prudence."

His brows shot skyward. Prudence? If ever he'd met a misnamed wench, it was this one, for a less prudent female he had yet to come across! Never shifting his gaze from the slender back she'd presented him with, he moved into the cabin, taking the precaution of locking the door behind him.

The tumbler was noisy, having seldom before been called into action. She whirled about and stared at him. "Why did you do that?"

"Lock the door? Shall we say I did it to protect your good name—Miss Prudence? Surely you wouldn't care to have one of your mates burst in here and discover you alone in a cabin with a man not your husband. Now, that would never do, would it?"

Mistrusting both his words and his tone, Pru was beginning to feel more than a bit uneasy. She'd gone along with him at first, knowing there was little else she could do. He'd caught her out fair and square, the only wonder being that it had not happened sooner.

"Nothing to say for yourself?" he taunted.

As Gideon moved closer, Pru began to edge away. Her fingers trailed over a rimmed cherry-wood desk, and she latched onto the ledger she found there. It had a hard enough spine—in a pinch, it could be used as a weapon.

"Don't even think it," he purred, and her eyes widened. This was definitely not going the way she'd envisioned. She'd pictured accusations on his part, admissions on hers—perhaps even an apology—and then instant dismissal. Which was precisely what she wanted, was it not?

She dropped the ledger. Gideon was a fair man, after all; leastwise, he was not apt to punish her physically. Certainly not now that he knew she was a woman. "All right, you have me," she said, and then wondered at the sudden flaring of his nostrils.

"Yes, I do...don't I?"

By this time she found herself backed up against what she thought must be a clothespress, cleverly fashioned to form one side of his desk, the foot of his bed extending from the other side. "Well, I'm sorry. Is that what you want me to say? It was all a mistake from the beginning, but you can't say I didn't hold up my end of the bargain."

Now that the effects of her immoderation were wearing off, she was beginning to grow angry. "There's no need for all this—this—'' She gestured impatiently toward the locked door.

Without moving, he somehow gave the effect of looming over her. Damn him, it wasn't fair! He had no right to intimidate her this way. "Well, say something!" she exclaimed finally.

"What would you have me say?"

Pru mopped her forehead with her sleeve. It was insufferably warm in here. "At least open the door!"

"I find it quite tolerable. If you're overheated, why not remove that heavy coat?"

She clutched the edges of her coat together and glared at him. He knew good and well why she didn't care to remove her coat! Her blasted binding was all but worn out, that was why! One deep breath and she would spring a dozen leaks, and that would be the end of everything!

But then, it was already the end of everything. How strange to think that there was no more reason to pretend— no more reason to bind herself until she could scarce breathe, no more reason to answer to a name other than her own, no more reason to go on with this damnable masquerade.

"How did you know?" she whispered, dropping onto the foot of the wide bunk.

Gideon moved to stand before her, propping one foot on the mahogany bed rail, and she kept her face studiously averted. He was too large, too near and entirely too masculine. "I saw you at the pond," he said after a considerable length of time had passed.

At that, her gaze flew up and locked with his. "You *what?*"

He shrugged. "I saw you. Same as you saw me."

"B-but you didn't know—that is, you thought I was a— that is, you were telling me how to—"

Gideon smiled. He was actually beginning to enjoy this. "Telling you how to make love to a woman? Aye, that must have given you a laugh. Tell me, how'd I do?"

She was blushing, which rather surprised him. He would have thought that such a creature had long since lost the ability to be embarrassed. "As a woman, surely you have an opinion," he pressed. "After all, you heard me—you sure as hell saw me. How would you rank me as a potential lover? Were you pleased with what you saw and heard, or do you need a reminder?"

She'd been asking for this, he told himself, and he'd damned well give it to her. Once he put the fear of God into her, she might think twice before she tried her tricks on another honest man.

"Well? Speak up, woman. You've enough to say on all other counts, surely you can think of something flattering to say that might weigh in your favor."

"What do you mean, in my favor? Surely you don't mean to—to punish me just because I—just because you—"

At the sound of her hesitant voice, the uncertainty that shone in her large, clear eyes, Gideon allowed himself a moment of quiet satisfaction. He finally had the upper hand. There'd been a brief spell when the little baggage had almost slipped under his guard, touching him in a way that he permitted no one to touch him.

Damn her conniving little soul, she deserved to be punished! And he deserved revenge for all she'd put him through—making him look the fool before his men!

She'd made her bed. Now let her lie in it. He would lead her to the brink of seduction, hear her beg for mercy, and then he would send her home with her tail between her legs like a whipped bitch.

"You mean to punish me, don't you?" Her shoulders drooped. Her mouth drooped. It was her mouth he stared at, until he caught himself up and tore his gaze away.

"Surely it won't be punishment," he said softly. Deliberately he leaned closer, until he caught the faintest drift of lilacs from her hair. Lilacs...*lilacs?* Who the devil ever heard of a whaler reeking of lilacs?

The woman was a seductress of the worst sort, wearing trousers that exposed her limbs from twat to toe before the whole camp. Reaching out, he grabbed her wrist and dragged her to her feet, relishing the fear that widened her eyes. Outrage and some unfamiliar emotion twisted his gut. "You knew, didn't you? Damn your wicked little soul, you *knew* I was there in the woods that day you stood and rinsed your hair, deliberately allowing me to look my fill!"

Pru trembled before him. This was a side of Gideon McNair she had never before seen. Stay calm, she told herself. You can reason with him if you keep your wits about you. "Now, Gideon, whatever you think it is that I've done, I'm truly sorry, but you'll have to admit that you've been as much to blame as I have. After all, I didn't ask to be kidnapped and taken—"

The quick widening and then narrowing of his eyes made her rethink her tactics. She could always resort to force if it became necessary. Her father had taught her a very effective way of discouraging a would-be attacker, just as he'd taught Pride to avoid the same sort of attack.

Despite herself, her gaze fell to that vulnerable place in question, and she was shocked to see that it was distorted beyond all reason. A thrill of something akin to fear raced through her body, making her eyes, had she but known it, darken perceptibly. She lifted her gaze to find him staring fixedly at her mouth, and she blurted out the first thing that came to mind. "You're going to kiss me, aren't you?"

After the briefest hesitation, he said, "Kiss you? Now what the devil makes you think I'd want to kiss you?"

Pru's head was in a whirl. A moment before, she could have sworn they were both furious. Now she was not so certain. "You had that same look that Albert used to get before he— Oh, blast."

The setting was all wrong. Besides, she hadn't had time to prepare herself. She had pictured herself soaked and bleached and softened, wearing a beautiful silk gown with a lace-draped neckline that would make her small bosom seem larger than it actually was. Her hair would be all soft and sweet-smelling, too, coiled on her head in a graceful, ladylike style, and perhaps she would have a lace fan to flirt with....

Instead, she was dressed like a whaler, and she looked like a whaler, and what was infinitely worse, she smelled like a whaler, for all the scouring she had done with French soap. Her skin was as brown as a berry from sun, wind and salt, and her hair was worn in the exact same style as Gideon's.

Damn and blast! How could she hope to make him love her? He wasn't supposed to discover her until she was ready for him!

"Why should you think I might want to kiss you, Haskell. I confess to being curious," Gideon prompted.

"Could you forget I asked that?" Her shoulders slumped again in defeat.

Ignoring her request, he went on as if she hadn't spoken. "Bless me if I can fathom why any man might want to kiss a sunburnt cutpurse in whaler's togs."

Something in his manner gave Pru the impression that he was not quite so angry as he'd been a moment before, which emboldened her to try to laugh it off. "Oh, well, I don't reckon any man would."

"Haskell?"

"Hmm?" Distracted, she wondered how she could salvage her pride before she lost that and more.

"What if a man did?" When her head came up, he went on to say, "Want to kiss you, that is."

She swallowed hard. "Oh, I—well, how would I know? That would depend on the man, wouldn't it?"

"Would it?"

He was toying with her now. She knew it, only she didn't know quite what to do about it. "What I mean is that it would depend on who he was, and whether or not I wanted him to kiss me."

"And if you didn't, and he kissed you anyhow?"

Her disdain at odds with her shabby appearance, Pru said, "I do have ways of defending myself, you know. My father taught me a thing or two before he died."

Amusement tugged at the corners of Gideon's stern lips. "Ah, you'd have been all of, what...five then? He died some ten years ago, I believe you told me."

"That would have made me eight," she said quietly. And then, thinking of the defensive maneuver she had resorted to on more than one occasion, she made the mistake of glancing at Gideon's crotch again.

Gideon's eyes widened as he divined her intent. "Oh, no. O-oooh, no! You wouldn't!" With a single whiplike movement, he caught her wrists in one of his hands, at the same time angling his body to avoid any possible danger.

"I don't know what you're—Gideon, you great ox, you're hurting me!"

His grip eased immediately, but he didn't release her. "By damn, it's about time someone taught you how to behave like a woman, you little heathen!" Before she could protest further, he dragged her against him and lowered his head, eyes blazing as his hard lips assaulted hers.

There was nothing at all playful about him now. It was as if the tension that had flashed back and forth between them like summer lightning had finally exploded. Catching a fistful of hair at the back of her head, he held her captive while he forced her lips open and thrust inside her, again and again.

Waves of dizziness swept over her. She couldn't breathe. She couldn't think. He was trying to suffocate her! The instant he moved his lips to her cheek, she twisted her head aside, gasping for breath. "No! Gideon, I—I've changed my mind! I don't like kissing, it hurts!"

His teeth sank into the tiny lobe of her ear, and she balled up a fist and struck him on the shoulder. For all the attention he paid, she might as well have saved her strength. "The sooner you learn your proper place, the sooner—"

"My proper place!" Pru gasped. He was nibbling his way down the side of her throat, and something—the rum she had consumed earlier, no doubt—was making her knees knock and her belly quiver. And the most troublesome thing of all was that it was not altogether unpleasant!

"Mmm-hmm," Gideon murmured. While he'd been dampening the skin of her neck and tracing the shape of her ear with his tongue, his hands had been busy removing her coat. Next, he went to work on the buttons of her shirt, and when the thing came off, sliding down to catch on her arms, he stared quizzically at the ragged linen bandaging her chest. "Let me see now," he murmured while she was still frantically trying to push his hands away.

She was strong, but he was infinitely stronger. "If I remember correctly," he ventured, "you tie this thing up under your left arm and tuck the knot under a fold of cloth, hmm?"

Her eyes widened, and she stopped fighting him. "How did you know?"

"Who'd you think undressed you the night you took a header off the bow of Toby's boat?"

Pru stared at him, unaware that his nimble fingers had already found her flat knot and twisted it open. "Pride? I mean, Nye?"

"Pride, is it? And what pride would that be?"

"My brother. His name's Pride, not Nye."

"More lies," Gideon said as he deliberately unwound the length of linen.

"No—that is, it was a game. But I don't suppose it matters now."

Leaving a single turn of cloth to preserve her dubious modesty, Gideon mocked himself for bothering. By all rights, he should have forced her to strip for him. She owed him something for the torment she'd put him through. "It was I who undressed you, woman. Knowing full well what I'd find, how could I allow anyone else to do it?" He refused to acknowledge her look of embarrassment. False modesty. It was a lie. Everything about her was a lie!

"Thomas—he must have guessed. When he dragged me back into the boat, he must have—"

"Thomas, the devil! 'Twas I who went down after you, with Crow one stroke behind me! 'Twas the two of us who got you into the boat, and 'twas I who held you in my arms until we reached shore! I alone put you to bed and stripped off your wet clothing, and then did my damnedest to ignore what I saw there!''

"Are you sure? I don't remember anything but being so awfully sick and leaning over the side." She clutched the single turn of her worn linen to her breast, and Gideon forced himself not to stare.

Unfortunately, both his patience and his better judgment were sorely eroded by this time. The hunger that had ridden him so relentlessly since he came upon her at the pond had taken its toll. "I don't doubt that you'd like to forget the whole affair. Failure is never pleasant to recall."

He refused to blame the brandy he'd insisted on giving her. That had been later—and besides, she'd needed a restorative. "Come now, enough talk! Let's see if you still have that heart-shaped mole on your belly, or if my eyes were only playing tricks with me."

She stiffened. "Gideon, you wouldn't! There's no call to take this any further. You've have your sport. Damn you, leave my trousers alone!"

But his hand was already on one of the two buttons that held the codpiece over her placket. "But y'see, that's where you're dead wrong, Haskell, my darling. I've not had my sport. Quit sulking now. You're not hiding anything I've not seen before, I assure you. Scrawnier than most, but female, all the same. Don't forget, you've already cost me my night's pleasure. Drucilla was a fetching piece, and she was more than willing."

With a surprising show of strength, Prudence drew herself up into a protective ball, wrenching her wrist from Gideon's grasp, which had loosened as he'd begun to unbutton her trousers. "Damn your bloody black soul, you lay one hand on me and I'll slit your miserable throat!"

"Using what, the sharp edge of your tongue? A formidable weapon, my little love," Gideon taunted, "but I may as well tell you, I don't kill easy. Better men than you have tried and failed. Now, come here and let me put into practice what I preached the first day we shared a bath."

"I'll see you drawn and quartered first,' she vowed. But her words lacked conviction. The memory of those scars she'd seen on his beautiful body was too fresh in her mind; the thought of him lying mortally wounded rendered her shockingly weak.

"Come now, darlin'—" He edged closer, and she stepped back.

"Don't call me that!" she hissed. "I'm not your darling, and we both know it!"

"No? Then what is it you claim to be?" He came one step closer.

"I never claimed to be one blessed thing!" The backs of her knees struck the edge of the bunk.

"You claimed to be a man," he countered, cutting her off when she began to sidle away toward his desk, which held, among other things, his heavy glass inkwell, neatly gimballed and stoppered.

"I never once told you I was a man! It was hardly my fault you mistook me for one. I merely went along with your own notion rather than argue with you."

Gideon's eyes widened at her outrageous statement. Either she was criminally innocent or she was taunting him, and knowing Haskell, he'd lay odds on the latter choice. His gaze fell to the baggy trousers he'd issued her when she first came to him. They'd hardly been new even then; by now, they were in far worse shape, three buttons shy of a full complement and hanging about her hips to reveal a stretch of impossibly small, white waist.

The trailing length of ragged linen was still clutched to her bosom, her shoulders bare and softly rounded above it, and Gideon fought against the power she wielded over him. God help him if she ever discovered it!

Deliberately, he began to stalk her around the perimeter of the small cabin. Another kiss, that was all he'd take, but he'd damned well make sure she was quaking in her boots before he released her!

Prudence drew in a ragged breath, her heart racing so hard she felt light-headed. She'd wanted him to kiss her, and he had. From the looks of him, he was going to do it again. She'd best make the most of it, as it was all she was ever likely to have of him.

With one fleeting regret for the silk gown and all the ruffled petticoats and embroidered chemises she had hoped to be wearing on the night she became a woman, she smoothed her hair, licked her lips, puckered and lifted her face to his. Somehow, she was going to have to make him forget the way she looked on the outside and see her only as she was on the inside.

However that was.

"Haskell, what are you brewing up in that wicked little noggin of yours?"

She opened her eyes and blinked. "I—what did you say?"

"The first time I saw that particular expression on your face, you ended up winning three shares off Ben and two off Thomas. The next time I saw it, you ended up taking Ned's seat as Toby's striker. Just what is it you're angling for now?"

"I don't have any particular expression on my face, and I'm not angling for anything!"

"No?" His smile was too artless to be anything but false.

"Well, if you'd rather talk than—"

"Than what, Haskell? What did you think I was about to do?"

She could feel herself flushing, and only prayed that in the dim light, under all her sunburn, he wouldn't notice. "Gideon—"

"What happened to 'Captain, sir'?" His voice was dangerously deep and soft. Like quicksand.

Her fingers wrapped around the glass inkwell, only to have him ring her wrist and force her to drop it. With his other hand, he grasped her chin, angling her face for his benefit. He was smiling the devil's own smile, and she clamped her lips tightly against his invasion. He might be stronger, but she had her own weapons.

The trouble was, there was nothing at all forceful about his kiss. It was seduction, pure and simple, and Pru, already fighting a losing battle against her own heart, went down without a whimper.

He bore her back down onto the wide bunk, lying half on top of her, but careful not to crush her. With the gentlest of strokes, he licked the line between her lips and explored the surface of her small, white teeth. When she felt his hand on her breast, she gasped, giving him complete access to her mouth, and there he began a dance so skillful, so coercive, that her head was soon reeling.

All too soon she was drunk from the taste of him on her tongue, the heat of his moist, satiny lips—so firm, yet at the same time, so very soft and beguiling. "Oh, glory," she breathed when he lifted his face to stare down at her, his eyes midnight dark with passion.

"Glory?" he echoed huskily. "I should hope so, my little darling. God knows, I should hate to think I've completely lost my touch from disuse."

They were both breathing heavily, staring into each other's eyes, and then, to Pru's amazement, he began to draw away.

"Gideon?" she whispered as he lifted himself to sit beside her. His back was turned to her, his shoulders heaving, and she knew as surely as she knew her own name that he'd been as affected by that kiss as she had.

With one finger, she traced a line up his taut thighs, and he jumped as if she'd touched him with a burning splinter of lightwood. "Didn't you like it?" she asked.

He turned to scowl at her. "Didn't I like what? Your hand on my limb? The whore, Drucilla, did it more skillfully."

Shocked at his cruelty even more than his crudeness, she sat up, unwittingly allowing the forgotten linen to fall away. "I meant my kiss, but if Drucilla does that better, too, why then, you'll just have to teach me. I learn fast, Gideon, you know I do."

He refused to look at her. Daringly, she took one of his large hands and held it in her smaller ones. She was quite strong. Her hands might not be soft and white and smooth, but they didn't lack strength. "Gideon, show me how."

His head fell back, and she thought she heard him sigh. Encouraged, she got up onto her knees and wrapped her arms around his waist, which brought her naked breasts directly into contact with his shoulders. He still wore his fine linen shirt, but the cloth was so thin she could see his dark skin under it, feel the heat and the hardness of his body.

Something inside her leaped into life. Her limbs grew heavy, a liquid heat seemed to flow through her body, centering near the pit of her belly.

Carefully, deliberately, she began to ease his shirttail from under his trousers. Acting purely on instinct, she ran her hands up underneath, stroking his bare skin.

He was so satiny, so warm. The scent of him made her want to—to consume him! To become a part of him somehow.

Gideon waited to see if his entire life was going to flash before his eyes. He'd always heard that happened in moments of extreme danger, and although he'd come close to dying more times than he cared to recall, it had never happened to him.

At this moment, he felt himself in graver danger than ever before, for reasons he couldn't begin to understand. He responded to the threat with anger. "Damn your wicked eyes, Haskell, either you're the boldest female it's ever been my misfortune to meet, or you're the—" He knew an instant of deep despair at the thought. "Or you're the most innocent!" It was hardly likely, but in any event, he'd better get out of here before he did something they would both regret.

Her small, capable hands were everywhere—on his back, his neck, his scalp. "Gideon, turn around," she said quietly.

Pru felt him stiffen, heard the raw rasp of his indrawn breath. Something akin to triumph leaped in her heart. He'd been about to leave her, and she'd been determined not to let him go—not like this.

He turned, and when she saw the dark blaze of passion in his eyes—a passion not unlike anger—she nearly regretted her decision to ask him to make love to her. What frightened her even more than the look in his dark eyes was the way her own body was responding. Wild, wicked, wonderful images filled her head, and she hadn't the least notion of where they came from. She knew a hunger that was close to starvation, knew in her heart that tonight that hunger would be assuaged in the only way possible.

Only how to proceed from here? He didn't seem particularly interested in exploring further. "Gideon, I don't mind if you want to—to, you know. Do that thing to me. I think I might even like it."

He turned to stare at her, leaving her to wish she'd thought of a more subtle way of phrasing her invitation. Annie had never mentioned this part of it.

"That is, if you . . . uh . . ."

Was that disbelief or disgust she saw on his face? In the midst of trying to fathom his strange mood, she was completely unprepared when Gideon reached out and yanked open her placket, sending a shower of small bone buttons across the cabin. By the time the last one had spun away into a corner, his large hand was splayed over the tiny swelling in the hammock of her belly.

So soft, so womanly—he hated her lies, yet he wanted her until he was sick to death with fighting it! One moment she seemed the most innocent of all creatures, the next she was acting the seasoned jade. What was she? Who was she?

With a sigh, he ripped off his shirt and flung it aside. What did it matter? She was here now—and she was willing.

Watching the centers of her eyes darken until they were nearly black, he moved his palm until it domed over the small nest of sable curls between her thighs. As he gazed down upon the treasures that had haunted him since that day at the pond, it occurred to him that the very contrast between her sun-darkened extremities and the creamy paleness in between made her nakedness seem all the more intimate.

You're so damned beautiful you make my heart ache, he told her silently as his other hand moved up to cover her breast. The lamp flickered as a light breeze came through the porthole. "You're thin as a rake, Haskell," he said aloud. "You've a need to eat more and work less."

He saw the pain flicker across her face and regretted his words. They were false. No, they were true, but it made no difference. Thin or fat, she tempted him as no woman had ever tempted him, and for the life of him, he couldn't say why.

"If I work less," she murmured, her words slurred as her eyes grew dim with desire, "I'll surely eat less."

At least he would pay her well, Gideon told himself. He would send her home with enough to set her up in some respectable business—though God knows what it might be.

And then he thought no more as reason was drowned under a tidal wave of urgent need. Lowering his head, he took the rosebud tip of one small breast between his teeth, swirling his tongue around the nub. He felt her stiffen beneath him, and smiled inwardly.

The scent of heated passion was all around them, mixed with the scent of lilacs, tar and salt air. How could anything so soft, so fragile and so responsive have been hidden away under layers of coarse canvas and cambric? How could he not have known?

Shaking with the need to restrain himself, he teased her with his tongue and his teeth, wanting to drive her to the ends of need—driving himself, instead. He had made himself a promise that before this night was ended, she would beg him to take her!

God help him if he ended up begging her, instead.

Lifting his flushed face, Gideon stared down at the small creature beneath him and marveled. How could such a woman, hardened as she must be from her life as a thief, a whaler and God knows what else, look so damnably innocent?

"Haskell," he whispered. She refused to open her eyes, and he stared down at the impossibly long lashes fanned out there and wondered again how he could ever have been so blind. "Open your eyes."

She kept them tightly closed. Playing another of her infernal games, he decided. Was she imagining he was someone else? The thought hardened his resolve to use her as she had used him, for convenience and amusement. She would have taken his purse for her own use, and she'd damned well had a good laugh at his expense.

But she wasn't laughing now. And God help him, neither was he!

Slipping his hand between them, he unfastened the last button on his own breeches and shoved them down his hips. When the last barrier was gone, he positioned himself over her, fearing that if he waited much longer he would explode on her belly and be shamed still further by her laughter.

"Open your eyes, Haskell," he repeated.

"I think if it's all the same to you, I'll just—"

"Open your eyes," he insisted, and pressed himself farther into the cradle of her parted thighs. She would damned well know who was mounting her this time!

"Haskell, my imprudent little darling, if you don't open your eyes I'm going to turn you over my knee and—"

Her lids flew open. He was kneeling between her thighs, resting his weight on one hand as he peered down into her face. The moment she opened her eyes, he smiled down at her. "There, that's not so bad, is it? If you're offended by my face, we can always blow out the lamp, but I've a wish to watch you."

His hand moved, and he was touching her, and she twisted, trying to buck him off, but it was no use. "Gideon, I don't know—"

"Hush, sweetling, let me pleasure you first. Talking takes the edge off a bit, but I vow it's no chore to hone it again...and again." At his intimate caress, she began to melt. And then she gasped. Reaching for something to hang on to, she caught at his shoulders and clung there, her short fingernails scoring his naked skin as wave after wave of the most incredible sensations swept her away.

"All warm and wet and ready," he whispered, his eyes heavy-lidded as he moved in closer. And then, just as his mouth came down over hers, she felt something smooth and hard and hot shoving against her private place.

She screamed silently into his mouth as she felt herself being split asunder. He froze in place—she thought she heard him swear under his breath, but she was hurting too much to be sure. And then, with a groan, he pushed himself into her, filling her until she was fit to burst. After a long while, he began to move, and then to move faster, deeper. She was no longer hurting, but she felt strange...exceedingly strange....

Just as something wondrous began to spread over her like a coral sunrise, Gideon cried out in pain. Something hot and melting shot into her, and then he shuddered and collapsed.

Dear God, she had killed him.

With great effort, and against his own will, Gideon dragged himself back to consciousness. After a moment, he rolled off the delicate body that was crushed under his and flopped over onto his back, flinging one arm over his eyes.

He heard her whimper as she rolled onto her side, curling into a tight, protective ball as far away from him as she could get. In the warm nest where she had been lying a moment before there was the clear evidence of her innocence.

She'd been virgin. He closed his eyes, his mind forming broken phrases that were half prayer, half oath. God forgive him, he had taken her innocence like a rutting stag, and there wasn't one way in hell that he could ever give it back.

"Lass—" He placed a tentative hand on the curve of her hip, and she shrank away from him. "Haskell, I'm sorry."

Words. What good were words when he had raped an innocent woman? Even piracy paled by comparison. "Did you hear me? I hurt you—what I did was wrong, and I'm more sorry than I can ever say."

Her voice muffled, she said, "At least you're alive. I thought I'd killed you."

It took him but a moment to realize the way her thoughts had run, and he smiled, his eyes bleaker than a winter storm at sea. "If you'd like another go at it—killing me, that is—I'd be glad to provide the weapon."

She gasped, and he knew it had been the wrong thing to say. Another go at it? The devil take his unworthy soul, he felt himself hardening again at the mere thought of having "another go at it." This time he wouldn't hurt her—he'd take all the time in the world—pleasure her in all the ways a man could possibly pleasure a woman, and only when she was weak with her own release would he take his, and not even then if she denied him.

"Will you send me home now?"

Home? Did she mean back to camp? To the fo'c'sle? To Portsmouth? "I've a cargo to collect before we can leave." The cargo could have waited. He wasn't ready to send her away yet, though he couldn't blame her for wanting to leave him. "Would you like me to move into the crew's quarters and let you stay here?"

"No, thank you." She sounded so listless he was sorely tempted to roll her over to see if she was all right.

All right? After what he'd just done to her? She was far from all right, but at least he could see that she had a place to recover away from a lot of rowdy, drunken men. "There's the sail locker. It's nothing fancy, but you'd have a mite of privacy. I could clean it up for you."

She turned over then, but she refused to look at him. Perhaps his face did offend her, he thought. It wouldn't be the first time a woman had turned away in disgust. But she'd seen him every day for months, and shown no sign that she noticed his blemish for good or ill.

Pru willed herself not to cry. She might have known it wouldn't work. Why should he want a woman who didn't know the least thing about being a woman? Even Drucilla was better at it than she was!

"I've a tub—I'll fetch it and see if there's any water left in the kettle," he said, and she nodded, still not looking at him.

Snatching up his trousers, he turned his back. Sulky little baggage! What had she expected him to do, offer for her? Pay her for what he'd taken? A virgin she might be, but that didn't mean she was innocent! No true innocent would have teased him the way she had, or flaunted herself before a camp full of men. Perhaps she had other tastes—and talents. He'd once heard of a whore who had sent hundreds of men away happy without ever surrendering her maidenhead.

Chapter Eleven

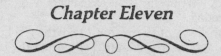

At first Gideon had thought to put into Portsmouth on the way back to camp and leave her there. But after due consideration, he knew he couldn't simply dump her off on the docks—not without knowing she would be taken care of. She'd be back at her old trade in no time.

Nye, or Pride or whatever his true name was, would have to go with her. If the lad wished to come back and work for him next season, they would discuss it when the time came.

Not even to himself would Gideon admit the possibility that he might find it impossible to put her ashore. Crow could take her. The half-breed had looked after the pair of them without seeming to since the night Gideon hauled them aboard and dumped them onto the deck of the *Polly*.

Besides, unless he missed his guess, Crow would welcome another chance to see the freed slave who claimed to be some sort of friend to the pair of them. It was an unlikely arrangement, and possibly not the whole of the truth. He had meant to get to the bottom of matters at one time, but now, the less he knew about those two, the better. God knows, the little witch had woven herself into his life already until he doubted he'd ever be entirely rid of her.

Gideon rubbed the back of his neck tiredly. At least he might be able to sleep without dreaming once she was no longer around to torment him.

Aye—first he'd get her out of his life, and then he'd set about getting her out of his dreams.

* * *

The *Polly* had scarcely dropped anchor back at the camp before Gideon was searching out Crow, who'd served as overseer in his absence. Quickly he explained the mission he had in mind. "You were wanting an excuse to get back to Portsmouth, weren't you?" he asked with a lightness he was far from feeling.

"The boy, he want to stay on. I take the girl home."

Gideon's eyes narrowed. He'd suspected the breed knew about Haskell, but he hadn't been sure. "How'd you find out?" If Crow had watched her bathing, too, Gideon thought he would likely kill him.

"A man cannot sleep beside a woman without knowing."

"Did Tolson guess, too?"

"Ben be a boy, not a man."

"Why the hell didn't you tell me?"

"Ain't be mine to tell," the half-breed said simply.

Gideon nodded. He would probably have done the same in Crow's place. But dammit, if he'd even suspected, he could have got rid of her before she'd ruined his life—and he hers!

"All right, Crow, I'll admit to being a blind fool."

Crow's face crinkled into a rare grin, which did nothing at all to improve Gideon's mood.

"Just take 'em away from here, will you? Both of 'em for now."

The breed said nothing, merely waiting for Gideon to say all that was on his mind. It was obviously no light burden he was hauling.

"I'll give you their shares and a bit more, besides. I wouldn't want her—them, that is—to go needy."

"Be cheaper to break her neck and try her for oil, Cap'n."

"Shut up, you damned black Indian, or I might just do it."

Crow chuckled and, reluctantly, so did Gideon.

It was Crow who told her. Pale and quiet, Prudence had gone about unpacking her meager belongings from her sea-bag, torn between disappointment and relief that Gideon hadn't veered by Portsmouth and left her there on the way back from Bath Towne.

Ben and the others had put her quietness down to too much kill-devil rum, which suited her purposes. She would not be with them much longer—a few days or a week at most. The camp was already largely dismantled, the men talking of heading for Hatteras and Ocracoke and Virginia for a break before the next season began.

"Best stow you gear back in you bag," Crow said just as the sun was breaking over the ocean. They'd got back to camp the evening before, and Pru had not seen hide nor hair of Gideon.

Not that she'd wanted to.

"Am I going home?" she asked numbly.

"Aye. The two of you, the captain say. We sail as soon as you be ready."

Pride burst in just then. He'd heard the news, gone to argue with Gideon and been told that he could come back in the fall if he was still of the same mind. "Hurry, will you? It don't take all that much time to stow a few rags in your bag. You won't even be needin' them once we get home."

Pru cast a worried look at Crow, but if he'd wondered at the careless remark about home, he said nothing. Numbly, she went through the motions of cramming her spare pair of breeches, her coat and her best shirt into her bag. The boots were beyond repair; she would leave them behind, as well as her blanket and her oilskins. Some other man would use those, and welcome. All she wanted to do now was forget Gideon and this whole miserable experience.

Even so, she could not help gazing around at the place where she'd worked harder than she had ever worked in her life—and found, perhaps, truer friends. Friends she dared not even bid farewell, for fear she would cry, and they would be embarrassed for her. Whalers didn't cry. Let them remember her as a lively gamester, a dreadful cook and a mate who had worked beside them until the last hunt.

Perhaps they would forgive her a single lapse. Thomas and Ben already had. And Crow. And Toby. And Bully and Lear...

Oh, Lord, there was Lucy, rooting the lid off the cask of salt mullet! "Gouge!" she called, but he'd already seen her and was coming at a run.

Waving, Pru blinked back her tears and hurried on to catch up with Crow and Pride. Only then did it occur to her that Pride had been planning to stay on and haul freight with Gideon until the next season began.

She had ruined everything.

They waded out to the shallop, which lay anchored inshore of the *Polly*. Pru heaved herself over the low freeboard unassisted and gazed back at the shoreline while Crow hoisted the sails. All too soon, the responsive little craft had heeled about and moved out into the tide.

Pru had thought perhaps Gideon might come to see them off, but then, why should he? He'd certainly made no attempt to speak to her since he'd brought the brass tub into his cabin and filled it with lukewarm water from the galley's huge kettle, insisting that she use it first.

She had. And then, dressing quickly, she'd thrown the covers over the small pink stain on his bed and fled to the fo'c'sle before he could return to his cabin.

Crow, one arm lying along the tiller, watched silently as the camp fell behind. He met Pride's gaze, and something seemed to pass between the two men before both set about the business of crossing the broad, turbulent inlet and running along a barren stretch of lowland to the village on the northern end of Portsmouth Island.

Pru was surprised at how much things looked the same, yet how much they had changed. Had the warehouses always been so rough? She'd once thought them neat and tidy, but then, things weathered quickly on the banks.

And the trees—somehow, she'd remembered them as being bigger than they actually were.

Some things never changed, though, she thought as she scrambled up onto the wharf, feeling almost shy after so long a time away. "Albert?" she called after the stocky figure disappearing around the corner of the grain warehouse.

She was sure he'd heard her, but for some reason he didn't stop. Probably on some crucial errand, she thought, such as finding out for his father what his mother was having for dinner.

For once there'd been room between unloading ships to come alongside the docks. Crow slung her seabag up onto the wharf and climbed nimbly after it. He seemed to be searching for something—or someone. Pru watched as he handed over something to Pride. The two of them spoke for several minutes in a voice too low for her to overhear, and she turned away in time to see Annie come out onto her front porch to shake a broom. The Duvaals' house was just across Haul Over Road and down a short path from the docks.

She waved, but unfortunately, Annie didn't see her, and Pru felt disinclined to call out. There'd be enough time to talk later.

Would Annie be able to look at her and tell what had happened? Did it show?

Several fishermen had been working at the end of the wharf. Now they had gathered into a knot and were staring, as if they couldn't believe their eyes. Pru smiled and waved, for she'd known them all since birth.

How odd! They didn't seem to see her. More likely, she reminded herself, they hadn't recognized her in her canvas breeches, with her hair in rats' tails and her feet bare.

Shrugging, Pru turned back to where Pride and Crow still stood. She frowned. Pride looked furious over something, and Crow—even he looked a bit concerned, although he wasn't someone to show his feelings.

Seeing her watching him, the tall half-breed made his way to where she was standing. "Here be you pay, little striker."

Pru whipped her hands behind her. "I'm not owed anything, thank you. The—the captain paid me along with the others."

"This be something more." Reaching around behind her, Crow pressed a bundle of coins into her palm. "Cutting pay. It be the end of the season. We share the spoils." He offered her what passed for a smile, and she felt like throwing herself on him and begging him to take her back to the others. Where would she find such friends again, friends who accepted her at face value without prying into her past? "Tell Lillah I be back directly."

She nodded and stepped back, her head held proudly. Not for the world would she let him see that she was hurting, for he might tell Gideon. She'd sooner die than have Gideon know that his sending her away without a word, no matter how much she had begged to go home, was cutting the heart right out of her body.

Both Pru and Pride stood and watched until the shallop gained the channel. For a moment, the westerly wind held her in irons, and then she came smartly about and disappeared behind a hulking merchantman that was lightering in barrels of rum and molasses.

Packs on their backs, they strode along Haul Over Road, passing first the Duvaals' turnoff and then a familiar grove of scrub oak, palmetto and cedar. Not slackening her stride, Pru swerved past the burned-out stump that marked the beginning of their own path. Tears stung in her eyes, and with a ruthless hand, she dashed them away.

Not until she reached the shelter of her own porch did it occur to her that it might have been wiser to send Pride on ahead to fetch one of her gowns so that she could change into it before she presented herself to Granna.

But it was not Granna who opened the door and stood there, arms crossed over her skimpy bosom, looking for all the world like a dark, avenging angel.

"You git in here, you shameless female!"

"Oh, Lillah, I'm so glad to be—"

"Glad, nothing!"

Pride had slipped by, evidently unnoticed, and was hurrying up the steep, narrow staircase, but Pru was not to be so fortunate.

"Is Granna all right?" she asked, inhaling the familiar smells of wood smoke, musty carpets, lavender and boiled fish.

"Lot you care, running off wit' a bunch o' wild men like you was one o' they common women down to the waterfront!"

Pru dropped her bundle. The familiar scents, along with the familiar sight of Granna's old hoop-backed chair and the settle where Pru and Pride had lain for hours listening to Urias's tales of adventure on the high seas, brought the tears to the surface again. All day long she had fought against them, determined not to give in to the aching emptiness inside her. But the smell of Lillah's corn bread finally did her in.

"Ohhh, Lillah," she wailed, and flung herself at the disapproving woman. "I'm so heartsore I could die! And I look so—so awful, and I stink, and he—he hates me...."

"Hush now, baby, git you'self into that kitchen. Lillah fill you a tub."

Pru sniffled and wiped her nose on her sleeve.

Lillah slapped her hand away. "Stop that! You home now. We got to get you cleaned up 'fore that Claude mon come back. That one put a spell on Mizzus, bad-bad."

Pru hardly heard the words as she dragged her bundle out to the kitchen, which was attached to the main house by a covered walk. The shelf that ran along the shaded side of the breezeway held pans of clabbered milk, crocks of larded fowl and salt mullet, a set of oilskins and a dry-rotted gill net that had belonged to Urias.

Suddenly, Pru was overwhelmed with exhaustion. It was as if she had raced through the rigors of the past few months all in a single day, and now she was watching it slip away into the distance, and no matter how hard she tried, she couldn't reach out and hold it back—not even long enough to hear that beloved voice once more, or to see those crinkling blue eyes and the blemished face that was more beautiful to her than any mortal had a right to be.

"Oh, glory, Lillah, what am I going to do?" she whispered.

The older woman slid the big copper tub into place and stood up, her dark eyes narrowing suspiciously. "You got a babe in you belly?"

"A *babe!* No!" Pru dropped her bundle and leaned against the massive old oak table.

"You be certain-sure o' that?"

Pru hesitated only the smallest moment, proud of the way she covered her dismay. "Of course I be certain-sure! Lillah, for goodness' sake, I've been working like a galley slave in a blasted whaling camp, not—"

Arms akimbo, the older woman looked her up and down, making Pru feel, not for the first time, that Lillah knew everything that went on in the world that was in any way connected to one of her people.

"You knows what a body has to do to make a baby?"

"I'm not a total ninny," Pru snapped. Of course she knew. Now that she thought about it, she'd known for years—at least as it applied to horses and dogs. Only when it involved people, when it involved longing and kissing and touching, why then, none of that seemed to fit.

She certainly wasn't able to take care of a baby, and she was reasonably certain that Gideon had no interest in becoming a father. Therefore, there would be no baby. Besides, a body had to be married to have a baby.

Lillah emptied one of the big kettles into the tub and set it on the hearth. With a look of sly amusement, she said, "You stink this way alla time you be gone, no mon ain' get close enough to make you belly swell up."

"That's all you know," Pru muttered under her breath. She shed the rest of her clothing and poked one toe into the tub. "Dammit, are you trying to scald me to death?"

"Maybe I leave you stinking like dead fish. Then that Claude mon maybe change he mind 'bout havin' you for he woman."

Waiting until Lillah had poured another kettleful of hot water and several dippers of cold into the tub, Pru lowered herself carefully into the high-backed tub. "If you mean that toad, Delarouche, you can rest easy. If he comes sniffing around, I'll be glad to send him on his way."

"Humph!" Lillah snatched a chunk of homemade soap and tossed it into the tub, and then set about collecting Pru's cast-off clothing, lifting the garments off the floor with the wash-boiling stick.

"Don't throw my things away!"

"They be fit for drawing off flies."

"Yes, well..." No matter how rank, how ragged and how ugly they were, they were a link with Gideon. The only one she had. "I might need them again," she muttered as she lowered her hair into the steaming water, her feet curled up against her hips.

Lillah snatched up the soap and set to lathering Pru's hair, her touch firm, but not unkind. Once she had finished and wrapped a coarse towel around Pru's head, she began scouring her body, starting with her ears.

Pru squealed and jerked away. "Dammit, Lillah, now you're trying to skin me alive!"

"Hush! You got a filt'y tongue in you mouf, girl!"

"You twisted my ear!"

"Huh! You got any notion what that Claude mon be doin' while you be off playin' boy-boy?"

"Well, you're still here. The house is still standing. Don't tell me he married Granna and ran off to Paris with her."

"You Granna, she be sleepin' in her bed so she be ready when he come tonight. He come *e-ver-y* night." Shoving Pru's head forward, Lillah commenced to scrub her back. "*An'* he sit, *an'* he sweet-talk, *an'* he pour out wine, *an'* he sweet-talk some more. Firs' t'ing Lillah know, that wicked mon done steal you, you gran'mama, you sewin' basket an' this ol' house, it all."

Pru's face was shoved under while Lillah finished scouring her backside. She came up sputtering. "What do you mean, he stole—"

"You hush, I tell you what I mean!"

And she proceeded to do so, painting a picture that had Pru shuddering in disbelief. "No, I don't believe it. Granna wouldn't do that!"

"Who know what that ol' woman do when she drink all that wine? She don' even need no laudanum no more, he fill her so full o' port wine."

"Yes, but to sign away our house? Why would she do such a thing? Wait'll Pride hears about this! He won't stand still for it, not for one minute! If I still had Papa's pistol—"

Lillah grabbed a foot and lifted it, causing Pru to fall back against the unforgiving rim of the tub. "You ain' heard the wors' t'ing yet. That mon say he own *you!*"

Righting herself with her elbows on the sides, Pru said, "What do you mean—he owns me?"

The sound of Pride's voice from the other end of the passage rang out cheerfully. "Pru! Lillah! Where the devil is everyone? Ain't there no food in the house?"

"Wait a minute," Pru yelled back. "I'll be out as soon as I get some clothes on!" Twisting around, she said hurriedly, "Lillah, could you get me some clean clothes? And what did you mean, Claude owns me? That's crazy."

The black woman stood, dried her hands on her apron and stared down at the shiny-faced girl in the tub full of filthy water. The look of sympathy in her eyes made Prudence feel suddenly naked. Vulnerable.

"He you new guardian, chile. He got papers say he own ever't'ing Urias Andros lef' behin'. You, the boy, the mizzus an' this house. Ever't'ing 'ceptin' Lillah. Ain' no mon own Lillah."

Chapter Twelve

In a quiet rage, Prudence stood still while Lillah worked with her hair. There was little that could be done with it, for it scarcely fell past her shoulders. Still, after twelve hours of sleep, a basting with eggs, honey and cedar-berry tea, another washing and a rinse of vinegar and rose water, it was once again thick, lustrous and sparkling with bronze and golden highlights.

"That mealymouthed buzzard dropping," she muttered.

Lillah yanked her head around, twisted the last rag and tied it. "Hush you mouf, girl."

"You think he's more than buzzard droppings?"

"You wiggle you mouf, you crack you face."

Catching a glimpse of her stiff white face in the mirror, Pru could not suppress a smile, no matter how irritated she was at the man who had come to dinner the night before and stayed until a shockingly late hour. Pru hadn't spoken a word to him beyond civil necessity. Pride had made some excuse and gone out the moment they left the table.

The thick mask on her face cracked and began to flake off as Lillah continued to scold her. Pru barely listened. She had been pummeled and pushed, larded and labored over since the minute she had set foot in the house, to the tune of Lillah's predictions of doom.

Hosannah had smiled vaguely and asked if she'd had a lovely visit at Hunt House.

"What made her think we were visiting Uncle John?" Pru asked now.

Lillah shrugged. "Mizzus, she hear what she want to hear."

"Why didn't you set her straight? Crow told you where we were."

There was no reply, for both knew that the old woman was beyond questioning anything that did not pertain to her immediate comfort. Lillah had confessed to having had more than one visit from Crow, who had told her only that his captain caught her two young charges in a bit of mischief and was teaching them a lesson.

"Oh, yes—Crow said tell you he'd be back." Pru had forgotten to pass on the message, her mind busy with more pressing concerns. Such as what was she going to do about Claude? Despite impeccable manners and a face any woman might call handsome, the man made her flesh crawl.

Lillah twisted the last bit of hair and tied it, muttering all the while. "That mon got wicked ways. I tol' him stay away from me."

"Is he bothering you, too? I can't think why. He wants something, I'm certain of that, but surely not from you."

For once in her life, Lillah looked puzzled, and slowly it dawned on Pru that they were speaking at cross purposes. *Lillah and Crow? Why, Lillah would carve Crow up in tiny pieces. She was as prickly as a Spanish bayonet, and for all his stoicism, he had a soft heart.*

Finished with Pru's hair, Lillah gathered up her sewing and sat down. She'd been working on a blue silk gown she had resurrected from Blanche Andros's trunk, but having aired it out, steamed it and resewn a place where the hem was torn, she was not satisfied yet.

Absently, Pru watched, her mind still on the Frenchman, who seemed determined to take over their very lives. He had said nothing at all about any guardianship the night before, and Pru had not dared to bring it up. Besides, she wasn't too sure of the law concerning guardians and women of her age. She was no longer a child, having turned eighteen a few weeks after she was captured.

"He said he would be calling around again this evening. Delarouche, that is—to discuss my future. As if my future had a bloody blasted thing to do with him."

"Hush you mouf, girl, 'fore I tie a string 'round you tongue! That wicked boy-boy talk."

"Well, no amount of wicked boy-boy talk will get us out of this mess," Pru muttered through her cracking mask. "Surely he can't claim anything Granna signed away while she was under the influence of all that blasted French wine. Can he, Lillah?"

Both women looked up at the sound of breaking glass.

"Mizzus!"

"Granna!"

Pru reached the old woman first and knelt by her side. Hosannah was in her favorite chair by the window, a shawl around her shoulders and another over her lap despite the warm spring weather. On the floor beside her lay a broken tumbler. Her hands were shaking, and tears streamed down the ruined old face.

"John? Where's John? Send my brother to me, at once, Sudie." Her chin quivered, and she stared accusingly at the dark woman who stood framed in the doorway. "Who are you? You're not my Sudie!"

"No, Mizzus, Sudie gone to fetch you brother. I be Lillah, come to take care o' you."

Seeing her grandmother in the bright morning light streaming in through the window, Pru was shocked at the disintegration of the woman who had raised her from a small child. In the light of candles and a single oil lamp the night before she had looked smaller, but much the same. Of course, she had seemed somewhat vaguer than usual, but no more than could be accounted for by the several glasses of port and, later, the brandy Claude had pressed on her.

But this was neither port nor brandy. At least, not directly.

"Granna, let me help you onto your bed. Shall I rub your ankles? Or I'll sing...you remember the songs you taught me when I was little?" She began to hum, her voice thick with unshed tears.

"I'm hurting, child. Go fetch John and tell him to send for the doctor. I need something to ease my joints, or I'll not sleep a wink."

The plaintive voice of a child came through the querulous tones of an old woman whose bent and swollen joints pained her without surcease. With a quick glance at Lillah, Pru nodded. Both women knew what to do. Lillah hurried out to the kitchen to fetch a kettle and a stack of towels, while Pru measured out a tiny dose of laudanum and stirred it into a glass of sugar water flavored with port wine.

"Here, love, drink this. Lillah's gone for your hot towels. In no time at all you'll be tapping your toe and calling for a fiddler."

"Claude is coming for dinner. Prudence, you'll have to remove that dreadful mess from your face before he gets here. And please do something with your hair."

Clear again, thought Prudence, stroking her grandmother's tiny, misshapen hands. It was like gazing out on a day when the sky was filled with small white clouds, with patches of sunlight and shadow racing one another across the face of the earth.

"I'll make you proud of me tonight, Granna. But perhaps we should send word to Claude that you're not feeling quite the thing."

"Nonsense, child! There's nothing at all wrong with me, and Claude promised to tell me about the lovely house he's going to build for us out on the point."

Pru's eyes hardened. That snake was up to something wicked, and for the life of her, she couldn't think what it might be. He in his fine satins and brocades, with ruffles dangling from every quarter—what would a man like that be wanting with an old house, an old woman and a set of twins who despised the very air he breathed? It wasn't as if they had anything left to steal, for the bloody bastard had already got to the sewing basket.

Not that he'd admitted it. Oh, no. When she'd got him alone the night before long enough to accuse him, he'd made a great show of shocked innocence. "Someone robbed you of needle and thread? But *mam'selle,* how terrible!"

If she hadn't been wearing a pair of her mother's old cloth slippers that were a full size too small, she would have kicked him where it would do the most harm.

Pride came home just past midday. He had managed to find work with one of the warehouses—a poor show indeed for one who should have been heir to nearly the whole of Portsmouth Island.

"You would work for Delarouche? I'd sooner starve to death," she told him.

"I hate his bloody gizzard, Pru, but he's up to something, and working in one of his warehouses is the best way I know to find out what he's about. I'll be working under Simpson. He's Delarouche's man, all right, but he's as dim-witted as ever. It'll be easy to get into the office. He still keeps the keys where Papa used to hang them. There's got to be something there—some clue. Notes, or a diary, or something." And at his sister's skeptical look, he went on. "Prudie, do you think Delarouche could've heard those old rumors about Papa's lost fortune?"

She snorted. "If we had a fortune, would I be sweating over a hot fire boiling down the wash while you're off clerking in some smelly old warehouse?"

"We might if the fortune was lost and we couldn't find a single shilling of it."

Prudence expressed her opinion of that theory in no uncertain terms. "All the same, he's after something. I'm going to tell him flat out tonight that Papa sold everything he owned and put it all into his ship and her cargo. Maybe then he'll go barking up some other tree."

"First, he'll have to believe you," Pride said, his expression making it quite clear that he didn't hold out much hope of that.

"I thought you were going to stay on with Gideon."

Pride's earnest brown eyes slid away from hers. He stroked the beard of which he was so insufferably proud and said, "Yes, well . . . a man can change his mind, can't he?"

"You didn't have to come back on my account, you know. It was me he sent home. You could have stayed on."

"Oh, sure, and who would have looked after you? An old woman so weak in the head she don't know her nose from next Thursday, and a sabre-tongued freedwoman who'd as soon walk out on the lot of us as not? You're only a girl, Prudie. You need some'un to look after you."

A blaze of color rushed to stain Pru's cheeks, cheeks Lillah had worked so hard to bleach and soften. "Are we talking about the same *girl* who used to bring home three geese to your one fish duck? The same *girl* who tried her best to teach you how to cast a fishing line without hooking your own stern end? The same *girl* who—"

"I'm talking about the girl who's going to end up being mistress to a smooth-talking devil from Paris if she don't watch her step."

Pru's eyes widened. "You think—you really believe I would do such a thing?"

"I believe you'll not have a choice unless I can dig up something to discredit the bleeding toad. Lillah claims Granna signed us over to him, along with the house and anything else we might happen to lay claim to. And I don't reckon she'd lie about something like that."

Pru dropped onto the bench outside the kitchen, where she'd been shelling seed beans. "We're eighteen years old now. I don't think it counts." Then she blurted, "God, how could Granna *do* such a thing? Does she think we're still children?"

"'Course she does—at least most of the time she does." Pride hiked a foot up onto the bench beside the bean sack. He had grown rapidly while they were away, his shoulders broadening, his arms and legs filling out. Even his face had taken on a more mature appearance. "For all I love her dearly, it seems to me Granna's never been real long on brains."

"That's not fair!" Pru protested. True, perhaps, but hardly fair.

He continued, unperturbed. "Likely comes of always having a man around to tell her how to go on—first her own papa, then her brother, Uncle John, then that poor old saint she married. Leastwise, until they either died or kicked her out of their house."

It was true, of course. Hosannah Hunt Gilbert had never been noted for her strength of mind, but neither the strength of her character nor the warmth of her heart had ever been questioned. The youngest child, she'd been spoiled by her parents and by her older brother—that is, until he married a jealous woman who lost no time in finding Hosannah a husband in the form of an elderly parson.

"We've got to get us all out of this mess she's landed us in," Pru said.

"I'm doing my best. It ain't going to help, though, if you go and murder the bastard before I can discredit him."

Frowning thoughtfully, Pru walked slowly home from an errand in town. It was a full week since Crow delivered them back home. Although she hated to admit it, she missed the whaling camp, missed living right on the beach, being lulled to sleep each night by the sound of the surf, missed watching the moon rise above the water, hearing the plaintive music of Crow's wooden flute over the cheerful noise of the men's yarning around the fire.

Missed knowing that at any moment, she might see Gideon standing slightly apart from his men, his pale hair blowing in the wind, sunlight glinting off his bronzed skin as he scanned the water for a sign.

By all rights she should hate the man, for he'd taken her too soon, before she was ready—taken all she'd had to offer, and when it was not enough for him, he'd sent her away.

If only they could have met under different circumstances, she thought, he might eventually have come to care for her. But she'd had her chance and lost it by being too bold, too inexperienced, too awkward, too—whatever she'd been, it was obviously not what Gideon had wanted.

Arriving home, she discovered two women of a coarse sort—women she vaguely remembered as working in one of her father's ordinaries. The two slatterns were doing a shabby job of polishing the pewter sconces on either side of the main fireplace.

Puzzled, she hurried back toward the kitchen, where Lillah was waiting for her. If the woman's eyes had snapped any harder, you could have heard the sound all the way to Ocracoke. "You see they women in my house? That wicked mon say Lillah not take care of you and Mizzus! He say Lillah go now, he send women to take her place."

"The devil he did! Where's Granna? What does she have to say about all this?"

"Mizzus be sleepin'. He bring her mo' brandy."

Faded India-cloth skirt swirling about her single petticoat, Pru stormed into the front part of the house. "We'll just see about this," she muttered. That bloody long-nosed fop had gone too far this time, bringing his women into her house and telling Lillah she had to go.

"Out," she said, pointing a trembling finger at the door. One of the women, a blowsy creature who had tugged her skirt up under her apron strings and was sprawled, toes turned out, on Granna's best hooped-back chair, wiped a filthy cloth haphazardly across the gateleg table.

"Monsoor Delarouche, he said we was to answer to him."

"This is my house, not Claude Delarouche's. You'll answer to me, and I say if you're not out of here by the time I get back, you'll be wishing you'd never left your mother's bellies!"

She spun around, with no real idea of where to go or what to do. She only knew that if she stayed there a moment longer, she might strangle those two bawds, wishing it were Delarouche's neck, instead.

By the time Pride came home, the women were gone and Pru had regained her composure. She had managed to persuade Lillah to stay on, but she knew that unless she put an end to the situation right now, it would only get worse.

"I'm going to have it out with that bleeding Frenchman," she announced before Pride even got through the door. "And I don't mind telling you, I'm looking forward to it. You say he sleeps aboard that brigantine that's anchored off Haul Over Point?"

"The *Saint Germaine?* Yes, but see here, Pru, if you go and get him riled, he's going to do something you're not going to like."

"If *I* get *him* riled! What about if *he* gets *me* riled? Papa would have called him out for far less than that! When I think about what that sneaking weasel has done to us—"

"So far, he ain't done nothing but put food on the table, send help to the house and tell us what he *could* do if he was of a mind to."

"*Nothing!* You call keeping poor Granna so sozzled she can hardly get out of bed *nothing?* You call sneaking around upstairs and stealing our savings *nothing?*"

"Shh, settle down now, or you'll get Granna all upset. She may be sozzled, but her ears are still as sharp as a bat's. If you'll just give me time, I'll take care of him, I promise. Hadn't you best see to helping Lillah set supper on the table?" he said, his manner placating.

Pru's eyebrows came together in a scowl. "We'll not have it on the table tonight. I'll eat with Granna in her room, and you can eat out in the kitchen with Lillah."

"You're begging for trouble, Prudie. Claude's coming, and if the food ain't on the table where he expects it to be, he's going to get mean."

"Let him. He'll find out what Urias Andros's daughter does when she uncovers a nest of cottonmouth moccasins."

Gideon crossed his arms around the spokes and leaned on the wheel, staring out over the calm moonlit waters of the

Pamlico Sound. Seven nights had gone by. Eight days and seven nights, and still he could not get her out of his mind.

Prudence. The most misnamed female of all time—and not Prudence Haskell, but Prudence Andros. He had learned from Crow that she was one of old Urias Andros's twins. God, the lies that pair had told him!

Orphans? They were orphans, right enough, but scarcely alone in the world. There was a grandmother somewhere in the picture. Only she must not be much of a force, for those two had been running wild as bucks when he caught them.

Cutpurses. How long had they been playing that particular game? If he hadn't deliberately set out to waylay them that night last winter, there was no telling what would have become of them by now.

An all too familiar pain began to gnaw at him at the thought of her falling into the hands of some rough sort. As pictures took shape in his mind of the fate she would undoubtedly have met had he not stepped in when he did, Gideon deliberately allowed his anger to come to a boil.

Anger, he had discovered, was as good a defense as any against the maddening dreams, the insidious longings that came upon him in the hours just before morning, when his control was at its lowest ebb.

Against the soft lapping of water against the hull, Gideon close-hauled his thoughts. Night watch gave a body too much time to remember, and remembering led inevitably to the night when he had learned to his dismay that his wicked little thief was, in one way, at least, still an innocent.

God help him, no matter what she was, he had done her a grievous wrong. His own past was not so clean that he could look askance at a girl who'd been forced, through whatever circumstances, into a life of thievery.

He would go back to Portsmouth and try to find her as soon as he had delivered his present cargo. There had to be some way he could make amends so that he could live with his conscience. A guilty conscience was a deuced intolerable thing.

And surely that was all it was that was keeping him awake at night, filling him with peculiar urges and longings for things he dare not dwell on.

Chapter Thirteen

Delarouche was dressed in a suit of satin brocade in a particularly noxious shade of green, with broad yellow satin cuffs and revers and a fall of lace at his wrists and throat. Pru deliberately wore her oldest gown, a faded sprigged calico fit more for dusting than for dining. For a wonder, Hosannah had not scolded her about her dress, for she'd been foggier than usual all day.

"No more wine, thank you," Pru said coolly. Lillah had been dismissed by Claude, who had then sent Pride on an errand to the warehouse, leaving the two women alone with their guest.

"*Mais oui,* the beauty of your eyes and the fragrance of your hair is more intoxicating than wine, *chérie.*"

A light breeze through the open window stirred the candles on the table, their flickering light glittering strangely in Claude's black eyes. Jumbie eyes, Pru thought—without light or life. She lifted her head. "The fragrance you're referring to, sir, is no more than swamp gas caused by thousands of dead creatures rotting away under the mud. They give off such a powerful stench that I—"

"Prudence!"

"Well, they do, Granna. When the wind's off the marshes, I can scarcely bear to breathe."

"Ring for Sudie. We'll have our coffee in the parlor."

There was no bell and no Sudie, but Pru held her tongue. Ignoring the question inherent in Claude's lifted brows, she murmured something about seeing to the matter herself and hurried out into the breezeway.

She simply had to get away for a moment! With naught but oily phrases and flowery manners, the man terrified her. His eyes seemed actually to touch her body, silently whispering all manner of wicked threats. Just the thought of his hands on her made her ill!

Pru stared out through the latticed walls toward the sound. She could have seen the water from the window in her bedroom, but from here, all she could see was the faint glow of reflected moonlight above the marshes and the low ridge of shrubs along the shore.

"Gideon, where are you tonight?" she whispered. She could picture him standing tall and strong on the deck of the *Polly,* or sitting atop the rail of the crow's nest, one booted foot braced against the corner post as he gazed out over a restless surf.

Not an hour passed that she didn't think of him. The pain of what he had done to her had faded quickly; remembered was the magic she had glimpsed, the sweetness of his touch, of his kisses—the way he had made her feel the moment before he had...hurt her.

"*Chérie,* your *grand-mère* has need of someone to attend her."

Pru gasped and spun around. He had slipped up on her so silently that she hadn't known he was there. "Then I'd best hurry." She tried to dart past him, but he barred the way, and she was revolted by the musky scent of his body, poorly masked by a cloying perfume.

"That is only one of the reasons why I took upon my own shoulders the burden of your father's responsibilities," he continued smoothly, barring her escape. "The honor of *la famille* Delarouche demanded no less."

"My grandmother doesn't need your precious *famille* Delarouche! She had Pride and me and Lillah. Please let me pass."

"Ah, but you seemed so eager to escape from your *grand-mère* only a moment ago. Or were you so bored with my conversation, *peut-être?*"

It was not boredom that had sent Pru scurrying for cover, although she was tired to the teeth of hearing that satin-covered, lace-bedecked blow toad boast of the vast Delarouche holdings and the proud Delarouche titles—not to mention all the illustrious Delarouches who had fought and died so heroically for the glory of France.

Pity there couldn't have been one more such heroic sacrifice, Pru thought bitterly. Despite the crest embroidered on his satin cuffs, the man was a knave. She knew it in the very marrow of her bones, yet she had no way of proving it.

Screwing up her courage, she said, "If you Delarouches are such an honorable lot, then why did you steal our money from the sewing basket? What would your heroic ancestors think if they knew you were stealing the bread from the mouths of widows and orphans?"

Delarouche reached out to stroke her arm, and Pru snatched herself away from him as if his very touch were venomous. "Get—your—filthy—hands—off—me!"

"Shh, *calme-toi!* I have stolen nothing from you, *mon petit chou*—do I not bring you food? Do I not look after your *grand-mère?*"

Pru exploded. "Damn you, I won't have it! You have no right to take everything we have."

Delarouche had been smiling. Now his lips curled in something other than amusement, and in spite of the warm night, Pru shivered. "Ah, but I am your guardian, *chérie.*"

"You're a bloody, conniving thief!"

Dark eyes glittered in the moonlight that flowed through the lacework walls. "Have you told your *grand-mère* that I have stolen monies from you? How do you know she herself did not remove the gold?"

Pru's lips clamped into a tight line. He had her there, and well he knew it. If she mentioned the gold in the sewing basket to Hosannah in one of her lucid periods, that woman would demand to know where it had come from in the first place.

"*Oui? Oui?* And what did *madame* have to say to that?"

Pru stared at a basin of clabbering milk on the shelf beside her, wishing she dared throw it at him. Wishing Pride would come home. Wishing Papa had never gone off and left them. Wishing...

"I am waiting, *chérie*. Did your *grand-mère* say she would loose the dogs to rend my flesh? Did she say I must hang for my sins? Did she say I must go and never again present myself *à sa porte?*"

Pru refused to look up, and Claude reached out and caught her chin, tilting her face. She shifted her weight to attack, but he stepped back too quickly. "*Non, non, mon méchant enfant,*" he warned with a mocking smile. "Now...why do you not tell me where the rest of the money is hidden, eh? You have teased me long enough."

"There is no rest of the money." She wrenched her face from his grasp and pressed back against the sharp wooden edge of the shelf.

"No?" His voice was patently disbelieving. "No more gold sovereigns? No more Spanish dollars? No more French—"

The front door slammed, and Pru darted away, her heart pounding in her chest. "Just get out!" she seethed. "Get out of my house and don't you *ever* dare come back! That's my brother, and he'll—"

Moving as swiftly as a blacksnake, the Frenchman caught her by the arm and brought her hard against his body, crushing her in his arms. Before she could regain her balance, he pushed his face toward hers, cursing when she twisted to avoid his lips.

"Let me go, or I swear I'll kill you! I have a gun!" *Forgive the lie, God, but I'll make it up to you.*

Approaching bootsteps rang out clearly on the heart pine floor, and with a soft oath, Claude released her. "I will have you yet, *ma petite,*" he vowed.

Pru slumped against the shelf, shuddering with revulsion. The oversweet scent of his heated body had made her want to gag, and she was still breathing heavily as she tried to wipe the touch of his hands from her arms.

"Did you know that I'm now eighteen?" She watched closely for a reaction, but there was none. The man was either clever at keeping his own counsel, or the guardianship had been merely a ruse.

They were still measuring each other for the next attack when Pride burst through the door at the other end of the corridor. "Pru? Prudie, are you all right?"

Claude leaned close to her ear and grated, "One day, *mon petit chou,* you will regret your treatment of Claude Delarouche. There is an infamous bordello in Jamaica, *chérie,* and after I have grown weary of your charms, I will sell you for the small sum they will pay."

Drawing himself up to his full five feet six inches, he smiled at Pride. "Did you find the papers I requested, Andros?"

"The box was locked, and as I lacked the key, I'm afraid I had no luck."

Delarouche shook his head reprovingly. "I should not have thought such a trifling lack would give you more than a moment's pause." And at Pride's look of shock, he went on to say, "After all, you are your father's son, *non?* A talented thief would not allow such a small thing as a lock to stand in his way."

For long moments after the Frenchman had left them, slamming the front door behind him, Pride and Prudence stared at the place where he had disappeared.

"Did he say what I thought he said?" Pride asked wonderingly.

"He called you a thief. Not only that, he called Papa a thief!"

"I'll call him out." Pride made as if to leave, and Pru grabbed his arm. He tried to shake her off, swearing in a manner that brought a blush even to Prudence's cheeks.

"Dammit, Pru, enough is enough! He's too slick to leave anything lying about where it might be found and get him hung, but a ball through the heart is as good as a gallows any day!'

"Listen to me. If you call him out, he'll only kill you, and even if he doesn't, the law will hang you, and then Granna and I will have no one! Do you know what he threatened to do to me?"

"He'll not be alive to carry out any threats when I get through with him," Pride said with a determination Pru had never before heard in his voice. "Leave it be, Prudie. I don't know what he's up to, but we can't go on this way. Now, Granna's snoring her head off in the parlor. We'd best see if we can lug her into her bedroom."

"Pride, just promise me one thing. You won't call him out. Promise me you'll not go back to work for him, for he's too clever for either of us to ever find him out. The only thing we can do now is—is—" She racked her brain to come up with a workable solution to an insoluble problem. "Never mind, I'll think of something."

"Delarouche and that cousin of his go by the Leaky Cask about midnight to collect the take. I'm going to wait until they're busy at that and then I'm going to row out to the *Saint Germaine* and see what I can find there. I doubt me they'll leave much of a watch aboard."

They had entered the house proper, and lowered their voices in case Hosannah had awoken in their absence. "You'll do no such thing. Of course he'll leave a watch aboard, maybe more than one. And just what am I supposed to do if you don't come back? Row out there and ask for you?"

"Oh, hell, I wish Gideon was here," Pride muttered. "I figured he'd likely be in and out of Portsmouth collecting cargo all summer."

Pru wished it, as well, from the bottom of her heart. Not only because she felt all hollow and aching inside without him, but because, despite the fact that he'd washed his hands of her, she would still have trusted him with her life.

It took both of them to get their grandmother into her bedroom, for poor Hosannah's joints were badly swollen, and she'd imbibed more than her usual amount of remedy. "I wish Lillah would live in. Shall I go fetch her?" Pride asked.

"It would take too long. I'll just slip off her shoes and loosen her stays and let her sleep in her gown tonight. Come morning, I'll tell her she's already been up for hours, and only dozed a bit in her clothes after breakfast."

"Cap'n, they be talk about the girl," Crow said as he joined Gideon at the helm. They were sailing with a crew of nine men, two newly recruited from the docks of Queen Anne's Towne in lieu of being jailed for fighting and general drunkenness.

"Talk?"

"Bad talk. Man talk. They say she live with whaling camp, she be no good no more."

Gideon swore quietly as he steered the long, high-prowed sloop through the treacherous currents of the inlet. Having sailed these waters since he was fifteen years old, he preferred to rely on his own abilities on that particular stretch of water. "Don't they know she worked as a lad? Didn't you tell them that?"

"You think they take the word of a breed?"

If there was bitterness there, Gideon chose not to hear it. Prejudice was an ugly matter, and Crow, being the spawn of an Indian out of a female slave, was doubly cursed. But Gideon had a more pressing matter on his hands.

He had ruined the girl. By keeping her on in his camp, even after he'd discovered that she was a woman, he had ruined her future.

Yet what sort of future could such a hoyden have had? Marriage to a decent man? Children? She'd been robbing sailors at gunpoint long before he'd ever laid eyes on her, if rumor was to be believed.

Still, according to Crow, no one seemed the wiser about her nocturnal misdeeds. As the daughter of Andros, who had once owned nearly everything on the island, the little witch had evidently been held in some esteem. At least until she'd been seen returning to the village with a whaler after an absence of some three months. The fact that Crow was known as Gideon McNair's man, and McNair's crew was known to be made up of reformed rakes, drunkards, thieves and runaways had done the rest.

The villagers could not be expected to believe that she'd been innocent until almost the very last. Gideon himself hadn't credited her with that. Why should they believe that not one of his men save Crow and himself had even known she was female?

Crow stood silently as Gideon went through the torment of the damned. There was no way he could undo what was done—no way save one, and he was not yet ready to face that.

"She be in trouble bad, Cap'n."

Gideon's heart froze for a small eternity. "In...trouble?" It wasn't possible. Not the first time. The only time. Besides, it was too soon to be sure.

"I see the way they look at her, those peoples. The boy, he know, too."

Swearing softly, Gideon tried to tell himself that he was not to blame—at least, not solely. The wicked scamp had been a threat to all decent, law-abiding men; she'd been a notorious little cutpurse! Besides that, she was a consummate liar.

All the same, whatever small chance a girl in her circumstances might once have had, he alone had destroyed. And if he'd gotten her with child, then he would have to accept his responsibilities.

"All right, dammit, I'll go see what can be done about the matter. *Make ready to come about!*" he shouted. As his crew scrambled to haul in the main, he spun the wheel, laying the *Polly* hard over onto a southwesterly course.

Crow was grinning as he watched young Ben race to trim the luffing jib. "Them Cullywangers up the York River be bound to wait a few more day for they fine furniture," h said, referring to the valuable cargo stored in the hold that was consigned to a prominent Virginia businessman.

Horace Cullywanger could plant his arse on a pork barrel for all Gideon cared. He knew for a fact that the man had trafficked with pirates in his day.

"We could take the girl up the banks to Hatteras, Cap'n. She be a fine help for Mistress Maggie."

"Maggie don't need no vixen like Haskell—Prudence, or whatever the devil she calls herself. Not with young Isaac at the impressionable age!"

Besides, Gideon had other plans for Mistress Andros. He'd been fighting a losing battle with himself for too long now. It was time he, too, came about and set a different course.

"You *what?*" Pru dropped to sit on the front step and stared at her twin.

"Dammit, Pru, I couldn't let him get away with it! It was an insult to our honor."

"Honor be damned, you don't know one blessed thing about dueling! All you're going to do is get yourself killed, and then where will our precious honor be?"

"As a matter of fact, I've been studying up on it. I'll need a second, of course, and a—"

"You'll need a brain, first of all. Pride, you can't even hit the broad side of an ox at five paces, much less a man at ten!"

"You want me to practice? Horrible waste of oxen, but—"

"Damn you, will you *listen?* If you've gone and got yourself in this mess, then I suppose there's no getting out of it. The slimy toad would likely come after you and run you through in your bed."

"Oh, there'll be no running through. I flat out told him if he choses swords, it'd be cold-blooded murder, for I'd never even held one in my hand, much less carved up a man with it."

"My God, you didn't!"

"You should've heard him laugh! He thought it was the funniest thing he'd ever heard."

"I'll wager it was," said Pru, wondering if she could appeal to the man's sense of fairness.

"But the upshot of it was, he chose pistols. I reckon he don't think much of my chances with a pistol, either. He didn't seem too worried."

Pru could have wept. "You ninny, of course he's not worried!"

"Well, dammit, it's better than the other. I ain't much of a hand at carving, but at least I've hunted all my life."

"Nor much of a hand at thinking," Pru muttered. "All right," she said after several moments had passed. "Here's the way we'll go about it. This time of year, there's considerable ground fog. If I go dressed as Haskell and wear my hair tucked up under Papa's old tricorne—"

"Oh, no. No, indeed, girl, you're to stay at home where I won't have to be concerned about your collecting a stray bullet in your bonnet."

"But it's the only possible way, don't you see? I'm an excellent shot, and you—well, this is no time to mince words—you never were nearly as good with a gun as I was, and there's naught to be gained by pretending any different."

Lifting his chin, Pride said, "If Papa had spent as much time teaching me as he did you, I'd have been twice the marksman you are. There's no difference in us but that Papa thought it was a lark to have a daughter who could ride and shoot circles around half the men on the island."

Pru stretched out her long legs, allowing the sun to soak through the triple layers of drawers, petticoat and calico skirt. "That shows just how much you know. In the first place, there's a great deal of difference between us, and in the second place, if you start shooting circles, we'll all have to run for cover."

She smiled at him, the hint of laughter in her gray-green eyes making Pride smile in response. If it would lift her spirit, which had been in sad repair ever since they came home, he would fight a dozen duels. "All right, Mistress

Vinegar-tongue, but we'll hear no more about your taking my place.''

Pru continued to smile. Vinegar-tongued she might be, but she knew enough to be silent when no good would come of further arguments.

Pride grew more and more nervous as the appointed day approached. Although he hadn't gone back to Delarouche's warehouse to work—indeed, both men seemed intent on avoiding each other until they were to meet at the clearing on the lower soundside—he kept a close watch on the waterfront from the window under the eaves in Pru's second-floor bedroom. He was doing so now.

Gideon, dammit, where are you? Pride had never needed a friend the way he did now, and Albert Thurston would no longer serve. After what his former best friend had said about Pru, Pride had been forced to blacken his eyes and ruin his bucktoothed smile.

Nor would the swollen fist he had gained in return serve him well when it came to handling whatever pistols the Frenchman provided. Like as not, Delarouche would come up with a pair of fancy weapons fit more for a lady's use than a man's, and the only guns Pride had ever shot were his father's old flintlock pistol and Albert's father's fowling piece.

Pride wasn't real sure of the rules pertaining to duels. Here in the colonies, except among the landed gentry, they were apt to be rather informal, but he'd feel a damned sight better if he knew all the Frenchman knew.

He practiced daily with an imaginary pistol, but it was not enough—not nearly enough. He had a notion that Delarouche, for all his foppishness, would be deadly with either sword or gun. He'd heard Jacques, that cousin of his, bragging one day about the duels the pair of them had fought growing up together back in France.

That was another thing. Jacques would be his cousin's second, and Pride trusted that pinch-mouthed polecat even less than he did Delarouche. There was something about both men that made his flesh crawl. He couldn't put his finger on what it was—not yet. But he would.

Though he had stopped working there, Pride had not given up searching the warehouses, despite what he told Pru. Waiting until both Frenchmen had returned to the ship for the night, he would let himself in the same way he had as a small boy playing with Albert.

Something he overheard just today indicated that Delarouche himself had conducted an exhaustive search of every inch of Andros property. Looking for what? A place to hide smuggled goods? It was certainly not unheard of for a warehouseman to seek to avoid paying the repressive crown taxes. Perhaps his father had been among them—Pride neither knew nor cared at this point.

But Urias's possible smuggling was hardly enough to explain Delarouche's accusations. If there was naught but a bit of dark-of-the-moon trading involved, why would the Frenchman be so determined to ruin them?

There was more than that at stake. And whatever it was, it was up to Pride to put an end to it, one way or another.

With narrowed eyes, he continued to scan the horizon, hoping against hope for a sight of Gideon's sloop. There were several vessels lying at anchor, awaiting their turn at the docks, but Gideon's was not among them.

Sighing, Pride had turned to leave the room when out of the corner of his eye, he glimpsed something that made him catch his breath and hold it. A single mast, rigged fore and aft, the staysail and jib a shade lighter than the main.

With a brief prayer of thanks, he let out a whoop and raced for the stairs.

Chapter Fourteen

The devil of it was that Pride refused to listen to reason. The meeting had been set for the following morning at first show of light, and still he refused to allow Pru to second him.

"Then, dammit, *you* second *me!*" she exclaimed, exasperated.

"Cry off, Pru. This ain't London, you know. Delarouche won't care if I have a second or not. It won't change the outcome."

Pru groaned. "Please, *please* let Haskell stand up for you. I don't trust that snake for one minute."

"Haskell's done you enough mischief already. If you must know, it ain't the first fight I've been in on your account since we've been back, Prudie. Likely, it won't be the last."

Pru went dead still at that. "What are you talking about?"

"Nothing. Nothing at all," he said hastily. "There's no law says a man has to have a second. If Gideon won't act for me—"

"Gideon! Is he here?"

"I saw the *Polly* headed in—leastwise, I think it was her. The sails looked the same."

Pru fought to still the sudden leaping of her pulses. What difference did it make if he were here or not. He had sent her away without a word of goodbye, much less a word of apology. He had to have known she loved him. After that first kiss, there was no way she could have possibly hidden it.

But at the moment, her own feelings were the least of her worries. A hundred Gideon McNairs acting as Pride's second could not make her brother a better marksman. "Pride, I've gone round and round, and there's no other way. You've simply got to allow me to go in your stead," she said flatly.

"Leave off, Pru. Women ain't allowed to duel. It's the law."

"Nor are men—legally, at least. What do you know of the law?"

"About as much as you do."

"Well, legal or not, someone has to go along to see that foreign devil doesn't prime your gun with black pepper."

Pride grinned broadly, reminding Pru suddenly of their father, who had been a handsome man, even in his middle years. "If I'm lucky, Gideon'll be there to see that I ain't cheated."

"I wish you would change your mind."

He tugged on a length of her hair, which she'd been drying in the late-afternoon sun on the bench outside the kitchen. "Never you fear, I'll come out all right. Claude's got to be thirty if he's a day. He's practically an old man."

Gideon must be all of thirty, Pru thought, and he was definitely no old man. But for the moment she would let it pass. She needed no further arguments, not if her plan were to succeed.

It was still pitch-dark when Pride rapped softly on Pru's door the following morning. She knew he'd been out the night before, when he should have been at home sleeping.

"Pru? You awake yet?" he called softly. As if she had dared close her eyes all night.

He stuck his head in the door, and she pretended to rub the sleep from her eyes. "Is it time so soon? Is Gideon going to act for you?"

"He didn't get in before dark. I waited, but the tide was out so far that he laid off and came in on the high tide. I'm off to fetch him now. Just thought I'd let you know, you don't have to worry about me."

Pru closed her eyes in a moment of despair. If it weren't so serious, a body might even think he was looking forward to it.

Boys!

"Will you wish me luck?"

She wished he would fall down and break his blasted leg, was what she wished! "You know I do," she said instead.

"Listen, Prudie, it's still way early yet, plenty of time for me to fetch Gideon. But happen I'm late, would you do this for me? Get word to Claude to wait, that I'll be along directly."

"I shouldn't worry about him crying off," she said dryly. "I'm sure he's looking forward to the chance to blast your lights and liver into the kingdom to come."

He grinned broadly, and with a jaunty salute, he was gone.

A few minutes later she heard him close the front door behind him, his footsteps clattering across the porch as he set out for their old skiff.

It occurred to Pru as she leapt out of bed that he might not have grinned quite so broadly if he'd had any notion what she had in mind.

It was for the best, she told herself as she crept into Pride's bedroom and removed a shirt from his clothespress. The buff nankeen breeches she borrowed were a pair he had outgrown this past winter.

Using a length of muslin that had been set aside for a night rail, she bound her breasts, taking care not to impair the free movement of her right arm. That done, she slipped on the shirt and knotted the stock high around her throat.

As for her feet, it was either wear a pair of her mother's cloth slippers or a pair of Pride's boots, which were far too big. She couldn't afford to risk tripping at the wrong time—better to go barefoot. In the fog, no one would be likely to notice that her feet were surprisingly small for a young man of eighteen.

Now all that was left to do was get there before Gideon and Pride did. She wasn't worried about the legalities of being a woman or of dueling without both parties being seconded. Nor, if she knew Delarouche, would he be concerned with anything other than dispatching his opponent at the very first opportunity.

And unless her timing went awry, then it was she who would give him that opportunity. She was counting on Delarouche's eagerness to make him early, and on lengthy explanations to delay her brother.

Casting an anxious eye at the sky, Pru was relieved to note that it had yet to show the first sliver of light. She still had some ways to go, for the local "settling grounds" was some distance away.

A nervous giggle escaped her lips as she let herself out the door. What if some other quarreling pair had made an assignation for the same time? Would she and Claude be forced to cool their heels while the other two settled their differences with fists, knives, swords or guns?

Not bloody likely. Within an all too short time, the Frenchman would be doing his damnedest to blow a hole through her chest—with that weasel-faced cousin of his most likely cheering him on!

The last thing she did before slipping out was to tilt the candle globe so that it smoked a bit. Running her fingers inside, she transferred the resultant soot to her cheeks, smearing it onto her chin in the hope that it would pass in the half-light for a short beard. Feature for feature, the twins were surprisingly alike, though Pride's face had lately taken on an angular look that Pru's lacked.

It would have to do. She would keep her chin buried in her stock, and her hat pulled low over her eyes. With any luck, Delarouche would be fooled. Most people, she had long since learned, saw precisely what they expected to see, and what man would expect to see a woman taking a man's place on the dueling grounds?

The clearing was no more than a small knoll rising slightly above the level of the surrounding marshes. Several large cedars and a few live oaks, shaped and stunted by the relentless winds, marked the edges, the center being flat and clear and perfectly suited for such an endeavor.

The marshes were still shrouded in the same mist that swirled around the trunks of the sprawling cedars. The air was surprisingly cool, for though there was now a glimmer of gray light on the eastern horizon, the sun had not yet begun to rise.

Following the narrow, white-sand path that ran between two broad marshes, Pru felt the beat of her heart all the way down to the soles of her feet. *God, let him come before Pride does. Let him come before I lose my courage and run away. Steady my hand so that I can spare the bastard's miserable life, for I've no wish to have the weight of his soul on my conscience, but God, please let me wound him in the most painful place you can think of so that he'll leave us alone from now on!*

Gideon heard the boy out, dressing as he listened. He'd been lying awake aboard the *Polly,* waiting until a decent hour to go in search of Prudence, when he heard the bump of a boat alongside the hull.

"So you see, we've no time to waste!" Pride said, having summed up the whole affair in as few words as possible.

"You say this Frenchman owns everything that once belonged to your father?" He pulled on his trousers over his smallclothes and fastened them up the front.

Pride snatched a white lawn shirt off a peg and shoved it at him. "Mr. Simpson was acting for Delarouche when he bought Papa's warehouses and ordinaries, but he didn't let on. The first we knew about it was when the Frenchman showed up last fall."

Gideon wondered if the boy realized that his father had also owned the island's best-known bordello.

"I think he fancies Pru. God knows why, she ain't the sort a man usually takes to, even if she is my own sister. Trouble is, she can outdo most men at most anything she sets her mind to, and a man don't like that in a female. All the same, when we got back here and Delarouche told me Granna had signed us both over to him, he sort of hinted—well, what I mean is, he let on that Prudie—hell, Gideon, you know what I mean!'

Gid buckled on a wide belt and reached for his knife. While the boy went on speaking, he debated whether or not to carry a gun. He would prefer to murder the bastard with his bare hands, but there were conventions to be observed in a duel.

"Of course, now that I'm eighteen, that don't count, but with a woman—I reckon that's a different matter. Could you hurry with those boots, please? You see, a woman—well, I reckon she has to belong to a father or a brother or a husband or someone like that, else who's going to protect her? Are you ready? Then let's shove off!"

Gideon sent him a level look. "If this French devil's as eager to have your liver as you say, he'll likely wait."

Leaving Urias's old skiff tied up to the *Polly,* the two men climbed down into the launch a few minutes later and commenced rowing towards shore. "Trouble is, if I'm not there," Pride explained, panting, "I've got a bad feeling Pru might do something crazy, and Delarouche'll think it's me, and—just hurry, will you? It'll be quicker to go along the shore instead of through the village. Make a set for that dead tree rising up out of the water below the village."

Both then were silent as they bent to their task. The distance was not so great by water, but Pride was sweating heavily by the time they hauled up the skiff on the shore and leaped out. He pointed. "Yonder grove of trees, that's the place," he whispered as he set off at a lope along the edge of the marsh.

With his longer stride, Gideon caught up easily. "What did you mean a while back, that your sister might do something crazy?" he wasn't even breathing hard, despite the fact that he'd just rowed a heavy launch near on two miles.

"I mean—you don't know—my sister! She's just wild enough—to want to protect me by—"

Gideon could feel the warmth drain from his body. "You don't mean she—" But God, yes, she would! It was exactly what she would do!

"I mean she's—likely out there right now—a-fixing to—get her fool head shot off!"

The image was shockingly clear in Gideon's imagination. For the sake of his sanity, he refused to allow himself to believe it. "Surely not even Haskell would—"

"Take my place? She did her best to—talk me—into it!"

"Sweet Jesus," Gideon breathed as he streaked past the younger man and raced toward the clearing. She wouldn't! That wicked little heathen! Once he got his hands on her, he was going to teach her a lesson she'd be long in forgetting!

Frantic, Gideon tried to recall every remnant of knowledge he had ever collected on the subject of duels. There was little enough, for among the sort of men he had associated with for the bulk of his life such affairs had been informal, to say the least. Usually a matter of hacking away until one or the other dropped dead.

The sound of two sets of pounding feet broke the early-morning silence. From some thirty feet behind him, Gideon could hear the air tearing in and out of Pride's lungs. He swore silently and increased the length of his stride.

"Gid, hurry! The sun's already showing on the horizon!"

Gideon didn't need to be told. He was well aware that an unscrupulous opponent might take advantage of its blinding rays.

"Cinq!" The nasal cry rang out in the stillness.

Five. They broke through to the clearing unexpectedly, just in time to see two ghostly figures pacing away from each other.

"Six!"

Six! Unconsciously, Gideon slipped his knife from his belt.

"Sept!" The word rang out clearly, masking the sound of Gideon's protest, and he started to run forward.

Before the next pace could be called, the taller of the two figures turned and fired. Gideon flung the knife at that very instant. Without waiting to see if it struck home, he raced across the clearing and fell to his knees over the prone form, still seeing in his mind's eye the look of hurt surprise on Pru's dirty little face the instant before she had crumpled silently to the ground.

"You filthy bastard! You shot her in the back!" Pride screamed. He stopped only long enough to be sure the fallen man was not going to move, and then he started after the second, who had slipped through the shadows without a backward glance for his fallen kinsman.

"Stay, lad! Let him go," Gideon called softly.

Pride wheeled around and ran over to where he knelt beside Pru's still form. "How is she? Is she still breathing? The murdering bastard fired on the count of seven!" Pride dropped to his knees beside his sister, his tears falling on her face. "She had no blasted right to go in my place! She was afraid for me, afraid that miserable bastard would k-kill me, and now he's—"

"Dead," announced Gideon, his voice marked by a calmness he was far from feeling. "And she'll be dead, too, unless you stop leaking all over her and help me get her somewhere safe." Cold to the marrow of his bones, Gideon eased the still form over onto her belly. She'd been shot in the back, just under her right arm. Still, she didn't seem to be bleeding too badly.

Carefully, he tugged her shirttail from her trousers and lifted it high up onto her shoulders. At the sight of a bright red stain seeping slowly through the layers of muslin, he squeezed his eyes tightly shut for a moment. He felt like crying. Cursing, laughing and crying at the same time.

"Um—that's only her binding," Pride told him, wiping his wet cheeks on his sleeve. "For her—uh, you know. Bosom."

"We'd best leave her bound up for now. At least it'll slow the bleeding."

"We'll take her home. Lillah'll know what to do."

Home. A pair of pitiful, homeless orphans. God help the poor fool who got tangled up with this pair, for he'd not be able to help himself, Gideon thought as he lifted the fragile creature into his arms.

Just before they left the clearing, Pride crossed to where the Frenchman had fallen. The handle of Gid's knife was sticking out of his chest, and he grabbed it and pulled, feeling his throat convulse when it jammed against the breastbone. Jerking it free, he cleaned the blade by stabbing it several times in the sandy ground. Someone would have to see to the remains, he supposed. The cousin, Jacques, could handle it. The same way he had handled counting off the paces.

Had they planned it between them? The count was supposed to have been ten. It was always ten! Even he knew that much!

"I don't know where you live," Gideon said quietly. "Would it be better to go by boat or by foot?"

Thankful for the distraction, Pride came about. "By foot," he said after only the briefest hesitation. It would be at least as quick, and there was talk enough on the waterfront of his sister's misdeeds without this. "I'll come back for the boat later."

Gideon carried her as if she weighed no more than a kitten. The bullet had gone clean through the fleshy part, grazing a rib, perhaps. It had come out alongside her right breast. Blood was beginning to seep through her shirt, and Gideon prayed with all his heart that she would not lose too much before he could cleanse the wound and bind a wadding tightly against it. She was going to be miserable when she woke up, but he was almost sure her lung wasn't torn. There was no bubbling sound when she breathed. And even if one of her ribs had been smashed, she would likely heal well enough as long as she didn't take a fever.

Soot on her face. God, what a little minx she was! As if a mere application of lampblack could disguise those peach-down cheeks, that stubborn little chin, those lips that had tantalized him even as her great sea-green eyes had laughed at him.

How the devil had she ever managed to fool him as long as she had? he asked himself for the hundredth time.

The answer was no more satisfactory than ever. He'd seen what he expected to see—no more, no less. The last thing he'd been interested in finding was a woman to love—

To love! Where the devil had that thought come from? Far from loving the chit, he could have turned her over his knee and tanned her backside for the merry chase she'd led him!

And was still leading him, he sadly feared. He had yet to meet another woman who could harden his loins, heat his temper and soften his heart, all the while dressed like a ragged waterfront urchin.

"How is she? Has she opened her eyes yet?" Pride asked anxiously. He led the way, as if by doing so he could somehow smooth the path.

The path was smooth enough, it was the distance that bothered Gideon. Pru was beginning to stir in his arms, a frown drawing her silken brows together now as soft little whimpers were beginning to accompany every other breath. "She's coming around. I'd like to get her settled before she wakes up completely. She'll be in considerable pain."

"I should have known. By God, I should have locked her in her room!" Trotting on ahead, Pride smashed a fist into his palm and swore as worry ate into him. "Even then, she'd just have gone out the window. Likely she did anyhow."

They turned in toward a weathered cottage, the peaked roof extending its shelter over a broad porch. There were two small glass windows in the front, and a smaller one up under the eaves on the side facing them, the whole, except for the massive chimney, sitting several feet off the ground on thin piers. In the back, a latticed breezeway led to an outbuilding Gideon recognized as a kitchen.

"This is it. Pray Granna is still abed."

But as luck would have it, it was Hosannah who greeted them at the door. On seeing a stranger bearing her bleeding granddaughter up the steps, she promptly uttered a shriek, dropped her cane and fainted. Pride dashed forward to catch her, and Gideon was left standing helplessly, his arms just now beginning to ache from carrying his burden some two miles from the clearing.

Lillah glided into the room, taking in the tableau in one glance. Without a word she turned and led the way up the stairs, leaving Pride to look after his grandmother, who had come to and was making pitiful little gibbering sounds.

"I bring kettle an' cloth," she announced. "That her bed. Wipe off her feet, they be muddy." With that pronouncement she left the tall, yellow-haired stranger to deal with Prudence, muttering to herself as she hurried down the stairs and out to the kitchen.

It was no more than she had foreseen in the castings she had read only yesterday. Trouble. Death. Not the death of one of her people, yet a death that would bring even more trouble in its wake.

Lillah knew who the yellow-haired man was. She also knew that if he were here, his man, Crow, could not be far away. A slow smile kindled in her dark eyes.

Let the boy look after the mizzus. Let the man, Gideon, look after the girl. It was time that young miss found someone with a stronger will than her own. Lillah had known the moment she looked into the eyes of the handsome man with the marked face that he was the man who had made that child into a woman.

Which was more than all Hosannah's preachments and Lillah's potions put together had been able to do.

It was the pain under her arm that awakened Prudence. That and the pounding in her head. She opened her eyes and examined the shadows that chased one another across the ceiling of her bedroom. The sun was low in the western sky.

Western? That meant it was evening. Had she overslept, then?

"Would you like a sip of tea?"

At the sound of the familiar voice, she lifted her head abruptly and cried out at the searing pain that streaked through her side. "You! How did you—what are you—"

"Yes, me. You'll learn the how and why of it when you're feeling better. Now, have a sip of this, and then close your eyes again."

Because she was thirsty, Pru drank what was offered, wrinkling her nose at the taste. "It's vile. Are you trying to poison me?"

Gideon smiled. It came to her slowly as the fog began to lift that he looked even more dreadful than she felt. His eyes were sunken and red-rimmed, his clothes looked as if he'd slept in them, and there was a bronze-colored stubble on his jaw that partially obscured the mark on his cheek.

"I slept the day away, didn't I?"

"Mmm-hmm." He sprawled in the chair, one of Granna's prized hoop-backed chairs from the parlor downstairs. His long legs covered half the width of Pru's bedroom.

"Might I know what you're doing here?" she demanded.

"Resting my bones until just now, when you woke me up. Do you need to use the pot?"

"Do I need to *what?*"

He shrugged. "You know—pi—"

"Hush! I know what you meant!"

"Then why'd you ask?" He still hadn't roused from his sprawled position since handing her the tumbler half full of some bitter-tasting tea.

"Because I—because you— Dammit, Gideon, what are you doing here?"

"I just told you. I've been sleeping."

"You mean you've been here while I was sleeping?" Pru drew the light counterpane up under her chin with one hand even as she felt beneath it with the other. She was not wearing her trousers—or her shirt. She was certainly bound up tightly enough, but as far as she could tell without looking, she wasn't even wearing her night rail!

He had seen her in far less, she reminded herself, feeling the heat creep up to stain her cheeks. "Gideon, I don't understand any of this, but I—'' She made the mistake of trying to turn over onto her side, the better to confront him. A cry of pain escaped her, and he was on his feet instantly.

"Easy now, don't move. If you need to shift, let me turn you, all right?''

She was whimpering, partly from pain, but more from fear. Only now were fragmented bits of what had happened coming back to her. "The duel—where's Pride? I want to see my brother, *now!*''

He held her down with one hand, stroking her hair back from her face with the other. There was no return of the fever that had flared up that first night, which was what they had all feared most. Pride had sailed with Crow for Queen Anne's Towne to fetch a doctor out to the island. They weren't expected to return before the following evening, at best, and unless the wind picked up considerably, it would be even later than that.

"Lie still, will you? There's a good girl. The medicine I gave you will start taking effect any moment now, and you'll rest easier, wait and see.''

Gideon watched her closely. Her lids were beginning to grow heavy. It had been a whopping dose, but the serving woman had said it was necessary. Knowing his little Haskell, it probably was, for she'd never been one to lie quietly and let others fight her battles for her.

Long after her last sleepy protest had died away, Gideon continued to stroke her brow, now and then allowing his fingers to trail around the gentle slope of her cheek and curl under her chin.

"So fierce,'' he whispered. "So ready to do battle for those you love, aren't you, my little fireball?''

She was far too fierce to be so fragile—far too fragile to be so fierce.

Gideon had now learned considerably more about the girl he had taken under his wing with the misguided intent of setting her feet on a more acceptable path. From what he'd seen in the Andros household these past few days, he'd been able to surmise a good bit more.

It was due in part to her father's upbringing and in part to her own reckless nature that she had ended up spending three months in a whaling camp, thus ruining what shaky reputation she'd had left.

Not that he discounted his own part in it. Still, under the circumstances, how could he have known? In the beginning he'd thought he was doing a good service for a pair of wayward lads. By the time he'd learned of his mistake, he was so deeply ensnared in her wicked spell he hadn't been able to call his soul his own, much less his mind!

He had come to Portsmouth to set matters aright. And now, damned if he hadn't ended up compromising her even more. How could he have known that a friend of hers by the name of Annie something or other would come rushing up the stairs and burst into the room just as Gideon was changing the dressing?

"Are you a doctor?" the girl had gasped, seeing him supporting her bare-breasted friend on one arm while he reached for a fresh dressing with the other.

"No, mistress, I'm a whaler," he'd snapped before he thought, and he'd known by the way she covered her mouth with her hand and backed out of the room that he'd as good as condemned them both.

All right, dammit, so he had compromised her and then sent her home to suffer for his sins. And as if that weren't bad enough, he had a witness to the fact that he'd just spent two days and a night sleeping in a chair in her bedroom!

What else could he have done? The old woman was a dead loss, the boy had gone for help, and he wasn't about to trust his little Haskell to some long-necked freedwoman who kept mumbling about castings and burnt chicken feathers and dried snakes' tails! If that was Crow's Lillah, then he could have her and welcome! Gideon had barred her from the room and taken over the nursing duties himself.

It wasn't the first time, he reminded himself as he fought back a yawn. After all, he'd delivered his own son, God rest the boy. He'd nursed his Uncle Will's swamp fever until that last mutiny that had put an end to the career of the *Morning Star* and her infamous crew. In all his years at sea, first as an honest seaman and then as a reluctant freebooter, before he turned to whaling, Gideon had treated more wounds than he cared to remember.

The least he could do was to look after the woman he was going to marry.

Chapter Fifteen

"Where's my grandmother?" Prudence demanded.

"She's settled in her bed by the window, so that she can watch all the comings and goings. Now give me your foot."

"Where's my brother?"

"Sailed aboard the *Polly* four days ago, gone to fetch a doctor. Haskell, don't be so damned stiff-necked, I'm only wanting to put your slipper on so you can sit up in a chair while your bedding is changed."

"I can put on my own slippers, and don't call me Haskell! Now, will you get out of my bedroom?" Lying flat on her back, feeling more helpless than she'd felt in all her eighteen years, Pru screamed for Lillah at the top of her lungs, and winced at the sudden pain.

Gideon reached under the light counterpane and located the foot in question. "Won't hear you. She's gone somewhere."

Pru kicked sharply, managing to free her foot, but the effort cost her dearly. Fresh pain shot all the way up her side, burning under her right arm like a hot poker. She swore softly and fought back tears. She was weak, hurting, helpless and frightened. It was a combination she could never abide.

Willing herself dry-eyed again, she lay on her back and glared up at Gideon McNair. Had she truly believed she loved him? The man was a despot. She had a dim recollection of being bullied into all manner of disgusting things at his hands. Turn this way, Haskell, turn that way—open your mouth, Haskell, raise your head.

She touched her hair, and her eyes narrowed in realization. He had actually braided her hair! Lillah would never have done such a lumpy, uneven job of it, and Granna's poor crippled fingers could barely manage to hold a tumbler without dropping it.

It was the first morning she had wakened without feeling as if her head were stuffed full of cotton bolls. The pain was worse, but her mind, at least, seemed clear. She'd sooner have the pain than the awful fuzzy-mindedness that had swaddled her since...

"Gideon, what happened? I remember hearing Jacques begin the count, but I don't recall firing."

"You didn't."

"Oh, no," she wailed softly, turning away to stare blindly at the wall. Then nothing was settled, nothing at all. They still belonged to Claude, and he could turn them out whenever he took a notion. Not for a single moment did she believe that tomfoolery he had spated about building them a house on the point. No man in his right mind would build a house right out on the ocean, where the storm tides would wash it clean away. For reasons of his own, he simply wanted them gone. Or dead.

"Prudence..."

Her name sounded strange on Gideon's tongue. She turned back to face him. He hadn't moved, but was still seated on the edge of her bed, a small silk slipper dangling incongruously from one of his work-hardened hands. He had shaved, she realized, with a dim recollection of having seen him at some time or other with a dark growth on his jaw. She recalled being surprised that it wasn't as pale as the sun-bleached hair on his head.

He looked far more rested now, and he'd changed his clothing. The plain white cambric shirt strained across his massive shoulders. It was turned back over his forearms, and she found herself staring at the hard muscular contours. His sun-bronzed arms were covered with golden-tipped hair that reminded her of the hair on his body.

Swallowing hard, she forced herself to look away, but even then, her senses betrayed her. She could feel his warmth. How could any presence so solid and reassuring be at the same time so unsettling?

Her nostrils flared at his clean, masculine scent. It was particular to Gideon. Her father had smelled of rum and the tobacco he smoked in the carved pipe that had been made especially for him by a pipe-maker in Maryland. Pride usually smelled vaguely goaty. As for the men at the camp, they'd all smelled the same—of whale offal.

"How long has it been?" she asked, meaning how long since the duel. How long since she'd disgraced herself by losing a match she'd thought sure to win.

"This is the fourth day."

At this news, she struggled to sit up in bed, only to be flattened by the pain in her side. "I missed, didn't I? And that miserable worm shot me! Oh, God, I'm so ashamed!"

Gideon reached for her hands, enveloping them in his much larger ones. "You damned well should be ashamed! That was a tomfool thing to do, taking your brother's place! Didn't you learn anything in all those months in my camp?"

"One thing I learned was to despise any bully who takes advantage just because he's big as a buffalo and happens to have been born male!"

"Show me a man—or a buffalo, come to that—who can win out over a mouthy female who fires off her tongue like a load of grapeshot on the least provocation!"

She ran a speaking gaze over the breadth of his chest. "With a target as broad as a buffalo, I could hardly miss!"

Gideon merely lifted his brows in a sardonic reminder of a large target she had not only missed, but failed even to strike at, and her brief burst of anger collapsed in a noisy sigh.

"All right, not with an iron, perhaps. But at least with a pistol, I'm a damned fine marksman. That's why I had to do it, don't you see? Pride would've flinched and fired wide of the mark."

"Or not fired at all. You didn't."

Another bitter reminder. She refused to meet his eyes, and finally sighed in exasperation. "Would you please stop hanging over me like a blasted thundercloud? You make me nervous!"

She hadn't meant to admit to that, but it was just as well. If he kept on hovering over her, treating her as if she had no more feelings than a side of beef, she would end up doing something supremely stupid. Like weeping. Or throwing herself at him again.

"We'd better get you dressed and on your aft end instead of flat on your back. It don't do to let the blood settle in one place."

"Lillah can do it."

"Lillah has all she can handle looking after your grandmother. You didn't do that poor old woman any good with your latest mischief, either. All she does it lie about in her bed ringing that damned bell of hers."

"Granna's not well. It's not her fault her poor joints are all swelled up. She hurts."

She also drank far more than was good for her, but Gideon kindly refrained from saying as much. And when she drank, she did foolish things, such as offering her granddaughter to a bastard who wasn't worth the dirt on the soles of her boots.

Again, he kindly refrained from saying as much. Unless he missed his guess, Hosannah Gilbert had already forgotten her own part in this whole unsavory business. God help that poor woman who had the care of her.

"Ready to get up?" he asked silkily, watching the play of expressions across Haskell's face. What was it about this contrary female that got inside him and tangled up his reason like a length of bindweed? The woman had been trouble from the first time he ever laid eyes on her, when she jumped out in front of him and shoved a damned blunderbuss in his face and commanded him to stand and deliver. She wasn't just headstrong, she was reckless!

So the little scamp had backbone—too much backbone and not enough brains was worse than no backbone at all. It had been known to get a person killed!

He stared at her morosely for several moments, and then he said, "Delarouche is dead."

Her mouth fell open, and Gideon's gaze was captured by a row of even white teeth that bracketed a small pink tongue. God help him! Moving abruptly, he got up off the bed and turned to stare out the window.

"But how? What happened? Gideon, tell me all of it!" For once in her young life, she looked badly shaken. It was all he could do not to gather her into his arms and offer her comfort.

"Delarouche fired on the count of seven. You were struck in the back, just under the arm, and you cracked your head when you fell," he said gruffly, "Nye and I got there just in time to see it happen."

"But Claude— How did he die?"

He waited a moment, not proud of having killed another man, even though the bastard had deserved to die a hundred times over for luring a boy into a man's fight and then cheating. "I killed him. It's done now, Has—Prudence. Best forget about it and work on getting back your strength. Lillah will be here soon to change your bedding, and I promised her I'd have you up a bit, but if—"

"Dammit, Gideon, would you stop staring out that window and look at me? I want to know the whole bloody business, not just the bits and pieces you choose to tell me!"

Pru glared at his back, miserable at having involved him in her problems, yet achingly glad he'd been there to save her. God knows what would have happened if it had been left to Jacques to see to fair play. He would likely have put another bullet in her back for good measure. "Gideon? Please, for I'll not rest until I hear the whole story."

He turned about then, his face hidden from her against the light. Damn him for being so tall, so strong, so beautiful, for she couldn't keep her thoughts where they belonged when he was present, even when her life depended on it.

"I told you, the Frenchman fired first, you fell, I threw my knife and went to you, while Nye—that is, Pride took off after the second."

"That would be Jacques," she murmured. "He's a bad one, Gideon. He'll not forget this, you know."

"Yes, well...he got clean away, and I've not seen or heard from him yet. Likely, he's ashamed to be related to a man who would jump the gun on a child."

"Hardly a child," she said quietly as a flush of warm color stole up to stain her cheeks.

But if Gideon had noticed her discomfiture, he chose to ignore it. "The Frenchman's ship is gone from the harbor."

"That would be the *Saint Germaine,*" Pru informed him after a deep, steadying breath. "She belonged to Claude, but Jacques sailed her for him." A thought occurred to her, and she tried to raise her head from the pillow, only to fall flat again with a groan.

Gideon was beside her in an instant, leaning over to slide his arm under her shoulders. "Come now, you can't do this alone, no matter how much you'd like to see the last of me. Hang on to my neck and I'll lift you. Would you like me to move the chair over by the window?"

"Yes, please," she whispered, more affected by his touch than by the agony in her side.

He lifted her first, and she clung to him, biting off the cry of pain that fought for release. "What did that wicked devil shoot me with—a cannon?"

"Shh, you're healing fast—that's why it hurts so." With his booted foot, he hooked the chair and moved it into position. Then he lowered himself carefully and settled her onto his lap.

"I thought I was to sit in the chair." Her voice sounded quivery, and she silently cursed the tremors that shook her at being surrounded by his hard, warm strength.

"You'd likely slide right off onto the floor, and then I'd only have to haul you onto the thing again and shore you up with pillows,'' he told her irreverently. But his own voice was none too steady.

Waves of dizziness assailed her as she struggled to hold her head upright for the first time in four days. She would have given all she possessed to have had a bath, to have had Lillah wash her hair until the highlights glistened in it, to have rubbed her body with perfumed oil and her cheeks with Spanish paper and to be wearing something delicate and feminine, instead of her plainest muslin night rail.

At least she was wearing something! She had a dim memory of waking to find him stroking her naked body with a cold, wet cloth.

Or had she dreamed it?

Gideon was undergoing his own sweet torture. He eased her away from his loins until she was in danger of sliding off his knees, and then drew her back again. Dammit, it wouldn't be the first time she'd felt a man's hard need pressing against her. All the same, she was in no condition for what he wanted—aye, needed, if he weren't to go right out of his mind!

"Maybe it'd be better if I settle you here alone," he muttered. "I'll fetch a pillow and a roll of blankets."

"This will do well enough. It's the shifting about that hurts." She settled against him, fitting the bend of his body as if she'd been made to lie against him. Gideon wished heartily he had a free hand to wipe away the sweat that beaded his brow. When he could trust his voice, he made some inane remark on the weather, which led to a discussion of the fine long season they'd had—which led to the chances of an early whaling season next year.

He closed his eyes and swore silently. Every spoke led back to the same old hub. Once more he saw a pale and dripping Haskell being handed into his arms more dead than alive, her small face so cold and white it had fair frozen his own heart. He would never forget the race back to camp, clutching her in his arms while he bargained silently with whatever gods there were to let her live.

If only she weren't so damned reckless! So damned vulnerable...

A dozen images flooded his mind before he could gain control of his thoughts again. Haskell kneeling under the cook shed awning, tossing bones with the men, laughing uproariously when she made her score, dancing about like a little gypsy the night they'd celebrated a kill after a long, dry spell. The day he'd come upon her bathing alone in the pond—when he had first discovered she was a woman.

A woman. She'd been a child! She was a woman now because of him, but he would make it up to her. If it took him a lifetime!

"Gideon!" A small hand tugged at his shirt. "Wake up. What's going to happen now that Claude's dead? Will there be any trouble?"

"Trouble?" Of course there'd be trouble. He'd been expecting it before now, but he didn't want her worrying about it. "Not likely. For all anyone knows, it was a simple duel. Two men met, and one of them died. As for the cousin—what's his name?"

"Jacques?"

"Aye, Jacques. He's likely halfway back to France by now."

"Still and all..." Pru couldn't leave it be. She felt as if something still hung over her head, but for the life of her, she didn't know what she could do about it. Gideon was right. It had been a duel, and one man had died. Surely not even Jacques would dare risk exposing his cousin's criminal behavior by reporting it.

"Woman, if you've a mind to worry about something, then worry about getting yourself mended. I've plans that won't wait forever."

But she was right. The sooner he reported the whole wretched affair to the proper authorities, the better he would sleep. Delarouche had been the biggest landholder on the island, and sooner or later, someone was going to have to settle his affairs. There was no real authority here, the nearest magistrate being across the sound. Still, even in a place such as this, a man could hardly get away with killing another without giving rise to a few questions.

Besides, Gideon had another reason for needing a justice. If he'd been in any condition at the time to think clearly, he would have sent for one along with the doctor.

"Do you suppose Jacques will inherit all Papa's properties?"

"I wouldn't worry about it if I were you. Best look to your own concerns," he told her, drawing his arms more closely around her, "which happens to be getting yourself well as quickly as possible."

"All the same," Pru mused, "four warehouses filled with all manner of valuable cargo. And two ordinaries..."

"And one bawdy house," Gideon teased. He looked at her face, his gaze lingering on one small feature at a time before coming to dwell on her lips. They were the exact color of a rose he'd seen blooming on a fence in Queen Anne's Towne.

"Quick Mary's Place. Of course I knew it belonged to Papa, but we always pretended it didn't. For Granna's sake, you understand."

He chuckled, delighting in the wicked grin that tilted her eyes ever so slightly. "Little witch," he murmured, and suddenly her face was much closer to his, her eyes hidden under the shadow of her lids.

"Oh, devil take it! I can't wait," he groaned.

The kiss was all she remembered and more. He tasted faintly of tobacco and coffee—real coffee, not acorn coffee. Ignoring the pain high up in her right side, Pru lifted her arms around his neck and held him the way she'd wanted to hold him for so long.

His lips twisted against her own softer mouth, as if he would brand her his. Even so, he was careful not to press against her wound.

It all came flooding back—the shocking intimacy they had once shared. The longings she had felt ever since—the restlessness that had kept her awake far into the night, remembering. Wondering.

Even if he hurt her a thousand times over, she wanted him to do whatever it was he had done before that had shown her a glimpse of something so wonderful, so awesome she couldn't begin to imagine it.

His mouth was by turns demanding and coercive, seductive in its sweetness, and shocking in its effects on her body.

"Gideon, please—" she gasped when he released her mouth to kiss her chin, her cheeks, her temples. She wanted him to kiss her mouth again.

Gideon's heart was pounding heavily against the breast that was pressed to his chest. The only sound in the room was that of her small whimpers and his ragged breath being drawn onto tortured lungs.

He could have wept when she pressed one small hand against his cheek and drew his mouth to hers again. God, if she didn't leave him be—if he didn't leave *her* be—he would take her here and now, and he couldn't risk it. It was too soon!

He savored her gently until he nearly exploded, and then he held her away, staring bemused at the clear, sea-green eyes that clung to his, at her soft, swollen lips, still glistening from his kisses.

Then, rising abruptly from the confining chair, he bent to lower her back onto the bed.

And then in a moment of madness, he came down beside her.

"Ah, God, sweet Haskell, you've bewitched me," he whispered hoarsely.

Pru beamed. "Then could we possibly do it again?" Her face flamed even as her hands trailed down his neck, over his shoulders, to rest on his chest. Her hot little palms were burning through his shirt as if he were naked, and he struggled against losing his wits.

"Don't be daft. You need to recover first," he groaned.

"Please? I was just getting the hang of it."

"Haskell, even if I wanted to—"

"Don't you?" She was tracing the rim of his ear.

"Aye, that's not the trouble. Dammit, stop that, woman! You don't know what you're doing!" He captured her hand and then, before he could think better of it, brought her fingertips to his lips.

"I know some of it, and you could teach me more. I—I think I'd like it once I got good at it."

A great sigh shuddered through Gideon's reclining frame. He closed his eyes, not wanting her to see the amusement there—or was it defeat? "It can be a pleasant enough pastime between a man and a woman. The first time's not much fun for a woman, I fear, though I've been led to believe it gets better with practice."

"Then can we? Practice, that is?"

This time, he couldn't hold back the smile. "It's too soon, love. You're not mended yet."

"But that's only one small place. The rest of me is well enough."

He could have laughed if he weren't hurting so damned bad. Why not? a small voice whispered. Why not take what he wanted, what she wanted, as well. He could take care not to brush against her wound.

It was the sound of footsteps coming up the stairs that saved him from making a mistake that they both might have come to regret. Lillah, no doubt, come to change her bedding, and now he would have to lift her up and hold her and be torn with need all over again.

He was sorely tempted to walk out of the house and keep right on going until he reached the *Polly*. At least he might be able to think straight. God knows, he wasn't able to where he was!

Reluctantly, he stood and tucked in his shirttail before pulling the counterpane up under her chin. Staring down into her eyes, he willed her to read what was in his heart—fearful all the while that she would, giving her such a power over him that never again would he be able to call his soul his own. His fingertips brushed lightly over her cheek, trailed down to the delicate angle of her jaw. They fell away, and he moved to stand beside the window.

"Prudie? You awake in there? Lillah says you're doing heaps better, but I brought the doctor. Can we come in?"

"Pride!" Pru shouted, delight spreading like sunrise across her face.

Gideon, his expression masked, stepped outside and closed the door behind him. After a moment, snatches of conversation came through the door, and Pru strained unabashedly to hear what was being said.

". . . my fee. Damned inconvenient, I can tell you!" She didn't recognize the voice, but it put her in mind of a buzzing hornet.

"She's been resting well. No fever, not since the second day." That was Gideon, the sound of his deep voice flowing through her with a quieting, healing effect.

"We came as soon as we could," she heard her brother say. "Blasted line of squalls had us blown halfway up the banks!"

". . . my fee. Triple the usual, and I'll have it now, if you please." The hornet again. What a nasty-sounding little man. Pru decided on the spot that she didn't like him, doctor or no. She'd much sooner have Gideon care for her. Or even Lillah.

"You'll get your damned fee—in gold!"

In gold? Where the devil did Gideon think they were going to get gold? The sewing basket was empty, thanks to that sneak thief, Delarouche. And now there was no chance to recover what he'd stolen from them.

When her bedroom door opened, Pru discovered that the little man was every bit as obnoxious as she'd suspected. Though to be fair, he looked as if he'd been seasick the whole journey and had yet to get his legs under him.

Ah, poor man. There were angry lumps on every visible portion of his body. She had to admit that the mosquitoes were unusually fierce, for the spring had been a wet one. She was on the verge of forgiving him for his testiness when he said, "Now there, girl, we'll just have a look at you! Sit up and disrobe, and be quick about it, for I mean to be well clear of this pest-ridden island before the sun goes down."

Her budding charitable feelings evaporated in a single whiff. "You, sir, may go straight back to wherever you came from, and devil take you."

"That I'm intending to do at my earliest opportunity. That young heathen damned near kidnapped me right in front of my wife and family! Here now, sit up so's I can see what ails you."

He lifted her, and while he reeked of strong spirits, stale tobacco and worse, she had to admit that his hands, though cold, were both steady and gentle.

Sullenly, she allowed him to unwind her bandages, sniff her wound with his sunburnt beak and examine it with a probing fingertip. Before she could quite recover from that, he was slapping a handful of some vile-smelling ointment on her, fore and aft.

Binding her up again, he snapped, "I'll not leave anything for pain, for whatever pain you're suffering is no more than your due, I suspect. I'll send up your woman after she feeds me, and then I'll be on my way. You'll likely live."

If she'd had something to throw after him, she'd have done it, and pain be damned. Too angry to sleep, she lay there and waited for Gideon to come back. Or Pride. Or even Lillah. Had they all deserted her, then?

She'd a good mind to take herself down the stairs and show them all that she didn't need any of them!

While Pru was lying in her bed, feeling restless and sorry for herself, Pride was closeted with Gideon.

"The talk was bad enough before, Gideon, and it ain't likely to get any better. I'd best send her away."

"Don't be too hasty. I've a feeling things will come around."

Pride scowled. Leaving the doctor to do his best, the two men had come downstairs and shared a glass of the brandy Delarouche had left. Pride had not spared a thought for the irony of it, his mind being too taken up with more serious matters. "I never knew what a nest of foul-minded buzzards they were—people I've known all my life—people who know Pru as well as they know their own families. How can they believe she'd go off and do the kind of things she's never even thought of doing here at home?''

Gideon had no answer. He knew what was being said, for Crow had apprised him of the situation some time ago. The devil of it was, they were partly right. The girl was no longer an innocent, but the fault was more his than her own.

''I never got a chance to tell you, lad, but I was headed back to set matters aright when you came after me to stand as your second. And then, after all hell broke loose, there wasn't time.''

Moving restlessly around the small room, Gideon poured himself another glass of brandy, and then stood staring out at the rain clouds moving in from the southeast. ''I reckon I'd best tell you—some yellow-haired chit came bursting in on us the day after you left. I was changing your sister's dressing, and she caught us—well, the thing is, it might have looked as if we were—uh . . .''

Pride swore. ''That'd be Annie Duvaal. For all they're supposed to be great friends, Annie's not one to hold her tongue when she thinks she's got the cat by the tail.''

Remembering the look of horrified fascination on the girl's face, Gideon could well believe it. ''That's what I was afeared of,'' he said quietly. ''You're the head of the family, I reckon, lad, so I'd best speak my piece to you. I mean to marry her. Haskell I mean—not the other one.''

''I kind of figgered you did,'' Pride said, and Gideon had the good grace to color. He wondered exactly what else the boy had ''kind of figgered.''

''Aye, well . . . I'd best give her time to mend a bit first. You might as well know that I've been wed before. Barbara was an Ocracoke woman—a widow. We had a son.'' He took a deep breath, but other than that, not a flicker of emotion showed as he said, ''I lost 'em both to yellow fever.''

''God, I'm sorry, Gideon.''

Gideon downed his brandy and set aside the tumbler. ''Well, it's past now. There's the morrow to think of, and this time a simple handfasting won't serve. To lay the talk, we'd best plan on the biggest wedding we can manage."

"Short o' using one of the warehouses, it'll have to be right here. We never got around to building a church."

Gideon stroked his jaw as he considered the most likely course of action. "You fetched out a doctor—likely I can fetch out an Anglican." Which would suit him better than a justice, for he'd about decided it would serve no purpose to involve the law in their private concerns.

"They say Anglicans is thick as ticks in Virginia," Pride offered, and Gideon nodded thoughtfully.

"Happens I've a hold full of furniture bound for a man up the York that's long overdue. We'll go about it this way, boy, if you've no objections. Tell your family first, and then tell the whole town they're expected to attend your sister's wedding come the first day of July. That should give me time to deliver my cargo, fill my hold again, take on a parson and get back."

"What if they don't accept? I've not had time to find out if things have settled down since I got back, but tongues were still a-clacking fierce before I left."

Gideon's face hardened into an expression Pride could never have imagined had he not seen it. "They'll come," he said softly, and the younger man had no doubt that they would—willingly or not.

Gideon handed over a bundle of trade scrip and a small bag of coins. "Buy what you need with this. Don't worry about Haskell's wedding gown. I'll take care of that."

"You've already asked her then?"

"Not yet, but I'm on my way," said Gideon, his eyes going a shade lighter as he turned toward the door.

But just then the doctor came into the room, and there was the fee to settle—which Gideon did—instructions to hear, involving both Pride and Lillah, as well as a number of unnecessary remarks about young heathens who had no respect for a learned man's time, privacy or station.

By the time Gideon managed to escape and make his way upstairs, Prudence was sound asleep. For a long time, he simply stood beside her bed gazing down at her. Was he making the biggest mistake in a lifetime filled with mistakes? Perhaps. Yet what other course was there? Even if his conscience had not demanded that he marry her, he could do no less. For better or worse, she had worked her way into his heart and soul, and there was naught he could do about it, even if he'd wanted to.

And seeing her lying there, her face composed in a misleading look of sweet submissiveness, he knew he would have it no other way.

Chapter Sixteen

Prudence was fit to be tied. It was bad enough that she hadn't been permitted to see Granna in more than a week. Not that she knew quite how it could have been arranged, for Hosannah was not fit to climb the stairs, and Lillah had threatened Pru's life if she set foot out of her bed.

"You'd think it was my leg that'd been wounded, not my—what-you-may-call-it!" she protested to Pride.

"Ah, now, Prudie..."

"I'm just so blasted miserable, and nobody comes to visit me, and Lillah is too busy looking after Granna and washing and cooking and all the rest to spare me any time."

But Pride knew it was more than that. Gideon had sailed without saying goodbye to Pru, much less proposing. As he explained when he came back downstairs the night he left, she had been sleeping so soundly that he hadn't the heart to wake her.

"You mean you didn't even speak to her?" Pride had asked.

"I told you—she was sleeping. I don't have all that much time, and it hardly seems the thing to wake up a woman from a sound sleep, propose marriage to her and then leave."

Pride had shaken his head. "Not that I've all that much experience with women, but if it was me, I wouldn't be taking too much for granted, knowing Prudie."

More than once since that night, Pride had been sorely tempted to speak out. Not that he would ever dream of doing another man's proposing for him, but at least he could say something to ease her mind, for it was plain as pudding that she thought Gideon had gone for good.

"Mr. Simpson said I could take up as clerk again if I wanted to," he told her. There was little other news in such a small place—nothing at all that might lift her spirits.

"Hmm? Oh . . . that's nice."

"It ain't all that nice," he retorted, only partly for the sake of argument. "I can think of a number of things I'd rather be doing than be stuck in a hole full of stinking hides, toting up figures and writing out receipts."

Something in the tone of his voice seemed to rouse her from the apathy that had lately alternated with fits of self-pity. "Do you ever wish you were back, Pride? At the camp, I mean?"

He nodded, toying with the book Pru had laid aside when he stopped by her room. "It suited me well. I'd go back in a minute if Gideon would have me."

To his great consternation, tears welled in his sister's eyes and broke through the barrier of her lashes to spill down over her cheeks. "Devil take it, Prudie, I'm sorry! I didn't mean to make you weep!" God, he hated tears! He never knew what to do, what to say.

"I'm n-not weeping, I was just—it was the sun coming through the window—oh, damn and blast the wretched man. I hope he trips over his big feet and breaks his blasted neck!'

"Hold there, now, girl. Gideon's not—that is, he's coming back."

"Why should he?" She sniffled and scrubbed her face with a corner of the sheet. "There's no reason he'd be coming back to Portsmouth, at least not until next season—and even if he did, there's no reason he'd want to see—to see—me-e-e-e," she wailed, as tears burst out afresh.

Which was why, a moment later, Pride found himself standing proxy for his friend and proposing marriage.

It took all morning, and even when he thought he'd convinced her, there were times when he had to convince her all over again. Finally, after three days of doubting and being reassured by a brother who was even beginning to have his own doubts, Pru settled back to get herself well enough to stand beside Gideon and pronounce her vows.

Pride came home from work each day looking more and more like a thundercloud, and Lillah grew stiffer and more snappish than ever, which Pru put down to the fact that Crow had gone again. But Pru blossomed. She allowed Lillah to unbind her wound and sit her in front of the window, turning her so that the sun could shine on both sides, telling herself that if there was the least bit of truth in Lillah's belief that sunlight would drive away the evil that could hide in the darkness under a bandage, it was worth trying. She intended to be fully mended in time for her wedding day.

When Pru was finally allowed to come downstairs, Hosannah dithered endlessly over wedding plans, as often as not talking as if it were to be held in the ballroom at Hunt House, with all her old friends and family present.

"Yes, Granna, the roses should be at their peak by then," Pru agreed gently. The most recent storm tide that washed over the island had killed the last of the poor struggling flowers Hosannah had brought with her from her old home, but the wild pink mallows would be in bloom, and honeysuckle made a graceful bouquet.

"I'll have Katie make up some of her lovely little cheesecakes and mince tarts. We'd best commence soaking out a ham before long. I'll remind her to pour a few bottles of Canary wine into the tub, for it does give a right wholesome flavor."

"Yes, Granna," Pru agreed. They could probably manage clams and shrimps and cold baked fish with tiny clabber biscuits, but she'd not eat a single bite of it, for she'd be far too excited.

Gideon loved her. She could say the words over in her mind a hundred times a day, and they still didn't seem real— nor would they until she heard them from his own lips.

On the other hand, if Pride were to be believed, he had said he wanted to marry her. And while that didn't necessarily mean he loved her, why else would he have sat with her day and night, doing all the tiresome, tedious things that had to be done while she was so ill?

Her father had loved her, and he'd made himself scarce as fish feathers whenever anyone in the family was sick. Did that mean that Gideon cared for her even more than her father had done?

Or was it simply a different kind of caring?

With a whole lifetime in front of her to learn the answers to all her questions, Pru hugged to her heart each precious memory of the time she'd spent with Gideon as she listened to Granna's rambling tales about hunt balls, whist parties, maypoles and cricket matches. Her mind wandering, she picked the stitches out of one of her mother's loveliest gowns, a rose-pink watered silk with a silvery sheen. Pride had said that Gideon would be bringing her wedding gown, but a bride needed more than one gown.

Annie Duvaal had finally come to visit again. Like everyone else in the village, she'd been invited to the wedding, and she was dying to hear an account of how Gideon and Pru had met, and especially what had taken place while Pru was away.

"But you were gone so long. Were you visiting his family?"

Pru murmured something, biting off a thread in the skirt she was hemming and hoping Annie would be satisfied with the evasion. Strangely enough—for there had been a time in their lives when the two girls had no secrets from each other—Pru was reluctant to confide the truth.

They talked of gowns and the few local swains, but even as they gossiped, Annie seemed on edge, glancing frequently out the front window as if she expected to see Gideon striding up the pathway at any moment.

"Your folks are going to come, aren't they, Annie?"

"What? Oh, yes, they'll be here. I don't reckon anybody'd dare miss it. After all, it ain't every day a body gets to go to a wedding where the bride's actually killed a man in a duel."

Pru stabbed her thumb with the needle and stared at her friend. "What do you mean?" she whispered when she could speak again. She glanced at the closed bedroom door. She'd just helped her grandmother in for her morning nap a few minutes before Annie came by.

"No more'n what everyone's talking about. It's true, ain't it? You did kill that Frenchman?"

"Is that what they're saying?" Dear God, so that was why Pride had refused point-blank to discuss the matter with her when she'd tried to find out why he was looking so thunderous lately.

"They say it was Pride that started it. Albert heard him talking about it while he was working the sheer hulk one day." The sheer hulk was a derelict ship half-sunk at one end of the wharfs, her deck cleared so that she could be rigged for hoisting cargo and swinging it from ship to wharf. It required two men to operate, and Pride and Albert still worked it together, despite their falling out.

"Annie, it was a duel. Pride might have challenged Delarouche, but he was more than provoked, I can assure you." Not for a single moment did Pru even think of implicating Gideon in the wretched affair. It had been her fight—hers and Pride's. She had stepped in to save her brother, and Gideon had stepped in to save her, but that was neither here nor there. "What else are they saying?"

Annie glanced nervously out the window and then leaned forward, her bunched ringlets dancing about her shoulders in a way Pru happened to know she practiced before a mirror. They had practiced it together, only it had never worked for Pru. "Well...they're saying it could have been a lovers' tiff. Claude was a handsome man, and he was known to be courting you even before your—uh, your..."

"Disgrace?"

"I didn't say that. All I meant was that everybody knew he was hanging around you when you ran off with that whaler. Lordy, I don't blame you for taking up with Gideon, Pru, for he's so handsome, even with that awful thing on his cheek. But then when Claude kept coming around after you got home again, everybody reckoned the two of you had words, and one thing led to another, and . . ." She shrugged.

Pru stood, dumping scissors, pincushion and gown onto the floor. "It was Pride who challenged Claude Delarouche, and it was certainly not over me! And for your information, Claude visited my grandmother, not me. I couldn't abide the snake!"

Annie's round blue eyes were perhaps a trifle too innocent, but Pru was past noticing. "If you must know, Claude said something unforgivable about Papa, and Pride was obliged to defend our honor. It's just unfortunate that—" she drew in a deep, uneven breath, her fists unconsciously knotted against her thighs "—that things turned out the way they did, that's all."

"Oh mercy, Mama just went past on her way home from visiting old Miz Daughtry. I'd best go now."

"But you do understand, don't you?" Annie was her friend, had been her closest friend all the years they were growing up. There were too few people on the island to spare even one friend.

"Of course I understand," the other girl said quickly, glancing over her shoulder on her way out. "That poor handsome Frenchman insulted your papa, and Pride called him out, and you ended up getting shot and the Frenchman died with a knife in his belly."

"His heart," Pru corrected before she could think. "Oh, devil take it! I don't know where you get all your information, but I assure you—"

But Annie was gone, and Pru didn't have time to assure her of anything. And even if she had, what could she have assured her of?

* * *

Lillah was increasingly tight-lipped as she went about preparations for the wedding. "Better that mon take you away from this place an' don' bring you back," she muttered one morning as she scoured the salt film off the front parlor windows with a pail of vinegar water. "All they filt'y tongues!"

"Of course I'll be back. Where else would I go?" Pru replied. In truth, she hadn't thought about it one way or another. At least not beyond the fact that her dream had really come true—Gideon loved her, and was coming to marry her as soon as he could find the preacher. Most couples settled for handfasting, and she took it as a mark of his respect that he would go to so much trouble.

Every day for a week, Pru had been expecting him. She'd spent hours at her window, watching for his sails to appear on the horizon, hours casting daydreams as she went about whatever light tasks Lillah provided her with—and still more hours dreaming away the nights.

By the time he came, she was exhausted from the waiting. She had turned out her mother's trunk, refurbished everything the moths and silverfish had left behind. In her oldest night rail—for she was saving her best for when she was wed—she lay sprawled across the bed sound asleep, with the light, warm breeze from the southwest blowing across her body.

Gideon had let himself in and tiptoed up the stairs in the darkness. Meeting Pride on the way in, he'd sent him along to the Leaky Cask to share a few drams with his old mates.

There was no light on in the house. Hosannah would have long since drunk herself into a genteel stupor. For once, Gideon was glad of the old lady's intemperate ways.

God, he had forgotten just how lovely she was! In the sliver of moonlight that fell across the bed, he could just make out her long, slender legs, one knee drawn up slightly as she lay on her front. One of her arms clutched the pillow, the other dangled over the edge of the bed.

Gideon slipped off his boots first of all, and then stripped off his shirt. Only then did he reach out and take her hand to lift it gently back onto the bed.

"Haskell," he whispered, leaning over so that his breath fanned tendrils of her hair. He breathed in the clean, womanly scent of her and felt his loins tighten, and then he spoke her name again. "Prudence, I've come back, little love. Wake up, for I've something to ask you."

Suddenly he felt a film of sweat dampen his back. Had he been a fool to take so much for granted? He should have asked her before he left. What if she wouldn't have him? What if she'd heard the rumors—the village would likely be abuzz with news of the wedding. What if she despised him for his high-handedness?

It had been a mistake to tell Pride to invite the village to a wedding when he hadn't even asked the bride. God, what a tangle he'd made of things! It had never occurred to him that she might hear about it before he could get back.

"Gi'eon," she muttered drowsily, and stirred in her sleep.

She had heard him. Or did she only dream of him? There was one way to find out. "Haskell, wake up, will you?"

He placed one hand on her back, feeling the incredibly fragile cage of her ribs. When he thought of those months in camp—all the slavey's labors and the risks he'd exposed her to before he knew—he could have wept! And even after he'd discovered her secret, he had not let up on her.

"Gideon, is it really you?"

She rolled over onto her back, and he found himself drowning in her huge, shadowy eyes. She was smiling. That was a good sign, wasn't it?

"I told you I'd be back."

"No, you didn't. You went away without even saying goodbye."

He wished now he had taken time to shave. He'd been in such an all-fired hurry to see her again.... "Shall I say it now?"

"Not unless you mean to leave me again," she whispered.

The last thread of his control broke, and he gathered her into his arms and buried his face in her throat. "Never!"

He kissed her then, coming down onto the narrow bed beside her to hold her against him as if to prove his vow. His mouth devoured hers with all the hunger, all the yearning bottled up inside him, and then it grew tender, and he made love to her mouth, telling her in the best way he knew what was in his heart.

Truly, he had never felt this way for any woman before—not even Barbara. It was beyond anything he had ever experienced, and he could hardly comprehend what was happening to him, much less put it into words.

But he could show her.

The room seemed to disappear around Pru as she lay in his arms, Gideon's lips moving over her cheeks, her temples, her brow. She was floating, not lying in the bed she had slept in all her life. That was not candle wax, juniper and lye soap she smelled, but the clean, musky scent of the man who had filled her empty dreams for so long, and now filled her arms.

Finally, he held her away long enough to draw her night rail up over her hips, and then he lifted her up and tugged it over her head. "I need to see you," he said, his voice rough with feeling. "I thought you couldn't be as lovely as I remembered, but truly, you must be the most beautiful woman in all the world."

Pru felt as if her heart would burst, thinking of how many times she had despaired of her looks, certain he could never find her even passable. "Then never light the lamps, for I'd not have you disillusioned," she said, the words ending on a sigh.

He took her hand and placed it on his chest. "Can you feel it?"

She nodded. Her fingers curled into his hard, satiny flesh, catching on the crisp hairs that swirled across the broad expanse before narrowing and disappearing under his belt.

Gideon's other hand was still holding hers. He stroked her fingers, caressing the soft flesh between them, and his thumb slipped away now and then to stray into her sensitive palm. "No more calluses?"

Pru shook her head. With lightning stabbing directly from her hand to her loins, she didn't trust her voice. When she could bear it no longer, she tugged her hand away. "Ouch, what are you doing to my hand? It tingles."

Gideon threw back his head and laughed aloud, and Pru rose from her pillow and pressed both her hands over his mouth. "Hush! For goodness' sake, do you want to raise the dead? If Granna ever caught you in here, and me stark naked, she'd—she would surely—"

"Force me to wed you?" he teased. "Ah, but my darling Haskell, I've a mind to do that, anyway." He caught her to him and held her there, her face pressed tightly against his throat. After a moment, he drew her onto his lap. "Remember that last day, when I held you like this?"

"Mmm-hmm?" She thought she would die of the sheer pleasure of being so close to him—or perhaps of something else, something that seemed to happen whenever he touched her this way.

"I thought I would die," he said simply.

She lifted her head and stared at him, goggle-eyed. "You, too?"

"You, too?" he repeated, and when she nodded, he laughed again. Easing her back onto the bed, he arose and quickly shed his remaining clothes.

Pru wished there was more light. She wished his back weren't turned to the window, so that she could see him better. What little moonlight there was only outlined his hair and his body in silver.

But then there was no more time to wish, for he lay down beside her, propping himself up on one arm so that he could stroke her shoulders, her waist, her breasts....

"What are you doing?" she gasped when he lowered his head to suckle her.

"Does it not please you?"

It pleased her all too well, she thought, as a flock of wild butterflies took to the air inside her belly. Daringly, she lifted her head and touched him with her tongue.

It was as if she'd set fire to him. "God, don't—sweetheart, I can't—"

"You don't like it?" she teased, drawing away to lie back on her pillow.

Gideon followed her down, his whole body tense and hard beside her. "That's the trouble," he said shakily. "There's a few things you don't understand, my wicked little darling. The first time we came together, I thought—that is, I believed—well, at any rate, I didn't take time to pleasure you as I should have." And when she protested, he laid a finger over her lips. "No, let me finish, for I've never told you I was sorry. In truth, I can't even say it now, for I'm not—sorry it happened, that is. But I'm sorry for the *way* it happened—sorry for hurting you. And sorry for what happened afterward. The talk, I mean. And fool that I am, I never even stopped to think that I might have given you a baby."

"I wish you had," Pru declared. "I would have loved a son just like you, Gideon."

Gideon's face revealed nothing, but he knew he would have to tell her about Barbara and the boy. Tomorrow would be soon enough. Tonight was made for more than words.

The finger that had closed her lips had fallen to the small hollow at the base of her throat. Now it set a course between her breasts, across the flat plain above her waist, and curled into the tiny dimple on her belly.

"I seem to remember a small heart somewhere around here," he murmured, lowering his face to her soft, sweet flesh.

Up came her knees, and she gasped.

"Too dark to see much, but I fancy I could taste it if I came across it." And he proceeded to lick her belly until she whimpered aloud, both her legs flailing helplessly on the mattress.

"Gideon, please, you mustn't!"

"What—here?" Ever so gently, he probed the nest of sable curls with his fingers. "Mustn't what?"

"Touch me—like that—" Again she gasped.

"Like this, you mean?" He found what he'd been seeking and stroked it with featherlike touches, taking care not to hurt her. She was so delicately made, all soft and moist, like the dewy petals of a rose.

Her fingers moved restlessly over his thigh, and just before he brought her to the threshold of ecstasy, he felt them close around his shaft.

Now it was his turn to protest. "Loveling, give me your hands—both of them. Quickly, before you push me too far."

With a final caress of his most sensitive flesh, she allowed him to take both her wrists in his and hold them over her head. And then he mounted her, unable to wait a moment longer.

Slowly, he warned himself, you've much to make up for. But when he felt her glove him so tightly, so hotly, his control was badly shaken. It was all he could do to hold back.

"Be still," he commanded.

"I can't," she wailed, and her hips lifted and twisted until he was out of his mind with need.

Reaching down to find her, he began to stroke, determined that this time he would take her where he was sure she had never been before. She was so incredibly responsive! Within moments, she began to whimper. He felt her convulsing around him, and all thought of control flew out the window.

Driving into her, he heard her cry out his name, and then they were both consumed in the raging fire. At the last possible moment, he rolled over onto his back, crushing her to him as he soared into oblivion.

"Haskell—ah, sweet—" he whispered aeons later. Thank God he'd thought to spare her his full weight, or she might have been crushed beneath him. He couldn't have moved now if his life depended on it.

* * *

It was the thunder that awakened him. A flash of lightning illuminated her still, sleeping face, and oblivious to the cool wind that blew across his naked body, Gideon gazed down at the miraculous creature who had changed his entire life over a few short months.

She was perfect. She was all the things he had longed for all his life without even knowing it.

And she was his.

Chapter Seventeen

Pride was waiting when Gideon came ashore again. He'd slipped out before daylight and returned to the ship, needing time to get himself together, for he'd rushed ashore last night with only one thought in mind—seeing her again. Holding her.

"Did Pru tell you I jumped the gun? Sorry, Gideon, but she was fit to be tied, and it weren't just on account of all the talk. As to that, she's been setting tongues to wagging since she used to climb out of her cradle and run all the way down to the docks wearing naught but a napkin, and that like as not soggy."

Gideon grinned broadly. As tired as he was, he was on top of the world after those precious stolen moments last night. "About time someone took a hitch in her breeches, then, wouldn't you say?"

"You found us an Anglican? I told you Virginia was crawling with the beggars."

"Right you were, only not a one of them was willing to leave his flock long enough to come this far down the banks."

"What about a justice? We could have settled for one o' them, couldn't we?"

"I'd have settled." Although not comfortably, Gideon added silently. "I got wind of one up the Albemarle that didn't mind traveling about for a big enough fee, only by the time I got there, he was already spoken for and gone, and I was of no mind to wait."

Gideon flexed his shoulders to relieve some of the tension that had gathered there. He'd not been able to sleep above two or three hours at a stretch the whole time he'd been gone. The truth was, he wasn't all that easy with the notion of tracking down a justice, even for his own wedding. It was his experience that they were an unpredictable breed. Given a choice, he would have much preferred a churchman. He reckoned he'd spent too many years looking over his shoulder, expecting at any moment to be called to account for having sailed aboard the *Morning Star,* to go seeking out a representative of the law, even now.

During the weeks he was away, Gideon had been free to think matters through. Piecing together all he knew, it had gradually come clear to him that Delarouche had borne some grudge against Urias Andros. With Andros dead, he had sought to avenge himself by murdering his son and ruining his daughter.

It was the thought of Prudence that eased the scowl from his face and the tension from his shoulders. Delarouche was dead. The rest of his verminous crew had fled, and Anglican or no, Gideon meant to claim his bride before anything more could happen to interfere with his plans. He should have spoken to her last night; instead, he'd taken the cowardly way and left her sleeping. At least no one had barged in on them this time, compromising her further.

"I'd take it as an honor if you'd stand up with me, lad," he said now. "Most of the crew's scattered, as I reckon they told you last night, but what's left will be there, for I've invited them all. Did you spread the word?"

Beneath Pride's tanned complexion, his cheeks grew red. "Uh—like I was trying to tell you, Gideon, I might have let something slip. To Prudie, I mean. You see, she was out of sorts, and Lillah was too busy to spend time with her because Granna's not been feeling up to snuff lately, and I wanted to make her feel better. Pru, that is—not Granna. I mean, Granna, too, but—what I mean is, I—"

"You what, boy? Get on with it. I've better things to do than stand around while you throw a half hitch in your tongue." But he was smiling, his thoughts leaping on ahead.

"Well, the thing is, I think I asked her to marry me. I mean you. Oh, hell, Gideon, you know what I mean! I'm right sorry if I offended you, but it was all I could think of to cheer her up. She had it in her head that you'd gone off and left her and weren't coming back, and I knew—"

"Well, hell, boy—don't keep me dangling? What'd she say? Will she or won't she?"

"She will!" Pride's grin bespoke heartfelt relief. "Once she took it in her head that I was telling the truth, she threw a hug onto me that damn near strangled me. I tell you, Gideon, you got to keep that woman away from oars. All that rowing she did for Toby last season primed her so she'd be a fearsome match in a fair fight."

Gideon let out a shout that drew the curious eyes of several nearby fishermen. "Wedding tomorrow at the Andros house!" he called out to them. "You're all invited!"

Shouldering the bundle he'd tossed ashore before he climbed out of the launch, Gideon leaped down onto the sandy cart track. "Don't hurry home, boy. Your sister and I have a powerful lot of catching up to do," he called over his shoulder as he hurried way.

Pride gazed after the man who was soon to become his brother-in-law. He suspected they'd done more than a bit of "catching up" the night before. Still, he didn't mind admitting he'd be glad to have a more experienced man at the helm. Being head of an otherwise female household wasn't all it was cracked up to be.

It was Pru who worried him the most. He just hoped to God she'd behave herself long enough to get decently married off.

Gideon was fixing to shackle himself to a female who would never in a hundred years be the kind of sweet, biddable woman a man needed for a wife. Pride only hoped he wouldn't lose his nerve and back out. Hell, she couldn't even cook fit to eat!

* * *

A bee droned in the swamp roses near the edge of the marsh. In the fragrant heat the harsh cries of gulls and fish crows went unheeded, as did the chatter of a flock of yellow-gray finches that flickered in the sun-dappled live oak tree. Somewhere nearby, the surf continued to whisper to the shore. The wind sighed through the tops of the stunted pines.

Oblivious to the sights and sounds around them, two people stood in the blinding brilliance of the noonday sun. Unaccountably shy after the night before, Gideon forgot his lines, while Pru, her fingers knotted together, stared everywhere but directly at him.

"I missed you this morning," she finally managed.

He cleared his throat. "I—needed to make myself presentable. Now I've come to say that if you'll have me without benefit of church or law, then we'll stand on your porch come morning and handfast before God and all his witnesses, and I vow it'll be the same for me as if we stood in the finest church in the world."

He was surely the most beautiful man in the world, Pru thought dazedly. Even exhausted and travel-stained, with half his face covered in whiskers, she'd thought him that. Now it was all she could do not to hurl herself into his arms. But if he wanted ladylike decorum, then she would damned well be a lady or die trying.

Demurely, she said, "I reckon you know from the way I acted that I'd have you any way I could get you, Gideon— and stay by you for as long as you'll tolerate me."

Was it only her imagination, or was that relief she saw on his face? "I believe you'll find I'm a right tolerant man, Haskell."

"I reckon I've been a sore trial to you in the past."

He merely lifted his brows.

"Well, I want you to know I plan to do better. Lillah's been teaching me to cook, and I'm already a fair hand with a needle."

"But a much fairer one with a knife, a gun or a deck of cards, hmm?"

He was teasing her. At least she hoped he was teasing. He was still standing an arm's length away, showing not the least sign of wanting to do more than talk. "Um…Gideon, do you suppose you could call me Prudence? And I'd be much obliged if you could try and forget the way we first met."

Crossing his arms, he stroked his jaw. It looked almost as though he were struggling against a smile, but she couldn't be certain. His hand was in the way. "Prudence," he repeated thoughtfully. "Hmm…I doubt me if ever a woman was more falsely named, but if it'll make you happy, I'll do my best to remember."

"And forget." She reminded him of the rest of her request, and he nodded. Please God, he would soon forget the dirty young cutpurse who had dressed like a man, cursed like a man and, more often than not, smelled like a cross between a fish house and a hog pen.

She, on the other hand, would never forget those days in camp, for it was there that she'd come to love this tall, beautiful captain, who led his men with a quiet authority that commanded their respect as well as their affection.

A lonely man, one who might share his body, but who did not so easily share his thoughts.

"Gideon—are you sure you really want to marry me?" He'd never claimed to love her; she'd not expected that.

And then, somehow, he was holding her, and her arms went up around his neck. She pulled his head down so that she could feel the texture of his skin against hers. She wanted to taste him again. She wanted to feel his body against her own without all the bother of clothes between them. But Gideon refused to be hurried.

"Would I be here if I didn't?"

And with that she had to be satisfied. For now.

As she strolled up the steps and into the house, Gideon's arm still around her waist, Pru told herself that even without the words, she was the luckiest among women. Most counted themselves fortunate if they could tolerate the men they married, much less love them. And she did love Gideon. She loved everything about him—his strength, his goodness, his beauty. She asked nothing more than to spend the rest of her days with him. Given enough time, she could teach him to love her in return—she *knew* she could!

Perhaps he already did, and didn't realize it, she thought wistfully. Why else would he have asked her to marry him?

"Pity it wasn't made up in red. Green makes you look too pale. I was never real partial to it, anyhow." Annie was on her knees adjusting a ruffle, while Pru peered at the image of the tall, slender woman in the gown of palest green taffeta. Both women were upstairs in Pru's bedroom, while the front yard of the Andros house was filled with guests, who had come mostly out of curiosity.

"I think it's the most beautiful gown I've ever seen," Pru said reverently. If it had been made of coarsest homespun dyed with onionskins, she would have loved it, for Gideon had brought it to her.

"I've a mind to ask Mama to send off for some red silk and make me up one just like it," Annie said, as she got to her feet and stared enviously at her friend.

Pru turned this way and that before the mirror, noting in amazement how green her eyes looked today; they were the exact color of the silk. And how very small her waist appeared in the basqued bodice above the full skirt. Could this lovely creature be the same Prudie Andros who, little more than a month ago, had been carving strips of blubber off a whale carcass and trying them out for the oil? The same one who had marched boldly into a waterfront tavern to drink and game with a crew of whalers?

"I look like a lady," she whispered.

Annie sniffed. "He's not getting the worst end of the deal, I reckon."

Pru turned to stare at her friend. "Who? Gideon? Well, surely you don't think I'm the one getting the worst end of the deal!"

Ignoring her, Annie continued to twiddle with her own best gown, adjusting the bright blue silk to hang smoothly under its pink overskirt.

It had always irritated Pru, the habit her best friend had of hinting at something and then backing away. But this was her wedding day. She refused to be irritated. "But you've seen him, remember? Leastwise, you told me you had. You said he was the handsomest man you'd ever laid eyes on."

Annie lifted her bosom with her hands so that it plumped up well above the ruffled edge of her gown. "Well, he is—I mean, if you don't mind that awful mark on his cheek." Pru bristled, but Annie forged ahead. "Even at that, I reckon he's a sight better than any man around here except Pride—but of course, he's your brother...."

"I *know* who Pride is, Annie! What did you mean about me getting the short end of the stick?"

Annie suddenly found a small blemish on one side of her chin that needed attention, and she squinted into the mirror.

Pru waited. She began tapping the toe of one small, ivory satin shoe. Hands on her hips, she drew in a deep breath. "Annie! Dammit, tell me what you were getting at!"

Annie shrugged, setting her bright gold ringlets to dancing about her ears. "I'm not getting at anything, Prudie. Honestly, I didn't mean a thing—only, you know how people talk...."

Pru's foot beat a tattoo on the heart pine floor. "And?" she prompted. "People talk? What does that mean?"

"Do you have a dab of rice flour I could dust over this place on my chin? Don't you hate it when one of these hateful things pops out just when you want to look pretty?"

Whirling about, Pru snatched up a muslin bag and slapped it into Annie's hand, sending up a fine white cloud. "If you don't tell me what you're getting at, you'll have more'n a ruby on your chin to fret over! Who's talking about what, and why should that mean I'm getting the short end of the stick?"

"Prudie! Ain't you ready yet? The whole front yard's filled up all the way out to the end of the path, and Gid's wearing a hole in the parlor rug!"

"We're on our way," she called down to her brother. And then she turned back to Annie, who was jutting her chin at the mirror to apply a judicious tap of the flour bag. "If you don't tell me what you meant, I'm going to let everyone know you stuff cotton bolls under your breasts to make them sit up so high," she threatened.

Annie's hands slapped protectively over her pale bosom, the top of which was generously displayed above her daring décolletage. "I only meant that everyone knows why Gideon's marrying you. That's all I meant, honestly, Prudie."

Pru's eyes narrowed dangerously. "Oh? And how could *everyone* know that? Gid's not a man to talk about himself, not even to me, and I happen to know him considerably better than you do."

"Don't it bother you that he could never truly love another woman, because he loved his first wife and his little boy above all? They say he near went crazy when they died." If she noticed how pale Pru had suddenly grown, she pretended not to. "I reckon you know how mad Pride got when the two of you first come back, and he found out how everybody on Portsmouth Island was talking about how you'd run off with this whaler, and he'd had to go chasing after you to try to make you come back, only you refused. Everybody knows that, but did you know your brother threatened to kill your whaler for ruining you, and that's the only reason he's here now to make an honest woman of you?"

Pru was too stunned to utter a word, but Annie was wound up and going strong. Thrusting out her freshly powdered chin, she went on to say, "And I s'pose you also know how everybody's saying you killed that Frenchman because he found out you were going to have a baby by your whaler, and—ow! Why'd you do that?"

"You've no cause to go saying those wicked things! They're lies, every last one of them!"

"Well, it ain't my fault if you don't like what you hear, Prudence Andros. You made me tell you what the whole village is saying.

Pru glared at the red-faced blond. "What do I care about what a bunch of nasty old gossips have to say? They don't know anything at all about Gideon, and not half as much as they think they know about me!"

"Prudie! Annie! Dammit all, if you ain't down here by the time I count to three, I'm sending Lillah up there after you!" Pride called from the bottom of the stairs.

With a furious look over her shoulder, Annie spun away and ran, skidding to a halt to descend at a more decorous pace, one pale, soft hand extended for Pride to take. Which he did, blushing and tugging with the other at the high stock Gideon had provided for him to wear with his own best shirt and coat.

Struggling to hide her bewilderment and uncertainty, Pru lifted her skirts above her ankles and went forth to meet her bridegroom.

The bridegroom who had been married before—who had been a father, if Annie could be believed. The bridegroom who was marrying her, not because he could ever love her, but only because he had ruined her reputation by kidnapping her and keeping her captive for three months.

"Your hands are freezing," Gideon whispered a few minutes later. They were standing on the front porch, and Pru stared at the hordes who had gathered to witness her wedding.

Hardly hordes by mainland standards, she supposed, but from the looks of it, not a soul had stayed at home. Nets were going unfished, lighters unloaded and meals uncooked. It was the Sabbath, she knew, but without a church or a minister, only a few held the day above any other day of the week.

Had they come to gossip? Had they come to see a wrong righted?

She was sorely tempted to step forward and set the record straight by telling them once and for all that she had *not* run away willingly with this man she was marrying. That she was *not* with child, by Gideon or any other man. That she was marrying for love, which was more than most of them could claim. And that she most definitely had *not* killed any man!

Oh, and what truth will you tell them? That you were only trying to rob Gideon, as you'd robbed so many others, and that he caught you at it and made you work off your debt? That you might well be with child, for your courses have not come on you in near on to six weeks? That you love Gideon more than you love your own life, but that he's marrying you only because he's far too honorable to do anything else?

And that Gideon, not you, killed Delarouche?

"Are you ready, darling?"

At the sound of Gideon's deep voice, Pru took a steadying breath and smiled up at him, not a hint of the turmoil she was feeling evident in her demeanor. "I'm ready," she said firmly.

They stepped forward to stand at the very edge of the porch so that the sun shone down on both their heads. Pru wore a slightly crooked headdress that she'd snatched up and jammed on her head just before she'd hurried down the stairs. The short veil attached masked her pallor, but nothing could mask the tremor of her hands as Gideon clasped them in his.

An expectant hush fell over the crowd. Even the children, who had been chasing the milk goat around her hobble, fell silent and turned to stare.

And then Gideon's voice rang out clearly, bringing goose bumps to every inch of flesh on Pru's trembling body. "Hear me now. Before God and all, *this* be the woman I would have for my wife!"

Pru took a deep breath and released it. They were all looking at her now. "Before God and all," she said, her voice gaining strength as she went along, "*this* be the man I would have for my husband!"

There was a chorus of, "So be it," from the throng, and then a ragged cheer went up. Gideon turned back Pru's veil and grinned down at her, his eyes as clear and deep as an autumn sky.

"Madam, the deed be done," he said, and then he kissed her chastely on the lips and stepped back.

"There be food and drink aplenty, and you're all invited to stay on!" Pride cried out, clapping his new brother on the back. Annie darted forth to kiss the air beside Pru's cheek, and steal a closer look at Gideon before she hurried out to help Lillah and the other womenfolk bring out the collation that had taken three days to prepare.

It was hours before Pru found a moment alone with her new husband, for it seemed that Gideon was bent on making the acquaintance of every single wedding guest, from the oldest to the very youngest. The little boys seemed particularly drawn to him, and Pru felt a deep sadness come over her when she thought of his once having loved and lost a son. Somehow, that was even harder to bear than the knowledge that he had been married before.

"Why so quiet, my docile little wife?" he murmured in her ear, having come up behind her silently. "Thinking up some new devilment?"

Pru turned, melting at the tender look on his face. He cared for her—she knew he did. It would have to serve until she could give him a child and teach him to love again. "Perhaps I'm practicing to be a meek and biddable wife," she told him.

He threw back his head and roared with laughter. "Come the day you're meek and biddable, woman, I'll know you've taken a fever. Now come and have a drink of wine with me before we slip away."

"We're going on a trip? Why didn't you tell me, dammit—I've packing to see to, and Granna to worry about, and—where are we going? Will I need rough clothes or fine?"

"Not too far," he told her, still laughing. "Lillah's put a few things in a bag for you, and Crow's halfway out to the *Polly* with them by now."

Gideon allowed his hand to trail over her cheek in the guise of rearranging her headdress. It was all he could do to keep from kissing her. Damn and blast the rules that said a man couldn't fondle his own wife in public! For tuppence, he would have laid her down right there under in the shade of the oak tree and loved her sweet body until she hadn't enough breath left to argue. But that was hardly the way to set about mending her reputation.

Easing her around behind a large woman who was holding forth on the proper way to preserve eggs, Gid leaned down until his mouth was brushing against Pru's ear. "You'll not be needing clothes, nor will I be needing a crew for where we're going, my sweet, biddable Haskell. All I ask is a strong anchor, a soft bed and a willing wench."

Chapter Eighteen

A broad band of coral streaked across the horizon, spilling its glorious fire out across the still water. In stark contrast, the dark silhouette of Gideon's sloop rode at anchor, her sharply raked mast lost in the bank of dark clouds that was settling lower by the moment. Pru stared down at her knotted hands, ignoring the spectacle.

"Likely storm before midnight," Gideon said over the noisy creaking of the rowlocks.

"I reckon."

Seated just abaft midship, he worked the sweeps smoothly, sending the sturdy boat skimming over the mirrorlike surface. When they were within a stone's throw of their destination, he came neatly alongside the sloop's leeward beam.

Painter in hand, he was up and over the side before Pru, with several heavy sighs, had gathered her skirts in her hands to stand. Then, having made the launch fast, he leaned over to offer her a hand.

"You might've given me time to change out of my wedding gown," she grumbled, trying to negotiate the narrow wooden rungs without tangling her feet in her wide silk skirts.

"Aye, I might've."

Thunder rumbled in the distance as she landed on the deck beside him. Shaking off his hand, she tugged at her neckline and brushed down her skirts. She had long since discarded the headdress, which had refused to stay put. Now, with a scowl on her face, she felt behind her for the once crisp ruff that had stood so proudly about her shoulders. It was drooping tiredly, and she felt every bit as wilted. This was supposed to be the happiest day of her life. So why wasn't she dancing for joy?

"Are you weary, sweetings?"

She cast him a look. If she were weary, he had only himself to blame, for he'd been the one to linger until he'd charmed every blasted soul on the island, from Old Lady Gaitskill, who never had a kind word for anyone, to the newest Burrows babe, who was cutting teeth and had howled incessantly until Gid took him in his arms.

And dammit, she could easily learn to hate that smile that twitched at the corners of his mouth without ever parting his lips. If a body wanted to smile, then he should damn well show his teeth!

With Gideon's hand warm on the small of her back, Pru stalked silently across the deck to the companionway hatch. Someone—Crow, she supposed—had opened it to relieve the heat that had built up below decks during the long, hot day.

That, at least, was a blessing. For tuppence, she'd strip down to her chemise and pantaloons and go over the side, she was that hot and bothered. Silk, for all it made a lovely wedding gown, was not at all practical for summer wear.

"Would you like me to lash myself to the mast before you mete out my punishment?"

They had reached the door of the captain's quarters, and Pru spun about and stared at him. "Would I *what?*

"I thought perhaps ten lashes should do it. Twelve if you're really determined that I should suffer, but I don't fancy having my back laid open in fly season, so I'd be obliged if you could make do with no more than an even dozen."

"I think you've gone soft in the head," she snapped.

"There's only one thing about me that's gone soft, lady, and it sure as hell ain't my head," he growled.

Before she could help herself, Pru's gaze dropped down the length of his powerful body. Cheeks flaming, she jerked her eyes upward again, only to discover that he was grinning broadly, two rows of strong white teeth on prominent display. He took her hand, and before she could snatch it away he placed it flat against his chest.

There he held it, against the steady throb of his heart. "If any part of me has gone soft, little prickly pear, 'tis this."

Suddenly, it was all too much for her: the long day of festivities, the sleepless nights of anticipation, the weeks of restlessness and uncertainty, of wondering if he would really come back for her. And before that, the months at his whaling camp, which had been both the most difficult and the most wonderful days of her life.

Before the first tear dripped off her chin, Gideon had gathered her into his arms and was swaying with her, murmuring words meant to soothe, but that only made her cry the harder.

"Are you so unhappy, little Haskell?"

"P-Prudence," she whispered, sniffing. "Yes—no—oh, how should I know?" she wailed, burrowing her face in the fine broadcloth coat he had worn throughout the day, even to row them out to the sloop.

Without speaking further, he lifted her into his arms and stepped through the cabin door, and Pru cried all the harder, remembering the last time he had brought her here.

Harnessing his own impatience, Gideon gave himself over to caring for his nervous young bride, sitting her down beside him on the bunk. How the devil was he going to manage the hundreds of tiny buttons that marched down the back of her dress? He was no lady's maid at the best of times, and this was hardly that. Since the night he'd left her asleep in her bed, he had looked forward to the time when he would have her all to himself, with no one to interrupt.

All in the world he wanted to do was to make love to her sweet young body until he collapsed. To sleep beside her and wake beside her and spend the rest of his life loving and arguing and exploring and sharing. And God willing, making babies with her.

She sniffed and hiccuped, and he stroked the back of her neck, causing the rest of her hair to come tumbling down over his hand. "There'll be warm water in the galley, and if you recall, I've a fine tub. You'll feel better for a warm soak and a bit of wine, love."

He tilted her face with the intent of kissing her, but one look at those enormous drowned eyes and he cursed under his breath. Dammit, did she have to look at him like that? So he was not the man of her dreams! He'd made no pretense of being other than what he was. Hardworking, honest and as decent as the average man, he supposed, but still only a whaler.

She deserved someone better. Andros had been something of a dark horse, but Hosannah Hunt Gilbert was from a prominent family with great holdings on the Albemarle. It had been plain from the first time he met the old woman that for all his Haskell's outrageous pranks, she was bred from gentry.

God knows, he could make no such claims for himself. If it hadn't been for him, she might have married a landed gentleman who would have given her a fine home and servants and a life of ease. Instead, thanks to his interference, she'd had no course but to marry a rough whaler, whose only home was a ten-foot-square cabin in a single-masted cargo ship.

The last button came off in his hands, and Gideon stared blindly at the tiny silk-covered ball. There were too many layers yet to be shed, and he suddenly knew he couldn't handle it. "Um—the water. That is, I'll fetch the tub and fill it for you, and then I can..."

He was out the door before Pru could stop him.

Had she truly wanted to stop him? Pru wondered. Wouldn't it be better to take the chance he had offered her to run away before things went any further?

She was still standing in the middle of the cabin, her gown billowing around her stocking feet, when the clank of a copper tub against the bulkhead announced his return.

Vainly, she searched his face for a hint of his feelings. If only he would take her in his arms and tell her everything would be all right. If only he loved her...

"Do you need any more help?" His mouth was clamped into an angry line, and she shook her head. "Then I'll fetch the kettles. There's fresh water in the *qaraba*." He indicated the big green glass jug mounted in a tilting wooden frame, and she nodded, feeling cold in spite of the stifling heat.

He lingered in the doorway for an inordinate length of time, and she pretended to work on a knotted ribbon at the waist of her outer petticoat. Finally he left her, and she sobbed out a fierce oath. "What am I going to do?" she whispered. How could she stand to live with a man who had married her only out of a sense of duty?

She hadn't wanted to believe what Annie said, but all day, seeing the way everyone looked at her, hearing their voices grow still when she came near, it had eaten at her. Had Pride truly forced him to marry her? It was Pride who had first brought up the subject. And after all, wasn't it her brother's duty, as head of the family, to find her a husband? He had challenged a man to a duel for disparaging the honor of their father. What might he do to a man who had disparaged the honor of his sister?

When Gideon came back with two enormous copper kettles, she was still standing in the center of the room, arms wrapped around her as she stared blindly out the dark porthole.

A flash of lightning illuminated the room, and with a muffled oath, Gideon strode across to the gimballed lamp that swung over his desk and lighted it.

Then he turned to her. "Do you mean to stand there all night?"

She stared at him, her eyes wide, her mind a complete blank. What was she doing here with this great, angry creature? Why was he looking at her that way?

"Haskell?"

She bit her lip. Married? Had she thought she wanted to be married? Dear God, she didn't even know how to go about it! She could barely remember her mother—she had never even known Grandpa Gilbert—she hadn't the least notion of how to go about being a wife.

"Gideon, we've made a mistake. You'll just have to take me home again, and I'll tell Pride to tell everyone that it was all a mistake—that we didn't truly mean it. You see, I don't even know—"

Ignoring her, Gideon emptied both kettles into the huge tub. He had shed his coat; now he rolled up his sleeve and plunged his hand into the water to stir it around. Pru watched the steam rise from the surface, not moving from where she stood.

"Soap," he muttered. Crossing to the drawer under his shaving mirror, he took out a round pat of French milled soap and tossed it into the bathwater. "I've no intention of running a halyard full of wet petticoats up the mast, so you'll oblige me by kindly removing your underwear before you get into my bathtub."

She had time to blink only once before his hands were at her waist, and he was untying ribbons and unbuttoning buttons, letting the lawn and starched muslin crumple around her ankles. Not until she was standing there in her chemise and pantaloons did she revive enough to slap his hand away, and by then it was too late.

"If you've made up your mind to show me just how stubborn you can be, wife, then know this—I once stood toe to toe for five and a half hours with a man bent on carving out my gizzard. He moved first, and lost an ear as a result."

Her chin fell and she stared at him. "You're daft."

He nodded, a grim smile playing over his face. "Likely. Don't let it bother you, for you'll not be forced to spend overmuch time in my company."

She wanted to ask what he meant, but was afraid to. Did this mean he, too, knew their marriage had been a mistake? "I'd as soon go back home now, if it's all the same to you."

She caught her breath as he jerked at the waist of her drawers, splitting them down almost to the knee. Before she could gather the gaping sides over her nakedness, he lifted her in one arm and completed the job of ripping them off.

She stood trembling and wide-eyed before him, naked from knee to waist, her stockings dangling and her thin, beribboned chemise skimming the top of her hipbones. "You bloody basta—"

His mouth came down on hers, shutting off her voice. She hammered at his chest as he ground his teeth against hers, bruising her lips, twisting her face to suit his needs.

And then, with her fists raised for another attack, something happened inside her. She lowered her hands slowly, and they were no longer fists. As Gideon's kisses turned from fierce domination to slow seduction, her hands curled over his shoulders. At the first touch of his tongue against hers, she slipped her arms around his neck, bowing her body against his hardening muscles, and murmured his name against his throat.

"There'll be no going back, love," he whispered. "If you'd rather stay ashore, I'll build you a house of your own, but have me you will. You're my wedded wife, and there'll be no untying that knot."

Before she knew what he was about, he had lifted her off her feet and deposited her, still in her stockings, garters and chemise, into the tub.

"Gideon, you're crazy as a loon!" she shouted, laughing, but dangerously near to tears.

"Aye, that may be, but even a loon knows how to manage a witchety looness."

"Looness?" she gurgled, reaching under her hip to retrieve the bar of soap.

He took it from her and laid it aside. Tenderly, he lifted one foot after the other, peeling her sodden hose and wringing them out. Then he worked the chemise over her head and wrung it, too, laying them all in his shaving basin.

"To fly from your mast?" she ventured.

"Aye, I might just run them up. 'Twould send a clear enough message."

She knew well what message that would be. "What did you fly from your masthead the night you—the first time I—"

"The night I took your maidenhead?"

Snatching up the soap, she began working up a lather, concentrating on the cloudy swirls that spun away from the fragrant bar. "No—don't tell me—I don't want to know," she muttered.

Taking her head between his wet hands, he turned her face up to his, and he was smiling. The old, sweet smile that made his eyes seem so clear and blue she could have dived into them and never reached bottom. "I might as well have run my heart up the masthead for all to see."

Hope leaped inside her, and she commanded herself to snuff it out. It was hard enough keeping her wits about her without harboring false hopes.

Somewhere along the line, Gideon had found a washcloth, and now he took the soap from her and began to bathe her throat, her shoulders, her arms. Taking one of her hands in both of his, he lathered it, rinsed it and then lifted it to his lips. When he sucked one fingertip into his mouth, Pru moaned and slid deeper into the tub, closing her eyes.

Light flashed against the portholes, and a moment later, thunder growled in the distance. Ignoring it, Gideon discarded the dripping cloth and slid his hands down over her breasts, wet and slick with soap. Her nipples beaded at his touch, and Pru caught her breath.

"Gideon, I don't think you should be doing this," she said weakly.

But when he asked her why, she couldn't think of a single reason. And then his hand was slipping down under the surface, stroking her belly, ringing her navel, and lightning flashed again.

Pru shuddered and closed her eyes. Her thighs tightened and then went soft as she felt his touch ease lower. Slowly, slowly, his fingertips combed through the wet curls nestled at the joint of her thighs. She raised her eyelids partway and stared at him, breath coming harshly from between her parted lips.

Lamplight shone down on his face, making his pale hair gleam like spun gold. His jaw was once more clean-shaven, the mark that was so much a part of his male beauty glowing darkly. She wanted to kiss him there. She wanted to kiss him everywhere!

"Your eyes look black, Gideon," she told him.

His fingers explored the vulnerable folds of her womanhood, and her own eyes widened. "So do yours, my little love."

She stiffened. "Gideon, please—"

Gently, inexorably, his touch so light she thought she might die, he circled her again and again, and she felt herself expanding, filling with heat, aching, swelling... *wanting!*

She cried out, and he lifted her from the water, holding her dripping against his fully clothed body. Lowering her onto the wide bunk, he quickly stripped off his clothes and lay down beside her.

"Would I could think of all the pretty words a man should use to woo his woman," Gideon whispered. "Alas, all I can think of is having you under me, of being inside you, feeling your sweet body holding me so tightly I near lose my mind—and then losing it."

His voice sounded strained, but at least he could speak; it was more than Pru could do, even if she'd known what to say. He was leaning over her, one of his hands gently shaping her breast. Bright streaks of pleasure shot through her body, and she lifted her head and brushed her face against his chest, loving the feel of the satiny, slightly damp flesh, the crisp hair and the rock-hard muscles underneath.

Tentatively, she searched for the small brown disks that had long fascinated her, knowing that he was as sensitive there as she was. She had not to wait long, for the instant her fingertips found what they were seeking, he stiffened and caught his breath. She felt the rise of a small hard nugget and daringly caught it in her teeth.

It was as if he'd been struck by a bolt of the lightning that danced all around their small haven. Pru was delighted. Her hands began straying on another exploration, following a line of silky hair that bisected his hard, flat belly.

"Ahhh, love, you'd dare the devil in his own den, wouldn't you?" he said hoarsely, gasping when her fingers closed around the rigid shaft of his manhood.

Before Pru could answer his challenge, he had covered her hand. For one long moment, he pressed her fingers more tightly around him, and then he brought her hands up to his lips as he moved over her.

She was more than ready for him, yet he took her slowly. "Easy, love," he whispered when she lifted her hips to meet him. "We've all night . . . we've forever."

But Pru was beyond caution. Driven wild by his skilled caresses, she bucked and twisted beneath him until he plunged into her hot, wet depths. Gasping her name, he rode her fiercely, and she wrapped her legs around him as her fingers bit into his sweat-slick shoulders.

"Are you with me, love? Hurry—faster, faster—*ahhh!*" he cried out.

Caught up in the white-hot ball of exploding pleasure, she could only cling to him mindlessly, shaken to the very depths of her soul.

Some time later she awoke to feel a light, cool breeze blowing across her naked body. The storm had passed, leaving in its wake a light, refreshing rain.

Gideon roused just enough to draw a thin cover over them both, and then he gathered her against him, back to front, and murmured drowsily in her ear, "Rest a while, my love. Storm's over."

His love. She would believe it because she must, because she knew now she could not go on living if she thought he had only married her out of a sense of duty.

But that was no "duty" she had just experienced. Nor was it duty she felt stirring against her buttocks even now. Nor duty that moved his hand so that it cupped her breast.

"Sleepy?" Gideon whispered.

She wriggled her hips, delighted at the instantaneous effect, and then pretended to snore softly.

"Then I'll take care not to disturb you, my poor sickly darling." Ignoring her unconscious snort, he reached one hand to her hip, lifting her thigh and drawing it back so that it rested on his own.

Before she quite knew how it had come about, she found herself seated astride his lap while still lying on her side, which was pleasurable enough, but when she felt his hand slip down her buttocks and reach around to caress her in that special place, her breath caught in her throat and her eyes widened.

He couldn't—he wouldn't—

He did. Slowly, thoroughly and with utterly shattering results.

The sun was pouring in through the porthole when next Pru opened her eyes. She ached in every part of her body, but it was a delicious ache—a drowsy, warm, wonderful ache that she knew she would treasure for all her days.

"I'm hungry," she said, surprised to discover that she was starving.

Gideon had evidently been awake for some time, for he had bathed and shaved, and was dressed in a pair of fresh trousers, barefoot and shirtless.

"I emptied the tub and refilled it. No hot water, but if you sprout goose bumps, I know a dandy way to warm you."

Propping herself up on her elbows, Pru grinned at him. From some deep well of wisdom, she recognized the moment of pure happiness and treasured it as if it were a golden sunbeam caught for a fleeting instant in the palm of her hand.

"You already bathed me last night. Now it's time to feed me. Unless you're trying to starve me into submissiveness?"

Gideon gave a bark of laughter. "Submissive! You? Darling, I fear the world's not ready for a meek and submissive Haskell."

Coming onto her knees, she lunged at him, and he caught her and swung her up into his arms, still laughing. "Still...while the coffee boils, I might try kissing you into submissiveness, hmm?"

Puckering her lips nicely, she closed her eyes and lifted her face. When nothing happened, she opened one eye. "Well? What are you waiting for?"

With a groan, Gideon gave himself up to temptation. He was well and truly harpooned. The coffee could boil over and the pot boil dry for all he cared. Still smiling, he took her puckered lips between his teeth and bit down gently. She howled, he laughed, and they were rolling on the bed when they were startled to hear the sound of a boat scraping against the hull mere inches from where they lay.

"Were you expecting the crew back so early?" she asked, struggling to cover her disappointment.

Gideon shook his head. "I vowed if I saw hide or hair of a single one of 'em before midweek, I'd fire on 'em."

"Pride, then. Oh, no, do you suppose something's happened to Granna?" She sat up, clutching the sheet to her bosom, and Gideon drew her into his arms.

"You wait here, love, I'll go up and see. Likely it's naught but Crow, come to bring more food. Lillah sent enough to feed an army yesterday, but..."

He was halfway up the companionway when a pair of legs in black hose and buckled shoes appeared at the hatch opening.

"Gideon McNair?" an unfamiliar voice demanded.

"Aye. Who wants him?"

"In the name of the king, I arrest you for the murder of Claude Delarouche, citizen of France."

Chapter Nineteen

The first thing Pru saw after she scrambled into her gown and flew up the companionway was a brace of high-booted men wearing bandoliers and swords, their backs turned to her. Gideon was listening to a third man who was dressed all in black, his white wig slightly askew under a faded black tricorne.

Who the devil were they? What did they want? Why were they accusing her husband of murder? Everyone knew that duels, while not strictly legal, were invariably overlooked as long as no one actually raised a complaint.

She wanted to fly to his defense, but something made her pause. Still as a mouse, she watched. From where she was standing, she couldn't hear much of what was being said, but when she tried to move closer, the two armed men blocked her way.

"...hold a hearing *mumble mumble*...authority *mumble*...witnesses present and *mumble mumble mumble*..." So said crooked wig.

Gideon's back was turned to her, any reply he might have made lost in the light wind that had sprung up.

"...*mumble* pistol found...*mumble* knife...*mumble* interference..."

She was seething with anger. Who had brought them here? Who would have dared? Pride had told her when she pressed him that before sailing for a doctor he'd hurried back to the clearing to retrieve anything they might have left behind, but both the pistol she'd dropped and Claude's body were gone. They'd assumed that Jacques had returned, claimed the body and fled in shame before anyone could accuse him or Claude of attempted murder.

Gideon stood tall and erect, his bronze shoulders bared to the morning sun and his blue trousers fitting his long, muscular limbs like the finest kidskin glove. His head was bare; his hair, which he usually wore clubbed at the back of his neck, blew freely in the wind.

Pru's gaze moved past her husband to the small man who was pointing a bony finger at him. He had the dusty look of an underclerk about him. Probably the smell, as well. His face was pinched, his skin too pale, and his eyes darted constantly, as if he expected to be set upon by cutthroats at any moment.

And then, suddenly, the two guards moved up behind Gideon and grasped his arms.

Pru leaped up the last step and flew across the wet deck. "You let him go! Let him go this minute, do you hear me?"

"Tell your doxy to cry off, or we'll arrest her, too," said the taller of the two guards.

Turning, Gideon commanded her quietly to go below. "This doesn't concern you."

She slapped at the hand that would have held her back, and there was a small scuffle. The next thing she knew, Gideon was lying flat on the deck, having been clubbed by the larger of the two guards.

Pru fell to her knees and lifted his head onto her lap, daring a single one of the intruders to lay a hand on her. "You listen to me, you bloody bas—" Some lingering shred of common sense stayed her tongue at the last minute. "You busybodies! Gideon is my husband, and he's done nothing wrong. I'll slit the throat of the first man who says he has, I warn you!"

Seeing the looks they gave her, Pru heartily wished she'd taken time to pin up her hair and put on a pair of shoes, but it was too late now. In her haughtiest tone, she warned the two guards to stand back. "If you've hurt him, I promise, I'll see you hang."

"Mistress McNair, if that be who you are," the fidgety little justice snapped, "kindly stand back! This is none of your concern."

"It is, too, my concern! How *dare* you set foot on my husband's ship and accuse him of wrongdoing! I don't even know who you are!"

Furious, she watched the clerkish little man's nose turn red as his lips disappeared altogether. "Madam, I have the honor to be Joshua Beading, esquire, duly appointed justice of the peace. Your husband has been accused of the unlawful death of one Claude Delarouche."

Gideon was beginning to stir. Pru clamped her hand over his face and pressed his head back onto her lap. "There's obviously been some mistake. I'm sorry to have to inform you, but you've been sent on a fool's errand."

"That's for me to decide, madam. Kindly remove yourself and let us get on with the king's business."

Before Pru could finish delivering her opinion of a king who taxed his subjects beyond all that was reasonable and then hobbled them with all manner of restrictive laws, Gideon sat up and groaned. Brushing Pru's hands away, he muttered, "Be still, woman."

"But Gideon—"

He silenced her with a single look.

In the end, the five of them were rowed ashore by two armed crewmen of His Majesty's Royal Navy.

For Gideon's sake, Pru tried to hide her fears, but by the time they reached the docks, where scores of people had gathered, she had bit her lip until the blood flowed.

Her wedding guests. Bitterness filled her heart as one of the guards handed her up onto the wharf. Yesterday they'd all come to hear her vows and feast at her table. Today they had come to see her taken away in disgrace.

Because she was the guilty party, not Pride, and certainly not Gideon. Pride had issued the challenge, but she'd been the one to carry it out. Whatever Gideon had done had been more than justified by Claude's treachery, and she would waste no time in telling them the truth of the matter.

"*Il a abbatu mon cousin!*"

"For God's sake, Delarouche, speak the king's English!" cried the justice of the peace. "We'll not get done at all if you can't make yourself understood."

Jacques! Pru spun about, trying to see the man who had been party to the attempt on her life, but the crowd was milling all around her, blocking her view.

"They kill my cousin," he accused in the familiar nasal voice. And then Jacques Delarouche stepped out of a doorway, a look of triumph on his pockmarked face.

"You bastard!" Pru screamed. Elbowing through the crowd, she hurled herself at the dandyish captain, who jumped back, his smirk quickly disappearing.

And then someone caught her by the shoulders and slapped a hand over her mouth. She struggled. Kicking back, she felt her bare heel make contact with a shin, and struggled all the more frantically. "Mffffpft!" she sputtered, and bit down hard on a finger.

"Oww, dammit! One more word out of you and I'm going to hoist you up with the sheer hulk and let you swing there until the cormorants peck out your blasted eyes!"

Pride! Pru went limp with relief. And then Pride was holding her hard, and she was weeping and trying to talk, and he was muttering there-theres, while the crowd continued to mill about them, pushing for a closer look at the man who was being tried for murder only hours after his wedding day. Such a thing had never before happened on Portsmouth Island, and already tales were being formulated that would be passed down for generations to come.

When she was allowed to speak again, Pru whispered, "But how did they get here? Who told them?"

Pride lowered his mouth until it was close to his sister's ear. "That damned cousin of Delarouche's, I reckon. They showed up at the house before the sun was even up good, two guards and that sanctimonious little pissant. They were a-banging on the door fit to wake the dead. I told 'em I didn't know where Gideon was, but I reckon there was plenty to point out the *Polly* and set 'em on his trail. I was headed out to warn the two of you, but one of the guards saw me just as I was shoving off. He threatened to hole Pa's skiff and take me into custody, and I figured that weren't going to do none of us any good. It'll be all right, Prudie, I swear. They can't hold a man for protecting a woman against scum like Delarouche.''

''I just wish it'd never happened. I wish—I wish all these people would go home!'' Pru buried her face in Pride's shirt and shuddered. All around her were people she had known all her life, come to watch the spectacle. ''They're like vultures! Don't they have a shred of decency?''

''They're just curious, sweetings, that's all. They don't mean no real harm.''

''We have to *do* something! We can't let them take him away!''

She was churning inside, wanting to hit out at something, wanting to shout out the truth—but knowing that a misplaced word could be even more dangerous to Gideon than a word not spoken.

''They're not taking him anywhere—leastwise, not yet. This is only a hearing, to see if there's anything to the charges.''

''A hearing!'' Hope leapt in her heart. ''Then they'll have to hear anyone who has something to say about the matter, won't they?''

''Now, Prudie...''

She slapped away his hand and climbed up on top of a stack of hides. ''Where— Oh, they're over by the door of the grain house. They've dragged out Mr. Simpson's desk. Damned them. They wouldn't even give Gideon time to get dressed!''

Pride patted her back and warned her again not to interfere. ''I'm going to work my way up to the front,'' he said. ''You stay here where you can watch what goes on. If things look like they're going awry, I'll signal you, and we'll think of something to do.''

"Are you going to tell them?"

He refused to meet her eyes, and Pru knew with a sinking feeling that her brother was about to take all the blame onto his own shoulders. And it was wrong! She should be the one to go down there and confess. But how could she do that? If she claimed Claude had shot her in the back, then the justice would want to know how she could have turned around and thrown a knife with such unerring aim and force that it had killed a man.

"Pride, wait," she cried, but he was already lost in the crowd.

A sharp rap of wood on wood brought about an instant silence just then, and Justice Joshua Beading's thin voice rang out clearly. "Did you, Gideon McNair, challenge one Claude Delarouche, now deceased, to a duel on or about June seventeenth of this year?"

Gideon opened his mouth to reply, when Pride stepped forward. "He did *not,* sir. I was the one who challenged the bastard to a duel. Gideon McNair only served as my second."

There was an angry outburst of French, and Pru stood on tiptoe as the crowd surged closer around the small tableau, blocking her view. Exasperated, she tucked her skirt up in her waistband and jumped for the eaves of the grain storage warehouse.

Scrambling up onto the roof, she missed what happened next. By the time she had levered herself on her hands and bare feet halfway up the roof so that she could see the small group gathered in the shade of the shed roof that covered the entrance of the main warehouse, Jacques and a rough-looking seaman wearing a single gold earring had joined them there. Pride, Gideon and two guards stood on one side, the two Frenchmen on the other, giving Pru a clear view of the proceedings. The justice was the only one facing her. As the others were facing him, they stood with their backs to her.

Hardly daring to breathe, Pru tried to read what was going on inside their heads in the way they held their bodies. For all the tension she sensed in him, Gideon might have stepped outside his hut for a last pipe and a look at the sea before turning in. But even from where she was seated, Pru could tell Pride was rigid with anger. How many times had she tried to teach him to stand easy? How many times had he tensed up at the last minute and fired wide of the mark or given away his hand at cards?

Her gaze returned to Gideon, and her heart melted. *Gideon, I love you so! I won't let them separate us, I swear it! If they take you, they'll have to take me, as well. If they hang you, they'll have to hang me!*

As if she'd actually reached out and touched him, Gideon turned and lifted his face, staring directly into her eyes. She thought he smiled, but she couldn't be certain.

Suddenly, the justice stood and began waving his arms at the two Frenchmen, who had approached his desk. "Wait a minute, wait a minute, you're both jabbering at once, and I can't understand that heathen tongue! First we'll hear from you!" Turning, he pointed a finger at Gideon. "You've not answered my question yet. Did you challenge the deceased to a duel?"

Pride stepped closer to Gideon and said something Pru couldn't hear. Gideon's eyes glinted, but Pride shook his head and jutted his chin. Even without the words, Pru knew what was happening. Gideon wanted to shoulder the blame for the entire affair, but Pride was not going to allow it.

"No," he said quietly, turning back to face his interrogator.

"Were you present at the fight?"

"'Twas a duel, properly challenged and properly accepted. I was there, but I'm sorry to say I was late in arriving."

"Did you kill Claude Delarouche?"

There was an outburst of French from the seaman with the gold earring, and Pride, his face mottled with angry color above his short beard, pointed at the strange seaman and shouted, "You weren't even there, dammit. Shut yer bleeding trap!"

And then, before the guards could lay a hand on him, he stepped past the two Frenchmen and placed his hands on the tall, tilt-top desk. "Sir, it was my quarrel, and I can tell you exactly what happened. I challenged Delarouche to an honorable duel for insulting my pa and threatening my family, but the bastard fired on the count of seven, and—"

"You were hit?"

"Well, um—not exactly."

"Was that when you threw the knife?"

Cutting his eyes at Gideon, Pride swallowed hard and nodded, and there was another spate of chattering from witnesses and onlookers. The justice picked up the belaying pin some kind soul had provided him with and slammed it down, setting Mr. Simpson's desk to rocking. His dignity wasn't helped by the fact that each time he bobbed his head, both wig and tricorne shifted farther to the east, and the fact that the desk was a clerk's, meant for a tall man to stand at; Justice Beading, even standing, was not a tall man.

"Now, we'll have the straight of it, or I'll haul the lot of you off to the courts of oyer and terminator and General Gaol Delivery!'

He glared at them all, one after another. Pru's heart swelled when she saw the way Gideon looked back at the man, neither arrogant nor afraid, but with the natural dignity that was so much a part of him.

Justice Beading cleared his throat at great and impressive length. He jabbed a finger at Pride. "You, boy—you say you challenged the deceased?"

Pride had time only to nod his head before the man pounced again. "Why?"

"I told you—he insulted my father."

"What'd he say?"

"That Pa was a thief."

Pru began inching down the steeply sloped roof. She had to stop this farce. Pride had nothing to do with it. Too many people in the village knew which twin had been shot.

"And was he?"

Pride's head reared back. "Hell, no, he weren't! My pa was the finest man—"

Down came the belaying pin. There was another outburst from Jacques, which tapered off to a sickening smirk when the justice pinned him with a beady glare.

"Now—you say the deceased fired on you."

"Fired early, on the count of seven," Pride accused.

"Then pistols were the weapon of choice."

Pride muttered something that Pru did not quite catch.

The justice leaned forward, a cold smile stretching his thin lips. "Then would you tell me, sir, why the deceased ended up with a knife in his heart? A proper duel, you claim? Not so, say I. It was a wicked murder, and I'll be taking you both back to Queen Anne's Towne to stand trial. So be it!"

In the furor that broke out then, Pru lost sight of Gideon. Then the guards forced the crowds back at gunpoint, and she saw him talking earnestly to the justice, who was nodding his head, but looking as if his breakfast had turned sour on him.

She lost no time in slithering off the edge of the roof, dropping down onto the stack of hides. "Let me through," she cried, shoving and elbowing past the fishermen and their families, who were looking at her with sympathy she neither wanted nor needed. "Move, dammit, let me though!"

Annie Duvaal caught at her hand. "Oh, Pru, what are you going to do? They'll take Pride away, and he didn't do nothing wrong, he never would!"

Not even slowing up, she said, "Quit whining, Annie. I'm going to tell that little cowbird exactly what happened, since neither of those two mule-headed men of mine can tell the truth from a pickled herring!"

Leaving her friend gawking behind her, Pru plowed through the crowds, reaching the king's official just as he was ordering the prisoners to be taken aboard the Royal Navy frigate that lay anchored and waiting. "You just hold on there!" She jabbed a forefinger into the chest of the guard—the big ugly one who had coshed Gideon on the head earlier that morning. "You lay a hand on my husband

and you'll be walking funny for a solid week!'' Spinning around to where the justice stood gawking, she said, "You want the truth? I'll tell you the truth!"

"Now, Mistress McNair—"

"Shut up! You think you know everything? You don't know anything at all! Pride Andros might have been the one to challenge that snake, but *I* was the one went to meet him, not my brother. And *I* was the one he shot in the back, as anyone on this island can tell you. God knows they've been prattling about it long enough! What's more, that sniveling excuse for a man—" she jabbed a thumb at Jacques Delarouche "—he watched it happen and didn't do a blasted thing to set matters straight! Left to him, I'd be dead and buried. Any scoundrel who'd shoot a man in the back would have put the next ball through his head, only luckily for me, Gideon and Pride got there in time to stop him!"

When Pru had first charged onto the scene, Jacques had been calmly filling a pipe, his bearing one of self-congratulation. Now he began to sputter, and she rounded on him.

"A fine second you turned out to be! You're no better than that filthy cousin of yours, and that's the truth! The pair of you deliberately set out to ruin—"

Breaking off, she covered her mouth with her hand, eyes wide and staring. "Wh—where did you get that pipe?"

Jacques looked dumbly at the ornate pipe in his hand, then back at her. And then he began looking around as if seeking an avenue of escape.

Pru bore down on him as he began to edge away. "Tell me!"

Muttering something under his breath to his compatriot, he dropped the pipe, and the seaman tried to kick it over the edge, but Pride broke free of the guard and snatched it up.

"Good God, this is Papa's pipe," he said wonderingly. "But how—"

Stepping around from behind the desk, the justice took the thing from his hands and peered suspiciously at it, at Pride and at Prudence. "I don't know what you think you're about, young woman, but I'll not be taken in by your attempts at trickery." He made as if to hand the pipe back to Jacques Delarouche, and Pru dived at his arm, sending the pipe skittering away.

Albert Thurston caught it, examined it and said excitedly, "Bless me if it ain't Mr. Urias's old briar root pipe. Look, Pa, it's still got the initials and all. Mr. Urias, he set some kind of store by that pipe, he did."

At that, Beading took it back and scowled at the blackened and much-worn surface. The bits of inlaid ebony glowed darkly, but most of the ivory was now stained a dark brown. The scrolled design was worn away on both sides, but there in the very front was a faint trace of what appeared to be entwined lines. Upon closer examination, they proved to be the initials of Urias Andros.

It was a jubilant company that gathered at the Andros house that night. Albert Thurston had found his way back into the family's good graces, but Annie was ignoring him to simper at Pride, who was making a good pretense of ignoring her, in turn.

"Imagine, after all this time," Hosannah kept murmuring.

"I told Mr. Duvaal a hundred times that there was something funny about all them foreigners a-swarming over this place all of a sudden like," said Mrs. Duvaal.

"Pirates," Albert marveled, basking in the small part he had played in the drama. "To think if you hadn't seen that pipe, and that woman of yours hadn't heard that Jacks feller jabbering fit to be tied—why, we'd likely never have found out who murdered poor Mr. Urias and his crew."

Most of the village families had lost at least one member when Urias's *Pride of Portsmouth* had gone down with all hands. Now they were rejoicing that justice had finally been served.

Pru leaned back in the circle of Gideon's arm, only half-listening. How strange that such fierce independence, irritating small-mindedness and genuine goodness could abide in the same very ordinary bodies. Her friends. Her neighbors. Her kinsmen. Come tomorrow, tongues would be flapping again, going on about the unseemly behavior of that Andros girl and her whaler, who'd spent the whole evening wrapped up in each other's arms, right out there in plain view of the whole community.

But for tonight all shared the feeling of having seen a belated justice prevail. Children drowsed in their mothers' laps, pipes were lit and drawn on with quiet satisfaction, and rum flowed freely. Hosannah blossomed under the excitement. Crow and Lillah stayed out in the kitchen for the most part, now and then bringing in a fresh trencher of wild plum dumplings or crisp fried fish roe.

"Tired?" Gideon murmured. They were seated on the second stair, all the other seats in the house, including the hearth, having been taken.

"Worn to a frazzle, but I doubt I'll be able to sleep a wink."

"I wasn't necessarily thinking of sleep."

Turning her head ever so slightly, she pressed her lips against his arm. Such a strong arm. Such a trustworthy arm. It had saved her life more times than she cared to think about.

"I never knew Lillah spoke French," she said.

Gideon grinned. "Neither did Delarouche, to his sorrow."

It had been the brief exchange between the two Frenchmen just after the pipe had been discovered that had brought matters into the open. The seaman had told Jacques he should have known it was bad luck to smoke a dead man's pipe. Jacques had tried to claim that his cousin Claude had found the pipe in one of the warehouses, but the other man had blurted out the truth in his own tongue.

It had been Lillah who had stepped forward to translate. Pru had not even known she was present. "He say, you fool, I tell you t'row dat t'ing away, but you not listen! You hang fo' pirate, I no hang wit' you!"

Only after charges and countercharges had been shouted, and the guards had taken the two Frenchmen into custody did Justice Beading hear the entire tale from beginning to end.

"So you see," Pru had put in after Pride told of the loss of her father's life, the lives of his crew and the fortune he had sunk into the purchase of the spanking new schooner and huge cargo of finest quality lumber, furs and tobacco, "Claude had been scheming to get back at Papa, because he claimed Papa had cheated his father out of a fortune. But Papa told us years before he died that they'd both been cheating. Only thing was, the Frenchman was drunk, and Papa wasn't. Cheating's an art, and old Delarouche was too drunk to be artful. Papa had no choice but to either win or call him out, and drunk as the man was, that'd be murder."

There'd been a loud murmur of agreement at this, for all knew that Urias Andros was basically an honest man, who had never, to anyone's knowledge, used his unquestionable skills against an honest man.

"If it hadn't been the duel," Pru had elaborated, "Claude would have thought of some other way to hurt us. It had eaten on him, you see. He'd grown up hating Papa, believing it was all his fault, and even after he killed him, he wasn't satisfied. He thought we still had a fortune hidden away somewhere just waiting to be discovered. Why, he even wanted to know where Mama was buried. Probably wanted her rings and any other pretties she'd been buried in."

There was no point in bringing up the gold sovereigns that had been stolen from the sewing basket; it would require a lot of embarrassing explanations, and that part of her career was ended now that justice had been done.

Gideon had stepped forward at that time to take her into his arms, right there before the entire village, justices, guards and all. Picking up the tale where she'd left off, he said, "The only thing Delarouche hadn't counted on was that the woman he intended to marry for her fortune was wild as a buck, too headstrong to let someone else fight her battles for her. My wife waited until her brother had gone after me, and then she disguised herself in his clothes and set out to meet Delarouche. It was barely light, you know, and foggy, and I'm forced to admit, the woman is a bit too bold for her own good. Before things could be set aright, the bastard nearly killed her, thinking she was her brother. It was plain he meant to murder the boy and then marry Prudence for what she'd inherited. He'd have ended up murdering them both if—"

"If Gid hadn't come along in time to put a kink in his plans," Pride put in.

They'd had to go over the whole tale from beginning to end twice more before the little man had been satisfied. Meanwhile, most of the audience had wandered off, some to go fish their nets, others to prepare the evening meal.

And now they'd all gathered under Urias's roof once more to toast a proper end to the entire affair.

Crow slipped through the shadowy hallway and said quietly to Gideon, "The boat be ready, Cap'n. Me and my woman, we stay ashore tonight if that be all right with you and your missus."

"Thanks, Crow. Can you be ready to sail day after tomorrow?"

The half-breed appeared to consider this, and then he nodded. "I go wit' you this time. Might be I stay here nex' time, build me a fine big house way south. Maybe fish some, maybe work drifters some, maybe sail wit' you some."

Gideon nodded, and Pru smiled up at the man who had come to be her good friend. "Tell Lillah if she wants to go along home now, I'll look after Granna."

She peered through the smoke and lamplight at where Hosannah held court from her favorite hoop-backed chair. Annie was tenderly tucking a shawl around the old woman's swollen knees, carefully not looking at Pride, who sat across the room in clear view.

Pru noticed that her brother was taking it all in, his expression giving nothing away. It occurred to her that he was the man of the house, the head of the family. Soon, he, too, might be marrying.

She sighed. It seemed only yesterday that he'd been a wiry lad, racing along the waterfront with a wooden sword in his belt as they played at being those two legendary adventurers, Haskell and Nye.

"Ready to go?" Gideon murmured in her ear.

"Just a bit longer, love," she whispered. "Granna'll be dozing over her toddy most any minute now. I think I'll ask Annie to help me get her to bed. I don't believe she'd mind at all."

"Mmm-hmm... Meddlesome little witch, aren't you?" Gideon smiled, his lips brushing her temple.

"I'm sure I don't know what you mean."

"Don't you?" Without bothering to see if they were being observed, he drew her up onto his lap and kissed her soundly.

They were both quite breathless by the time they drew apart. Pru placed a hand over her heart to contain its clamor, and Gideon covered her hand with his. "I'm almost afraid to think about what our children are going to be like, with your blood and mine running rampant in their veins."

Gideon had told her about Barbara and Adam, his infant son, as soon as they'd got home from the hearing. At first she had resented the woman who was his first wife, but somehow, as he described their brief life together, she'd been grateful to the woman who had been there to help Gideon when he most needed someone.

As for his son...she'd felt his sorrow, and could only hold him, saying nothing. That had not been the time to speak.

But now her eyes glowed with the secret she had to share. Leaning forward, she brushed a kiss over the stain on his bronzed right cheek. "You've not a thing in the world to worry over on that account, Captain McNair." Taking his hand, she placed it on her belly, daring anyone in the room to take offense. "Lillah says they're both going to have your beauty and my brains. It's a perfect combination, don't you agree?''

His groan was lost in the sound of her clear, ringing laughter.

Several people, on the verge of taking their leave, looked around and smiled. Hadn't they always known that the wild Andros girl would settle down once she met a man strong enough and foolish enough to take on the job of taming her? Few remembered Blanche Gilbert, but they'd all known and respected Urias Andros. He'd been a sound man. Not perfect, mind you, but then, who among them was?

* * * * *

Take 4 bestselling love stories FREE

Plus get a FREE surprise gift!

Coming in March from

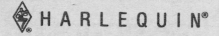

HARLEQUIN
American Romance®

THE ROMANCE THAT STARTED IT ALL!

For Diane Bauer and Nick Granatelli, the walk down the aisle was a rocky road....

Don't miss the romantic prequel to WITH THIS RING—

I THEE WED
BY ANNE McALLISTER

Harlequin American Romance #387

Let Anne McAllister take you to Cambridge, Massachusetts, to the night when an innocent blind date brought a reluctant Diane Bauer and Nick Granatelli together. For Diane, a smoldering attraction like theirs had only one fate, one future—marriage. The hard part, she learned, was convincing her intended....

Watch for Anne McAllister's I THEE WED, available *now* from Harlequin American Romance.

ITW

COMING NEXT MONTH

#71 SUN WOMAN—Lindsay McKenna
Kuchana, an Apache scout, and U.S. Army sergeant Gibson McCoy
were captivated with each other from the moment they met. But before
their love could be fulfilled, they were forced to surmount the fierce
hatred and bitter prejudice that surrounded them.

#72 RANSOM OF THE HEART—Kate Kingsley
Well-meaning swashbuckler Arturo De Leon attempted to rescue
penniless Louisiana belle Danielle Valmont from vengeful pursuers—by
kidnapping her. But Danielle was neither grateful nor cooperative, and
they were soon battling each other and their mutual attraction from
New Orleans to exotic Tangier.

#73 MARI—Donna Anders
For young New Englander Mari Webster, loving Hawaiian rancher
Adam Foster was like a slice of paradise. But when tradition and the
contradictory wishes of others proved to be obstacles to their love, Mari
wondered if she'd soon be mourning a paradise lost.

#74 MISSION OF MERCY—Kathryn Belmont
Mercy Randall Wright fought her attraction to whaling captain Samuel
Starbuck. After all, she was a married woman. Or was she? As the
search for her missing husband continued and days on the whaling
vessel with Starbuck became months, Mercy grew less certain of her
husband's fate and more certain of her heart's.

AVAILABLE NOW: